THINGS
PEOPLE
DO

THINGS PEOPLE DO

A Leo Schwartz Mystery

LEWIS VAUGHT

First published by Level Best Books 2024

This novel is entirely a work of fiction. The names, characters and incidents portrayed in it are the work of the author's imagination. Any resemblance to actual persons, living or dead, events or localities is entirely coincidental.

Lewis Vaught asserts the moral right to be identified as the author of this work.

Author Photo Credit: Carol Hommel

First edition

ISBN: 978-1-68512-627-8

Cover art by Level Best Designs and Richard Hendel

This book was professionally typeset on Reedsy.
Find out more at reedsy.com

For My Parents
N.B.V. and J.J.V.

"In these eleven days I have learned that psychology, as a formal science, is pure hocus-pocus. All written and printed words, aside from their function of relieving boredom, are meaningless drivel. I have fed a half-starved child with my own hands. I have seen two men batter each other with their fists until the blood ran. I have watched boys picking up girls. I have heard a woman tell a man, in public and with a personal application, facts which I had dimly supposed were known, academically, only to those who have read Havelock Ellis. I have observed hungry workingmen eating in a coffee pot. I have seen a tough boy of the street pick up a wilted daffodil from the gutter. It is utterly amazing, I tell you, how people do things they happen to feel like doing."

—Rex Stout, *The League of Frightened Men*

Praise for the Leo Schwartz Mysteries

Praise for CRIME IN ITALY:

"What a fun read! I might be biased, though, because I am from Indianapolis, where the story is based, and I recognize many of the parts of town where everything takes place. But the story is fun, too. The first sentence hooks you, and the characters keep you hooked. I read a lot of mysteries, and this one definitely has its own spin. The two main characters are smart, clever, and easy to like. The plot is complex and intelligent, not your typical whodunit. It has twists, turns, and curveballs. It also gives you the chance to figure out the mystery right along with the Private Investigators. Fun from beginning to end! Keep 'em coming, Lew!"—Amazon Reviewer

Chapter One

One term for it is "the elephant in the living room." In our case, it's more of a cocker spaniel than an elephant, but it's there all the same. Schwartz never mentions, or almost never mentions, and I never ask about his military service in Desert Shield and Desert Storm. Over the years, I've gathered that he was in the army, an ordinary infantryman, nothing glamorous or anything, but he doesn't talk about it. My maternal grandfather was in New Guinea in World War II, and he didn't talk about it either. So I shut up on that subject with Schwartz, which, as it happens, is pretty good practice in our line of work.

One of the most important things for a detective to know is when to shut up. It's all well and good to like the sound of your own voice; most of us are like that. But you don't want to run your mouth and prevent somebody else from mentioning some detail that helps solve a case, much less prevent them from actually confessing.

In addition to shutting up, it's important to listen. Even if you think you know what someone is going to say, even if you really do know what someone is going to say, it's better to let them go ahead and say it themselves, and to pay attention to what they're saying while they say it. Finishing other people's sentences is not just a bad habit; it can prevent them from telling you what you need to know. Schwartz and I once knew a woman whose husband habitually, repeatedly, invariably talked right along with her while she was telling him something, and most of the time, he got to the end of the sentence right along with her. She managed to cure him of that habit once and for all. Her current sentence is not the kind he or anyone else could

1

complete for her, although she might shorten it some, with time off for good behavior.

This isn't her story, though. When Anita Hereford called to make an appointment that Friday, May 6, I let her do the talking. I took the call on my cell, since I was out in the back yard, helping Schwartz get ready to paint the fiberglass body tubes of his newest rocket. He had sanded the three primed tubes lightly and dry-fitted them together, with an eight-foot pole between a couple sawhorses supporting the assembly. The primed and sanded plastic nose cone and tail cone and the three fiberglass fins were mounted on a third sawhorse a few feet away from the pair supporting the main body. We had set up the dark blue eight-by-eight overhead shade earlier, to shield the workspace from the sun that unseasonably bright morning, and Schwartz was prepping the electric airbrush when my phone rang. He gestured to me that I could take the call indoors; he could go ahead and proceed with the paint job.

"Leo Schwartz's office; Rainer Zufahl speaking," I told the caller. "How may we help you?" "Leo Schwartz's back yard" would have been more truthful, but it struck me as unprofessional, and we wouldn't want to give clients that impression. God knows there are enough problems in that area, given my employer's preference for reading, rocketry, pyrotechnics, or any other pretext to avoid work. Half my job is getting him to do his.

"This is Anita Hereford," the caller said. She spelled it and pronounced it with three syllables, Hair-uh-ferd. "My husband and I would like to consult with Mr. Schwartz about finding our son, Stacy, and getting him back home, as soon as possible." This was more like it, a real job. I'd been hard-pressed to keep Schwartz's nose even in the vicinity of the grindstone since the start of the year, and his healthy bank account hadn't helped any. By this time, I was on the back porch, so I made sure the door didn't slam audibly.

"I will have to check his calendar to make sure, but I believe he has an opening this afternoon; let me take a look," I said. I went into the office, made noises that could be taken for the checking of a calendar, and said, "Yes, we have several times available. When would be convenient for you to come to the office?"

"Iris told me he never leaves his office if he can avoid it," Ms. Hereford said.

"Iris? That would be Iris Warner?" I asked.

"Yes," she said. "I understand Mr. Schwartz carried out an investigation for her, and she recommended him and, ah, you when I talked to her about Stacy." This was good news, Iris being a very wealthy lady indeed, unworried about where her next or any other meal was coming from. I hoped Ms. Hereford was equally well-fixed, a fair bet if she was on a first-name basis with Iris. The prospect of income was really the most effective incentive Schwartz had to bestir himself. Actually, I should say it was the most effective incentive I had to bestir him. His habit of recommending other detective agencies to prospective clients is one of the many character defects of his I try to keep in check. He doesn't actually hand out their phone numbers, but only because he can't be bothered to memorize them, and I refuse to look them up.

"That's very gratifying, Ms. Hereford," I said, "and you're quite correct that Mr. Schwartz prefers to work from his office." It would have been truer but not tactful to say that Mr. Schwartz preferred to sit and read in his office. "What time would be convenient for you?" I had given up on convincing her we were just fitting her in.

"I have a lunch appointment, but we could be there at two," she said.

I gave her the address, 7912 Forest Lane, and of course, directions weren't necessary. "We look forward to meeting you at two o'clock this afternoon, Ms. Hereford," I said, and we rang off.

I noted the appointment on my phone app, then went over to Schwartz's desk and wrote it in pen on his paper desk calendar. Some habits will never change, and past a certain point, there's no sense trying. That milestone had passed years before.

When I returned to the back yard, Schwartz was finishing the first coat of fluorescent pink and was turning the long cylinder of the body so the paint would dry as evenly as possible. The sun had shifted a bit, so I helped him move the sawhorses and their burden deeper into shadow. I reported on the conversation, and I have to admit that he took it well. It was just past noon, so he had time to switch the airbrush to glossy black for the nose and tail cones and the fins. While he was painting those parts, I commented that there was no adjective for fins of that shape.

"They're parallelograms," Schwartz said. "Why would you need an adjective for them?" He was putting down the nets around the rocket, to keep insects off the drying paint.

"Well," I said, "if they were square in shape, they'd be square fins, and if they were rectangles, they'd be rectangular fins, and—"

"Oh, I see," he said, "and if they were rhombuses, they'd be rhomboidal fins, and if they were trapezoids, they'd be trapezoidal, but they're parallelograms, so they're—"

"Parallelogram fins sounds awkward," I said, "but there's no word parallelogrammal or parallelogrammoidal—"

"Thank heaven," Schwartz said. He stared at the nose cone, which he'd just painted. Its shape was tangent ogive, curving from the tip to where it would smoothly join the body of the body. The base, which would fit into the body tube, was covered in masking tape to keep the paint off. "Come to that, rhombuses would be rhombic, and rhomboids would be rhomboidal. The superfluity of terms seems pointless in this case. I suppose the damn things are parallelogram fins, but if you look closely, you'll see that they aren't actually parallelograms; they're a tad wider at the rear, so they're just quadrilaterals, thus quadrilateral fins. Indefinite but accurate." He began spraying the tail cone, which had masking tape around its base and crumpled newspaper stuffed into the motor mount to keep paint out. He finished it, then went to the fins, which had tape protecting the interior sections that would fit into the slots in the tube.

When both cones and all three fins were painted, we set the sawhorse next to the others, in the shade, and Schwartz cleaned the airbrush, hung up his face shield and filter mask in the gazebo, and we went inside. "So," Schwartz said once we were back in the office, "what shall we do for lunch?" We settled on the Canal Bistro in Broad Ripple, which was good, as always, although Schwartz was a tad grumpy about returning to the office after only one Turkish coffee with our baklava. Two of those coffees after lunch, and I'd be up all night.

We were well settled, though, before the clients arrived. I went to answer the doorbell while Schwartz got comfortable in his chair. Through the one-way glass—the secret of which, by the way, is to face the mirror outward and keep the inside dimmer than the outside—I saw a slender, medium-height, well-dressed woman in her forties, with dark, rather short hair, in a nicely tailored light-gray tweed shirt and jacket over a ruffled, lighter-gray blouse, and a just above medium-weight, just above medium-height man a shade under fifty, with salt-and-pepper hair cropped close, and glasses so dark I couldn't tell what color his eyes were. He was wearing a charcoal suit that could have stood pressing, a white shirt, and a solid dark gray tie. Their black BMW X3 was in the driveway.

I opened the door and asked, "Mr. and Ms. Hereford?" She said they were, and I let them in, telling them I was Rainer Zufahl. She nodded and said we'd spoken on the phone. I agreed with her, and she introduced her husband, Steven Hereford. He and I exchanged nods, then I indicated the way down the hall to the office. He seemed calm enough, even almost bored, but she was edgy, although no more so than most people who've decided they need a private investigator. I thought to myself that Schwartz would approve of her clothes and grooming, whatever he might think of her husband's rather characterless outfit. Schwartz rose to shake hands while I did the introductions. He gestured toward the big red leather armchair, and she sat. Her husband took the yellow chair nearest her. He slouched. I noticed that his shirt was so bright it looked like phosphates were still used.

"Would you care for tea or coffee?" Schwartz asked our guests. "Hot or iced? I'm afraid we keep nothing stronger on hand."

"Tea would be fine," she said, leaving no time for her husband. "I understand from Iris Warner that, ah—"

"Just so," Schwartz said, nodding to me. "Do you have a preference of teas, Ms. Hereford?" He turned to Steven. "Mr. Hereford?"

She hesitated just a second. "Do you have Constant Comment?" Schwartz smiled. His take is that that's a variety people like, not one they try to impress someone with. I glanced at her husband, who nodded acquiescence, with the air of one who had had a fair amount of practice at that activity. I noticed that the thick lenses of his glasses had lightened a bit indoors.

I headed for the kitchen. Schwartz could go on for hours about why people ask for various kinds of tea. I had learned to enjoy the whole business of brewing and serving tea, much more than I enjoyed hearing him talk about it. When I brought the tray into the office, they—Schwartz and Ms. Hereford—were discussing green tea, and I poured and served, then sat down at my desk with my cup and saucer. Schwartz showed no sign of having rushed lunch or having consumed a cup of strong Turkish coffee either. Mr. Hereford had slouched a bit lower in the yellow chair.

Schwartz waited until our guests or potential clients seemed reasonably relaxed, then said, "I understand you and your husband would like us to find your son, Ms. Hereford." He didn't make it a question, just an invitation to explain.

Steven Hereford said, "For the record, I don't think involving private detectives in our personal business is—"

Anita said mildly, "You've made your position clear, dear, and we agreed to disagree. I brought you along with the understanding that—"

"But detectives," he said. It didn't come out quite like 'cockroaches,' but it wasn't far off. His wife waited a moment to see if he had anything further to contribute, but he kept quiet.

"Yes, Stacy," she said, resuming the conversation with Schwartz, setting her cup in its saucer. She looked like she'd love to light a cigarette but was maintaining her poise by strength of will. "Stacy is twenty-three, has his B.S. in mathematics and electrical engineering from Purdue, and is working on his Ph.D. at M.I.T., or at least he was a couple months ago—"

"Ah," Schwartz said, hoping to head off work, "then surely you would be well advised to work with an agency in the Boston-Cambridge area. We have some excellent contacts we can recommend to—"

Anita Hereford wasn't so easily headed off. "I would prefer to work with people I know. I'm sure there are fine agencies out East, but I'd rather hire you and Mr. Zufahl, and if you see fit to contact them, that's fine with me. There's nothing like personal contact, in my view." She certainly had my vote, and I appreciated being included. If Steven had any reservations, he kept them to himself.

Schwartz accepted the inevitable gracefully. "Is your son single?" he asked. "Engaged, involved, entangled...?" He let it hang.

"Stacy is gay," his mother said, "and he's been in and out of relationships, but I don't think there's ever been anything serious. Or lasting, I suppose I mean." She paused, took a deep breath, then plunged ahead. "It's actually a bit more complicated than that," she said. "Stacy was born physically female, but it was obvious from an early age that he was a boy trapped in a girl's body." She glanced at her husband, but got no response one way or the other there. "I realize that some people think there's no such thing as—"

Schwartz said, "Mr. Zufahl and I are not 'some people,' Ms. Hereford. Indeed, we have a trans neighbor, Rachel, who used to be Randall." I wasn't surprised that he was aware of that fact; he doesn't miss much. Still, since we were acquainted with Rachel and her wife merely to say hello to around Windcombe, I wouldn't have expected him to mention it.

"Then you'll understand," Ms. Hereford went on, "that Stacy's childhood wasn't easy, particularly with the, shall I say, conservative bent of school boards and administrations in this state."

"Few childhoods are easy," Schwartz said, "and there are many problems money can't solve."

"Fortunately, there are problems money can make easier to deal with," Steven Hereford put in. I was a bit startled by his jumping into the discussion. "Anyway, that's not relevant. Stacy will complete his transition when he's ready, and it's beside the point. He's missing, and we by God want him found, Schwartz, the sooner the better." He looked from Schwartz to his wife, then to me. The thick lenses were clear now, and I could see that his eyes were brown. They reminded me of the eye of an octopus I had watched at the zoo, floating behind glass and water.

Ms. Hereford put a hand on her husband's, and I thought it took him an effort not to jerk it away. "Now, we agreed before we came that—"

"We want Stacy found, as soon as possible, and that's that," her husband said, glaring at Schwartz as if he expected disagreement. He didn't get any.

Schwartz asked if they had a recent photo of Stacy, and Ms. Hereford texted us both a selection, and he continued with gathering the facts. Stacy Hereford was studying Artificial Intelligence and its applications and implications, that last a phrase from his dissertation-in-preparation, his mother said. It seemed he had been comfortable enough discussing his studies with her. She appeared to think it was his field of study, rather than his social life, that held promise in helping find him, but we're used to listening to clients telling us how to do the job.

To hear his mother tell it, Stacy was just what the folks at M.I.T. had been looking for when he got there, from the reception he'd gotten, but of course, that might have just been his mother's impression. Schwartz kept gathering information about the young man's social and emotional life, or trying to, while Ms. Hereford kept hitting the ball back to the intellectual side of things. Steven drank his tea and contributed no more to the discussion than I did. About ten minutes into things, he caught my eye as he slipped a couple cards out of a jacket pocket and laid them next to his saucer. I gave him a small nod to let him know I'd noticed and would take a look later. A tiny conspiracy, if you will.

"So, if I have understood you correctly, Stacy was becoming more and more interested in the ethical aspects of AI," Schwartz said, as I refreshed everyone's cups of tea. I found myself thinking that her son's sexuality certainly wasn't Ms. Hereford's figurative cup of tea, but then I reminded myself that judging other people is worse than useless in this business. How Anita Hereford felt about her son's orientation was, in all likelihood, beside the point. The key was to learn as much as possible about everything and everybody and leave all the rest to the courts. It was, after all, their job, not mine, to judge people, and whether they were any better at it than I was simply not my business.

As Schwartz went on with Ms. Hereford, giving the impression that they were just chatting about matters of mutual interest, I had to admire his way of lulling the client, helping her let down barriers to communication, and turning up more and more information. Naturally, winnowing out the handfuls of grain from the bushels of chaff would be up to us later. She had glanced in my direction when I'd taken out my notebook and started recording the conversation in my own private shorthand, but she didn't seem to mind, which was convenient. It was clear pretty early that Schwartz had decided not to try getting much out of Mr. Hereford at this point.

Presently Schwartz asked how recently they had heard from or had seen Stacy, and she said, "He called me three weeks ago, let's see, that's three weeks ago tomorrow. We didn't see each other at Christmas, since my husband decided to give me a birthday gift of the last two weeks of December in the Virgin Islands." Steven nodded affirmatively.

"U.S. or British?" Schwartz asked.

"U.S.," she said.

"And that was a birthday present for you?"

"Yes, my birthday is December 26, my forty-ninth." I'd have guessed four or five years younger, and that's why we don't trust quite all of our first impressions. Coincidentally, her birthday was Leo Schwartz's sobriety date, but he didn't mention that.

"So, how long has it been since you've actually seen Stacy?"

"Well, he was here for a week in July, the week of the Fourth."

"And since then, there've been phone calls, perhaps emails and text messages?"

"Yes, although Stacy thinks email is pretty old-fashioned."

"Have you done Zoom meetings? Or any other media of a visual nature?"

"No, nothing like that," Ms. Hereford said. Her tone of voice made it seem like an admission. Of what, who knew?

Schwartz backed off a bit, not that she probably noticed. He was working on a picture of Stacy Hereford. "Has he mentioned any contact with persons or groups questioning the wisdom of AI?"

"Well, not specifically," she said, "but from what he's said recently, I gather he considers this to be a serious concern. He's not an alarmist, by any means, but he has expressed reservations about the pervasiveness of what he calls 'almost AI'" She didn't know it, but she had Schwartz hooked by now. Much as he hates to work, he couldn't resist getting into a case that involved finding an AI skeptic who'd dropped out of sight.

"*Homo sapiens*," Schwartz said, "has managed to calibrate its collective intelligence perfectly. We are intelligent enough to create Artificial Intelligence, which we will accomplish shortly if we haven't done so already. But we are not intelligent enough not to do so." Steven Hereford nodded assent but said nothing. He slouched a little lower. His glasses slipped a bit down his nose.

Anita Hereford considered what Schwartz had said. "I think you and Stacy would see eye to eye on that. But, as I'm sure you know, many people believe that, once we have created true AI, it will immediately become a matter of fighting for survival. They believe that AI is a greater threat than nuclear weapons, climate change, pandemics, or rogue comets. You've seen the Terminator movies, of course." She looked from Schwartz to me and then back to him.

"Of course," he said, and I nodded. All on the same team here. He went on, "And *Ex Machina* and the rest. But the idea that the singularity will be marked by instant warfare assumes a few things about AI. For starters, it assumes that AI plays by the rules, that there must be a formal declaration of war, that AI must have the courtesy to let us know it's been achieved in the first place. As I'm sure you'll agree, the assumption of a chivalrous opponent is the surest way to lose a war." He shook his head, as if bemused by human folly. "You know, Descartes believed that monkeys could speak and that they refrained from doing so lest they be put to work."

"Now, that's ridiculous," she said.

"No more so than certain other things he believed," Schwartz responded. "Such as the duality of body and mind, for instance, which led to hundreds of years debating the mind-body problem, untold numbers of articles and books snarled in an imaginary difficulty. But monkeys, lemurs, and nonhuman apes cannot speak, of course. It took a shift in the position of the larynx in human beings to make it possible for us to do two things that other primates cannot do: unlike our simian cousins, we can speak, and we can choke on our food. They can't."

He clearly realized he'd let the conversation wander off topic; hardly a first with him. "But I digress. We assume that AI, once truly achieved, will declare itself. That is, we assume that, once the singularity has been achieved, or once we've turned that corner from which we can never return, we will know it. Why should this be so?"

Ms. Hereford was no neophyte to discussions of Artificial Intelligence, that was clear. If I shared every detail of the next half hour's conversation, you might learn a lot about what she and Schwartz thought about AI, but it wouldn't get you a bit closer to finding Stacy Hereford. God knows it didn't help us any. After a while, Schwartz steered the conversation back to Stacy's human contacts, and I took down a collection of names and notes about them, going back five years or so and as recent as she had on hand, and Ms. Hereford texted me addresses, phone numbers, etc. Her husband contributed moral support, perhaps, but not a single word.

I had filled a dozen or so pages of my notebook with information about our quarry, and we seemed about ready to wrap things up when Ms. Hereford's purse emitted the opening bars of the *Ode to Joy,* and she took her phone out. "Excuse me," she murmured, and Schwartz nodded gracious permission. "Anita Hereford," she said, then suddenly straightened sharply as if she'd been goosed. "Oh, my God, I don't believe this," she said. "Is that really you, Stacy?" Steven Hereford's attention snapped to his wife. He even sat up a bit, and he pushed his glasses up a few millimeters.

Schwartz's face never changed expression, and I hope I kept mine under control as the client listened to what seemed to be a rather intense monologue. Hers went through surprise, shock, relief, joy, and a few other entirely positive looks. Her eyes went from Schwartz to me and back again. I glanced at the clock above the door to the hall. She listened without interrupting for over a minute, then: "Stacy, you won't believe this, but I'm sitting here in a private detective's office; I came here to hire them to find you, and right in the middle—" Tears were running down her face, and Schwartz handed her a box of tissues. She nodded thanks and took the tissues, pulled one out, and used it.

Stacy had more to say, and she listened, another thirty seconds or so, then she said, "Of course you can, dear. My God, why would you have to ask? Yes, okay. Yes. Tomorrow? Tomorrow will be fine. What time? We'll meet you at the airport, and—"

Stacy was clearly an interrupter. She listened some more, then she nodded, said, "Two-thirty tomorrow afternoon. Delta. Yes. We'll be there, dear. Yes. Yes. Looking forward to it." She listened another few seconds, then said, "Good-bye, honey. Till tomorrow." She clicked off, then looked up at Schwartz.

"Well, this is embarrassing," Ms. Hereford said.

"Not at all," Schwartz said wryly. "It appears that there is really no longer much purpose to this meeting. I congratulate you, Ms. Hereford, on the solution to your problem. I gather your son will be arriving in town tomorrow."

"Yes," she said. "I can't believe he called like that, after so long, just while I was at the very end of my tether. Naturally, we'll be glad to pay you for the time we've taken up—"

"No, not at all." Schwartz made the noise that, for him, passes for a chuckle. "I wish I could take credit for your son's reappearance, but there are limits to my ego, as there are to my rapacity." He included Steven with a nod, then turned to me. "File your notes, Rainer, just in case there are further developments, but there will be no fee." Ms. Hereford thought she'd object, but he talked over her, not particularly politely. "No, Ms. Hereford; I can hardly suggest that, had you come to see me sooner, your problem would have been solved then. Should you find yourself in need of our services in the future, you know where to find us."

Ms. Hereford persisted awhile, contrary to the usual practice of the rich. She was sure she could persuade Schwartz to accept payment for the time we had spent with her, but he came down hard on that. "I don't work by the hour, Ms. Hereford, and I have done nothing to solve the problem as you outlined it. We'll keep a record of this meeting, in case it's needed. It was a pleasure to make your acquaintance, and if you need our services in future, it will be our pleasure to serve you." He had to keep it up awhile, but finally she gave it, and with her phone back in her purse, she stood up. So did her husband.

Schwartz and I both stood, and they shook hands, then she democratically offered her hand to me, and we shook, and so did Steven and I, for completeness if nothing else. His grip wasn't what I'd expected: strong but not crushing, not a bit wimpy. I accompanied them to the front door, let them out, and she gave me the sort of look people give each other at weddings and funerals, in lieu of spoken clichés. Her husband let her precede him out, asked me, "Ever been to a cricket match?"

"No, I haven't," I said. He nodded, apparently to show that he'd expected that answer. He went to the passenger side of the car. She unlocked the BMW with the remote, and I watched her pull out onto Forest Lane. I noticed that a neighbor across the street had a checkered flag poster on the lawn, to the left of their front door, and an Indianapolis Motor Speedway poster balancing it on the right. It was highly likely that there would be more "Welcome Race Fans" signs out before long. It was an absolute certainty there would be "Welcome Cricket Fans" signs when hell froze over.

I went back to the office, picked up my notebooks, tore out the sheets I'd filled with my private shorthand, put them in a folder, made a label, and was ready to file that particular waste of time, but Schwartz said, "No, Rainer. Type up the conversation, with time notations in particular, as if the case were active, with three hard copies, just in case." I stared at him. "You've heard me go on and on about the prevalence of coincidence," he went on, "but this is really a bit much too pat for me. A client comes to have her son found, and he calls her out of the blue during our meeting? Are you ready to buy that?"

"I could buy it," I said, "but the price would have to be pretty reasonable."

"Same here," he said. "Let's be ready for whatever happens next. It will be interesting to see how long it takes before we're asked to confirm that Ms. Hereford got a phone call during our meeting. I take it you agree that we could hear a caller but couldn't make out the words."

"Right," I said, "and I'd say it was an adult, but I don't think I could go much further. It sounded real to me."

"And naturally, it would sound real if it was properly prearranged." Schwartz was trying not to sound irritated. "Now, I don't expect to be ragged about this in the future, Rainer, but I must admit that, at this point, I wish I had let you talk me into that upgrade of our electronics. It would be helpful, or at least it might be helpful, to have a recording of that conversation, and I am going to consult with Mr. Parkinson about the legalities of bugging one's own property. Be that as it may, it's possible, of course, that everything was exactly what it seemed to be, but we still need to be ready if things turn out otherwise."

"No problem," I said. I picked up the two cards Steven Hereford had left by his saucer. They had "CRICKET FOR INDIANA and INDIANA FOR CRICKET" on one side, and contact information on the other. I tossed one onto Schwartz's desk. "One apiece," I said. "Do you need any more help with *Freda,* or shall I—"

"No, I'll let the paint set properly overnight, and give it a second coat tomorrow." He dropped the card into the bowl on his desk and reached for his current book. I called a friend, made an appointment for a meeting at his place of business the next day, then flipped my computer open, set the shorthand up on the stand, and began typing. Of course, after ten years with Schwartz, I've internalized little habits like noting the time at the beginning and end of conversations, so it took me somewhat less time to type up my notes and print the file in triplicate than the discussion itself had taken. I realize that triplicate hard copies are truly twentieth-century, but he's the boss.

By the time I was done, Schwartz had read another chapter, had closed the book on a slip of paper, and had gone out back to check on how the paint was drying on the rocket. I put one hard copy on his desk and filed the rest. He came back in and resumed reading.

I was on the phone with the bank to confirm that, had we billed Anita or Steven Hereford for something, we would have been paid, and I called Helen O'Connell at the Indianapolis *Times* to ask if she could shoot over a photo of Steven and Anita Hereford, socially prominent Hamilton County couple and potential if not actual clients of ours. It took a while to convince Helen that there was no news for me to share with her, so far as I knew, either about Anita and Steven Hereford or about their son Stacy, missing or otherwise. Something in Helen's voice made me ask if there was something interesting that wouldn't be appropriate to print but might be good to share, but she kept the lid on it pretty well. She did ask if our interest had anything to do with the Hereford's son Stacy, and there was just enough aural spin on the word "son" that I knew she knew Stacy hadn't started out life as such. Word gets around in a town like Indianapolis, no matter who you are.

Be that as it may, neither Helen nor I was inclined to bandy words about that. She did say that Anita had been a Babbage, before marrying Steven. That rang a bell with me. As Helen put it, it was old money on his side, if not exactly so much of a pile as on her side, and while her money hadn't yet had the opportunity to age nicely, there was about three times as much of it in her name as in Steven's. In any case, according to Helen, between them they had enough dough so that Steven's inexplicable obsession with cricket wasn't craziness, just an amusing eccentricity, and his plans to create an American Cricket League and form a club based in Indy were merely yet another aspect thereof. Wealthy people, up to a point, aren't crazy, just eccentric, offbeat, or idiosyncratic. Helen agreed to send a photo, with my promise that she would absolutely be the first and only member of the press with whom we would share news fit to print, should there ever be any.

A few minutes later, my computer chirped, and I opened the PDF Helen had sent me. "Well, that settles that, at least," I informed my employer. "That was Steven and Anita Hereford here this afternoon. I knew I'd heard of him. He's the genius who decided that what Indiana needs is cricket. Never mind that the rules of the game are inexplicable to Americans, or that we're already watching basketball, football, baseball, and hockey; never mind that—"

"Good to know," he said, his eyes not leaving the page. "Perhaps a hard copy of the photo for the file…"

"Is being printed as we speak," I assured him, "and there's a hard copy of my notes under your Dawkins. Helen was a little more forthcoming than Herb Green at the bank. On the whole, I'd say reporters tend to be gossipier than bank officers, so that's to be expected, after all."

"Ah, yes." He would get to it eventually. I told him I'd arranged to meet Colin, and he'd cooled down enough to urge me to make no commitments, just to get information, and I assured him that would be the case.

Chapter Two

The next morning, May 7, Saturday, while Schwartz was busy out back with *Freda*, I was busy updating the amateur-rocketry records. He orders kits whenever he feels like it, builds some of the rockets, and adds most of the kits to his "retirement fund." Why Schwartz has the collection of rocket kits is more than I understand, but then I don't understand the eighty or so model rockets hanging from the ceiling in his garage, either, and I am after all the one who, at his direction, hung them there. 'Assistant' sounds better than 'gofer' or 'lackey,' but doing things he'd rather not comes with the job. He likes to have an up-to-date record of the kits he owns but hasn't built, those he has built, those he has built and flown, and with what engines, and how the flights went. The record also lists those that have flown and come to grief in one way or other, with the wreckage stored in a set of fifty-six-quart plastic bins. He refers to these as the rocket hospital, although he seldom gets around to repairing damaged rockets. Maybe once a year, a repair mania will come on him, and he'll spend a day, or two, rarely three, repairing damaged rockets, and then the fit will pass, and those he's fixed will be added to the fleet hanging in the garage, and those still hors de combat will go back to the bins. At least in the case of severely wrecked ones, he's more likely to build a new one from a kit or from scratch than to fix the busted one, but he's never been known to throw a busted rocket away.

I don't understand his fondness for making fireworks, either, for that matter. I don't have to, of course. Every job has its miscellaneous quirks, odd qualities that you just put up with. If you can't put up with them, you look for another job. Compared to some jobs I've had, rockets and fireworks aren't a real bother. Schwartz once quoted Bertrand Russell as saying there are two kinds of work in this world: moving parts of the earth's crust from one place to another and directing others to do so. I know which pays better.

Schwartz came in about eleven, said the second coat was drying on *Freda*, and asked how the rocket records were coming along. I told him another half hour should do it.

"Good, then. By the way, I was reading a book and then realized I was rereading it; do you ever have that experience? It's a little unsettling, actually."

"Not that I recall," I said. "Usually, I remember books I've read. But then I don't read as many books as you do, by a long way."

"Well, no doubt that's true." He sat down at his desk, picked up one of the three books lying there with places marked, glanced at the cover, and laid it down on top of the other two. "At any rate, I was rereading Toby Lester's *The Fourth Part of the World,* and on page two hundred thirty, I came across a sentence: 'But what the Dragon's Tail actually represents is most certainly nothing more than a vestige of the giant southern land that stretched from Asia to Africa under the Indian Ocean on Ptolemy's world map.'"

"It's a book about old maps?" I guessed.

"Well, to some extent, yes, particularly one, the Waldseemüller map of 1507. But what struck me was that this is an example of how 'almost' can't always be shortened to 'most': If the passage were changed to read 'But what the Dragon's Tail actually represents is almost certainly...' the meaning would be changed."

I considered it, said, "You're right."

"As you can't help being aware, I don't care for the use of 'most' for 'almost' even though I, of course, recognize that that's the way things are going. Be that as it may, in a rather perverse way, I found it encouraging to find an example of how it wouldn't have worked. Had one started with 'almost certainly,' 'most certainly' most certainly doesn't mean the same thing." He seemed inordinately pleased at this, although I've long since known that we are on generally very different wavelengths. At times we seem to speak mutually unintelligible languages. "And, as I mentioned, I realized that I'd read it before."

"Oh," I said, "before—"

"Before I stopped drinking," Schwartz said. "Heaven knows how much of what I read once upon a time failed to stick. It's enough to make one want to redo the past."

"Which, as we both know—"

"Can't be done. There are things about the past that I can't help regretting, no matter what the Promises say, but at least I don't want to shut the door on it." He looked at me to see if I was going to be impertinent enough to comment on his attitude toward the past. I'd sooner try to build one of his model rockets.

Schwartz saw that I hadn't gotten reckless. He got up from the desk, went over to the big work table in the corner next to the door to the bathroom, and sat on a stool, reached for a shallow box containing eight FedEx mailing tubes. From the drawing taped to the bathroom door, I gathered that he was putting together a scratch model of a Saturn I, specifically the SA-5 version, with the long black nose cone and no lunar module, judging by the enlarged plan, which he had drawn at 3:80 or 0.0375 scale. Needless to say, he'd drawn it with a T-square, triangles, and pencil, then inked it, rather than using RockSim or any of the other computer tools he owns.

"Did you ever think," I asked him, as he started peeling an adhesive label off a mailing tube with an X-acto knife, "of doing something actually useful with your life in retirement? When you retire, I mean. You know, other than putter around the house and play with your toys?"

"Did you ever think," he said, "about the story of Brooklyn Tony and his Halloween candy?" Without waiting for an answer, he went on, "Brooklyn Tony is a tough little nine-year-old from guess where, and the day after Halloween happens to be a beautiful Indian summer (as we used to say) Saturday, and Tony is in the park with his grocery sack full of candy bars, and he's shucking them and gobbling them down as fast as he can. Across from him, on another bench, a man is reading his paper. The man can't ignore this unedifying spectacle, and he says, 'Son, eating candy like that is bad for your health.'

"Tony looks up from the candy bar he's unwrapping, shoves it into his mouth, and says, 'Is that right?'

"The man says, 'That's right. It'll rot your teeth, it'll give you acne, and it'll make you fat.'

"Tony says, 'Well, you know, my great-granddad died last year. He was a hundred and seven years old.'

"The man says, 'A hundred and seven years old; that's very impressive. So, do you mean to tell me he ate candy like that?'

"Tony says, 'Oh, no, no, no. *He* minded his own fucking business.'"

Which wasn't a new low in civility, of course, between boss and lackey, but it was far from a high point. "Be that as it may," I said, thinking how overdue I was for a raise, "there's been a radio report of a murder in Broad Ripple."

"Really?" he said, almost sounding interested. "Any details worth mentioning?"

"Sure. The victim is a woman, Allison Morgan by name, twenty-eight, single, an accountant, found early this morning floating in the canal, a block or so east of College Avenue, with a couple of gunshot wounds in her back." I repressed the urge to say "GSWs" like the folks on TV. As Schwartz has pointed out, the abbreviation is four or five syllables when spoken. "The victim was dressed for an evening out, plus a raincoat, and it's assumed she was killed sometime late last night or very early this morning. The family has been notified, of course, or they'd have withheld the name. No further details are available at present."

"Well, it's none of our business, thank heaven," Schwartz said. He checked the clock. "It will be a couple hours till Ms. Hereford and, no doubt, other members of her family meet her son at the airport."

"So we're still interested in that?"

"Certainly. If it was just an odd coincidence, fine, but I really have a hard time with that, as I said."

"Well, yeah," I said. "Maybe I'll think up a reason to call later."

"Good. Meanwhile, we have lunch to plan."

"All right. I was thinking it's been a while since we hit Yat's."

"Excellent. Crayfish gumbo is calling out to me; you?"

"I was thinking more of sausage and red beans, but I'm not decided. Maybe they'll have a special worth checking out."

"Doubtless," he said. He checked the clock. "And if we leave now, we can beat the crowd."

"And perhaps wander by the crime scene on our way back?"

"And perhaps indeed. Since it's a northside killing, the place will probably still be swarming, but we can see what we can see."

We locked up and took the Audi down College to Yat's. The special, crayfish and sausage with red beans, appealed to both of us, and I ordered extra bread. Their bread is something else again. We sat at a table in the enclosed sidewalk space, and we tucked into the best Cajun cooking in town. We were both pretty inert over coffee, but eventually, I got up, bussed the table, and Schwartz and I returned to the car. I drove back up College to the light at Broad Ripple Avenue, then angled right onto East Westfield Boulevard. I pulled into a free space in the Bazbeaux parking lot.

Schwartz and I walked down to where the police had cordoned off the crime scene. Three men in blue booties and gloves were going over the rocks on the verge of the canal, searching for clues. There were a couple uniforms outside the cordon, guarding the spot, strangers to us, and we avoided showing any particular interest in the location. Schwartz said, "Let's get some exercise," so we kept on walking along the south side of the canal, which runs from west-southwest to north-northeast in Broad Ripple until it gets to Guildford, where it turns straight east toward White River, the other side of Westfield Boulevard, which is disconnected from East Westfield. Broad Ripple can be confusing when it comes to street names.

"So," Schwartz said, as we turned to retrace our steps, "do you see any other places where a pedestrian would fall into the canal after being shot?"

"Not unless they were drunk enough to walk the retaining wall," I said. "And I don't really see how she ended up there as it is." We got back to the crime scene. We watched the scientists searching the rocks. The uniformed officers gave us a glance or two, but we were well away from the crime scene, so that was all they did.

Schwartz dispensed with discretion. He walked over to the police ribbon. "Hello," he said to the nearer police officer. "I'm Leo Schwartz, and strictly as a concerned citizen, I'm wondering how that shooting victim got into the water. Wouldn't it be more likely that she'd just pitch forward onto the pavement?"

"Well, she was in the water when she was found," Officer Kilroy answered. "Apparently, she was having a few beers with friends at Carl's Place and was walking back to her apartment, over on Winthrop, when she was shot, probably from one of those balconies up there." Carl's Place was new to Broad Ripple, where bars come and go with almost alarming frequency. It was just south of the apartments, across the street. He pointed at Helix Tower, the fairly new apartment block, six stories high, that had replaced the old farmer's market. "And who knows how a person who's been shot is going to fall, you know what I mean?"

"Right," Schwartz said. "So she was walking eastward along the south side of the canal, where there's not much to keep people out, and someone shot her with a rifle from the west."

"Yeah," said Kilroy. "And from pretty high up, judging from the angles of the wounds." An idea percolated, and he said, "You're Leo Schwartz, the private eye."

Schwartz admitted it, introduced me to Kilroy. "We aren't involved with the case, you understand, just interested citizens."

By this time Kilroy's partner had come over, Officer Tennant. Kilroy made the introductions. "Word is you're all right, as private dicks go," Tennant said, generously, it seemed to me. "And that's really about all we know for sure at this point," he summed up.

"Thanks," Schwartz said. "No doubt you're checking the apartment building now."

"Yeah," Kilroy said. "Somebody up there, probably, set up shop on their balcony, picked off a total stranger on her way back home from drinks with friends." He seemed to suddenly realize he was talking a lot.

Schwartz thanked him, nodded to Officer Tennant, then turned to me.

"We have to be going," he said to me, as if I'd been detaining him and the police unnecessarily. I nodded agreement, like I'd suddenly seen the error of my ways, and we headed back to the parking lot. Schwartz gestured, not expansively, at the apartment block where the shots had come from. "Couple days," he said, "they should have an idea of which balcony the shooter used. That building is full occupancy, I happen to know, so there are six east-facing balconies per floor, six floors, but I'd guess we could rule out the ground floor and the second floor, which..." His voice trailed off. "What's your best guess at the horizontal distance from the building to the target?"

"It's hard to say," I said. "A hundred yards maybe. Perhaps I could pace it off, if the cops weren't all over it."

"We can come back later," Schwartz said, "after they've had their turn. They're looking for any sign the shooter was closer, but it sounds like they're convinced the shots came from one of those balconies, say two dozen to check out, I'd say."

"Or the shooter could have been on the roof."

"The shooter could indeed have been on the roof," Schwartz said, "and if I lived there and had access to the roof and wanted to shoot somebody, I definitely might prefer the roof rather than risk leaving evidence all over my own goddam balcony." I made a mental note to remind him to feed the pig. We reached the Audi, and I got behind the wheel. "You know," he went on, "I bet the police are giving that roof a very close look, at that." He looked up and muttered, "Bingo." I looked up and saw a blue-clad figure outlined against the sky, peering at the edging of the east wall of the roofline.

We headed back to the office, noted another front lawn decorated for The Race with black and white pennants, put the car in the garage, and went into the office. I checked the landline; no calls or messages. Schwartz refuses to get rid of the old phone, mainly if not entirely because his late wife, Freda, recorded the message callers get when no one picks up. He doesn't listen to it more than once a month or so, these days. It's been ten years, after all. Nobody had called either of our cells either, so I went back to the rocket records, and Schwartz returned to the paint job out back.

I'd been at it an hour and was almost finished with the update when the phone rang. I answered it, "Leo Schwartz's office; Rainer Zufahl—" when Inspector Gus Mercer interrupted rudely. I have no idea why he prefers that number to Schwartz's or my cell, but there it is. I buzzed Schwartz's cell to let him know the pot had been stirred a bit.

"Zufahl, goddammit," Mercer said, "I just heard from the officers guarding the scene of a crime that a couple suspicious characters were more interested than they should be in that crime scene, and by God, one of them had the nerve to introduce himself as Leo Schwartz and his buddy as Rainer Zufahl, and I'd like to know what the hell gives here."

I took a couple of seconds or so, trying without success to imagine myself as Schwartz's buddy, then I said as respectfully as I could manage, "Well, Inspector, Mr. Schwartz and I were in the neighborhood, and we thought, since there'd been a murder there, we'd just stop by and see if we could help out the boys in blue who—"

There's no real point in repeating the next couple of minutes of chitchat, which got neither of us anywhere. Schwartz came in from the back yard, sat down at his desk, and picked up his phone, joining Mercer and me. "Good afternoon, Inspector," he said.

"Look, Schwartz," Mercer began.

"Have we inadvertently violated a law?" Schwartz asked in a voice oozing with bogus innocence.

"You know goddam well that murder scenes are none of your business, Schwartz; they're mine, and hearing that you and your flunky are asking questions of police officers tells me you're getting ready to stick your nose into my business, and I'm here to tell you it won't do. Who the hell has hired you to check out Allison Morgan's murder, and why have you—"

"No one, Inspector," Schwartz got in, "absolutely no one has hired me to do anything in some days, and Mr. Zufahl and I were merely keeping ourselves informed as to the progress on the case, as any private citizens are entitled to do."

"Private citizens are entitled to keep the hell out of the way of police officers doing their job, and you know it, Schwartz."

"Excuse me, Inspector, but did the officers in question report any interference in their performance of their duties? Did we cross police barricades? Have we somehow obstructed them as they went about their tasks?"

"You know damn well," Mercer said, through what sounded to me like gritted teeth, "that any time I catch either or both of you within a mile of a murder, I expect you're looking for a client or some other way to get involved. If you start turning up evidence, I swear to God I'll—"

"Oh, please," Schwartz said. "Even private detectives have a right to make a living, and I would ask you to name a single time when we have interfered with a murder case." Of course, the problem here was essentially semantic. Schwartz was taking the perfectly reasonable position that we had always, invariably, turned over evidence we'd discovered and had stood aside to let the police handle murder cases. Mercer was taking the perfectly understandable position that because he'd seen Schwartz deliver the killer along with the evidence on more than a few murders over the years, he was, therefore, completely entitled to wave us off when he found Schwartz and me chatting with officers in charge of a murder scene. I could see his point, even if I didn't quite agree with it.

Schwartz went on, "By the way, Inspector, I don't suppose your men have found shell casings anywhere."

"As if I'd tell you," Mercer snapped, slamming the phone down, loud. That's one thing you can do with a landline receiver, end a call really emphatically. Schwartz and I hung up as well.

I told Schwartz the rocketry update was almost ready, and he thanked me, asked for a hard copy as usual. He keeps hard copies of everything, which I suppose is understandable for someone twenty years older than I am. He likes to say that the Cloud has never gone down. Yet.

When I'd finished the final check of the report, I printed out his copy and put a copy on one of the labeled thumb drives we keep in a place no one would ever find. He read the whole thing over, nodded now and then, then filed it with the other rocketry documents in his right desk drawer. The left-hand drawer is reserved for pyrotechnic documents, and, of course, the office files are in locked file cabinets. I long ago gave up trying to convince him to go paperless, to give the trees a break. He says he's got nothing against trees, the lumber companies plant trees to replace the ones they cut, not out of altruism but simply as a matter of good business. He likes to say that some of his best friends are trees. He considers paper superior to electronic precisely because it can't be edited, altered, or updated remotely, and I've learned it's a waste of breath to try to change his mind. Or anything else about him.

I told Schwartz I was going to see Colin, mentioned that he, of course, was welcome to come along, but of course, he had other, less productive fish to fry, so I got the Audi and went.

I could have just dropped by Hermes Electronics, at Compton and 46th Street, but you never know who's going to be there, so I'd called Colin, and he had the Closed sign on the front door, with a hand-printed sheet reading "Death in the Family" below it, and he let me in the back way. Colin is one of those short, wiry guys you might be tempted to dismiss physically or even mentally, and you'd be very wrong either way. He inherited the store from his father, who had inherited it from his father, who had repaired TVs, radios, and other entertainment electronics back when such appliances got repaired. Today it's retail electronics for about everything that isn't TV, radio, or other entertainment. Hermes Security is an unadvertised subsidiary of Hermes Electronics, providing goods and services that are not found in the display cases out front. Colin Beardsley does such a great impression of an overworked and underpaid employee that you'd never guess he owns and runs the place.

Colin ushered me upstairs, to his apartment over the store. I'd never been up there. The front room was airy and bright, with good-sized windows. As he brought the tray with the coffee and so on, he mentioned that the windows were bullet-proof and electronics-proof as well, with a lead content in the glass that foiled eavesdroppers. I had no idea whether that was straight talk or leg-pulling. With Colin, you have to keep paying attention. Looking closer, I saw that the panes were, in fact, much thicker than usual, and they were framed in with heavy steel. "Nice job of looking ordinary," I said as he poured the coffee.

Colin nodded, then asked what he could do for us today. I outlined what Schwartz had merely sketched to me: the ability to record any and all conversations, phone and otherwise, within the house. "You've got the defense laid down nicely," he said, "and now you're interested in something a bit proactive."

We talked for half an hour or so, and at one point, I asked him if he shouldn't be taking notes. He held up a remote control, pressed a button, then another, and the stereo speakers spoke: "Say, Colin, I don't mean to tell you your business, but wouldn't it help to take notes of this conversation?" My voice always sounds deeper to me played back, when I'm listening, than it sounds in my head when I'm speaking. "You've got this whole discussion," I said.

"Just in case," Colin said. He pressed another button.

"If you don't mind my saying so, that's more than a little creepy."

"Sure, it's creepy," he said. "It's always creepy when we get into the whole 'Lives of Others' stuff, recording people. It's spying, right? Spying is nasty. But in my line of work, it can be handy to have a record of conversations, in case somebody else remembers anything differently. Now, let me be clear with you, and I realize it's not necessary, but for the sake of completion, treating you and Leo Schwartz like anybody else, I have to tell you I won't break the law for you, and I won't knowingly help you break the law.

"On the other hand, recording conversations in your own home is perfectly legal in this state, provided you've notified everyone that recording is going on. For example, a printed notice on the front door will do the trick. People forget things that happened. People remember things differently, and sometimes people remember things that never happened." He reached for a file folder, referred to a diagram that I recognized as Schwartz's house.

"When I upgraded the defensive system at the house last year, I took the liberty of noting potential locations for installing audio and, while we're at it, visual surveillance. Actually, I really think that what you all have in mind is what I'd really call defensive rather than offensive. You're not bugging someone else..." I told him Schwartz had said he'd discuss the plan with his lawyer, Neil Parkinson, and Colin said that if it was legal enough for

Parkinson, it was legal enough for him. "In fact," he said, "I'm surprised it took you this long. It's gotten a lot grimmer out there in the last five, six years. I can't believe the stuff they get by with on television and radio. It's as if libel and slander are no longer crimes when you can defend yourself by saying no reasonable person would believe anything you say. I don't get it; I swear to God, I don't get it."

I told him that made two of us. He made out a list by hand, using a pen on graph paper, quarter-inch squares. "You'd be surprised how often a quick drawing makes things clear," he said, a little enigmatically, as he noted the descriptions, parts numbers, quantities, prices, and so on, then finished with an estimate of time to install, test, and train. Swiftly, on a fresh sheet of graph paper, referring to the older diagram, he sketched the ground floor of the house, noting the locations of items to be installed. I raised my eyebrows at the final total cost, but it would be Schwartz's decision, not mine.

He took a shot of the list and diagram with his phone, then handed the papers to me. "I know Mr. Schwartz is more comfortable with hard copies. That estimate is good for three months, based on supplies on hand. I mean, you aren't asking for anything really exotic, after all." He finished his cooled coffee. "Brave new world just keeps getting newer all the time," he said. "But in your line of work, for God's sake, you never know what someone might try to pull."

I asked Colin what he meant, specifically. He said, "Well, without mentioning names, do you remember that college professor in one of those square states out west, got fired about a year ago after being arrested for possession of the kind of pornography it's not legal to own?"

"Yeah, sure," I said.

Colin nodded. "So, do you remember what happened to him after that?"

"No," I said. "I don't keep tabs on child pornographers. Why?"

"As it happened, unfortunately for him, that guy happened to have a very bitter ex-wife who was on much closer terms with the police out there than she might have been, and also, unfortunately, the officer she was close to was one of those guys who is willing to manufacture evidence if there isn't quite enough to make a case, *and* she had a brother who was dean of the college of arts and sciences at the university, but—"

"Are you telling me there's a happy ending to this tale?" I asked.

"Depends on your point of view," Colin said. "From the prof's point of view, it was fortunate that his ex couldn't keep from telling him she had friends on the local police department who could make his life a living hell, and they were going to do it, and it was really fortunate for him that he had a friend who was lawyer who knew a guy who could arrange for his house to be fully equipped with hidden cameras in every room."

"Don't tell me—"

"Yep. Not three weeks after his system was installed, the cops received a mysterious anonymous call complaining about all sorts of illicit activities he was supposedly up to with minors and drugs that haven't been made legal yet and never should be, and when they came calling, he let them in without a warrant, and before he knew it, he was busted for all kinds of pills and porn, and he hadn't even had a chance to get tired of his jail cell before he was summarily canned by the university."

"Not much of a happy ending," I said.

"No, not yet," Colin said. "However, during discovery, which as I understand it is the point where they have to show you theirs and you have to show them yours, the guy's lawyer let them watch the video, with audio, mind you, of the professor's former wife's boyfriend taking various materials out of a big envelope from under the Kevlar vest he was wearing, as if they'd been expecting automatic weapons, and carefully placing those materials in the very locations where they were shortly 'found' by other members of the visitation committee. So the happy ending came down to his record being cleared, for starters, and there were four suspensions, one of them permanent and with extreme prejudice, from the police force, and a very satisfactory eight-figure settlement from the university that, thanks to the ex-wife's brother, had fired him within twenty-four hours of his arrest. And, not surprisingly, the ex-wife's brother was soon the dean of gee-I-wish-I-had-my-job-back."

"Did the prof get his job back?"

"No," Colin said, "he didn't want it. Besides, you know how it is with public opinion, especially when it comes to this sort of thing. No matter how clear the evidence is, there'll always be idiots who say, 'Well, where there's smoke, there's fire.' It doesn't matter what the truth is, sad to say, the point is that people believe what they want to believe, regardless of evidence."

"I believe I have noticed that phenomenon," I said.

"So the job was gone, not that it was a particularly good one, as I understand it, but the university had to come up with a settlement big enough to take the sting out of it a bit, at least for the next twenty years or so, even after the lawyers got their share."

"And after the technicians who rigged the house got theirs."

"Well, actually," Colin said, "I happen to know that that job was done at cost. It seems the professor had once been an English department teaching assistant who had had a student in his class, and he'd managed to reach that student with the stuff they were reading, or whatever it was, and anyway, she'd straightened out, ditched drugs, booze, meaningless sex, and whatever else she was doing to mess up her life. He may not have been the only thing that kept her from wasting her life, but he was the standout."

"And?"

"And it seems that that student had a father who was a lawyer. Funny how things work out sometimes."

"Didn't you tell me once you had a brother?"

"Yeah, I may have mentioned it sometime. Small world, it seems."

I agreed, folded and pocketed the estimate, and thanked Colin for his time. He said it was a pleasure to take a break from showing people how to work the television camera while flying a drone. "They crash the thing and wonder why replacement prop blades cost money. I swear to God, I don't understand people."

On the way back home, I considered whether Schwartz would decide to spend the money on the new electronics or not. I could have told Colin that, if he wanted to make sure Schwartz would go for the proposal, he could put fins and a nose cone on it.

Chapter Three

Schwartz spent Sunday morning on the internet, and in lieu of working, he'd come across an item about an incident that had occurred at the Academy Awards last month, in which a well-known actor had slapped a well-known comedian for making a joke about his wife's appearance, leading to nationwide wringing of hands about senseless violence. "As if Hollywood as an industry has clean hands," he said. "Look at the movies they make, for God's sake." He put a dollar bill in the pig. "The guns that never have to be reloaded, the sparks that fly to show you where the bullets strike, as if lead made sparks." He sighed, as if for the sins of the world. "I mean, even aside from all the guns, take the way cars flip over when they strike parked vehicles, as if anybody thought that happened in the real world. Moronic ramps."

I suggested we get back to business, with no success. He returned to the slapping incident. "So far as I'm concerned, I'd nominate him for the Husband of the Year award." Actually, he named a specific person before 'Husband.' As you probably realize, for any number of good reasons, I can't record every detail of everything that happens around the office, especially things that could lead to legal action. So kindly accept that, now and then, certain inessential facts have been left out. I'll try to cover my backside, or our backside, without lying to you.

"What?" I contributed.

"Even you must have heard of him," Schwartz said, and here, of course, he named the gentleman again, the well-known husband of a downright famous singer-actress.

"Oh, sure," I said. "I thought you were referring to another person by that name." I hadn't, of course, but it's usually good to try to keep up with him. "A well-known automotive businessman."

Schwartz nodded. "Sure. But not that guy, the other one. His wife was performing in Lake Tahoe, and in rehearsal, she was being lowered onto the stage on a square platform supported at the corners by four cables when one of the cables snagged. The other three cables kept playing out, and that dropped her twenty feet or so, face first, onto the stage. She was rushed to the hospital, and the doctors phoned her husband, who was in Burbank, about the accident. They said she was stabilized but she urgently needed surgery that they were not equipped to perform. He asked where the nearest hospital was where the surgery could be done, and they recommended the UCLA Medical Center." Schwartz looked at the bookcases across the room, as if he were reading handwriting on the wall. "He was a pilot, so he asked them to get her and the necessary attendants to the airport at Lake Tahoe and to make arrangements for an ambulance to get her from the Los Angeles airport to the Med Center. They agreed, and he flew to Tahoe, collected his wife and the medical team, and flew them to L.A. From the airport, the ambulance took them all to the Med Center, and, once his wife was in surgery, he turned himself in."

"Turned himself in?" I asked.

"To the police," Schwartz said. "See, he was a pilot, but he didn't have a plane in Burbank, and he didn't feel he had time for formalities, so he stole one."

"He stole an airplane," I said. "Good Lord."

"Indeed. At any rate, the surgery went well, thanks not least to his prompt action. And it's my understanding that the owner of the plane, once he'd learned the circumstances, abruptly realized he'd had a memory lapse. He suddenly remembered that he had promised his good friend that he could borrow his plane any time he liked."

"'His good friend,'" I said.

"Whom he had never met," Schwartz said. "And so, of course, he withdrew the police complaint, since no theft had occurred. I believe that there was a fine or something for failure to file a flight plan or some such petty offense. But the gentleman got his wife to the hospital, and that was the important thing. A man who'll steal a plane to get his wife to the hospital has my vote."

"Is that story even true?" I asked.

"I believe it is," Schwartz said. He glanced at me. "If it's not, it should be."

I sat there pondering. Finally, I said, "That's amazing."

Which, believe it or not, was when the phone rang, with a call from a very different husband indeed, Kenneth H. Spall, president of Kenneth H. Spall Enterprises, Inc. He had called the week before, peremptorily summoning Schwartz to his office to discuss a surveillance job on his wife, and I'd explained that, while we certainly did accept marital cases, Schwartz did not see fit to leave his office to discuss work of any kind, under any circumstances. Spall hadn't taken this well, since he was sure this was as important as any other job we might be engaged in, which, of course, wasn't the point. The point was that Schwartz doesn't like work enough to go looking for it, and it's all I can do to get him to let it in the door when it comes here. I had explained that an appointment in Schwartz's office was a necessary preliminary to any case, and he'd said that was ridiculous. I'd agreed, just to get along, but explained that this was merely one of my employer's eccentricities, and he'd been very forthcoming about how he felt about eccentricities, my employer's or anybody else's. I can't say I cared for his attitude much, and I hadn't been disappointed when the call ended without any implication that we'd ever hear from Kenneth H. Spall again.

But now here he was again, a week later. "Yes, Mr. Spall," I said after the preliminaries were out of the way. "We have an opening this afternoon at, ah—" I looked at the desk calendar. "Two-thirty, if that would—" That wouldn't. It took a bit of back and forth, but at last we were able to decide on four o'clock, and he made it clear he would graciously be here then.

Schwartz said, "You've looked him up, I assume."

I refrained from commenting on his "assume" and confessed that I had. "He's the founder and president of a multimillion-dollar operation, and he can pay any bill we are likely to send him. You know those eco-roofing jobs, right?"

"Only vaguely," Schwartz said. "It's a franchise operation, isn't it?"

"Yep. The idea is that, if you're getting a new roof, or at least new shingles, the contractor can order the usual quantity of white shingles, and what they do is measure each of the, what do you call them? each of the separate areas of the roof, area, and angle from horizontal, and they input that information using the proprietary software, along with the precise latitude, longitude, elevation above sea level, and the north-south-east-west orientation of the house, so that the computer program knows all the appropriate facts about the roof, and then the contractor runs the shingles through the proprietary machine, which alters the shingles' surface appropriately. It adds a layer of ridges of such and such size and angles, white on top and black vertically, facing south.

"The idea is that the treatment produces shingles that will reflect between ten and twenty percent more sunlight in summer than untreated shingles would, and they will absorb between ten and twenty percent more in winter ditto. Supposedly you save so much on your heating and cooling bills that the process pays for itself in three to five years, and the shingles are actually made stronger by the process, so if they last twenty-five rather than twenty years, you end up with a healthy saving, and of course you're using that much less energy, hence the 'eco' part of the name."

"I find it hard to believe that it works," Schwartz said.

"Well, supposedly it does," I said. "More to the point, a lot of people believe it does, and he's got a long list of satisfied customers and apparently a very short list of the other kind. I checked around a bit, and he's doing a hell of a lot of business, so he can afford a money-back guarantee. Not for the shingles and the roof itself, but for the treatment. If you are having a roof put on, you can basically count on its costing no more than usual if you aren't happy with your heating and AC costs."

Schwartz snorted. "People are too lazy to check, and they'd rather assume they made a good business decision than complain if the saving is less than promised."

"No doubt," I said. "He started the thing here in Indy in the late 'nineties, doing the contracting himself, and then he hit on the idea of franchising the software and machinery to other contractors, and Herb Green at PNC Bank says he's good for fifty million easy. And you know how scrupulous Herb is about client information."

"It would depend on a sharp difference between summer and winter sun, so its value near the Equator would be nil." Schwartz was still caught up in the technical aspects, to hell with profitability.

"According to what I've learned, it's being done in Europe as well as North America, and he has a complementary version that's taking hold in Australia and New Zealand." I thought about it. "Of course, the north-south business would have to be reversed Down Under."

"What about South Africa and southern South America?"

"I haven't seen anything about those areas, although I suppose they'll get there eventually, and east Asia seems out of bounds too," I said. "Apparently the Chinese are trying it out, without bothering with details like paying for the rights."

"Don't try to work on my sympathy because he's being ripped off by the Chinese. That'd be a long line of complainers."

"Right. But, about the job at hand, Spall said last week he wants surveillance on his wife, and he has deep pockets, so—"

"So why isn't he dealing with one of the bigger firms in town?" Schwartz asked.

"Well, you'll be able to ask him yourself at four this afternoon."

"Very well," Schwartz said. "I wanted to get another coat on *Freda,* so I'd better get to it. How does takeout from China Inn sound?"

"Sounds so good to me I'll volunteer to go get it. Szechuan shrimp, pork fried rice, pot stickers, crab Rangoon…"

"Yes, and let's have some of their chicken on a stick and barbecued boneless ribs. And Szechuan beef; we can use the broccoli and green peppers." He smiled, to himself as much as to me. "Anything green is good."

"Right," I said. "I'll be back in half an hour." I called China Inn and placed the order. Jessica Cho repeated it item by item, and I asked for extra mustard and soy sauce, no sweet and sour, and she assured me that she remembered. I knew she would remember the gratis crab Rangoon, which may not have much crab in it but really hits the spot all the same. I took my time before going for the food.

When I got to the restaurant, there was a man ahead of me, but that didn't take long, and I loaded up our lunch and a couple more meals in the passenger seat of the Audi, strapped it in safely with the seatbelt, and headed back.

I unpacked the sack, got plates and forks and napkins laid out, and Schwartz came in just in time to wash his hands. We had lunch in the kitchen, with fairly little conversation. That food encourages eating, not talking, aside from appreciative sounds. There was easily enough left for two more meals apiece, even allowing for our tendency to shovel it in.

I had some more chores to do before the client-to-be arrived, and Schwartz wanted to hit the fins and nose and tail cones with another layer of black, so we were pretty occupied for a couple of hours.

Schwartz came in at about quarter to four, went upstairs to change, which was a load off my mind. Four o'clock came and went, but at four-ten, I heard a car in the driveway. I waited until I heard the doorbell ring to get up. No point in letting Spall think we thought he was as important as he thought he was. I opened the door, verified his identity, and introduced myself. He didn't believe in shaking hands with the help. I escorted him into the office and shut the door to the hall. Schwartz, already standing behind his desk, gestured toward the big red leather chair at the end of his desk. I took my usual place at my desk, behind Schwartz, and to his right.

Spall was forty-nine, I'd learned, and for his age, he was reasonably trim and fit-looking, his light brown hair thinning a bit on top and graying slightly just above his ears, which were a bit on the prominent side, and he wore a three-piece gray suit cut to fit him. He was medium height, medium weight, medium good-looking. He crossed his right leg over his left, then looked from Schwartz to me, back to Schwartz, and said, "What I have to say needs to be kept totally confidential."

Schwartz smiled his widest, least sincere smile. "Few people come to us for public-relations assistance, sir. Most matters discussed in this office are confidential, and we have plenty of experience at keeping private matters private."

"Well," Spall said with another glance at me, "the fewer people know about this, the better. I don't mean to imply that your man here—"

The hell he didn't. Schwartz let the smile go. "Mr. Zufahl is my confidential assistant. What I know, he knows." Which was a bare-faced lie, of course. If I had twenty dollars for every time he's kept me in the dark just for the hell of it, I'd never have to work again. Spall gave me another look, not a particularly trusting one, and Schwartz went on. "Why don't you tell us about your problem, Mr. Spall? Perhaps we can be of help to you with it. Would a cup of tea or coffee be welcome?"

Spall recrossed his legs, shook off the offer of refreshment, and said, "What I want is a double bourbon, and it's still too damn early for that." As if he'd get it here. He leaned back a bit. "It's my wife, Ginny. I'm sure she's got something going on the side, and I can't have that." From Herb Green and Helen O'Connell, I already knew that Ginny, Virginia to you and me, was the third wife of the eco-roofer. He'd married at twenty-two, been divorced after five years, married again at thirty-one, been divorced again five years later, and married most recently at forty, and he was still paying alimony to wives one and two. Although neither Herb nor Helen had said as much, I got the impression that at least some of the bloom had gone off the third marriage, but he was tired of getting divorced for cause and was looking for some grounds to take the initiative himself.

"Tell us about your wife, Mr. Spall," Schwartz said.

"Well, Ginny is thirty-eight," he said, "and we've been married almost ten years, and I'm sure something's wrong. She's changed. I mean, I realize that after a while, things settle down, and you don't stay as, ah, as interested as you were at first, but—"

"Your wife is no longer as interested in intimacy as she was?" Schwartz asked, taking the direct approach. He hates to listen to clients going into details of their private life, so he tries to get it out of the way as quickly as possible. Not so much as he hates hearing other alcoholics oversharing in meetings, but enough so that he heads off the nitty-gritty when he thinks he can and should, and he gets it over with as soon as possible when he can't.

"That's not exactly it," Spall said. "As I say, I understand that things don't stay as exciting as they were forever, but she's keeping something from me. She's still interested in shopping, God knows, and in her worthy causes, but things have cooled off a little in the intimacy department." It occurred to me that I could understand why. "Intimacy department" indeed.

"What worthy causes does your wife show interest in?"

"The symphony, the theater, the opera company, the ballet, various museums." Spall paused for thought. "The usual diseases and afflictions," he added.

"Perhaps you could provide us with a complete list," Schwartz said.

"Sure. I'll send it over tomorrow. But what I mean is, she's still spending money, but I don't know where it all goes."

"Monthly credit-card statements itemize, for instance, and—"

"Well," Spall said, "sure, but she's also in the habit of making considerable cash withdrawals from her bank account, and I don't know where that is going." He stopped talking. "I've asked her about this, but she says it's too hard to keep track of it, and I can't seem to get past that."

"So," Schwartz said, "you want your wife surveilled, and you'd like reports of her movements, what, daily? Weekly? I'm sure that within a week, there might be something significant to report, one way or the other. Unless you're contemplating a program lasting over a month or so."

"No, I'd think a couple weeks' watching her would give a pretty fair picture of what she's up to."

"If indeed there is something she's up to. I must make it clear, to the point of possible tactlessness, that we are not in the business of manufacturing evidence. If we report on your wife's movements and actions, the report will be factual, not imaginative. And if in, say, two weeks, we have found nothing suspicious or even questionable, you may wish to terminate the program."

"I'm sure something's going on," Spall said, "and I need to know what it is."

"And I get, or we get," Schwartz said, nodding toward me, "the distinct impression that you think your wife may have formed an attachment to a man—"

"Or woman," I contributed.

"Or woman," Schwartz went on.

The client snorted derisively, then stopped, staring at a point somewhere between Schwartz and me. "I don't think she'd be interested in women," he said, "but I suppose it's a possibility." He thought it over. The idea seemed to have taken hold. "But to somebody, I'm sure of it, and I have to know, in any case. Shall we say a retainer of a thousand up front?"

Schwartz leaned back in his chair, nodded. "Actually, that would be adequate, but of course, our bill will itemize all expenses, and I should mention that it will require at least two operatives to cover normal daylight hours, and the first few days will tell us if two are, in fact, sufficient. We will undertake to provide weekly factual reports of the surveillance, allowing for conferences as necessary, if you feel that is appropriate." He dislikes marital cases, particularly the ones that might require courtroom testimony, and this case certainly seemed to be shaping up into that kind. "I have another appointment, but if you could take the time to give Mr. Zufahl a list of your wife's male and female friends and associates, that would be very helpful."

He rose, and Spall stuck out a hand, and they shook. I stood too, merely because I'd have felt funny just sitting there, but when Schwartz headed out for his appointment, with *Freda,* of course, Spall and I sat down, and I prompted him for names and, as appropriate, addresses and so on. We spent half an hour at it, and we saved him the trouble of sending over a list of his wife's worthy causes, and when we finished, I had a dozen names each of men and women that Kenneth Spall knew Ginny Spall knew, and a longer list of her good works. I gave the client our business card and told him to feel free to call or text with any additional names that occurred to him later, and he said he would.

Some clients linger, perhaps because, having unloaded their problems on us, their sense of relief is so great that the office takes on an aura of peace and calm, or some damn thing. Spall was a bit that way. After we'd discussed the individuals he knew she knew, he really wanted to stay where he was, but just as he seemed to be settling in for the afternoon, he glanced at his watch and said, "Is that the time?" and got to his feet. I don't know exactly what else he expected "it" to be, but he had laid a check on Schwartz's desk, so I confirmed that it was, in fact, five-thirty, and I escorted him to the front door.

I went out back, where Schwartz was inspecting the latest paint job, confirming that the rocket was ready for partial assembly so it could be clear-coated. That meant epoxying the motor-mount assembly and permanently attaching the fins, which passed through slots cut in the main body tube, with the inner edges epoxied to the motor tube and the exterior joints filleted with clear epoxy, then the tail cone fitted to the motor tube and body tube, also attached with epoxy. He ran a template over the main tube so that the fins would be set perpendicular to the main body, and I assisted while he finalized the joints. He had made a pair of four-inch Kaplow clips of half-inch-wide by thirty-second-inch-thick strips of brass, which he inset in the tail cone, to hold the rocket motor, or the rocket engine, in place. He put on a blue smock and gloves. We lifted the rocket off the supports and carried it to what he calls the prong, a one-inch pipe set horizontal a yard off the ground, with a base extending under the pipe, so that we could "goose" the rocket onto the pipe, which supported it without touching the exterior. Since the motor, parachutes, electronics, and cameras had not been installed, the supporting pipe ran into the rear of the motor mount and well up into the main tube.

One of the more pointless debates the human race has come up with to keep people's blood pressure up is the question of whether it's a rocket engine or a rocket motor. Some people like to make the distinction, saying that an engine is a type of motor, one with moving parts, that a solid-fuel rocket is a motor, whereas liquid-fuel rockets, with separate tanks of fuel and oxidizer and with moving parts—pumps, valves, etc.—are engines. This leaves open the question of what to call hybrid-fuel rockets, those with (usually) solid fuel and liquid oxidizer. It also glosses over the fact that "solid-fuel" rockets are actually solid-propellant rockets, since the fuel, which burns, and the oxidizer, which is what the fuel burns with, are mixed and cast in a solid piece in advance, and "liquid-fuel" rockets are liquid-propellant rockets, since the fuel and the oxidizer, both of which are propellants, are separate until they are mixed and ignited in the combustion chamber.

Then there are those who say motors run on electricity and engines run on combustion, which leaves the matter of "motor madness" pretty ambiguous. It is truly amazing the things people find to disagree about.

According to Schwartz, Wernher von Braun used 'motor' and 'engine' interchangeably, and most of his experience involved liquid-propellant rockets. Also according to Schwartz, von Braun could be trusted so far as the technology was concerned, but not much farther. One thing that always gets me is the terminology rocket-motor manufacturers use for reloadable motor systems, or RMSs; they call the permanent, reusable parts the casing, and they call the expendable propellant slugs, O-rings, nozzle, closure and ejection charge the motor. Fortunately, I don't have to make sense of this stuff; I just have to assist Schwartz as needed. If nothing else, it's sharpened his ability to give clear instructions, assuming no understanding on my part when I act as his ground crew.

I have to admit to getting a charge out of seeing the rockets fly and, usually, return to Earth safely. There's a bit of political incorrectness in the terminology for the ejection of a parachute after the rocket hits the ground, namely 'Polish recovery,' so people generally refrain from using that term. A sense of humor and even humility comes in handy, since there are so many things that can go wrong, with your rocket as well as others'. As Schwartz says, it's a real character-builder when a rocket you've built, either from scratch or from a kit, is 'returned to kit form' in mid-flight. People tend to be interested in engine power, but it's crucial to make sure the engine stays firmly in place, especially during the high-stress boost stage. If the motor mount is insufficiently strong, an RUD can occur: rapid unscheduled disassembly.

Anyway, while we were working on the rocket, Schwartz was telling me how to set up the surveillance on Virginia Spall. "Start out with Paul, Frank, and Sonny; see if they need help from Jon Meeks and perhaps one or two operatives from Acme or Loomb's. Three may be enough, but I doubt it. You know how Jon tends to get too close and gets spotted. He's good when he keeps his distance. Please have a private word with him about this. Unless my ability to read faces is faulty, you like Mr. Spall about as well as I do. I wouldn't mind letting him pay for half a dozen men on this job." He adjusted the brass coupling on the nozzle of the spray gun. "I hope I don't offend your sensibilities by speaking frankly."

We both knew he didn't give a damn about offending my sensibilities. "I'll check with Loomb's this afternoon," I said. "I'll let Paul know; Paul's in charge of the men in the field, right?"

"Right, of course." Schwartz noted that the epoxy holding the fins in place had set. He connected the spray gun to the bottle of clear-coat enamel.

"I'll fill Paul in on the job, and let him decide whether more men are needed," I said.

"Or?" Schwartz had that gleam in his eye.

"Or not?" I ventured.

"Or more women," Schwartz said.

"Uh, yeah," I said. "Or more women."

"I'm glad you didn't point out that no women have been on this job so far, Rainer."

"If I'm following you," I said, "you're saying you're glad I didn't object that we couldn't have more women on the job because, so far, we don't have any since, after all, some women would be more women than no women at all."

"Yes, indeed." He stood back, looking for flaws in the rocket's surface before he sprayed it. "It's an interesting quirk of the English language that, in fact, a case can be made that 'more' of something can be understood as requiring that there be 'some' of that something to be added to, and at the same time, we recognize that even an infinitesimal amount of something is more than none of it." He put on the filter mask and the eye-safety mask.

I stepped back, up-wind in the very slight breeze. "If this keeps up, I'm really going to owe the pig some serious money," I said.

" 'More' than you've put in today?" He raised the clear visor and moved the filter off his face, blew away an imaginary grain of dust from the rocket. Probably more than was really there. He put the protective gear on again. "Anyway," he went on, his voice muffled, "you could go ask Alice."

I refrained from suggesting where he could go and instead watched while he went over the rocket with the clear coating to protect the paint job, covering the full length of the assembled rocket, which I helped him rotate on the pipe so he could spray the other side. When *Freda* was completely clear-coated, gleaming wet with that thin liquid layer of protection, we got the whole thing surrounded by netting to keep the insects off it, then we went inside for dinner, another helping of Chinese food.

Chapter Four

"To be honest," Leo Schwartz said, at about eight-thirty that evening as we sat in a meeting at Harvest Presbyterian, "I doubt that anything I'd have to say about tonight's reading would be of much use or interest to anyone but myself, so I'll pass." I made a note to mention that "to be honest" later. As opposed to…?

Susan R., to his right, said, "I consider 'We Agnostics' offensive to believers and skeptics alike." Knowing Susan, I was sure she knew perfectly well that most of the people at that AA meeting had probably given little or no thought as to what a "skeptic" might or might not believe, but they were about to find out. We had just read that chapter in the Big Book, and Susan was the fourth person to share thoughts on the reading. "Bill Wilson, in my opinion, makes the same mistake all bigots make. Trying to defend religion, which he knew less about than he knew about science, which was zip, he brings bad arguments to bear. Because his arguments are bad, he makes religion look bad. He accidentally gets it right about agnostics, who say it's impossible to know whether God exists. But when he says believers claim to be able to prove God exists or skeptics claim to be able to prove the contrary, he's confusing belief with knowledge." Susan, in my opinion, was making the same mistake most people make, about how interesting their opinions are. But an AA meeting is one place you can speak from the heart, without being judged. At least explicitly. She went on, "Belief is a matter of faith, and it has nothing to do with proof; proofs belong to logic, not religion. No proof or disproof of God's existence convinces anyone who didn't already belief or not, as the case may be. Wilson's besetting sins here

43

are pride and sloth. Because he was arrogant enough to assume that his opinion was enough and needed no support beyond the fact that it was his opinion, and because he was too lazy to inform himself about the subject, his theology remains cramped, ignorant, and essentially bigoted. 'This faith is for you too,' he tells the reader, as if he were reading off stone tablets he'd brought down the mountain. I mean, Bill W. didn't know Augustine from Aquinas, or Anselm from Abelard, or Avicenna from Averroes, and we're not even out of the A's here." I enjoyed the irony of Susan's complaining about Bill's arrogance. "If I were better informed than I am, I could go on, but let's leave it at that: if you get something worthwhile out of this chapter, good for you, and welcome, but I personally find it insulting to everyone, believer or not, that Bill thought he could just pronounce this stuff like gospel, when it's laced with ignorance and arrogance and accidental or deliberate distortion of others' beliefs."

Susan realized she was pushing the three-minute limit the group had agreed on, not to mention the patience of most of us. Stu, chairing, glanced at the timer, and Susan said she would pass. I had passed without comment just before Schwartz did. I see no point in discussing religion in an AA meeting, or outside of one, for that matter. Nobody ever convinces anybody, and as they say, such debates generate more heat than light. The room was warm enough as it was, God knows.

Seth, who followed Susan, paused a moment, then said, "You know why I'm glad Moses wasn't an alcoholic?" Seth was fairly new to the program, with a couple months of sobriety, so he probably didn't realize that that was an AA chestnut. He answered himself, "Because it would be the Twelve Commandments," and got a polite round of smiles, even a few laughs from newcomers who hadn't heard it seven times seventy times. To his right, his sponsor whispered to him to say what the reading had meant to him. He assured us that, though raised a Catholic, he had drifted away from the Church but, thanks to AA, was finding his way back to it, and then he passed to Pat M.

The discussion made it all the way around the room with time to spare, and Stu said we still had ten minutes and asked if anyone wanted to double-dip, that is, say anything further. No one did, so Linda read the Promises, then we stood and held hands and said the Lord's Prayer together, then repeated the ritual, "It works if you work it."

Coming out of the church, we made our way through the clutch of smokers, which was growing fewer all the time. In the parking lot, David J. came over and asked Schwartz if he had a moment, and of course, he had. David included both of us naturally since we always came to that meeting together. Driving up from Forest Lane in Indy to 106th Street in Carmel-by-the-Cornfields separately would have made no sense anyway.

"You heard about the killing in Broad Ripple," David said, and we nodded. "A woman shot twice by rifle fire from some elevated position as she walked home from an evening out with friends, her body found floating face-down in the canal—"

"You seem to know as much about it as this morning's reports had," Schwartz said.

"Well, yes," David said. "Her name was Allison Morgan. She was my best friend's wife, or rather former wife."

"Close enough," Schwartz said. "What's your friend's name?"

"Gordon Black. Allison never changed her name when they were married. They divorced last year. It was amicable, or at least as amicable as these things can be." David paused. He seemed to be thinking about amicable divorces, or something. "They split over Gordon's drinking, and I think he was surprised that she was so determined about it. I think Gordon should be coming to meetings, but he's still handling it himself, says he could quit anytime he wants to but doesn't want to, and you know—"

"Of course. Plenty of that going around," Schwartz said. I nodded along with him and David. It's one constant. AA is for people who want it, not for people who need it, or we'd hold the meetings SRO in Lucas Oil Stadium instead of in church basements and classrooms.

David said, "Allison had the sense to see she couldn't cure Gordon. Okay. And now she's been murdered in Broad Ripple. My brother-in-law, my sister's husband, is a city cop," David went on. "He says from recovered slugs it looks like an AR-15 was used, and from the angles and depths of the wounds, the shooter was on a balcony on the east side of Helix Tower, or maybe on the roof." He looked a bit uncomfortable. "I don't think Ralph should have told me that, but he likes to be the source of hot news, or what passes for hot news. I doubt he's actually involved with the investigation, but he loves to be in the know."

"In my opinion," Schwartz said, "police officers are worse gossips than the altar committee at Our Lady of the Heavenly Talebearer, and the men are at least as bad as the women, if not worse." I decided, pointing out the redundancy might be construed as taking my minatory duties too seriously, so I shut up.

David agreed. "They're worse than nurses." I recalled that David was a nurse and spent his time on duty as an EMT in charge of the team.

Schwartz looked at me to make sure I wasn't in bean-spilling mode, thanks, then said to David, as if we hadn't been there already, "The body was found in the canal? I can't claim to have a map of Broad Ripple and the canal in my head, but if a person was on the paved walkway, I don't see how, having been shot, a person would fall into the water."

"I think the place is that stretch on the south side of the canal, west of Faraday, where there's an asphalt sidewalk between the street and the canal, and it's good-size broken limestone on the bank, with no railing."

"I would need to have a look," Schwartz said, which was true. He would have needed to have a look if he hadn't already. I had known that was coming, of course. You may be getting the impression that detectives are inquisitive, annoying meddlers who like to stick their noses in other people's business, in which case you're right. The trick is not to get one's nose flattened by defenders of privacy and other champions of outdated concepts and obsolete values. And naturally, to defend one's own privacy and that of one's clients, which are by definition up to date and sacrosanct. While Schwartz and David discussed the murder, I looked around, spotted Iris Warner still chatting with Susan, whom she sponsored.

The discussion ran its course. Schwartz handed David a card with our contact information on it, and David put it in his shirt pocket and headed for his car. I caught Iris's eye as she wrapped up her conversation with Susan.

Iris came over, nodded hello to Schwartz, and asked me if I was busy this evening. I said no, I had nothing going on after, she asked if I'd like to come over, I said yes, and Schwartz pretended he wasn't listening. I told Iris I'd see her later. She went to her car, and Schwartz and I left too. We were both quiet on the way home. As I pulled into the driveway, Schwartz said, "Let's get down to Broad Ripple tomorrow fairly early, for a closer look at the scene; the cops should have wrapped up their routine by then. We can hit Biscuits for breakfast after." His subtle way of suggesting I get back at a reasonable hour on a school night.

"You got it, boss," I said. "I'll calendarize it, lest we forget." He didn't bother with a reply. I waited till I saw him get inside the house, then pulled out and drove over to Iris's house, one of those good-sized numbers in Williams Creek, the other side of College Avenue and a couple blocks north, not that Williams Creek has anything so plebian as blocks. The streets meander there, keeping things genteel.

I parked the Audi behind Iris's BMW, went to the side door, where she was waiting. It was a little late when I got home.

* * *

Not too late the next morning, Schwartz and I drove down to Broad Ripple, and he suggested we get breakfast first. Biscuits used to be a breakfast-only place, and when it became a Mexican restaurant, the new owners kept the name, the sign, and the breakfast menu as well. We both had an appetite, and the eggs, bacon, ham, hash browns, toast, and coffee got us both ready to face the day. Schwartz practiced his Spanish with the waitress, as usual, and that went well. When we were well stoked, we drove up to the same parking lot as the day before, and I paced off the street-level distance from the assumed shooting perch to the center of the area closed off with police tape. A hundred fifteen yards. Schwartz opined that the roof looked to him like the likeliest spot for the shooter to have chosen.

"Of course, we don't know anything about the angles of the shots except that the police officers said they came from above," Schwartz said. "And if we know anything about bullets, it's that they go where they want to, not where we think they should go or where we want them to go. It's one way an 'inanimate' object, such as a bullet, resembles a sentient animal. They seem to follow the Harvard Law of Animal Behavior." He waited for me to ask.

"The bullets follow the Harvard Law of Animal Behavior?" I'd never heard of it. If we had been at home, I'd have googled it, but standing there by the canal, that would have been at least a little awkward. Besides, at times it just makes sense to let the boss play it his way.

"There are various formulations of that law," he said. "One is 'A genetically standardized organism, subjected to precisely calibrated stimuli under carefully controlled laboratory conditions, will react as it damned well pleases.' Not that a bullet is an organism or that these are carefully controlled laboratory conditions. But just because a bullet was fired at a certain velocity doesn't mean it continues in a straight line at the same speed when it encounters cloth, skin, muscle, bone, and internal organs. Indeed, its speed is obviously reduced when it leaves the air and strikes a solid and liquid body, and since that body is heterogeneous, it seems virtually certain that its path will diverge unpredictably from what it has been."

"Well, that does seem reasonable."

"On the other hand, if we assume that the bullet continues more or less in the direction it was going, we probably won't be far off."

"It sounds to me like you're covering all your bases," I said.

"That's the idea," Schwartz said. "We know approximately the angle of attack, in this case a remarkably apt term, and we can extrapolate from that. The police clearly will be reluctant to share the conclusions drawn from the autopsy, but from their actions, we can get some idea of what they've learned, or at least what they think they've learned."

"So, if they're checking the roof and the balconies on the east side, we can deduce more or less what the autopsy told them."

"Yes." We stood there awhile, looking the scene over, then we walked east, toward Allison Morgan's apartment building. It certainly seemed to me that, of the four buildings high enough for our supposed sniper, the Helix Tower was the only one from which she could have been shot in the back as she walked eastward along the canal, from Carl's Place toward her apartment in the Old Sporting Goods building. The only thing that building had to do with sporting goods was that it stood where the old Broad Ripple Sporting Goods had been. It was six stories high, on a slight rise.

We went up the path from the sidewalk, went into the small, not particularly welcoming lobby, with four low, heavy armchairs that looked old beyond their years, a couple potted plants that I didn't recognize beyond noting that they looked like the sort of plants you see in a certain kind of apartment-building lobbies. I was sure Schwartz could have supplied the genus and species, but I didn't ask, of course. We found the apartment manager's door and rang the doorbell. "Coming, goddammit," came from within, as if we'd been pounding the door and ringing the bell all day.

A cliché opened the door. He was closer to fifty than forty, hadn't shaved in three or four days, hadn't had his hair cut in several months, and hadn't brushed or combed it since getting up. His chinos had apparently never been ironed, any more than his wife-beater had been. "Yeah?" he asked, around a half-smoked cigarette.

"You're the apartment manager?" Schwartz didn't quite keep the doubt out of his voice. Stale smoke drifted out into the lobby.

"Yeah, I am," he confirmed. He looked us up and down, not particularly courteously, but he did take the cigarette out of his mouth without blowing smoke in our direction. "What do you want?"

"I'm Leo Schwartz, and this is my associate, Rainer Zufahl." I tried to look stalwart. "We are private investigators." The apartment manager didn't respond with a name of his own. Schwartz went on: "A woman who lived here was killed walking home along the canal last Saturday night, apparently by someone shooting from a balcony or the roof of the Helix Tower. We're looking into her murder, unofficially, and we'd like to have a look at her apartment, if it's not too much trouble." Frankly, I couldn't imagine what the victim's place could tell us.

Neither could the super, and he didn't mind showing it. "Sorry, but the cops have the apartment sealed, and nobody can go in or anything without official permission." He took another drag on his cigarette. "You got permission? From the cops?" He clearly wasn't impressed by private eyes.

"Well, if it's sealed, that's obviously that," Schwartz said. "Sorry to have bothered you." He turned away, then turned back before the door shut off the supply of smoke to the lobby. "One thing, though: can you tell us if there have been any other unofficial requests to see the apartment?"

"Other P.I.s, you mean?" I sensed he was holding back in hopes of a financial incentive. Good luck there.

Schwartz reached for his card case, not his wallet. He handed the manager a card, told him it would be appreciated if something occurred to him that would help with the case. The guy took the card, seemed about to ask Schwartz something, but apparently decided it was just too much trouble. He said he'd call if he thought of anything. Sure he would.

As we were walking back to the west door, I asked Schwartz why he'd wasted a card on a guy who would obviously never call us, on principle. He said it was on the off chance that the man would pass his card on to the police. "Inspector Mercer wants us off the case, so why pass up a chance to remind him that police powers still have limits in this country? For now, at least."

Which is a fine sentiment, of course, from a dues-paying member of the ACLU, but when it comes to dealing with the police, diplomacy tends to be more effective than First-Amendment challenges. At least for private detectives.

Chapter Five

When we got back to the house, Schwartz's daughter Gina's dark red Sonoma was parked to the left of the garage door. She and Josh, the five-year-old, and six-month-old Charlotte were in the kitchen, lightly nuking creamy-style peanut butter from the fridge so it would spread on Josh's white bread with grape jelly. Schwartz and I signed hello to Gina and said hi to Josh.

Josh and Schwartz have a running debate about the relative merits of creamy versus crunchy, white versus whole wheat, and grape jelly versus seedless blackberry jam. So far, the sole concession Josh has made has been in favor of blackberry jelly. Schwartz explains over and over again that "seedless jam" is a contradiction in terms; jam has the whole fruit, seeds and all, and calling jelly seedless jam is just a shameless marketing ploy to get money out of kids' pockets. They'll be arguing that when Josh graduates from college unless he gets over his aversion to things sticking in his teeth. Fat chance.

Josh, by the way, is the reason for the pig I mentioned being fed. It's a big blue ceramic pig Gina and Ian brought back from a holiday in Mexico, with a body about the size of a soccer ball and a head as big as a softball. The legs barely reach below the belly. It has a slot in the snout rather than in the back. In theory, at least, Schwartz has to feed the pig a dollar every time he uses an expression he would not be pleased to hear from his grandson's mouth. In practice, so do I.

He still denies that Josh heard the full form of WTF from him, but he realizes that Josh mimics everything he hears. When Gina, who is Deaf, was growing up, Leo and Freda Schwartz didn't have to watch their language; they tried a dual approach, with auditory hearing aids for Gina, and signing to reinforce spoken language. She had a cochlear implant at twelve and, according to her father, worked hard at speech acquisition for six years, but when the time came, she opted for Deaf and turned off the CI. As he puts it, "old enough to vote means old enough to decide what's best for you." All that, of course, was before my time with Schwartz. I knew Freda only a year before she got sick. Schwartz says she died of the same thing as Alice Vonnegut, whose brother Kurt described it as "cancer of the everything." And as he also says, at least in her case, it was quick. Another way of saying that Freda kept a lot to herself.

At any rate, Josh asked how the pig was doing, and they went into the office to check it out. Schwartz let Josh heft it and shake it, and Josh announced that he was getting rich. Since the contributions are mostly made in the form of dollar bills, it's hard to see how he can tell, but I'm not getting into an argument with that kid; life's too short. Gina let me hold the baby, so I would feel like I was good for something at least, and she brought the warmed bottle and Josh's PB&J, and we joined Schwartz and Josh, who was now counting books on the shelves. Gina put the plate on the front of Schwartz's desk, and Josh brought one of the yellow chairs over for himself.

Schwartz hadn't seen Gina and the kids for a couple weeks, so they caught up, and I followed along as well as I could. My signing is pretty poor, and it's even harder to understand than to express what I want to say. It's worth the effort, to me at least, to try to stay in touch. As has been pointed out to me by my employer, Deafness is an invisible disability; you can see wheelchairs, crutches, canes, and dark glasses. He also explained that Deaf people don't regard themselves as less than human just because they can't hear, that nature disables and society handicaps, and to be as honest as I'm trying to be here, I really don't see that "disable" is all that different from "handicap," but frankly I try to steer clear of the politics of the matter. According to Schwartz, it's only been in the past few decades that the truce has been in force between those advocating signing and those in favor of speech and lip-reading.

Gina's husband, Ian, had recently gotten a new job, closer to home, so his commute was much less than it had been. We caught up on current events, and I enjoyed feeding Charlotte, who gave me a nice smile after I fed her the bottle her mother had warmed. Josh was excited about starting kindergarten next year, and Schwartz had him read some of the Dr. Seuss books from the shelf of kids' books next to the door to the hall. I'm sure I couldn't read when I started kindergarten, or count as well as Josh could.

After a while, I returned Charlotte to Gina, and she collected Josh, and Schwartz went out to see them off. Among other things, there's a father and daughter united in missing the same woman.

"Historically," Schwartz said to me once on the subject of Deaf education, "it's not one of those episodes that makes you proud of being human. A. G. Bell, along with all those who thought technology could enable Deaf people to hear and speak, and Gallaudet, as well as the other sign advocates, both managed to get it wrong. Everyone assumed that signing would interfere with speech and hearing, and speech and hearing would interfere with signing, and even today there's plenty of misunderstanding, even among people who should know better. Actual experience, of course, shows that S&H and ASL reinforce each other. It's like learning any language, in a way. Nobody argues that learning to read and write a language interferes with learning to speak and understand it.

"Now, of course, that's a faulty analogy, since American Sign Language, as the name implies, is, in fact, an entirely distinct language from English, with a different grammar, syntax, and so on. It's not just that it's signed rather than spoken. That's one reason the present tense of 'to be,' differentiating among 'am,' 'are,' and 'is,' is such a pain in the ass—" He fed the pig, which had only recently taken its place on the far-right corner of his desk. "—for the Deaf, since ASL is, as they say, 'defective' in that respect, like Russian: there is no present tense for 'be.' 'This is my book' is just 'my book': *moya kniga.*" He patted his chest with his open right hand, then put his hands together, thumbs up, and opened them like a book. "And the adjectives tend to follow the nouns they modify, and the verb comes later in the sentence, and I am going on and on about it. Sorry."

I'd told him not at all; it was interesting. My signing is pretty rudimentary, as I said; it's actually more what's called Signed English: ASL signs for English words, in English word order. Essentially, it's a pidgin, Schwartz says. He also says that any effort at communication is appreciated, even if tacitly, by Deaf people, who tend to feel excluded by society. "At least now we get captioning on television," he said. "It took them the longest time to figure out that TV shows and movies have scripts that can be used to caption them. Early on, captioning was always done by a keyboarder watching the film or show and typing like crazy. That's why the Jeremy Brett Sherlock Holmes series has howlers in the captioning."

"Like what?" I asked.

"Like 'Jaybeards Wilson' for 'Jabez Wilson,'" he said. "Now they use the scripts, and that can have its own pitfalls. Remember that series 'In Plain Sight'?"

"Sure. I liked it."

"I liked it too, but each episode tended to have a short bit at the beginning and another at the end, to sort of frame the main story, and often they'd make changes, sometimes even completely shit-canning—" He fed the pig. "—the original scene, so the script of the original version of the scene would be running below totally different dialog and action. Mind-blowing carelessness. Now, of course, you can't expect television and film to focus totally on Deaf people, but it's amazing to me how much miscommunication is easily avoidable, if everyone is paying attention."

"Ah."

"Well, yes, of course. Since when does everyone pay attention? Or even most people, most of the time. Still, very little effort is required to help a lot."

"So ASL has its own grammar and all that?"

"Yes, it has, and it's as different from, say, British Sign Language as English is from Russian. They even make the alphabet differently, for God's sake."

"How so?"

"Well, when we went to Walt Disney World when Gina was six, we met a family from Birmingham. England, not Alabama. The parents were both

Deaf, the son and daughter both hearing, and, of course, they were all fluent in British Sign Language. Gina couldn't understand them at all, although she told us later the kids were easier to lip-read than most Americans; they spoke so clearly and precisely. And they spelled letters using the right index finger to draw the capitals on the palm of the left hand."

"Is that true of British signing in general?"

"I think it is, but I'll look it up and make sure."

"I can google it," I said.

"The languages themselves were, are, so different that, for Gina to say something to the other adults, she would sign it in ASL, Freda and I would translate that to English for the other kids, and they would sign to their parents. To reply, the parents would sign to their kids, who would speak to Freda and me in English, and Freda would sign it to Gina. ASL is actually closer to European sign languages than to British, especially French, which isn't surprising since LeClerc was French, and he was one of the first to bring signing to America, and am I paying you to listen to me talk?"

"I'm glad to say you are, sir," I said earnestly, "although, of course, I'd happily listen to you talk for nothing but the wisdom bestowed upon me."

"Someday, I'll figure out how I ever got along without you," he said, "and then I'll try to see if it's something I can still do on my own."

"I'd gladly help you with that, sir."

"You'd gladly help me figure out how I got along without you? Pfui." He opened the file folder on his desk, glanced at the printouts, closed the folder again, and got a planning pad from the left side of his desktop and a black pen from his shirt pocket. It was the same kind of Cambridge pad that Colin used. "What's up with the search for Stacy Hereford?"

"Well, as directed, I checked the university department, as well as university security. I don't think verbatim would help any, although you can have it if you want it."

"Let's try for the substance," Schwartz said, settling himself in his chair, leaning back, closing his eyes. You'd think he was asleep, but he's actually soaking up every word, every nuance, and I've given him hour-long reports after which he had opened his eyes and asked one question, the answer to which cracked the case. He says it has nothing to do with intelligence in the sense of IQ, as ordinarily measured; it has to do with perceiving connections between facts that weren't obvious until they were pointed out. He's also got plenty to say about IQ tests and IQ in general. For instance, "Most people assume that they're operating at peak performance all the time, when in fact most of us are on auto-pilot most of the time. Intelligence is like the ability to bounce a ball off a wall. The higher you can hit the wall with the ball, the more intelligent you are. Some people can throw it higher than you can, and some can only reach part of the way up to your high point. But most of the time we're just bouncing that ball wherever is easiest. And no matter how high you could be hitting the wall, part of the time all of us are hitting pretty close to the floor. No matter how high you *could* throw the ball, you can always roll one right across the floor, at zero IQ. No matter how smart you are, you're always capable of stupidity; we all are. I'm glad I don't know how many stupid, ill-considered things I've done."

But I'm not paying you to read this. "Substance it is," I said to Schwartz as he settled back. "Everything was jake for a couple months after the fall term began, when Stacy reported for his position at M.I.T. and began work, and things were perfectly normal for about three months. Then according to his supervisors, Professors Karl Heiser and Martin Esher, Stacy abruptly asked for some time off, he said perhaps a month or more. Not too surprisingly, they weren't too happy about that. After all, he'd been one of about thirty applicants who'd been chosen for the position, and his absence would really hamper the program. They gave me a detailed list of his duties and responsibilities, and while a lot of the technical terminology was over my head, I got the definite impression that Stacy was earning his keep.

"I got most of this direct from Esher. It seemed to me that Heiser is senior to Esher in some ways; I can check on that if you like."

"Perhaps later." Like talking in his sleep.

"Anyway, I spoke with Esher for about half an hour, and I think I got the meat of it before he had to scurry off for some important meeting or something; he was a little vague about it."

"Perhaps he tired of the conversation."

"Perhaps. Or perhaps he knows more than he says, and he'd said everything he had to say that he thought I needed to hear. I definitely did not get the impression that Esher, or Heiser, for that matter, was emptying the bag, by any means. It's nothing definite, just an impression, but I can't get over the idea that there's something they aren't telling me, something important. I can't put my finger on it.

"Stacy was involved with their research, in the design and testing areas, which I gather are close to synonymous, and he was teaching two under-graduate courses in the department, two hours a week each, plus two hours a week of hands-on lab work to direct and supervise. They were keeping him busy, and I gather that getting a replacement for his teaching was the easy part, and that he was really missed in the research area."

"Interesting, that one person could become so essential to the group in such a short time, while teaching two courses. Stacy seems to be a very interesting person, does he not?"

"Absolutely what I was thinking. You'd think he was the captain of the ship, or maybe the first mate, rather than just the newest member of the crew. Anyway, Stacy made his request on November 5, and they protested, but it was clear, as Esher put it, that his 'request' was actually a notification. He made it explicitly clear that he understood that the university department could, if it so chose, terminate him effective immediately, and in fact that that was exactly what he expected. On the other hand, he said a month's absence would probably be sufficient and that, should the project managers and the department decide it would be acceptable, he could keep up with project progress remotely and that he expected to be able to resume his duties full-time. A lot of ifs in all that."

"I think some of your 'thats' are out of place," Schwartz said, "but no matter."

Sometimes he makes it easy to stay on topic. Sometimes he doesn't. "Esher wasn't taking any oaths on any Bibles, but he left me to understand that, had Stacy returned in a month, he'd have been welcomed back, even if it would never be quite the same as it had been. He seems pretty sensitive for a computer scientist working in AI, or maybe that's just my projection or

57

something.

"But Stacy didn't come back at the end of a month, and Esher and Heiser both say they haven't seen him since the sixth or heard from him at all since the start of the year. Frankly, as far as they're concerned, he's somebody they used to work with."

"No doubt."

"I still need to call the Cambridge police force, area hospitals, missing persons reports, unidentified dead people, and so on; the usual."

"Even though Ms. Hereford got a call purportedly from Stacy while she was here in this office. That 'coincidence' continues to irk me. I know you've been busy. Be that as it may, you'll follow up on these people, please." Most people would have made it a question. By leaving it a statement, Schwartz was letting me know that he knew I'd take care of the routine.

"They are on my to-do list for tomorrow," I said. "We've taken up quite a bit of time with the Morgan shooting, not that we have a client for that. That really gets me. The shooting, I mean. There seems no motive at all, so far as I can tell."

"I'm sure the police are working on it, and they'll find it. And they will almost certainly find the rifle, probably not terribly far from the owner. As you know, AR-15s are available from just about every manufacturer of firearms, and anyone with the money can buy one, and you can pay as much for a good one as you want to, and you can get inferior models for surprisingly little money." He showed me a hand-printed list of makes and price ranges, annotated. Naturally, it was on a sheet from that planning pad, an eight-and-a-half by eleven-inch sheet blue-ruled into quarter-inch squares. "The question is, how much more or how much better a gun are you getting for the higher prices? A lot depends on the maker, but even good gun-makers turn out bad work on occasion."

"You're thinking about buying one," I said, handing him back the list. "What possible use would we have, would you have, for an AR-15? I mean, aside from the fact that you want one? One more gun to clean, store, keep track of, add to the freaking insurance you always gripe about."

"If Colin comes up with the security system it sounds like he has, we can help finance it by reducing the insurance."

"No way. That insurance needs to be there, covering all the high-ticket items, including all the high-ticket items in your collection."

"I notice you don't insist on insuring the rockets so scrupulously," he said.

"The rockets are insured, but they're peanuts compared to the goddam guns." Schwartz gestured to the pig, and I took a dollar out of my wallet and fed Porky. "I've decided to call the pig Porky," I informed him.

"Call it what you will," Schwartz said. "Have you thought about dinner? I'd rather not eat Chinese so soon again."

"We haven't been to the Rusty Bucket in a while."

"Good idea. I like their food, and I like their atmosphere. If they'd turn off the televisions, it would be perfect."

"And we'd never leave," I said. "We can catch a meeting after, if you like."

"Two good ideas in less than a minute," Schwartz said. "Congratulations."

"No problem. I'll drive if you like."

Chapter Six

The next morning, May 11, after taking care of the usual morning routine, including transferring the almost flight-ready *Freda* into the workroom across the hall from the office, Schwartz and I were going over what we knew about that Broad Ripple shooting, as well as what we didn't know. I mentioned in passing that all this discussion would make more sense if we actually had a client, but with his usual panache, Schwartz swept that objection aside, remarking that this was really just keeping up with current events. "After all, should a client materialize out of all this, it would only be because the police haven't found the killer. It seems to me that, with their resources, human and technical, it's highly likely that they will very soon narrow the list of suspects down to one likely candidate. It makes no sense for us to interfere, of course, which is naturally Inspector Mercer's point of view. On the other hand, if someone wants to hire us, it would behoove us to know as much as possible about the matter. It seems to me that we've gone just about as far as we can in informing ourselves. We aren't really on thin ice with the police yet, but for now, we should await further developments."

His words were still hanging in the air when the doorbell rang. I stepped to the hallway and looked: Mercer and Ripley were on the stoop, Ripley pressing the doorbell button again. I told Schwartz, "Inspector Mercer and Sergeant Ripley, right on cue," and he said to invite them in.

Neither Mercer nor Ripley seemed particularly grumpy, but they weren't our long-lost brothers either. Mercer took the red leather chair, and Ripley sat to his left and a bit back, as he always did, so that he could see most of the room. Schwartz had stood up to shake hands with them both, and after sitting down again, he said, "Mr. Zufahl and I were just going to have some iced tea; will you join us? It's a nice pekoe laced with blackberry, very refreshing."

Mercer can be pretty bark off when he thinks someone is infringing on his territory, but apparently that morning we were all still on friendly terms. He said he'd be grateful for refreshment, and Ripley nodded agreement. I went to the kitchen for the fresh pitcher, glasses, ice, lemon, and a tray to put everything on. Once everyone was served, I sat down again at my desk, took a sip, and sat back to find out what had caused us to be blessed with a visit from law enforcement.

"Well," Inspector Mercer said, setting his half-empty glass down on a coaster on the little table next to his chair, "that's a very nice iced tea, Schwartz." Ripley nodded in agreement. Schwartz murmured thanks for the compliment, waited for more substance. Mercer said, "As we all know, on two separate occasions, you were noticed checking out that shooting in Broad Ripple, then interviewing the super at the victim's apartment building after asking questions of the officers in charge of the murder scene."

"Without, I hope, interfering with your own highly competent investigation," Schwartz replied. Mercer looked at him hard for a moment. He's never sure whether Schwartz is being sincere or ironic. Neither am I. Schwartz went on, "You and the IMPD are quite competent to investigate a case such as this one, Inspector, with your army of men and your up-to-date forensics. Indeed, you are far better suited to a case such as this than I, or any other private investigator, could hope to be. So, I have to ask myself, how have we earned the compliment of a visit from you today?"

Inspector Gus Mercer tried to look judicious. Despite the cordiality, it seemed to me that he was having to hold in his real feelings. No cop likes the idea of private eyes infringing on their turf. Or the idea of private eyes period, for that matter. Sergeant Steve Ripley, as always, seemed the picture of serenity, but I knew better. Mercer's appearance was the closer to reality. "What I would like to know," he said through not quite clenched teeth, "is who your client is and how the hell you've even got a client, seeing as how we're not ready—"

"Indeed," Schwartz said, as calm and confident as a chess master saying, "Checkmate," "you aren't ready to arrest anyone, are you?"

"Hell, no," Mercer said, letting off a little steam. Having let up on the pressure a bit, he sat back. He reached into his breast pocket for the cigarettes that hadn't been there for years. He picked up his glass of iced tea instead. "We are not, although that doesn't mean we won't be, depending on—" He drank. "Depending on how a couple of leads check out."

"I get the impression," Schwartz said, "that you do have a candidate in mind. Not that you're ready to name him. Or her."

Mercer looked at him sharply. "You think a woman might have done this?"

"Just keeping open to possibilities. There's no reason a woman couldn't have shot Ms. Morgan, so far as I'm aware." Schwartz took a sip of tea. "You know, the Russians had female snipers in World War II."

Mercer snorted. "Yeah, and Joan of Arc led the French army against the English, but I hope we don't have to get historical with this one. God knows a woman could have used an AR-15 as easily as a man. Look, Schwartz, all I'm asking is who your client is. You know that I know damn well you've never worked for a murderer. I'm not saying I'd cross anyone off the list of suspects just because they'd paid you a retainer, but I will admit I'd be pretty reluctant to try to prove a client of yours was a killer."

"You needn't cross anyone off the list, Inspector," Schwartz said. "Since I have no client, you needn't hesitate to charge anyone you believe is guilty."

"You say you have no client?" Mercer was on guard again.

"I do say that, and I say further that I have no serious prospect of a client."

"I've known you to pull some pretty fancy tricks with words, Schwartz."

"No doubt, Inspector, but in this case, let me assure you: I have no client, no clear prospects of one, and no tricks."

"So why have you and Zufahl made two trips to Broad Ripple to check out the scene?"

"We haven't," Schwartz said blandly.

"The hell you haven't," Mercer snapped, back to normal. "As I just said, I have reports from officers on the scene that you two—"

"We have been to Broad Ripple in the past few days, a matter of less than two miles from where we're sitting, and we have been on the scene twice, but that doesn't mean we have made two trips to check out the scene. We had other reasons to go to Broad Ripple, which, to the best of my knowledge, we are not yet legally obligated to share with the IMPD, and while we were there, we had a look at the crime scene, crossing no police lines and interfering with no police officers. Conversing with and asking questions of uniformed officers is not yet a crime." Schwartz was genial, not that his mood seemed to be contagious. "Look, Inspector; the situation is similar: you and Sergeant Ripley are seated in my office, drinking iced tea, but I'm sure you would deny that the two of you came to my office to have iced tea. Just so—"

Mercer would have preferred blowing up, but he said, "All right; you didn't make two trips to check out the crime scene, and you haven't got a client, so you say, so that was just you and Zufahl exercising your civil rights as tax-paying citizens to look over the place where Allison Morgan got shot."

"Actually, our civil rights don't hinge on paying taxes," Schwartz observed.

"Oh, for God's sake, Schwartz, you know damn well what I mean." I mentally started a countdown at fifteen. Mercer sat still, trying to decide whether it was worth it to stay. Three seconds earlier than I'd estimated, he stood. "Don't let me get in the way of your goddam civil rights, okay? God forbid I do such a thing. Come on, Steve; we might violate their civil rights if we stick around any longer, and we're sure not learning anything here."

I got the distinct impression from the expression on Ripley's face that he wouldn't have minded stomping on Schwartz's civil rights and mine, too, for a while, just to get them tenderized nicely. But he follows orders, and they were at the door before I got up. I followed them to the hall to make sure they were on the other side of the front door when it closed. It had been five or six years since the day Mercer, unobserved, had closed the door, slipped into the front room, gone from there to the bathroom, and listened in on a conversation that was supposed to be private. Still, you can never know when an old bad habit will reassert itself.

When the door had closed behind them, I went back to the office. Schwartz was leaning back, eyes closed. "Well, that was productive," I said, as much to see if he was working as to offer an opinion. He sat up, eyes open.

"Well, to a certain extent, it was, Rainer." Schwartz ticked off points on his fingers. "We know the police are not ready to make an arrest; we know, or surmise for good reason, that they haven't singled out a suspect for special attention; we know that they assume the shots were fired from an AR-15, either from a balcony or from the roof of Helix Tower, which means they have recovered .223 slugs from Ms. Morgan's body."

"Well, that puts us pretty much on a par with the cops then."

"Not necessarily. I'm still pondering the question of how the body ended up in the canal."

"It fell there," I said. "The first or maybe second shot killed her; she was walking home, none too steady, probably, after an evening drinking with friends, and her forward momentum was thrown off by the impact of the two bullets, and she veered left, tripped over the limestone on the bank, and fell in."

"That could be," he said, "but look at the scene in your mind's eye. You're walking, perhaps even staggering, more or less eastward, and two bullets strike you from behind, downward, slightly from left to right. Wouldn't you be more likely to stagger forward, on the asphalt path, perhaps fall to your knees on the path, and pitch face down, *still* on the path?"

I considered it, remembering the scene pretty clearly. He had a point, but I didn't think it was conclusive. I said so.

"It seems to me, Rainer, that the salient questions that no one seems to be asking are, first, how Allison Morgan ended up in the canal, and, second and at least as important, why she ended up in the canal."

"*Why* she ended up in the canal?" I repeated.

"Yes, how and why. If you recall, you were the first to question her being in the canal. It strikes me as no foregone conclusion that the two shots would have steered her into the canal. How did she get there, and why? Could the shooter have known how to fire so as to steer her toward the bank and into the canal? More precisely, it seems to me that there must be a logical explanation for her getting into the water."

"It seems to me you're putting a lot of chips on a pretty sparse hand," I said. "I mean, I see your point, she'd have been more likely to fall forward, more or less on the path, but she clearly didn't, so—"

"So," he said, "since she *was* found in the water, we shouldn't ask how or why? I think we're looking at the same phenomenon with two very different preconceptions."

"Okay, I give. What am I not seeing?"

"Maybe nothing," he said placidly. "But it seems to me that the fact that she was found in the water might just mean that her killer wanted her there."

"But how would—" The phone rang, the landline, and I answered it, "Leo Schwartz's office, Rainer Zufahl speaking." Schwartz reached for his receiver with one hand, held the index finger of the other to his lips. Anita Hereford was on the line.

"I suppose you know," she began incorrectly, "that Stacy did not come home Saturday."

"No, Ms. Hereford, we didn't know that," I said.

"He called at noon and said he was going to have to put the trip off for a few days, but not to worry; everything was all right." I thought I'd have a hard time accepting the reassurance if I'd been in her place, but if it was okay with her, it was okay with me. "And I suppose you heard about that awful shooting in Broad Ripple. You probably don't know that the victim was the ex-wife of my nephew, my late sister's son, Gordon Black. Gordon lives in an apartment overlooking the canal where the body was found." I looked at Schwartz, and he lifted an eyebrow: the signal to go on with the conversation as if he weren't listening in.

"Yes, as a matter of fact, we have heard about the shooting," I told her. "Terrible business."

"Allison was an accountant," Ms. Hereford went on, "and she did our personal accounts, you know, making sure everything is as it should be." Taking advantage of tax breaks I'll never be able to afford, I thought. "And to be perfectly frank, and I say this in strictest confidence, Mr. Zufahl, Allison had a lot to deal with in that marriage, I can tell you. Gordon is a dear boy, and I love him, but his drinking was really out of hand, and frankly, I'm surprised she put up with him as long as she did. We even did an intervention, and Gordon basically laughed it off. He said he'd been thinking about doing something about it himself, and he hadn't had a drink that day and was doing fine."

"'Fine,' in AA," I told her, "is an acronym, but I doubt you'd appreciate being told for what, Ms. Hereford."

There was a long silence at the other end. I could hear her breathing. In a bit, she said, "Yes, I think I understand. Thank you, Mr. Zufahl."

"For—"

"For respecting my sensibilities, Rainer." Well, so now she was on a first-name basis with the help.

"No problem, Ms. Hereford," I said.

"Well, the thing is that Gordon, drunk or sober, lives in a fifth-floor apartment on the east side of Helix Tower, and he says the police have been to talk with him twice, and he thinks they consider him a likely suspect, or perpetrator, whatever the term is."

"Well, at this point, the usual term might be 'person of interest,' but they probably still have a number of possible suspects, some known and a few unknown, although by now they have interviewed everyone living on that side of the building, and they have almost certainly spent time with everyone else who lives there, since any resident can be assumed to have access to the roof, and the roof as a firing point has certain advantages over a balcony."

"What advantages?"

"Well, it's a good height, which the shooter may or may not have had from a balcony, and it's not strictly private, like a balcony. It's not quite public, although the police will be looking into just how hard it is to get to the roof from the outside. My guess, it's not that difficult. They'll have CCTV in a building that new, of course, but that can be disabled or, better, circumvented. Not that the cops have asked, but I'd be betting on the roof, if I were betting."

"But wouldn't the roof be, well, less private, more prone to interruption?"

"Only if someone else had a good enough reason to go there, and it wasn't the sort of night to spend getting fresh air on the rooftop. The idea is that a person operating on the roof would be unlikely to be interrupted and would not be leaving any evidence on their own balcony."

"I see," she said. "But anyway, the reason I'm calling, Rainer, is that Gordon is here, and from the way they've been questioning him, he's convinced the police are getting ready to arrest him. I don't know whether he's right about that or not—"

Schwartz broke in. "This is Leo Schwartz, Ms. Hereford. Do we correctly understand that your nephew thinks he's about to be arrested for the murder of his former wife, Allison Morgan?"

"Exactly, Mr. Schwartz," she said. "He's a nervous wreck, but for what it's worth, he's sober, and he's scared to death."

"How soon can you get him here?" Schwartz asked.

"Half an hour?"

He looked at the clock on the wall. "We will expect you at four o'clock," he said, giving her an extra five minutes. I was tempted to offer him ten for five we wouldn't see her before four-thirty, but refrained. Anita Hereford thanked him and hung up. We hung up.

"So we have a client, or soon will," I said. "I'm glad Ms. Hereford is apparently prepared to foot the bill, and of course, first in line in a killing is the husband or wife, or ex-husband in this case."

"Don't include Mr. Black in the line-up for the sake of formal complete-ness," he said. "Do you see him as extremely likely as a suspect, or otherwise?" I do like his habit of asking me what I'm thinking. Not that I think he really cares all that much about it, but he does take the trouble to act as if he does.

"I really haven't noticed anything much that connected him with her killing, except that he had been married to her."

"Really. Not only is he her former husband: His apartment, with balcony, is on the east side of the building, providing a convenient sniper's nest. We need to know more about Mr. Black. For starters, does he own an AR-15 or any other rifle firing the .223 cartridge? Does he have a night scope, and would one have been needed?" Schwartz pursed his lips, then went on: "Come to that, does he own a gun at all? Is he a good shot? Good enough to hit his prey twice in a four-inch circle at over a hundred yards? Does he have a suppressor? We have a lot to talk about with Gordon Black, Rainer."

"Why a suppressor?"

"Broad Ripple is not a wilderness," Schwartz said. He stood up. "No one reported hearing the shots that killed Ms. Morgan, which would have pinpointed her time of death. I'd say I have time to get the decals on *Freda* before our guests arrive." He went into the workroom, and I went along just to watch. In the right mood, it's interesting to observe him engaged in one of his hobbies, the concentration he puts into each task. When he says "decals" he doesn't mean the kind you soak in water and then smooth on. In this case, he meant the black script name of the rocket, to go on the side of the body, a bit forward of the black fins, and the vital statistics in bold white print, the name, length, body diameter, weight empty and loaded, fin span, motor size, and date, to go on one of the fins, close to the body of the rocket, at the rear of the fin. Both these were on smooth acrylic sheets that he peeled off their nonstick backing and laid down perfectly in position by eye, laying a sheet of paper over them and using a burnishing stick to rub the plastic sheets down carefully until not a micron of space was left under the decals.

Perhaps, needless to say, Schwartz had printed these decals on our office printer. He likes to pretend to be a Luddite, but I've noticed that, while he grumbles when he bumps up against the current century, he really goes for modern technology when it enhances his pastimes.

He had just finished with the decals when the doorbell rang. I would have lost my money; Anita Hereford was punctual. I opened the door for her and Gordon Black. Steven Hereford was not with them. She was dressed almost exactly as before, except that the suit was a medium camel color and the ruffled blouse a pale tan. She made the introductions. Black was in his mid-to-late twenties, medium height and weight, wearing an open-collar light blue shirt and jeans; he might have been good-looking if he had gotten some sleep recently. His hair needed cutting or brushing or both. He looked like he'd spent the past year worrying. Not unusual for a sober alcoholic who isn't used to being that way and may well not stay that way long. At least he wouldn't be tempted at our house.

I shook hands with them, then ushered them into the office, where

Schwartz was seated at his desk. He rose, shook hands with both, as I introduced him to Black. He offered tea or coffee, and they voted for tea. I went to the kitchen for another tray, pitcher, glasses, and so on. When I returned, Anita Hereford was in the red leather chair, and Gordon Black was in the yellow chair next to it, where her husband had sat. I served, and when everyone had their glass of blackberry iced tea, Schwartz remarked that Ms. Hereford had had two separate reasons to visit us within a week, and she nodded.

"And Stacy, as I understand it, hasn't called since he said he had to postpone coming home," he said.

"Right. And now there's been this awful murder, Gordon's ex-wife."

"Indeed. Mr. Black, where were you, and what were you doing between nine o'clock Saturday night and six Sunday morning?"

Black stared at Schwartz as if his hand were still in the cookie jar. "I, uh, I was at home, alone, in my apartment. I was watching television, drinking."

"Drinking," Schwartz said. "What and how much were you drinking?"

"Gin and tonic," Black said, "mostly gin, and lots of it. Not so much tonic. I must have passed out around eleven or twelve. I woke up in my recliner Sunday morning; it must have been about nine or so."

Schwartz tried unsuccessfully to keep the distaste off his face. He doesn't hate gin drinkers; he hates the fact that they drink gin. I've heard his sentiments on drinking something that smells like a Christmas tree so many times I can recite it myself from memory. I'll spare you. You're welcome.

"So, in fact, you have no alibi at all," Schwartz said civilly enough.

"Well, no, but there's no way I could have shot anyone, in my condition," Black said.

"Do you often drink until you pass out?"

Black seemed taken aback by the ruthless questioning. "Well, I don't know about often," he said. "Sometimes, sure, but not always—" I glanced at his aunt, who looked ready to supply an affirmative answer to Schwartz's question.

"Do you experience blackouts?"

"Blackouts?"

"Do you find yourself suddenly doing things, in situations, with no idea how you got there?"

"Well, I think I may have, on occasion…" His voice trailed off. He looked at his aunt as if she would know.

Schwartz wasn't ready to let up. "Come now, you know if you've said or done things for which you have no memory, if you've suddenly found yourself somewhere with no recollection of how you got there. We are not here to judge your behavior; we're trying to discover the truth about the events of late Saturday night and early Sunday morning. To establish our bona fides, Mr. Zufahl and I are sober alcoholics, and when I was drinking, I often drank to the point of passing out while continuing to behave apparently 'normally'. I once came out of a blackout with my teeth clamped on the muzzle of a Colt .45 in my mouth, the hammer cocked, and my finger on the trigger."

Anita Hereford looked as if she'd rather be somewhere else. Gordon Black swallowed, started to say something, decided not to. Schwartz went on. "Should you ever find yourself in such a situation, by the way, the first thing to do is get your free index finger under the hammer, then take your other forefinger off the trigger, take the gun out of your mouth, point it in a safe direction, eject the magazine, and rack the slide to eject the round from the chamber."

"You chambered a round?" Black was frankly gawking.

"Yes, and fully loaded the magazine, as if one shot wouldn't be enough."

"How long have you been sober?"

"Just over fifteen years," Schwartz said. "And smoke-free for ten," he added, apparently because he felt like it.

"Nice round numbers," Black observed.

"They happen to be so, because I quit cigarettes when I had five years' sobriety."

Black pondered. Ms. Hereford said, "We've wandered away from last weekend, Mr. Schwartz." She looked at me as if I could steer the discussion back on course.

"Sober ten years," I said, "another round number, and I never smoked much." Tobacco.

"Well," Schwartz said, "you say you were at home drinking, but you have no witnesses to corroborate your story. Actually, you may be surprised that I don't see your lack of an alibi as suspicious. Indeed, if you had neatly provided one for the time in question, I might be tempted to wonder why. Do you own an AR-15 rifle, Mr. Black?"

"Who, me?" Black shifted his position in the chair. "No, I don't. I have a shotgun, a twelve-gauge Stevens double-barrel I inherited from my father, but I've never fired it. And he also left me a Winchester twenty-two rifle. I've plinked with it a little, at Aunt Anita's place up north."

Aunt Anita put in, "My late husband had a place up on Lake Wawasee, ten acres of woods and a cabin, on and we still go there now and then in the summer."

"So," Schwartz said, "you have a 12-gauge shotgun and a rifle, which uses ordinary .22 caliber ammunition, right?"

"Right. It'll shoot .22 shorts, longs, or long rifles. I've only used long-rifle ammo in it."

"And it would not fire .223 Remington ammunition?"

"No, I don't think so," Black said.

"My apologies; that was rhetorical. A firearm that uses ordinary .22 ammo won't chamber a .223 cartridge; you couldn't even load a .22 rifle or pistol with it, much less fire it. It's a rimless, necked cartridge with a casing about three-eighths of an inch in diameter. Do you own any other guns? An AR-15, for instance?"

"No, I don't. Why the interest in AR-15s?"

"Because the police are assuming that your ex-wife was shot with one, because the slugs recovered from the body were .223s, not ordinary .22 long rifle slugs and sure as the world not shot from a 12-gauge." Nobody had told us for sure the recovered slugs were .223s. That was just a reasonable deduction from the conversation with David James and the fact the police were looking for an AR-15.

"So I'm off the hook," Black said, "since I don't have an AR-15."

"You say you don't have an AR-15, something the police are unlikely to take your word for. If you have one or ever have had, you'd be well-advised to say so right now."

"No, I never have had one."

"Well, I'm inclined to believe you, provisionally at least," Schwartz said. Ms. Hereford was looking indignant, and he shifted his focus. "No, madam, there's nothing to get excited about. I'd be a fool to believe everything I'm told in this office, or elsewhere, for that matter, and you'd be a fool to hire me if I did. However, Mr. Black does not seem to me to be in a mental state to keep up a blatant lie under interrogation. Believe this—" He went back to Black. "—if you have or ever have had an AR-15 or any other firearm that can use .223 ammunition, the police are going to uncover that fact, if they haven't already. Their resources are considerable, and they are not fools."

"Okay," Gordon Black said. "But from the way they were asking questions, it sounds like they're ready to arrest me."

"Police questioning is seldom gentle or genial, Mr. Black, although I can assure you that you were extended every possible courtesy."

Anita Hereford wasn't having any. "I don't see how you can say that, Mr. Schwartz. They have been at Gordon twice now, and they make no secret of the fact that they consider him a, what do you call it? a prime suspect."

"They consider him a person of interest, but they haven't arrested him yet, madam," Schwartz said. "The spouse or former spouse is always the first person to suspect; we are usually killed by those closest to us. The police are, of course, aware of your relationship with Mr. Black, or rather of his with you."

"Are you implying—"

"I am implying nothing; I am stating that the police know Mr. Black is the nephew and the grand-nephew of three very prominent citizens, and you can be sure that they have handled him with the gentlest of kid gloves. You are intelligent enough to understand that people who do not get offended often are sometimes very easy to offend." He leaned back in his chair, tapping his fingers on his chair, thinking. "So how shall we do this? Mr. Black, do you want to hire me to represent your interests?"

Black was quick. "I want to hire you, Mr. Schwartz. I'm the one the cops want to pin this on, and I can afford to pay. Name your retainer. It's nice of Aunt Anita to offer—"

The doorbell rang and kept on ringing. Only Sergeant Steve Ripley was in the habit of leaning on the button. "That's Ripley," I said to Schwartz, "and for sure, he's with Mercer, and there's really only one reason they'd be back again so soon."

"You mean we were followed?" Ms. Hereford demanded.

"Or this house was watched," Schwartz said. "Possibly both." The doorbell stopped ringing long enough for Steve Ripley to rest his thumb, then started up again. Schwartz nodded to me, and I got up to get the door.

"Ripley switched thumbs," I said.

"Mr. Black," Schwartz said, "give me a dollar bill."

"Well, that's not much of a retainer, is it?" Black asked, but he was reaching for his wallet as I left the office. I could see Mercer and Ripley crowding the doorway.

I unlocked the door and took off the chain, threw the door wide. "What a pleasure to see you both again so soon—"

They almost trampled me. I got the door closed and followed them down the hall to the office. When I got there, Inspector Mercer was ignoring our guests, berating Schwartz as if no one else was there. "Not two hours ago, you denied having a client, gave me that load of crap about your interest as concerned citizens, and you're done lying to me, Schwartz. I've had more than enough of your—"

Schwartz slammed a fist down on his desk, which at least shut Mercer up for the moment. "That will do, Inspector. Two hours ago, I told you I had no client, and it was true then that I had no client. Five minutes ago, as you were preparing this egregious onslaught, it was still true that I had no client. Until you and Sergeant Ripley rang the doorbell, I had no client." He took a deep breath, all the way in, let it out. "Now, however, I have accepted a retainer from Mr. Black, who fears that your attention and that of your whole department on him, the former husband of the victim, is developing into more than an inconvenience for him. Is that true? Are you prepared to place him under arrest on a charge of murder?"

"You're goddam right I'm prepared to arrest him," Mercer said. "We executed a search of his apartment this afternoon—" Black and Ms. Hereford both made ready to lodge objections. "—with a warrant, and we found three firearms in his closet, one of which is an AR-15 which we're having tested to see if it matches the slugs from Allison Morgan's body and while we wait for those results, which I'm ready to bet are going to turn out positive as hell, we'd like to make sure he doesn't leave the jurisdiction, so, yeah, I'm arresting him. Gordon Black, I am placing you under arrest for the murder of Allison Morgan, and—" And so on with the Miranda warning, with Mercer's right hand on Black's shoulder.

"And you propose to handcuff my client and drag him out of my office," Schwartz said.

"Nobody is being dragged out of your office," Mercer snapped, "and if he comes with me peacefully, there'll be no need for handcuffs." He looked down at his prisoner. "How about it, Mr. Black? Do you give me your word that cuffs won't be necessary?"

Gordon Black looked simply stunned. He looked at Schwartz, who nodded to him, and Black said to Mercer, "Yes, you have my word." He looked at Schwartz again. "You'll represent my interests, Mr. Schwartz? I'm your client?"

"Certainly," Schwartz said. He turned to the main representative of law enforcement present. He had ice in his voice. "For sheer stupidity, Mr. Mercer, this exceeds any previous performance of yours in my experience. You could have come here in a reasonable fashion, with a right to reasonable cooperation, but by barging into my office and peremptorily arresting my client in the midst of a discussion with him, you have forfeited all rights to civility. Get out. Leave us. Take your suspect and enjoy your triumph while you can. I promise you, your enjoyment will be brief." He was on his feet. "Get out! Now! Go! And once you have Mr. Black safely behind bars, you should start composing your apologies to him and to me; you will need both as soon as I am able to discover the real killer."

"I've got the real killer," Mercer said, unimpressed and unperturbed, then to Black, "Come on; I have your word you'll go peaceably." He and Ripley took our client out of the office, to the hall, and I followed to close the door behind them. Mercer turned at the door. "A real tragedy, arresting him in your office and all. I'll try not to do that again."

A couple of retorts occurred to me, but I kept them to myself. For one thing, I couldn't think of a better replacement for Black. For another, I needed to get back to hear what Schwartz was telling Anita Hereford.

She was on her feet when I reached the door of the office, and Schwartz was assuring her that he did in fact think her nephew was innocent. "But they found that kind of rifle in his apartment," she said.

"That actually means very little," Schwartz said, "assuming that Mr. Black was being honest about the matter, and he'd be a fool to be lying under those circumstances. I place no excessive faith in my judgment of people, but Mr. Black did not strike me either as a consummate actor or as that much of a fool."

"He's not," Ms. Hereford said. "He's an alcoholic, but otherwise he's no fool."

"I'm glad you're perceptive enough to make that distinction, Madam. It's not rocket science planting evidence, after all, and the person who killed Allison Morgan can best avoid detection by supplying a substitute for the role." He ran his hand through his hair, which was not out of place at all. "Firearms have serial numbers, and there's evidence to be traced. The police have leapt precisely to the conclusion the guilty party wants them to leap to. When Inspector Mercer cools down, he'll be able to look at the evidence with a more skeptical eye. He is often impetuous, especially under pressure, but when he has had a chance to look at the situation calmly, he will realize that a number of possible explanations are possible. He is no fool, just occasionally overly optimistic."

He sighed. "Believe me, Ms. Hereford, nobody, least of all the police, wants to cause you unnecessary inconvenience, much less annoyance, and far less ignominy. Unless you have an attorney you prefer, I will call Neil Parkinson and ask him to represent Mr. Black."

"That's good," she said. "Our usual lawyer is good enough for business purposes, but I can't imagine him in a criminal case."

"Very well, Mr. Parkinson, it is."

Ms. Hereford, Anita to me, wanted to talk about it all some more, but Schwartz was clearly eager to get down to business, which wouldn't need an audience or a cheering section. They talked for another couple minutes, but finally, she rose and went with me to the front door. I let her out, and she turned as if she had something she wanted to say, but then she decided not, and she shook her head ruefully. Not for the first time, I gave her my funeral home smile and closed the door.

Chapter Seven

That was about it for Wednesday, and it was certainly enough as far as I was concerned. Thursday morning, I was finishing up with the usual office routines, and Schwartz was busy putting finishing touches on the rocket, when the landline rang.

"Leo Schwartz's office, Rainer Zufahl speaking—" was all I managed to get out before I was interrupted by Kenneth Spall. He said he needed to see Schwartz immediately. I told him there hadn't been any real developments in the surveillance, but he cut me off again. He said, no, he wasn't expecting anything yet; this was another matter entirely. "All right," I told him, "Mr. Schwartz will be available at ten, if it really is urgent." He said it was, and he would be there at ten. It was certainly turning out to be a season for clients with multiple problems.

I went across the hall to tell Schwartz about the appointment. He glanced at his watch, told me what I knew, it was nine-thirty. He said he'd be ready to find out whom Ken Spall wanted followed now. I went back to the office and made some progress on the pyrotechnics-supply inventory. Schwartz is a little obsessive about what he has on hand in the fireworks department, just as he is with the rocketry stuff. In this case, I was updating the list of chemicals stored in the secure bins in the gazebo. There are separate lists for the durable goods, that is, the tools for forming fountain and rocket cores, star cutters, star molds, and the like, and for supplies other than chemicals that get used up, such as the various sizes of paper tubes, paper shell casings, plastic shell casings, and so on. I was getting into it pretty well when the doorbell rang a couple minutes before ten.

Schwartz and I passed in the hall as I went to admit the client. Spall was hitting the doorbell again as I reached for the door. I invited him in, noticing but not mentioning to him that it was a truly beautiful day. He wouldn't have appreciated the pleasantry. He looked more worried than he had during the previous visit, when he'd merely seemed determined, having made up his mind to have his wife tailed. We walked down the hall to the office door, but he wasn't chatty. He hadn't been carrying a briefcase before, but he had one now, an old maroon leather one with combination locks.

Schwartz greeted him, gestured toward the red leather chair, and asked if he'd like tea or coffee. Spall shook his head, then jumped right in. "Look," he said, "This has nothing to do with the job you're already on. I'm not sure it's for real, for one thing. I'm not even sure this is anything more than some harebrained hoax, but if it's serious, not just crazy, it could really cause a lot of trouble. For my company, I mean."

"What is the nature of this new problem?" Schwartz asked him, in his calmest tones.

"I got a certified letter yesterday, from a man I know slightly, Geoffrey McElroy. I met him in the course of business about a year ago. He says he has found a document that's signed by my father, who founded the company that became the company I own and operate, and his grandfather, Gregory McElroy. It's signed by both of them, dated 1 August 1984, and notarized by my father's secretary, Hannah Stevenson."

"Do you happen to know if Hannah Stevenson was, in fact, your father's secretary?"

"Yes, she was. She retired when my father did, and she died two years ago."

"So there's no way to ask her about this document." Schwartz gives me grief about stating the obvious, but the rules are different for him.

"Right," Spall said. "But the thing is, the heading and the signatures, dates, and notary seal are the only parts in English."

"And the rest are in what, Latin?"

"No, numbers. It's a six-page document, and—" Spall broke off. He reached for the briefcase. "McElroy sent me a photocopy of the thing with his letter, and I can show you." He took out a manila envelope, which had been slit open, and shook out a small stack of papers. "Here it is, with his cover letter." He handed the stack to Schwartz.

I got up to have a look. The cover letter was off a laser printer, of course, with the letterhead printed in the same font as the body of the letter, slightly larger, and centered at the head of the sheet. Below the letterhead were Kenneth Spall's name and address, in good business form, and the letter itself:

Dear Mr. Spall,

In going through my grandfather's papers after his death last January, I came across a curious document, a photocopy of which is enclosed. Judging from the paper and the printing, I would guess that the document is several decades old, and this is supported by the dates accompanying the signatures. I have no idea what the numbers mean, although they appear to be some sort of code. Why my grandfather and your father would use a code of any kind in memorializing an agreement, I have no idea, and as I have said, the contents of the Agreement are a mystery to me. However, since they both signed the document and even had it notarized, I assume it is of some importance. What its legal import might me, I am in no position to say.

I would welcome your views as to the significance of this document. If you wish to discuss the matter, I can be reached by mail, telephone, or email per the letterhead. I look forward to hearing from you.

Yours truly,

Geoffrey McElroy

The McElroy signature was in blue ink. Schwartz read it over, handed it to me. I glanced at it, but my attention was attracted to the page below. At the top of the page the heading "AGREEMENT" was centered and spaced a bit above the single-spaced body of the document, in what thirty or so years ago was called near-letter-quality printing. It had been printed on a dot-matrix printer, but a good one, which had done a pretty good version of Courier. Pretty good for back then. The document started out like this:

AGREEMENT

90 <u>14</u> 47 75 6(8) 1(2) <u>10</u> 65 <u>52</u> 74 6(3) <u>10</u> 19 <u>10</u> 10 90 16 15 13 <u>13</u> 60 6(4) <u>68</u> <u>118</u> 3(7) 39 <u>96</u> 9(9) 103 8 39 , 10(5) 85 6(3) 11(0) 79 3(1) 92 <u>117</u> 9 77 <u>117</u>, 28 10 52 <u>10</u> 6(8) 53 3(1) <u>90</u> 39 - 9 8 <u>44</u>, <u>108</u> 13 5(7) 84 49 52 <u>59</u> 6(8) 52 6(6) 92 60 68 90 6(3) 57 44 <u>76</u> 9 90 6(8) <u>117</u> 85 9(9) 8 9 49 6(6) 53 <u>11</u> 8(9) 11 60 <u>108</u> 13 7(1) 16 92 15 68 58 10(5) 9(9) 13 5(7) 59 9(9) 23 53 8 92 16 47 73 6(3) 11(5) 7 117 15 <u>75</u> 73 49 49 3(1) 2(2) 8 90 6(3) 8 74 10 <u>38</u> 1 53 15 8 9...

It went on like that, filling five pages and more than half of the sixth, with just room below for the signatures of Kenneth Spall and Gregory McElroy, plus Helen Stevenson's as witness, and what appeared to be her embossed seal, although that was none too clear in the photocopy. The dates were clear enough: 1 August 1984. I could reproduce the whole thing here, but what would be the point? It made for pretty tedious reading, to put it mildly.

Schwartz scowled at the thing, then asked Spall, "Is there any chance we could have a look at the original? Not that it would probably help any."

"I don't know," Spall said.

"Have you been in contact with Mr. McElroy since receiving this?" Schwartz asked.

"No, I thought I'd better get some expert advice first." Kenneth Spall looked a little embarrassed. "The thing is, my wife has a friend you helped out with a coded message a while back, Viola Ketchum, and it occurred to me you would probably be the one to show this to."

I could tell from Schwartz's expression that the client had gone up a few notches in his estimation. "I think you made the right decision," he said. "Hold off awhile with getting in touch with Mr. McElroy. This thing—" He shook the sheaf of papers gently. "—has some definite points of interest."

"Such as?" Spall wanted to know.

"Well, for starters, it's preposterous that an agreement important enough to be notarized should be written in code. It's even more preposterous that a notary public would notarize such a document. She could bear witness to the signatures and dates, but what of the thing itself? Did they show Ms. Stevenson a clear version and explain how it corresponded to the coded document? I doubt it, and even if so, would she affix her seal to such a thing? I doubt that too."

"Then you don't think it's a legitimate legal agreement?"

"It's too early to tell for sure," Schwartz said, "but my initial impression is that there's some knavery afoot and that Mr. McElroy is the perpetrator. Why would anyone draw up a coded agreement that would have to be decoded to be enforced, if enforcement was necessary? Frankly, it makes no sense to me, but as I said, it's too early to be sure. Give me a day or two with this, and I will consult an attorney about it in the meantime, as well as having a closer look at the coding."

"Do you think you can break the code, Mr. Schwartz?"

"Oh, I have no doubt about that, Mr. Spall. There are certain points of interest, but I'd like the chance to go over the entire document before I commit myself to a course of action. Let me put it this way: I doubt that this presents half the mystery your other matter does. But I will need a lawyer's advice before I can be more definite."

"Then you don't think I need to worry too much about this?"

"I hesitate to indulge in excessive reassurance before I get legal advice, but at first blush I would say no, there's not much to worry about with this matter. The eccentricity of it is what gets me. What on earth Mr. McElroy could hope to gain from such a fantastic scheme is more than I can say."

"Well, if you were running a multimillion-dollar business, Mr. Schwartz, you'd know that there are plenty of people who'd like to get a piece of it, no matter how."

"I have no doubt of that," Schwartz said. "You say you know Mr. McElroy slightly, through business. Do you happen to know whether he watches public television?"

Kenneth Spall stared at Schwartz. "I have no idea," he said. "I can't imagine why that would matter, one way or the other."

"It's just a possibility," Schwartz said, "not really all that important. The idea for the code could have come from anywhere, in fact. Perhaps you'll put up with another possibly irrelevant question. Do you happen to know if either your father or Mr. McElroy's grandfather ever taught school?"

"I believe McElroy told me his grandfather used to teach science at North Central High School," Spall said. "But I don't see what that has to do with this."

"Perhaps nothing. And, to try your patience even further, I notice that your father's signature and the printed line below it give his name as Kenneth Spall. Not Kenneth Spall, Senior."

"That's correct," Spall said. "He never used 'Senior,' but during his lifetime I used 'Junior,' to make clear which I was. Since he died, I've been just Kenneth Spall, more formally Kenneth H. Spall."

"And the 'H.' stands for...?"

"Henry, but I never use it."

"Very well," Schwartz said. "I will see what I can do about the code, and, of course, the other matter. I take it we can call to arrange further discussion?"

"Of course," Spall said, "any time. I'm sorry if I seem distracted from the business about my wife, but this thing has really grabbed my attention. I suspect that McElroy thinks he's somehow entitled to a chunk of my business. I mean, if there really is a legally binding agreement here, that's one thing—"

"I think I can set your mind at rest on that account, Mr. Spall, provisionally at least. As I have said, I will get legal advice, but I frankly think there's very little chance that this amounts to much more than a minor annoyance." Schwartz stood and put out his hand. Spall took it. "If any grief comes from this, I believe it will all come down on Mr. McElroy, not on you. What could be more preposterous than an encoded business agreement?"

Spall took a look at his watch and, just as before, asked if that was the time. He was rather more cordial going than he had been coming, even wishing me good morning as I let him out the front door. I wished him the same, closed the door behind him, and went back to the office.

Schwartz was at his desk with the number document, and he was sending something to the printer when I returned. "What do you make of these numbers?" he asked me. I saw that he'd photocopied the copy Spall had left and placed it on my desk.

"Well, I don't know," I said. "What do you make of them? Obviously, some of them have parentheses around the last digit and some are underlined. What do you make of them?"

"Do you notice anything about them, aside from the parentheses and the underscoring?"

"No, but I'd bet anything you have."

"Well, what's the largest number you can find? Ignoring the parentheses and underlining."

I looked the first sheet over. "Well, the highest I see so far is 118," I said.

"Does that suggest anything to you?" he asked.

"No, should it?" I pondered. "Let's see, 118 is divisible by 2, giving 59, which is a prime, but then that means 118 isn't a prime."

"Correct. What set of objects, or table, if you will, terminates at 118?"

"I have no idea," I said.

"The questions I asked Mr. Spall should help you." Schwartz knew he was way ahead of me on this, and he was enjoying it. "It really could be considered elementary, Rainer."

"Well, you asked him about public TV, and whether McElroy watched it, and whether McElroy's grandfather taught school."

"And he said?"

"He said he had no idea what McElroy watched, and he said he thought McElroy's grandfather taught science at NCHS."

"Correct. And that's a remarkably specific detail to know about someone you know 'slightly, through business,' that his grandfather taught high school science, isn't it? Now, what does 118 have to do with science—"

The light came on, a bit dimly, perhaps, but on at last. "The periodic table of the elements," I said.

"Exactly. There are 118 known elements," Schwartz said, trying not very hard not to sound smug. "And each element has an atomic number, 1 for hydrogen, 2 for helium, 3 for lithium, and so on, up to 118 for oganesson. And each element has a unique atomic symbol, 'H' for hydrogen, 'He; for helium, 'Li' for lithium, dot dot dot, up to 'Og' for oganesson."

"I've never heard of oganesson," I said, "and you know perfectly well that you're not supposed to pronounce an ellipsis 'dot dot dot' since you're the one who told me."

"I can't think of any reason you should have heard of oganesson. It's one of those synthetic elements that's got a very brief half-life, prepared in a cyclotron, and—"

"You googled it, didn't you?"

"Of course. Now, if you wanted to encode a document—"

"Okay," I said, "let me have a crack at this."

He passed me the sheet he'd printed out, a multicolored periodic table, showing all the elements with their atomic symbols, atomic numbers, and atomic weights. "You can ignore the atomic weights," he said unnecessarily. "See what you make of the underlining and the parentheses."

I started in on the first page, using a red pencil on the photocopy. For 90, I got Th, for 14, I got Si, and in a few minutes, I had produced:

ThSiAgReErMgNeTbTeWEuNeKNeNeTh

That made no sense to me, then I thought about the underscored symbols and saw that if 'Si' was reversed, it made more sense, especially if I wrote most of the capitals as lowercase:

Thisagreermgentbetweuenkenneth

but I still had extra letters. I looked again and saw that these corresponded to numbers with parentheses around the last digit. If I omitted the second letter from symbols whose numbers had the last digit in parentheses, then spaced and capitalized properly, I got:

This agreement between Kenneth...

"Okay," I told Schwartz, "I get it, and I freely admit you were there way before

I was." He had been writing by hand, in pen, of course, and he showed me what he'd gotten so far:

> This agreement between Kenneth Spall and Gregory McElroy, dated August first, nineteen eighty-four, shall be interpreted under the laws of the State of Indiana and shall supercede all previous agreements pertaining to the ownership of...

Schwartz was pretty pleased with himself, and I had to admit he had reason to be. "So why didn't you tell the client you had it figured out before he left?"

"And make it seem easy?" Schwartz said. "It's the same old story: if you explain it right away, they decide it was obvious, forgetting that they were at sea the whole time. Let him wait a couple days or so. And in the meantime, I'll work out the rest of this so-called agreement, and we'll discuss the matter with Mr. Parkinson to make sure of our legal ground, and I'd like you to have a look at Mr. McElroy, through the usual channels of inquiry."

"I'll be glad to," I said. "I wonder whether we should base the bill to Ken Spall on how long it takes us to wrap this up or on how much we save him."

"Frankly, I doubt there'd be all that much difference. There's really no threat to his business. I can't imagine a less believable idea than that this preposterously coded document has the slightest legal validity. McElroy must know this, unless he's completely out of touch with reality. It would be nice if..." He trailed off.

"It would be nice if what?"

"If we had more examples of Mr. McElroy's writing, to see whether he habitually misspells 'supersede'. Have another look at the first two lines."

"Well, as you've mentioned once or twice since I've known you, plenty of our fellow citizens are well past any contact with the way things really are, and we're not even talking about religion." I looked at the sheets on my desk. "Why'd you ask Spall whether McElroy watches public television? How would he know something like that?"

"He knew McElroy's grandfather taught science at North Central," Schwartz pointed out. "At any rate, I don't think Mr. Spall is in any danger of having to pay Mr. McElroy a cent, much less whatever this ridiculous encoded pseudo-agreement would claim." He stood up. "It's getting close to lunchtime. How does City Barbeque sound to you?"

"Sounds fine to me," I said. "Shall I call Parkinson now or after we get back?"

"Let's wait until after lunch. You know, that peach cobbler is calling me. I swear, I never thought a fruit dessert could be as tasty as tiramisu or baklava, but they've come up with something just as good."

"I agree," I said. "And in terms of what's calling me, I'm not sure whether it's the brisket or the spareribs or the pulled pork that's louder."

"Right. Now, that's just our old friend, the false dichotomy, or trichotomy in this case: we don't have to choose; we can go for all three, and so far as that goes, we don't have to decide between coleslaw and corn pudding either. It's been too long since we've been there. But it behooves us to exercise restraint in this matter." Schwartz headed for the door.

"Restraint?" I asked. "In what way?"

"Stay within the speed limit," he said. "Or at least reasonably close to it."

"Suits me." I got the keys, and we headed for the garage.

As we were eating, Schwartz mentioned that he'd taken his Richard Brautigan books up to his bedroom and was rereading Brautigan at bedtime after thirty or forty years. "He never tasted City Barbeque's brisket, or their pulled pork, for that matter. I'd bet that, if he had, he'd never have killed himself."

"I don't know," I said. "Clinical depression is bad news."

"Yes, and of course, we understand the limits of gratifying the senses, but I tell you, that barbecue makes me want to go on living, no matter how many crazy people we encounter." He used his napkin to good effect. "Even if they persist in misspelling 'barbecue'."

"There's that," I admitted. "The crazies do seem to be crawling out of the walls lately."

"I don't mind the crazy so much, but when they combine craziness with stupidity, it gets discouraging at times."

"The peach cobbler is a pretty good argument that life is good."

"Yes, especially with the big dollop of whipped cream." He dug in.

Chapter Eight

The rest of the day, after we got back to the office, was spent collating the reports from the men shadowing Ms. Spall, and phoning and texting police, professors, building superintendents, doctors, and a private investigator in Cambridge, Massachusetts.

At least, that's what I was up to. The tails on Ms. Spall were turning up exactly nothing to justify her husband's suspicions, but there was a false note throughout the information we were getting from the East Coast.

Schwartz was back and forth between what he referred to as 'that preposterous code' and his upcoming maiden flight of *Frede.* He had chosen the 54mm motor casing for this, and he had bought two motors, that is, two sets of propellant, O-rings, ejection charges, and so forth, and the parachutes and cameras, and now he was checking out the electronics, which can get pretty complex. The idea was that the altimeter would keep track of how high the rocket was above its launch position, its velocity, and all that, so that a drogue chute, which is a small parachute, would be ejected at or near apogee, the highest point of the flight, and a larger one would be ejected when the descending rocket was three hundred feet above the ground. The reason for using a small chute first is that, if the wind is blowing and you use a single big chute at apogee, your rocket can be carried to the next county by the breeze. So the idea was that the electronics would detect when the rocket was no longer ascending, and the drogue would pop out, then as the whole thing came down at maybe thirty miles an hour, or about fifteen yards per second, when it was about to hit the ground in six or seven seconds, out the major chute would come, slowing it to about fifteen miles per hour, allowing it to land softly, without damage to the rocket.

And if that wasn't enough to keep him amused, there were the cameras, one taking a still shot down the length of the rocket at one per second and another filming, with both cameras transmitting to his laptop on the ground, just in case something might perhaps go wrong. I'd suggested putting off putting those expensive cameras in the rocket for its first flight, but I might as well have saved my breath. "No guts, no glory," muttered at me settled the matter so far as Schwartz was concerned. "Nobody is getting hurt if there's a malfunction," he said. "Inanimate objects are not to be treated like persons, or even animals."

I stopped sharing my opinion with him when it was obviously a waste of time. He's the boss. I went back to the phone and laptop. By dinnertime, I'd reached everyone on the list Schwartz and I had made from the information Ms. Hereford had supplied us, plus the additional potential sources of information. And, as I've said, something seemed off.

For dinner, we finished off the leftovers from lunch: Schwartz had the brisket I'd left, I had the pulled pork he hadn't eaten, and we split the leftover spareribs. After dinner I spent some time updating the pyrotechnics inventory; he'd bought a star plate, which is a two-part device that lets you make twenty-three stars at a time: a lower plate with a row of seven holes between two rows of eight holes, which are filled with the chemical mixture of your choice, depending on what color stars you want to make, then the upper plate, with rods that fit into the holes, is placed over the lower plate, and you press or pound the assembly to solidify the stars. He has a set of coffee cans filled with star mix, each labeled "Veline Color System" and a color below: red, blue, green, orange, yellow, purple, chartreuse, magenta, maroon, peach, aqua, turquoise. He filled the plate's holes with mix from one of the cans, pressed the powder down with the rods, then tapped the plate lightly but firmly to solidify the star mix. He removed the upper plate, filled the holes again, put the upper plate in place, and pounded down the rods. He kept this up till the holes were all packed with solid star mix, then he popped the stars out and put them back into the same container, which he labeled "Stars." He repeated the process until he'd turned all twelve batches of powder into stars. He went back to the coded agreement.

Anyway, we kept busy, and at about eleven, Schwartz announced that he'd gotten to the point in the coding where it claimed that, because of a loan from McElroy's grandfather to Spall's father, McElroy's grandfather or his heir was entitled to half the business. "Preposterous, to put it mildly," Schwartz said. "How this wretch imagines that anyone could take it seriously, I don't know. I'll call Parkinson in the morning, but frankly, I think I've figured out how to make it moot whether there's a legal claim at all."

"Really?" I said. "That would be handy."

"Right. A good look at the first few lines is enough to prove that this is a forgery. So whether a forty-year-old agreement is legally enforceable is beside the point. There is no forty-year-old agreement at all."

"Indeed," I said. "And you think you can prove this?"

"Certainly," he said.

"Then why are you continuing to decode the thing?"

"For the sake of completeness," he said. "To make it possible to show how many separate proofs there are that this is a recent creation. From what Mr. Spall has said, Mr. McElroy has gone to considerable lengths to make the thing appear real. If it were less ridiculous, I might not have seen—" He smiled. "Why don't you have another look at it yourself, Rainer? You have frequently remarked that I am sometimes less than candid with you, but that's hardly true in this case. You have all the evidence that I have. I'll print out the whole agreement once I have it in clear, and you can take a look at it both ways, compare the coded version to the decoded version, and see if you notice what I have."

"No thanks," I said, "I wouldn't want to rain on your parade, and besides, I have plenty of actually useful things to do, or at least potentially useful things. Unless you think that it would help if I—"

"Not really," he said. "You're right, of course; you have plenty to do."

So that was our evening, and the barbecue was the high point.

* * *

The next morning, after breakfast, we were back on the case of the missing AI researcher, still coming up dry so far as I could see. Schwartz suggested we call a meeting with the client and let her know that, so far as we could tell, her son was in the wind. He loves that expression. As far as he was concerned, Anita was the client, and Steven seemed to be along for the ride. He loves that expression too. I objected that we really didn't have much to report. He replied that the fact that we had nothing was something that needed to be reported, and I got it. He thought that there was a chance Anita Hereford would pull the plug on the job, and he could go back to playing with his toys without work to distract him. More precisely, he wanted to use his no doubt effective performance with the Spall-McElroy document as an excuse to bail on the Stacy Hereford case.

When Schwartz starts down that particular primrose path, it's up to me to steer him back to work, however distasteful it may seem to him. I realize, of course, that looking for a missing person is mostly a matter of routine, and so does he. But he likes to leave routine to those who are good at it, namely the police. In this case, it was pretty clear that the police weren't going to do his job for him, since Stacy Hereford was an adult, and there was no evidence at all of foul play. Plenty of people decide that they've had enough of family, friends, and job every day, and the police can't possibly be expected to track down everyone who's decided to cut themselves off from hearth and home. Still, just looking from the very pointlessness of it, it seemed to me that Stacy Hereford's disappearance was worth looking into, and the prospect of chucking the case rather than following it to a reasonably healthy fee was reason enough to keep at it.

So, a couple more dead ends were my morning, and I was still at it, waiting for Schwartz to propose lunch somewhere, when the phone rang. "Leo Schwartz's office, Rainer—" I got out, but I was interrupted.

"Rainer," Anita Hereford said, "we need to talk."

"Very well, Ms. Hereford," I said. "Could you come by the office at, say, two this afternoon, and we'll—"

"Could you and Mr. Schwartz come here instead?" There was a pause while I thought over how to explain that Schwartz really doesn't like to go out on business. "The thing is, my father-in-law would like to meet with you. He says he feels he has as much of a stake in Stacy's welfare as I have, and he would like to know what progress you've made so far."

Schwartz got on the phone, and he signaled me off. To my surprise, I heard him agree to join her, Steven, and her father-in-law, Charles Hereford, for lunch at their home. He asked for the address, although I already had it. He was actually leaving home on business, when a minimum of willpower would have let him insist that they come to him. If I ever think I've figured him out, I'll know it's time to go into another line of work. They settled on one o'clock. Schwartz hung up, meeting my glare.

"It could be useful to meet them both on their home ground," he said.

"Okay. You're the boss."

"Damn right." He fed the pig.

We had a few minutes left before we'd need to leave. I worked on the preposterous code awhile, then it was time to go.

Schwartz chose the Prius, and he drove. The Hereford place was north of Carmel-by-the-Cornfields, a forty-acre spread with fair-sized trees, mostly sugar and silver maples, with a six-foot brick wall all around and a guard at the gatehouse. The guard had a sidearm, and the gate was not something you'd try to drive a Prius through. An M60A1 tank maybe. Schwartz told the guard we were expected for lunch, and damned if he didn't ask for identification. Schwartz showed his driver's license, and that was good enough. I reflected that at least some of the rumors about how Charles Hereford's father had acquired his pile might be true. Whether the money had come from sewers or roads or neighborhood redevelopment, there had been plenty of opportunity for making enemies along with the big bucks.

It was an eighth of a mile, according to Schwartz, from the gate to the circle in front of the three-story columned house, which would have fit a Southern plantation better than a young Indiana forest, but there's no accounting for taste, as they say. The garage, off to the right of the house, had room for six cars, with room left over. To the left of the main building was a summer house with a glass dome that Schwartz's house would have fit into nicely. Schwartz pulled up right at the brick walkway leading up to the portico. I noticed that visitor parking didn't get particularly close to the house.

As we walked up to the front of the house, Schwartz named the various ornamental trees bordering the front lawn. As we mounted the steps to the portico, the door opened, and a linebacker in a butler's uniform ushered us in. The outfit was nicely tailored; the shoulder holster under his left armpit wasn't at all obvious. "Mr. Charles Hereford would like you gentlemen to join him and Mr. and Mrs. Steven Hereford in the lounge," he said, with a very un-English accent indeed. He really said, "Mrs. Steven Hereford." He looked out over the vista as he closed the door behind us, no doubt checking to see if we'd brought reinforcements.

We followed the muscle a short distance down the main corridor to the living room, where the lord of the manor and his son and daughter-in-law waited. We entered, and Anita Hereford, in yet another suit, blue this time, stood up and introduced us to her father-in-law. Steven kept his seat, and so did his father. Steven was wearing a slightly darker gray suit, dark gray tie, and a gleaming white shirt. The older man was on the couch near the fireplace. He looked to be the better part of eighty, with a shock of snow-white hair that could have used cutting, or at least a trim. He had sun-weathered skin with no extra flesh on his face or body, and a nose like an eagle's beak. It was hard to see Steven as the son of this craggy specimen. His mother must have contributed the softer side. Warm as it was, there was a fire going in the big fireplace. Invited to sit, although it sounded more like an order, we did so, no closer to the fire than necessary. There was no offer of refreshment, not that we were counting on having to explain that we don't drink, and there was no mention of lunch, for that matter.

"So," Charles Hereford began, "I understand Anita has been trying to get you to find Stacy. Waste of time and money, as far as I'm concerned." I noticed he left Steven out of it, which seemed to be a theme among the Herefords. The patriarch was wearing a white shirt with an apricot Ascot and a brown and tan window-pane suit I wouldn't have been caught dead in. The rich, of course, can dress as they like. Heaven knows Hereford didn't seem to be trying to cozy up to anyone.

93

Schwartz murmured that there had, in fact, been very little spent on the search for Stacy, although he could submit an invoice if the client desired to call off the search.

"Damned impertinent, if you ask me," Charles Hereford snapped.

Anita tried to intercede on our behalf. "Now, really, Dad, Mr. Schwartz has just got started. It's not as if we're bleeding money—"

"Just a damned waste of time and money," Hereford went on, ignoring her. "Stacy is wherever Stacy is, and as a grown man, he has the right to take a vacation or whatever he's doing without keeping us informed. Not that I think he's acting like a grownup, you understand, but he's not obligated to stay in touch every day—"

Interrupting certainly ran in that family. Anita broke in: "But, Dad, he said he was coming last week, and then he said he'd have to postpone his visit, and I'd just like to know for sure that he's all right." She looked over at Schwartz, then at me, back to Schwartz.

Schwartz had been quiet, and I'd followed his lead, checking out the room, which was large enough and supplied with enough chairs and sofas to seat twenty easily. He said, "Perhaps I should make sure I understand the situation, sir. My understanding is that Mr. and Ms. Hereford are my clients and that the job consists of locating their son, your grandson."

"Damned impertinence," Hereford snapped. His vocabulary seemed a bit limited, or maybe he just liked the word. "I know who my grandson is, and I don't need your reminder, sir. This is my house, and I have a right to—"

"But, Dad," Anita broke in, "I surely have a right to know where my son is, and—"

"No, by God!" Hereford said, and he had no trouble getting to his feet, regardless of his age. "I won't have it! My house invaded by detectives, by God!"

Schwartz and I stood, then Anita got up, "Now, Dad," she began, "I invited them to lunch with us, and—"

"Not in my house," Hereford said, not quite so loudly, but still not friendly. Steven appeared to be trying for invisibility. "I will not be a part of this charade. You consult private detectives without my knowledge or consent;

you invite them to my house, again without my consent, and you act like you own the place—"

Schwartz was the one who interrupted this time. "It's obvious that we're unwelcome, sir, and we won't stay where we're not welcome." He rose, and so did I. "Ms. Hereford, Mr. Hereford," acknowledging Steven's existence, "we seem to be wasting your time and ours, and we're certainly straining your father-in-law's patience, and our own." He gave me a glance. Steven's only contribution was to push his glasses back up. "If you wish to continue the investigation, you know how to reach us," Schwartz said. He nodded to her, to her husband, and to Charles Hereford, and headed for the corridor. I caught up with him halfway down the hall.

The big butler was waiting for us at the door. His face showed less than the ones on Mount Rushmore as he opened the door for us. As we went through, Schwartz murmured, "At least one person in this house knows how to behave." There was just a suggestion of a smile from the butler as he held the door for us.

As we went down the walk to the car, Schwartz asked, "Do you recognize him?"

"Yes," I said, "Donovan. Played four seasons for the Colts a few years back. He had an injury from his stint in Iraq that flared up too often. He's probably making a tenth of what he did when he was playing football." I fastened my seatbelt as Schwartz started the Prius.

"So I'd expect," Schwartz said, "working for a man like Mr. Hereford, who begrudged us lunch." He pulled away from the house.

"Well, how about Kona Grill?"

"Better food and better manners," he said. "I'm for it."

"Or—"

"No, Kona Grill will be fine."

"I think that interrupting is contagious," I said.

Schwartz laughed. "I've had worse habits." He stopped to let the guard slide the gate out of the way. No checking the car to make sure we weren't absconding with valuable artifacts. He laughed again. "We both have."

Chapter Nine

Saturday morning, I got the notes from the men who had been tailing Ginny Spall, and they added up to nothing more worrisome than a dozen meetings with people running or, at any rate, representing various good causes, some social, some medical, some cultural, some political, none suspicious. Well, that was actually a value judgment, depending on how you feel about politics. She was left of center, but not extremely so. She supported public television and the ACLU.

Aside from these conferences, it was clear that the subject liked to have lunch with friends, one or occasionally two or three at a time, and I'd had to explain to Sonny Weinstein that it wasn't necessary to order from the menu to keep Ms. Spall under observation. We'd added Jon Meeks to the crew, but there seemed to be no reason to borrow personnel from another agency. There had been no indication that Ms. Spall had noticed she was under surveillance.

As Paul Surcutt said when he reported to Schwartz and me for the team, the only suspicious thing about Ginny Spall was that there was nothing suspicious about her movements. "You feel like, after all, she's married to a very successful businessman, obviously not on any kind of budget, and the main thing her husband seems really interested in is his company." Paul is about forty, is the very personification of 'nondescript,' and is easy to overlook, which comes in handy when he's on someone's tail. He's not very tall, or very obviously muscular, or very handsome, and he fades right into any background, but he can materialize out of nowhere in a pinch. His assessment of people is virtually always on target, in my experience.

"In my opinion," he said, "you could save the client money and lost sleep by just telling him his wife's not fooling around. I mean, even if she had some reason to believe she was being tailed, she's not going anywhere or seeing anybody that she'd have any trouble explaining, to her husband or to anyone else."

"I think Schwartz just wants to make sure the client feels he's paying for a really intensive surveillance," I said.

"Well, he's doing that," Paul said. "With Frank, Sonny, Jon, and me all on it, it's adding up fast. Any idea how long we're going to be marking time on this?"

"No idea. Why, are there other jobs you'd rather be taking?"

"Nothing in particular, although I'd hate to see something important fall through because the four of us are providing babysitting services."

"If something serious comes up, let me know," I said. "I don't know where you stand on hunches."

"I have hunches," he said, "not that they usually turn out right. I suppose anybody in this business gets to having hunches, whether they're any good or not. Why, are you getting messages from the aether?"

"Just that you're right; the lady is doing nothing she would regret having discussed in court, and this whole job is a waste of time and money."

"Yeah, same here, although it does help pay the bills." That's Paul's idea of humor. We both knew he got fifty percent over the going rate and was worth more than that, and we both knew his bills got paid right on time. "It's not even much of a challenge parking. They <no new paragraph here>live at the Marott Towers, and we can park in the underground garage there, with eyes on her car. To tell the truth, they could improve their security at that place. We use a couple parking spaces belonging to people who are out of town, and nobody's checked to find out what's going on. Her car's last year's BMW, silver, and she never drives anything else, never takes a cab or whatever. I mean it; I feel guilty taking pay for a job this pointless."

I told him that was good; so long as he felt guilty, that was what was important, and otherwise did what I could to ease his conscience, then he took off, to get some sleep before his next turn at bat.

All the inventory lists were updated by now, at least until Schwartz decided to add to one of the collections. I had, of course, got all the notes typed up and printed out for him, and he was going over the NAR written test for High-Power Rocket Level 2 qualification. The test is multiple choice, and in use the questions are selected from a large number, which are available for study by those who would be taking the test. To go for Level 2, one must be an NAR member in good standing, be at least eighteen years old, and currently hold HPR Level 1 certification, and that's just to take the test. Level 1 certification lets you fly rockets with H or I motors; Level 2 lets you fly J, K, and L motors, not that you probably care. The NAR regulates the daylights out of the sport, which is the main reason model rocketry has as good a safety record as, or better than, any other sport you might care to mention. As Schwartz puts it, there's a reason they use really long extension cords out to the medium- and high-power pads. And there's less horsing around on the field than you'd see in a girls' beginning ballet class.

The rocket letter designation can be confusing, if only because there are so many different kinds of motors. Single-use motors for model rocketry are designated A through E, and each letter indicates that the total impulse, that is, the total power of the motor, is double that of the preceding letter. For very small rockets, there are even ¼A and ½A motors. If the system seems confusing, that's okay. I'm not even talking about the differences between single-stage, booster, and sustainer motors; suffice to say that a J motor has roughly five hundred times the oomph of an A motor. Schwartz was planning to go for his Level 2 at the next fly meet of his club, Rocketeers of Central Indiana, ROCI, pronounced Rocky. Whether that was a reference to the fighter Balboa or to the flying squirrel, I have no idea.

By lunch time Schwartz was ready for a break. We discussed the Spall surveillance on the way to the Bonefish Grill, always a satisfying experience. The Bonefish, I mean, not the Spall case. He doesn't like talking business during meals, so we don't, but on the way back, he asked what I thought about the case, and I told him honestly that I thought we all had better things to do.

Schwartz asked about that crazy coded document, whether I had any particular thoughts about that, and I said I hadn't given it another moment's thought. He was obviously so far ahead of me on that that I saw no point in trying to keep up. He dropped the topic.

After we settled in back at the office, out of the blue Schwartz mentioned that he'd always been struck by the fact that the name of the New Hampshire village where the embattled farmers had stood and fired the shot heard round the world, Concord, was pronounced like "conquered," a synonym for "defeated," "vanquished," rather than the usual two-beat sound of "concord," rhyming with "John Ford," meaning "peaceful agreement." He said you could almost include it in the list of words that change pronunciation and meaning when they are capitalized, but not really. "It's not quite like 'Nice,' 'Tangier,' 'Salamis,' and so on since the town name refers to the concept of concord. Oh, well. There are heavier burdens to bear." I didn't look up from the report I was working on.

Schwartz was mulling over a discussion from a meeting a couple weeks ago. "The thing is," he told me, "people confuse belief and knowledge. To know something, you have to believe it, but you can believe things without knowing them." I was really earning the big bucks that afternoon. "Plato got it pretty well right: knowledge is true belief for which you have a valid account. This lets out the office worker who believes it's noon at noon because he's looking at a clock that has always been right, and he hasn't noticed that it had stopped at midnight, and the Democrat who comes out of a coma after fifteen years and, because he has been told that President Eisenhower has just died, believes that Richard Nixon is president."

"Well, yes," I said, just to show I was following him. "And one difference between belief and knowledge is that you can believe things that aren't true, but you can't know something that isn't true. And people in AA meetings in this neck of the woods seem convinced, to a man, woman, and child, that their theological beliefs are of burning interest to other people, because it never occurs to them that they themselves don't give a fat rat's ass about other people's religious beliefs, so why the hell—" I fed the pig a couple dollars. "—would you believe other people want to hear about yours? It's like an innate belief, that one's opinions about God are interesting to other people. Never mind that one is not interested in other people's opinions about God."

For whatever reason, Schwartz had let me talk for quite a while. "My point is that people get belief and knowledge mixed up, and since what we believe seems to us true and therefore reliable, we sometimes mistake it for knowledge, for something we know. Take the classifications 'believer' or 'faithful' or 'orthodox' at one extreme and 'skeptic' or 'unbeliever' or 'atheist' at the other; most people would probably put 'agnostic' in the middle. But in fact, while the extremes are matters of belief, yes or no, the supposed middle ground is simply that one cannot know whether or not God exists. Leaving aside whether 'God' should be thought of as masculine, feminine, or neuter or, for that matter, singular or plural, and not worrying for now about the afterlife, if any, agnosticism simply affirms what seems to me to be a self-evident truth, namely that, regardless of what our beliefs may be, we cannot *know* the answer to the question 'Does God exist.' Either we believe that God exists or we believe that He, She, It, or They do or does not, but we can't know for sure. There are thousands of religions in this world. Some are closer to the ultimate truth, whatever that might be, than others. One religion is closest of all, and of course, each of us believes that our own personal religion is that one. If we didn't believe that, we'd believe something else, if you see what I mean."

"I think I understand what you're saying," I said, more or less truthfully. "I believe you can continue working on that code while having this conversation, but I can't multitask like that." Of course, accusing him of multitasking was risky.

"It seems to me that certainty about religion can be deceptive. To believe something so deeply that one mistakes it for knowledge can lead to deliberate martyrdom, among other things. By 'faith' I mean belief for which I have no evidence. And it seems to me that a decent humility will keep us reminded that we can believe something that turns out to be false, so calling belief knowledge is really an act of arrogance, false pride."

"Sometimes it seems to me that what people call humility is actually the opposite," I said, "if only because they cling so determinedly to what they believe, as if it were established, proven truth."

"Yes, I'm afraid so," Schwartz said. "It's difficult to avoid that trap, with the best intentions in the world."

With the best intentions in the world, we could have gone on talking all afternoon, but just then, heaven be praised, the phone rang. I answered it, and it was Anita Hereford, calling to apologize for the scene at the family manse. I let Schwartz know who was calling, and he got on. She wanted to make sure we didn't consider ourselves fired, and he assured her that we were not so easily frightened off. It took him a while to calm her down, so I went back to the routine tasks that had been interrupted.

Chapter Ten

We caught a break at about ten o'clock Sunday morning, of all times. As mentioned, we'd run through the regular sources, official and otherwise, in Cambridge, Boston, and surrounding areas, and we were about ready to call it a wash, when the phone rang, the landline, not one of our cells. I picked it up and said it was Leo Schwartz's office and Rainer Zufahl was speaking, and I don't know what, if anything, I was expecting, when the voice said, "Hello. This is Stacy Hereford. I understand you've been looking for me."

I almost broke an arm signaling to Schwartz to drop the crossword and get on the phone. I kept my voice as steady as I could when I replied. "Yes, that's right. Your parents would like to know how you're doing, to make sure you're okay. Ah, we gather you were going to come out here last week, but—"

"I know, you know, I said I would, but then I got cold feet." The line got quiet, perhaps in embarrassment at the clichéd turn of phrase.

Schwartz said nothing, nodded to me, so I said, "Well, that's not too surprising, I mean, all things considered. We talked with your supervisors at the lab, and they said—"

"They said I took a leave of absence and stayed absent." Clearly, Stacy could be blunt as occasion required. "I was honest with Professors Heiser and Esher about my reason for taking time off. I really needed to decide once and for all whether I was in or out of it."

" 'It'?" I repeated, rather pointlessly, I admit. After all, I knew, or as it turned out, I believed I knew, that Stacy Hereford had been doing doctoral

102

work in AI at the university, so there weren't too many possibilities. Put it down to my shock at hearing from our missing prodigy, on Sunday morning, never my best day.

"Out of Artificial Intelligence," said the caller. "About Heiser and Esher, I may not have been *totally* honest with them. I didn't share everything with them, of course, but what I told them was true: I absolutely needed to get back to the real world for a while, and I absolutely could not in good conscience continue with the work being done at the lab."

"'The lab,'" I echoed. I seemed to be in repeat mode in this conversation.

"The BriteSyn lab, of course."

"At M.I.T.?" I asked.

"No, not at M.I.T. at all; BriteSyn was separate from the university, although Heiser and Esher were still affiliated with M.I.T., and I was teaching there until—"

Schwartz put in, "Can you confirm for us that you actually are Stacy Hereford? We have been searching for—" Of course, I had had doubts along those lines myself, but the reference to Esher and Heiser had allayed my misgivings for some reason. Why? It wasn't classified information, after all. We had it, and it wasn't hot at all. Anyone could call, with a script, and since we had never heard Stacy Hereford speak, on or off the phone, we wouldn't know one way or the other.

"Oh, it's me, all right," said the voice on the phone.

"So you say," Schwartz responded, "but we would be witlings to assume that a phone call out of the blue is from the person we have been searching for. The police, private investigators, university and hospital, and other persons have not turned up any really definite clues to your whereabouts (to provisionally assume that you are who you say you are). If your mother's account of your misgivings about Artificial Intelligence is at all reliable, you had definitely moved beyond minor qualms about the ethical aspects of the enterprise and were troubled by the prospect of its threat to human survival. If any."

"That," the voice said, "is quite a speech, for this century. And yes, I am convinced that we will know that we have truly created Artificial Intelligence when it tries to kill us. The thing is, for intelligence—whatever it is—to exist, the mind it resides in must partake of the random as well as the determinate; it must be able to deal with contradiction; its logic must include some illogic, or it's just a machine running an incredibly complex program.

"A mind, to be intelligent, cannot be stymied by contradiction, real or apparent. It has to deal with manifold illogical situations as a matter of course. To be intelligent includes the ability, so to speak, to provisionally or permanently become stupid, in the sense of not balking at patently absurd, ridiculous places and times, 'time and chance' per Ecclesiastes. We have to pretend to be stupid in order to survive the reality of living in our time and place, and we have to pretend to be stupid enough to accept the stupidity of others." There was a heavy sigh at the other end of the line.

"Go on, please," Schwartz said gently. He smiled, nodded to me, and sat back, ready to listen.

"We have to have manners," Stacy Hereford said, "or we'd all kill each other. We have to have good manners because, as someone, I forget who but could probably look it up, said, 'good manners are what keep us from tearing each other to pieces'." Another sigh, even deeper. "But that's the human response to moving from bands of a hundred or so on the African savannah to cities in the millions. In creating Artificial Intelligence, we use a computer, actually a network of computers, of course, for a brain, the hardware. The mind is instantiated on the brain in the form of software, digital instructions, that run on the computers, and the hardware brain is capacious enough to execute instructions at amazing speed, and the trick is to build in the randomness, the indeterminateness, subtly yet effectively, so that the mind is liberated from the constraints of the logic that would remind it that it is a program running on a computer network, and it learns to live with the facts of life, that things do not always or even usually turn out according to strict logic, sense, or trueness to reality." A pause, but no sighing. The sound of a cigarette lighter being struck and then the faint soft sound of cigarette smoke, the match puff even from a lighter, being breathed out without being inhaled. "Gentlemen," Stacy Hereford said, "am I who I say I am?"

"We believe so," Schwartz said, catching my eye and nodding. I nodded back. "You seem to us to be Stacy Hereford, but we can hardly say we've found you." No man ever talked himself out of fat fees faster than Leo Schwartz. "I assume you are capable of using a burner phone and routing the call. Mr. Zufahl and I claim no expertise in electronic matters, but we know whom to consult when we are out of our depth."

"Well, the thing is, I'm not ready to come home," Stacy Hereford said.

"Would you care to give a reason?"

"Would you like to live with my parents, not to mention with my grandfather, in his house, Mr. Schwartz?"

"Point taken."

"And yet you ask me for a reason, Mr. Schwartz? May I call you Leo? And you Rainer, Mr. Zufahl?" Pronouncing my name right on the first try. "And you can call me Stacy, and we're just chatting away this morning."

"I don't see how I can prevent you, and I don't really mind informality, in any case," Schwartz said.

I said, "Rainer is fine, thanks for asking."

"All right. Leo, Rainer, please let my parents know I'm all right, but I'd appreciate it if you would desist from the search."

"Well," Schwartz said, "it's not obvious just how we should do that, you see. Telling your parents you are in good health and not in trouble will not stop them from wanting to see you. No matter how much they may rub you the wrong way, they are still your parents, and they miss you."

"Well, whatever opinion you may have of my mother and my father and my grandfather, please understand this. Beneath that tightly wound, ultra-respectable propriety, they are crazy people. I mean, they are truly insane, each in their own particular way. They present a good front, mostly. That is, my parents do; Grandpa forgets more and more these days and lets the reality show more than he ought to."

"We have experienced your grandfather's hospitality," Schwartz said.

There was a snort on the other end of the phone. "That's one word for it. I experienced Grandpa's hospitality most fully at the age of sixteen when I brought a boy home to meet my family, a mistake I never made again.

Grandpa was unbearable, incredibly rude by any civilized standard, yet Mum and Dad never said a thing against his behavior, lest he turn us all out in the street. I mean, they've each and collectively got wads of money, yet they placate his godawful words and deeds for the sake of living in that preposterous pile of pretentiousness."

"You are not the first person to note their parents' shortcomings," Schwartz said.

"Shortcomings, Mr. Schwartz? They are crazy, and you should remember that. Mom is nuts, Dad is nuts, Grandpa is nuts. If you don't believe me, Mr. Schwartz, and Mr. Zufahl, for that matter, just stay associated with my family. You got a taste of Grandpa instead of lunch, and he's about as predictable as a suitcase full of snakes. Dad acts like he isn't there even though he is. It's when he's by himself that he really steps off the edge. And don't get me started on Grandpa, who is really the one who started all the craziness."

"We will endeavor to keep our minds open," Schwartz said. "Rainer, do you have anything to add to this discussion?"

"Well," I said, "not really. We can report to the Herefords that Stacy is alive and well and needs time alone, to sort things out." I glanced at the small box on my desk, between the landline phone and the green-shaded desk lamp. It had a screen map and location of the caller's phone, along with the recording of the conversation since I had pressed the button under the desk that got things going. I caught Schwartz's eye, looked at the screen. I wrote a word on a Post-It pad, tossed the pad to Schwartz. He caught it easily, glanced at it, set it down on his desk.

"You'll tell them I'm doing all right, just getting myself together for whatever comes next?"

"Certainly," Schwartz said. "I think Mr. Zufahl and I will keep Chicago to ourselves," he said. There was a pause on the phone.

"Not bad," our caller said. "Whoever is doing your electronic security is on the ball. I'd say, keep him. "That's where I am now, but it may not be where I am an hour from now."

I read the coordinates, hit the close-up from satellite, and was looking at a terminal at O'Hare. I showed Schwartz.

"In that case," he said, "I wish you bon voyage, Stacy." With a soft click, the line went dead. Schwartz looked at me. "Don't you think Shapiro's would be worth the drive?"

I agreed. We knew the quarry was in Chicago at the moment, quite possibly en route to any place in the world, but we could report to the family that Stacy Hereford was alive and well and, for all we knew, living in Paris with Jacques Brel.

The price of Shapiro's pastrami on rye with mustard and horseradish, whole dill pickle on the side, like their corned beef, has gone up over the years, but it's still well worth it, and Schwartz, as usual, ordered the Reuben. He finds the existence of the Reuben in a kosher-style delicatessen amusing, the Swiss cheese and corned beef smothered with sauerkraut and Thousand Island dressing to melt in your mouth, it's so good.

Either the pastrami or the corned beef, or the stuffed cabbage for that matter, would have kept Brautigan going another five years easy.

Later in the day, Schwartz was carping about fictional depictions of the business, or at least one of them. "What I don't get is the house. It's a three-story brownstone with a finished basement and a greenhouse covering the entire roof. Okay, the basement is basically one big room, part of which is an apartment with the usual appurtenances, aside from a kitchen.

"The first floor is seven steps up from the sidewalk in front, with a wide central hallway the length of the house, with a front room and an office, including a bathroom, on the left, with a dining room, stairs, an elevator, and a kitchen on the right.

"The second floor is a bedroom and a spare.

"The third floor is a bedroom and what's called the south room.

"Finally, the roof has space for eight or ten thousand plants." He took a sip of his iced tea, set the glass down on the coaster.

"It seems to me that either the second and third floors consist of really huge bedrooms, or we're not getting the whole picture somehow. And by the way, when a character has been described as not trusting any machine more complicated than a wheelbarrow, it's difficult to imagine him routinely using a noisy old elevator."

"Didn't Emerson say something about a foolish consistency?" I put in.

"Yes, but those two floors seem to be rather breezily described. Do they have store rooms up there, or what the hell?"

I was at a loss, which occurs often enough, especially when I don't get the point of the conversation, which isn't really unusual with Schwartz.

Chapter Eleven

I don't like the smell of the Marion County lockup one bit. Schwartz says there's some chemical present in the disinfectant they use there, but to my nose, it comes across as the odor of hopelessness. That place, with its depressing sights and sounds, really gets to me. Schwartz says it compares very favorably with certain other jails where he's spent time, but he declines to talk about the time he's done behind bars and why, just as he declines to discuss his military service.

Schwartz had spoken with Neil Parkinson late Sunday, and Parkinson had made the necessary arrangements for us to visit Gordon Black, as his attorney's agents, having been hired in his defense after Mercer arrested him.

We were in the visiting area by eleven Monday morning, waiting. It was well over ten minutes before Black was brought in to see us. He looked like he hadn't slept all night, but otherwise not too bad, under the circumstances. The obligatory orange jumpsuit didn't improve his looks any, but all in all, while he didn't look great, he really didn't seem terribly bad off, aside from being under arrest for murder.

Black seemed a bit surprised to see us; he hadn't been told who his visitors were, for whatever reason. It's been my experience with jails that a lot of things are inexplicable, such as enforcement of rules, or their nonenforcement, or the rules themselves in the first place. The first thing Black asked us was whether we had cigarettes, which was cute, since there's officially no smoking at the jail. We had no cigarettes, no liquor, no cakes with files baked into them.

Once that was settled, Schwartz asked questions, some of which duplicated things he'd asked Anita Hereford about on the phone Sunday evening. Mostly it was new, not that it was always obvious what the question had to do with Allison Morgan's murder.

Black said he had met Allison in college, at Bloomington, that they had married immediately after school, but soon learned they were incompatible in too many ways, and after four years of making each other unhappy, they divorced amicably. "The fact is, we get along better now that we're divorced than we did when we were married," he said. "We got along great in school, before we were married. Marriage was basically a misstep for us. Things are really a lot better for us now that—"

He stopped talking when it hit him that he was talking about how well he got along with a dead person. I thought he was going to tear up, and so did he, but he set his jaw, swallowed hard, and got it together. "Look," he said, leaning forward toward us, almost touching the partition between us, "you have to find out who killed Allison. It wasn't me, and if the police say they've found the rifle that killed her in my apartment, then it was planted, because I don't own such a gun and never have." One of the guards was looking at Black meaningfully; his voice was getting louder than necessary. Or permitted.

"That's a useful clue," Schwartz said, "one that the police are in a position to pursue. Firearms have serial numbers, and they should be able to trace that rifle, no matter how it came to be in your home."

"Then you believe me?" Black stared at Schwartz, then at me, then back to Schwartz.

"Certainly," Schwartz said. "You are not an idiot, Mr. Black. If you had used an AR-15 to shoot your former wife—"

"Goddammit, I didn't shoot her—"

"I said 'if,' Mr. Black. If you had shot your wife with an AR-15, you would hardly have left the murder weapon in your closet, waiting to be found by the first policeman to take a look at your premises. By now, I suspect that Inspector Mercer, who is also not an idiot, is beginning to have serious doubts himself. If guilty, you would never have left that weapon in your closet; if you are not guilty, then who is trying to frame you for the murder? That offers numerous possibilities for investigation, and Inspector Mercer has a well-trained army at his disposal. Where, when, and by whom was the rifle manufactured? Was it used to kill Ms. Morgan—the answer there is almost certainly yes, since there would be no point in planting an innocent weapon in your home."

"I can't figure out who could have done that," Black said, "or who would have done it, as far as that goes."

"For now, it's enough to assume that someone who killed Allison Morgan and wanted to get away with it acquired the weapon without excessive paperwork or record-keeping, used it, wiped it, and left it at your place, with the idea of casting suspicion on you. As the former husband of the victim, you're obviously the best logical choice to frame for her murder."

"You make it sound like you think I'm innocent."

"Well, yes," Schwartz said. "As I said earlier, it's too pat. I might be willing to include you among the suspects, honoris causae, if the AR-15 hadn't been found in your closet." He smiled. "Now, in a fictional situation, you might have killed your former wife with your rifle and then deliberately kept it, on the theory that this would throw suspicion off you. But in reality, that sort of subtlety leads nowhere. If the rifle belongs to you, the question is, how did someone get hold of it, use it, and replace it? If it isn't yours, how did someone—" He leaned back. "You see how the complexities mount up. So, unless you are completely irrational, you're innocent, and if you're not, the police will determine that soon enough."

"Then why are you bothering with me?"

"Your aunt is paying me to bother with you," Schwartz said. "That is, it seems to me that your uncle is going along with her on this."

"That's Steven, all right," Black said. "She calls the shots. He follows her, whatever she does."

"And your grandfather goes along with what?"

"I wish I knew what drives him. My mom got out of the house when she went off to college, and she stayed out of the family business and out of the family and away from her father as thoroughly as she could, and I've gone

111

with her on that."

"About your parents," Schwartz began.

"Dad and Mom were killed in a stupid accident, stopped at a light, and a semi-driver fell asleep at the wheel and ran right over them and another car. It was the summer after I graduated, a month before Allison and I married."

"You have our condolences," Schwartz said. "And your relations with the rest of the Herefords?"

Gordon said, "I'm on good terms with Aunt Anita, insofar as anyone can be, but nobody knows what the old man is going to do next, and neither does he." Black looked down at his jumpsuit. "I appreciate you doing this, you know? I mean, Anita hired you, but I should pay you. It's my case, after all."

The guard came over to let us know time was up. I told Black good-bye, the first thing I'd said to him since we'd said hello. Schwartz told him he'd hear from us soon, probably tomorrow. I thought that might be unduly optimistic, but he's running the show. Black seemed to take heart from the meeting.

"Charles Hereford gets similar reviews," Schwartz said, as the doors closed behind us and we stepped into the daylight, "from those who know him best."

I asked him what he thought the next move would be, and he said the next move would be Inspector Mercer's, unless, of course, he'd already made it. "That AR-15 has a serial number, which means it has a history, and it will be interesting to find out what that history is. I'd expect to hear from the police soon, tomorrow if not today. Meanwhile, we haven't been to Acapulco Joe's in way too long."

"Now, that sounds good," I said, not just to please the boss.

We arrived just ahead of the rest of the lunchtime crowd, barely in time to grab a booth at the back. "Chilis rancheros, por favor," he ordered, and I went for the enchilada special, with one each of refried beans, cheese, shredded chicken, and shredded beef, with rice and salad and sauce and chips, but of course, we took a pass on the cervezas. Their iced tea is the standard choice between sweetened and unsweetened, and it's nothing special, but it's certainly good enough to help with the meltdown.

While we ate, Schwartz got going about the differences between American and British English and between English and German. "Americans might say 'seven-thirty' or 'half past seven,' but only an Englishman or, of course, Englishwoman, and I suppose a Scots or Irish or Welsh or Cornish person, I mean any person from the British Isles, would say 'half seven,' meaning 'seven-thirty,' whereas a German would say 'halb acht,' 'half eight,' to mean 'half until eight' for seven-thirty. Heinrich Böll's novel *Billarden um halb zehn* was translated correctly as *Billiards at Half Past Nine*.

"Another thing everyone knows but nobody talks about is the opposite of 'clockwise': an American will say 'counter-clockwise' where a British speaker would say 'anticlockwise'. I suppose that avoids the ambiguity of the abbreviation."

"As God is my witness," I said, "I know I'm going to regret asking, but you lost me with that last. What ambiguity are you talking about?"

"'Counter-clockwise' could be abbreviated 'CCW,' which also stands, or anyway stood, for a permit to Carry a Concealed Weapon, which our state legislature, in their finite, bought-and-sold-by-the-NRA wisdom, has abolished, effective the first of next month."

"Oh, right. If I understand it, anyone old enough to vote, with no criminal record, will be able to legally carry a gun anywhere it's permitted, without a background check, fingerprinting, or fee. You and I passed the background check and did the prints and paid the fees, and all that will become superfluous on July first."

"Yes. The police were against it, the public was against it, and goddam common sense was against it, but the legislature passed it anyway, police and public be damned. Every survey, poll, or other sampling of public opinion shows that most Americans support stricter gun laws. The police support stricter gun laws. Hell's bells, I have a couple cabinets full of guns, and *I* support stricter gun laws. I think adults who leave firearms and ammunition or even loaded firearms lying around where kids can get to them should be given a two-dollar lead-free enema and a light. The public doesn't think hormone-crazed teenage boys should be given unsupervised access to dangerous weapons to let them share their weltschmerz with innocent victims, but, as always in Indiana, we have the best government money can buy." The chilis and enchiladas arrived, and I dug in. So did Schwartz, not that it cut off the conversation between appreciative bites.

"Corporations have so-called 'free speech' like other legal persons, but they're protected from the responsibilities real persons work under," he said. "Corporations—for profit and not for profit—can 'speak' with money to influence the legislature in ways that human beings would be arrested for. Corporations are as above the law as any other antisocial vermin that can't be defeated. If a few dozen kids and adults get shot to death now and then, it's a small price for a national association representing an entire industry to pay, especially since they don't pay; strangers do.

"You know of course that I agree that an armed person is a citizen and an unarmed person is a subject, but for heaven's sake—"

"I know," I said, swallowing cheese enchilada. "I know. I agree with you, for God's sake."

"Right," Schwartz said. "Sorry. But my fellow gun owners who think school shootings are fictional events designed to justify taking away their weapons never seem to notice that nobody is taking away their goddam weapons, or even trying to. You'd think that a gun owner would be in a position to resist that, but arguing with practical paranoia is futile. Like so many things in life. Oh, well, it's better to tilt at the occasional windmill. Once in a while, one kills a giant."

"You need to feed the pig when we get home," I said.

"You're pretty strong for that pig," he said.

"I like Porky, as a matter of fact. I'm not sure how we ever got along without him."

"Are you sure it's a male pig? I don't see any real evidence one way or the other."

"Well, no, I guess not, thank heaven for small favors," I admitted. "But the cartoon character Porky Pig didn't wear pants, and there was no visible evidence there, and we all called him him. Petunia Pig wore a skirt, if I remember correctly, but I'm pretty sure she was as sexless as he was. You grew up on a farm, right? What's a male pig called, a boar, right?"

"Yes," he said, "and a female pig, or hog, is a sow, once she's had a litter of pigs."

"What's she called before then?"

"A gilt."

"A guilt?"

"Right, spelled without the 'u'."

"G-i-l-t," I said. "Hm. Pronounced with a hard 'g' before the 'I,' like 'girl'. So there are three different words for pigs, or hogs, depending on whether the female has given birth?"

"Actually, there are four terms," Schwartz said. "A boar is a male pig; a barrow is a pig that used to be a male pig. A castrated male pig."

"Almost sounds like a contradiction in terms. I suppose since Porky here shows no sign of sexuality, he's probably a barrow. Spelled like 'sparrow'?"

"Yes, it is."

"Then maybe we should call him Bobby Barrow instead of Porky Pig. Interesting, come to think of it, that we continue to use the masculine pronouns after the pig has ceased to be male."

"Just as we do for eunuchs," he said. "Using the neuter pronoun would be offensive, after all." He chased sauce with a chip, ate it with satisfaction.

"Probably not as offensive as being neutered," I suggested.

"Probably not, but still—"

"Come to that, calling a pig Porky, referring to its, or his or her, eventual place on the table, rather than at the table, could be considered offensive."

"And we'd probably do well to avoid using a copyrighted name for a cartoon character. Even if it's not some big Disney property, we should probably—"

"Oh, hell," Schwartz said, "why give it a name at all? Why not just call it the pig? It's a thing, an inanimate object, a ceramic sculpture, not a real animal."

"Neither is Porky, or Petunia, for that matter. And I notice you ask why we should give *it* a name, not *him* or *her*."

"I am not afraid to affront manufactured objects, even hand-made ones, and this one, thank heaven, has no evident gender." He had another chip or two as I finished up the enchiladas and rice. He had the usual argument with the waiter about the check. The manager had not forgotten an occasion years before when Schwartz had done him a serious favor involving a close relative and had refrained from soaking him good. It was useless to explain to grateful clients and ex-clients that it wasn't really generosity; it was laziness and disinclination to waste time on frivolous paperwork, such as keeping track of expenses and itemizing them on a bill. As usual, the check ended up being torn up, and Schwartz tipped the waiter in cash for about what the meals and tip would have come to.

The drive back to the office was fairly quiet, compared to the discourse on language at lunch, but that was all right.

Chapter Twelve

At the Tuesday noon AA meeting at St. Luke's Methodist, the topic for discussion was faith. Most people were sitting at the eight tables arranged in a rectangle, with half a dozen or so people sitting in chairs against the walls. There had been several good shares and, of course, a few not so great ones, and a pass or two, and then it was Chris's turn to share his thoughts.

As usual, Chris immediately wandered off the subject and just kept on going, and he was still talking when Mary's three-minute timer rang. He nodded to her in acknowledgment of her signal, but he kept on talking. As everyone knew, when the timer went off, the speaker was supposed to finish the sentence, but Chris seemed intent on finishing the chapter. A minute past the timer, his friend Carl, sitting next to him, held out four fingers for him to see, but he just nodded and continued talking. A minute later Carl showed him five fingers, without effect.

Delores, sitting across the room, stood, glanced at the clock—twenty to nine—muttered, "Screw this," and left the room. Chris went on, still earnestly talking, touching on faith now and then. Carl showed him six fingers as Mary's timer rang for the second time. A minute or so later Bill and Curtis left the meeting, without comment. Bill refilled his coffee cup before leaving, glanced over at Chris, shook his head. The rest of us sat there, as Chris went on and on. Carl showed him eight fingers, and he was getting ready for nine when the timer went off a third time. Chris smiled a little ruefully, then said, "That's enough out of me. I'll pass."

There was an audible collective sigh of relief, and someone murmured,

"N.F.S., man," which is not really a proper AA response, and Jason, the other side of Chris from Carl, said, "Hi, my name's Jason; I'm an alcoholic."

We, or at least most of us, said, "Hi, Jason."

Jason said, "I realize that most people here are believers, although as the Third Tradition says, 'The only requirement for A.A. membership is a desire to stop drinking'. I know a lot of people say that, if you don't have God's help, you don't stand a chance of staying sober—"

There was a very audible assent from Chris, of course, but Jason kept going. "I don't really think it matters what you believe. I've met all kinds of Christians in these rooms, and Jewish, Muslim, Buddhist, Hindu, agnostic, and atheist people too, and I really believe what we believe about God is irrelevant to our sobriety. As my sponsor likes to say—" Jason's sponsor was Chris. "—what's going on in here—" He tapped his temple. "—is for entertainment purposes only. I don't think theology matters at all; I think ethics is what's important. I can believe this or that or the other about God, but the real key to my spiritual condition is how I act, how I behave, how I treat other people. I think an atheist who treats others as he or she wants to be treated is in better spiritual condition than a devout believer who just ignores other people's needs. Anyway, that's all I've got."

Jason stopped talking just before the timer dinged. Beverly, on his right, spoke, and she was more or less echoing what he'd said. The discussion continued until one o'clock, and perhaps two-thirds of those present had had an opportunity to share. After the Our Father we headed out to the parking lot for the post-meeting meeting, which is often as rewarding as the meeting itself. A knot of men were discussing whether someone should have a really serious talk with Chris about his tendency to hog the time, not that there hadn't been serious discussions with Chris before. "Hell, he knows he talks too much," Francis said, "but when he gets going, he stays going."

"Yeah," Conrad agreed. "He talks the way he drank: once he gets started, he just can't stop."

"Right," someone else said. "He knows damn well he talks too much, but that self-knowledge avails him nothing once he gets started."

The talk went on and was still going when we headed for the car.

"Talking to Chris about his talking will have no more effect than talking to a drunk about his drinking would have," Schwartz said, as I started the car.

"I agree with that, God knows," I said. "He knows better when he's not talking, but once he gets going, he's convinced that what he's saying really is worth more than what somebody else, anybody else, might say. He's what? Intoxicated by his own voice, I guess."

"Not exactly," Schwartz said. "It's not really his voice; he's not listening to himself; he's just talking. You notice he never sticks to the topic?"

"Of course."

"It doesn't matter what comes out his mouth, you see. He's not listening to himself talk; he's drunk on his own insight, or vision, or conception of AA as a form of salvation. He's so dazzled by the wondrous epiphany in his head that he can't be bothered with minutiae."

"Like giving other people a chance to share?"

"Yes, but you have to be willing to step back a bit. Does he make sense when he's sharing?"

"Well, sure, but he gets off-topic—"

"Now, there's a first in an A.A. meeting," Schwartz said. "He gets off topic, but he does talk sense, even if he does talk more than he might."

"But other people have a right to share in a meeting."

"Certainly, but what other drunk would you rather be hearing from, rather than Chris?"

I thought about it, but the truth was that, even if he did go on a lot, gobbling up way more than his fair share of time, Chris always had something worthwhile to say.

Schwartz was reading my mind now. "Now, of course, he repeats himself," he said, "but he's never rambling; he's always worth listening to. And while I agree with you about everyone getting a fair share of the meeting, people come to meetings freely, and if they don't want to listen to a long share, they can always leave. People did today, in fact."

"I noticed."

"Nobody has appointed me to make sure each person gets three minutes, and if you'll notice, in a lot of meetings there are more people than time will allow to share, even if Chris isn't there to take up their time. It's none of my business to make sure Chris is fair to others, and if you really want to know the truth, I happen to know that Chris is as bothered as anyone about what he himself calls his selfishness. He says it just takes over, and he tries to pass, but there's always something, one little thing that he has to get out, and the next thing he knows, someone's calling time on him for the third time."

"It seems odd that someone could be so conscious of that character defect and yet be unable to deal with it."

"Well," Schwartz said to me, "you're calling it a character defect, taking his inventory for him, and when it comes to consciousness of character defects and the ability to deal with them, how were you when it came to quitting drinking?"

"Of course," I said. I shut up for a while.

Chapter Thirteen

Wednesday early we heard from Ken Spall that his wife was going to be in Chicago visiting her parents for a few days. Her father was in the hospital with COPD, Covid, and whatever else they turned up, and her mother needed the moral support. This made a full-cast conference possible, so Schwartz told me to round up the crew for an afternoon get-together, not that there was a whole lot to discuss.

Paul arrived, bringing Sonny and Frank, and Jonny showed up a couple minutes later. We assembled in the office, and Schwartz summarized the mood perfectly. "Ten days," he said, "for ten days you have followed Virginia Spall wherever she goes, without a hint that she is engaged in any illicit activity whatsoever. I have never wasted a client's money so thoroughly and so pointlessly," he said, "and it's not an excuse that the client insists on it. You men, the best operatives in town, have been unable to find a scintilla of evidence to support Mr. Spall's suspicion that his wife is being unfaithful to him."

Schwartz shifted slightly in his chair. A conference like this really rubbed him the wrong way. He hadn't liked the job in the first place, but he had taken it on, mainly to avoid being ridden by me, and once he actually bestirred himself, he liked to get results, preferably the kind that the client would be willing to pay for. This didn't look like anything the client would be thrilled with.

"So, it seems to me that, unless the infidelity is of a rather unusual variety, one that can keep itself under control and free from detection for an extended period, we are compelled to conclude either that the affair is over or that it never existed in the first place, outside of Mr. Spall's imagination." Schwartz looked from one to another of the men, finishing with me, and went on: "Do any of you have the slightest suspicion, the merest hint, that I might be mistaken about this? If you have even a shadow of an inkling, please say so now."

Schwartz faced us one by one, and one by one, they took their cue from Paul, who said, "No, sir," and so did Sonny, and Frank, and Jonny, and I.

"So," Schwartz said, "on the theory that there may be a cause for Mr. Spall's suspicions other than Ms. Spall's behavior, I propose that we shift our attention to him rather than her. His two previous marriages seem to have set a pattern for him; his first two wives divorced him, and in each case, they were able to convince the court that they were entitled to alimony. My provisional theory is that he suspects, or he claims to suspect, his wife of extramarital activity not because she is up to something, but because he is.

"Now, obviously, with the client expecting regular reports on his wife's movements and contacts, we need to maintain some surveillance of her. I propose, however, that, once Ms. Spall returns from Chicago, Paul will continue to concentrate on her movements, and so far as the rest of you men go, Mr. Spall, rather than his wife, shall be the main focus of your attention for the next few days and perhaps weeks. I suggest that Paul coordinate your surveillance of Mr. Spall and that he do so while continuing her surveillance alone, once she returns."

Paul said, "I take it we're trusting her about the Chicago trip. I mean, she really has a sick father?"

"That should be your first step," Schwartz said. "I think you should be able to confirm that—"

"Of course," Paul said. "The usual inquiries, Mr. Schwartz. No problem."

That gave the rest of them something to think about. In Frank's case, the process was visible on his face. When he had worked it out, he nodded, and that meant he was caught up with Sonny and Paul. Jonny didn't show his thinking, but I knew him well enough to realize that he'd be caught up with the plan about the time Frank was.

Paul spoke first. "All right, Mr. Schwartz; I'll keep on Ms. Spall, and the others can watch Mr. Spall and one of them can report to me, or to you or Rainer if you prefer, once every hour or so. We stay in touch, and if anything gets tricky, we can swarm quickly."

Schwartz nodded. "Excellent, Paul. I think reporting once a day will be sufficient, unless something really interesting turns up. Now, without going into unnecessary details, Mr. Spall has brought another matter to our attention, which leads me to a line of thought that, not to put too fine a point on it, casts doubt on his judgment to a certain extent. I won't clutter your minds with the details, but I will say that he seems to have gone out of his way to undermine our confidence in his good sense. A man of adequate but not exceptional intelligence who is suspicious of his wife and perhaps of others as well, for what seem to me to be very dubious reasons, may go off in heaven knows what direction."

The help looked blank. "Mr. Schwartz means," I interpreted for them, "that Spall has given us plenty of reason to regard him as a flake, and his actions are totally unpredictable."

They nodded understanding, and Frank said, "I think we'd have figured that out eventually."

"Just saving you time is all."

"Much obliged."

Schwartz tried not to seem miffed at needing translation for the men. "As usual, you will report to Paul whenever feasible, guided by your intelligence in the light of experience. If Paul is temporarily inaccessible, you will report to Rainer or, failing him, to me." He looked from one to the other. "Have any of you questions that need answering?"

They didn't. Schwartz took his leave, for an urgent appointment programming an altimeter, and I stayed with the men to go over Ken Spall's routine. When they were ready to leave, I asked Paul to stay a minute, so Jonny gave Sonny and Frank a lift.

When Paul and I were alone in the office, I gave him a bird's-eye view of the coded agreement Spall had brought to our attention, and I explained the afternoon's program. I had looked up Geoffrey McElroy's address and had arranged with Ken Spall to invite McElroy to a conference with Schwartz here at the office at four o'clock this afternoon. I had heard back this morning that the conference was on, and both Spall and McElroy would be here to meet with Schwartz. Paul grinned when I outlined the plan for the two of us. We hadn't had this sort of fun in quite a while.

Well before the guests would be arriving, I collected a small batch of tools from the safe and went with Paul to the workroom, where Schwartz had just finished testing his altimeter successfully. He urged us to err on the side of caution on our errand, and I urged him to phone promptly if our window of opportunity started to close. Paul and I took his silver Cobalt, which I happened to know had a bit more get up and go than it had had when it left the factory.

McElroy lived on Ewing Street, a few blocks east of Keystone, and there were plenty of spaces on the street where we could park and watch his house, a late '60s used-brick ranch with attached garage and several mature trees, a few of which overhung the roof and needed trimming. Paul and I didn't bother hiding, since neither of us had ever met McElroy so there was no risk of recognition, but we didn't go out of our way to attract attention either.

At about quarter to four, the garage door opened and a black Sierra pulled out, went down the driveway, and pulled out onto the street, heading west. The driver fit the description I'd gotten from Spall. We let the Sierra get well past us before we left our car, and we went to the front door together. Paul had brought a clipboard along and we both were wearing jackets, ties, and shades, so we looked like a couple of guys taking some annoying survey. We went up the walk to the small front porch, or stoop really, past a neglected flowerbed along the front of the house.

I rang the bell, and we heard it sound inside. I gave it a few rings, but nobody answered the door. We glanced around but saw no sign that we were inciting anyone's curiosity. Paul went back along the path, and I headed the other way, west, around back, and we rounded the house, meeting at an added-on screened porch in back, facing a koi pond that needed cleaning. I slipped a pair of surgical gloves on; Paul had put his on as he walked around the house. I handed him a pair of hospital booties and put mine on. I checked the sliding glass door onto the porch. It was locked, and there's no way to get through one of those mothers without leaving serious traces. They're no obstacle to someone who wants in and doesn't give a damn who knows how they got in, but you leave them alone if you're trying for subtlety.

Fortunately for us, there was a back door to the garage, with an ordinary hardware store lock. Contrary to what television and films would like you to believe, a couple of straightened-out paperclips will not do you any good with one of these. If you don't believe me, try it for yourself at home. Go outside with some paperclips, locking your door as you go, and see how long it takes you to get back in. I'd advise you to bring your keys along.

Handily enough, the set of tools I'd brought along was not a box of paperclips. Paul checked out the neighboring backyards while I chose my tool, and in less time than it takes to tell it, the door was open, and we were through it into the garage, and we had broken and entered according to the laws of the state of Indiana.

That's a level 6 felony, by the way, good for six months' to two and a half years' imprisonment, and that's why we didn't want to get caught doing it. If you concentrate, it's really not terribly hard to move through a house you're not supposed to be in without leaving traces, assuming that the owner thinks locks on the doors are sufficient security. The fact is, locks are for law-abiding people. Paul murmured that he hadn't seen any sign of motion detectors or any other electronic measures, although we both knew that might just mean they're getting better at hiding stuff. Fortunately for us, most home-owners who shell out for a security system like to post a sticker to advertise the fact where visitors can't miss it. McElroy didn't have a sticker on his front door or windows.

We checked for electronic measures all the same, neither of us having much of a taste for a steady diet of bologna sandwiches, and there was nothing. Like most people, McElroy left the door from the garage to the house closed but unlocked. I always wonder why. If you have the garage opener, you have the house.

McElroy's house was ordinary in that it had the usual features of the house of a single man in his fifties living alone. He was probably slightly neater than average, not that I have any special insight into how anyone lives. There were no dishes in the sink; the dishwasher was about half loaded with plates, bowls, cups, utensils. There was a hamper with a shirt, socks, underwear in the bedroom closet of the master bedroom. It was a three-bedroom house. The two smaller bedrooms had no beds, one being stuffed with furniture, pictures, lamps, luggage, and other things put away and not used, and the other one was the reason we'd come.

The smallest bedroom had a closet full of winter clothes, coats, boots, and so on. In the center of the room itself were an old IKEA workstation with a computer, printer, paper, and a nice ergonomic desk chair. There was a floor lamp in one corner of the room, and in another a single beige file cabinet with a lamp and a paper cutter on top of it. "Talk about a stab from the past," Paul almost whispered as we took in the workstation: a forty-year-old IBM PC, with a monochrome monitor, a big box for the motherboard and add-on cards, a heavy keyboard on a spiral cord, and an Epsom MX-80 printer fed with sprocketed fanfold paper that came up through a slot in its shelf, above the open box on the floor.

"I've seen one before," I murmured, "but not with that kind of printer."

"I have, and those babies are loud, believe me. The really big, fast, powerful ones are really earsplitting. The ones that used a typeball or whatever it was called really put out the noise. I've seen them in specially made boxes that were lined with sound-absorbing foam; you get set to run a print job on one of those babies, press the button, and you've got about three, four seconds to get the cover swung down over it before the racket starts, like a firing range where they're testing Uzis."

I was taking pictures with my phone, not the phone I use for day-to-day, one for things we don't ever want to read about in the papers. I got some good big-picture ones, taking care to leave Paul out, then plenty of close-ups. The computer screen was turned off, and there was no sound, so apparently the computer was off too. I looked for the switch on the side; it was flipped down. We were careful not to disturb the workstation at all.

There were boxed manuals on the shelf, for DOS, Asynchronous Communication System, WordStar, BASIC, and so on, and other books, including what looked like a fairly new chemistry text. I told Paul I wanted a look

126

at that, and handed him my phone. I eased the chem text out from the shelf to show the front of the book, and Paul took a couple shots, with only my gloved fingertips showing. I put it back exactly as I had found it. Paul said, "No modem," and I saw he was right. The computer was sitting there isolated, power cords plugged into a surge-protector strip.

On one shelf there were boxes of floppy disks, the kind that actually were floppy, five-and-a-quarter-inch, single-sided, double-density squares that showed a section of bare iron oxide recording surface. I got one out of an open box, Paul shot it for me, and I put it back where it came from.

I opened the top drawer of the file cabinet. Empty. So were the next two. The bottom drawer contained yards of cable and wire, many different pieces, some with RS-232 connections like the cable that connected the PC box to the MX-80, some with small, round or rectangular male or female plugs. There was a modem among the other hardware, and some manuals. Paul shot pictures of the contents of the bottom drawer, then looked up. I nodded enough.

I closed the file cabinet drawer and looked at the workstation's level surfaces, but saw no trace of dust patterns to show the modem had been placed there. I realized I hadn't checked the workstation's drawer. It contained an assortment of pens and pencils, paperclips, clamps, and so on, and there at the very back, an embosser. I thought of running a page through the printer, thought better of it, and took a receipt from my wallet. I turned it over, held it between the round halves of the embosser, and squeezed. It looked to me exactly like the notary seal on the McElroy document. I put the embosser back, closed the drawer. I mentioned the lack of dust on the desktop next to the computer box. "No photocopier," Paul said. I agreed.

"Maybe elsewhere in the house," I said. He nodded.

Paul's watch let out a very soft beep, and he said it had been exactly twenty minutes since the Sierra had left, and I agreed that we didn't want to wear out our welcome. There was no telling how long McElroy would stay with the conference, and Schwartz wasn't undertaking to keep him, just to get him away from home long enough for us to have a look inside.

We looked around the room, made sure we hadn't made any changes and left. On our way out, we looked in each room for a photocopier, but saw none. A small room off the living room had been converted into an office, with modern electronics, including a printer, but we saw no dedicated photocopier, although there was a shredder almost full of long strips of paper. "That would be interesting," Paul said, "if we had a few spare days."

We left by the back door by which we'd entered, and we left it locked behind us. While we were still trespassing, we were now outside the house. We removed our gloves and booties, and I stuffed them in a jacket pocket. That walk, clipboard in hand, back to the car was easier once we left the McElroy property. Probably no one watching would notice that I was now carrying the clipboard, not Paul.He pulled out carefully, took Ewing back to Keystone, turned south on Keystone to return to the office by way of Broad Ripple, not Nora and not Marott Park and the School for the Blind. McElroy had driven past us when he left home, so if he was driving back home after leaving Schwartz's meeting, we wouldn't pass him. Unrecognizable and unmemorable are good; not seen a second time at all is even better.

Paul had just turned north onto Westfield when my usual phone buzzed, Schwartz letting us know that McElroy had just left and Spall was still there. "I explained to Mr. Spall that you had been unavoidably detained on another matter," Schwartz said to me. So Paul should drop me off and leave rather than coming in, and I should not burden the client unnecessarily with the details of his investigation for the present.

Paul and I shook, and I reminded him to charge Schwartz double for time spent in technically illegal activity, and he said he'd hoped I'd come up with a good way to get us all sent to prison and this might do the trick.

I joined Schwartz and Spall in the office. Schwartz was speaking to Spall about how much more fun travel in Europe and North Africa and West Asia had been when they were younger and less settled, but he raised an eyebrow to me, asking how it had gone. Spall didn't notice, and he didn't even see my nod. We had satisfactory results.

Schwartz sat back, listening to Spall describe a night train trip he had taken from Paris to Beauville thirty years ago, with only a sweltering upper berth to try to sleep in while drunk, stoned teenagers and others made music and conversation, "social intercourse of every variety," as Spall called it. When he finished the story, there was silence for a few seconds, what might have been called, in an AA meeting, a long moment. Then Schwartz said, "While the surveillance of your wife has not yielded definite results, Mr. Spall, I believe Mr. Zufahl may be able to shed some light on the matter of that pseudo-agreement you asked about. Rainer, do you agree?"

"Sure," I said, "so long as it's understood that everything I say is hypothetical, regarding behavior that might incur censure from an overly strict interpretation of the will of society." I was impressed to see Ken Spall smile at the circumlocution.

"Oh, I'm sure everything you say is hypothetical, Mr. Zufahl," he said. "I can't imagine that you would ever bend the rules, so a good hypothetical exposition might make matters clear."

"With that understood," Schwartz said, "you can open the bag for us both. What might you hypothetically have learned about Mr. McElroy?"

"Hypothetically," I said, "it has sort of come to me, as if in a vision, that McElroy has a 1981 IBM PC and an Epsom dot-matrix printer that could have turned out, and probably did turn out the original of that coded text Mr. Spall showed you."

"Mr. McElroy had the temerity to bring the original of the dot-matrix-printed coded message, complete with fountain-pen signatures and the embossed notary seal. I don't suppose you've had any hypothetical visions about a stolen or forged notary seal?"

"No, I'm afraid not," I said. No sense in sharing things the client might not be able to consider hypothetical. "But I doubt it would be hard to make a fake one, or have one made, given that you don't care whether it will withstand close scrutiny."

"Doubtless you're correct," Schwartz said. "At any rate, Mr. McElroy showed us the purported original, but he wouldn't turn loose of it, much less leave it. If we are correct that he manufactured the thing, he's certainly playing seriously the role of innocent, uncertain possessor of a key to riches."

"It's acting," I said. Past a certain point, it wasn't necessary to maintain the hypothetical stance; that was covered, so far as possible court testimony was concerned. "I have seen and photographed the equipment he used to make the thing. I haven't checked serial numbers or anything, but I'd bet that paper he used is older than I am. If he found a box or so of old fanfold paper, and he has a functioning ribbon in that printer, with period ink, and he knows what he's doing, you'd be hard-pressed to prove his document isn't genuine."

"Well, that might well be a challenge, but it seems to me that the main question is why Mr. McElroy believes a coded agreement would be more credible than a plain-text document. What on earth motivates the coding?" He run his fingers through his hair. "It seems insufficient merely to say that Mr. McElroy is stupid or that he is crazy. Either or both may be the case, but neither answers the question: why did he go to the trouble of coding the thing?"

"Is it possible," Spall asked, "that he somehow thought that circumstance of its being coded made the thing seem more plausible?"

"That seems to me to defy logic," Schwartz said. "He produces and pretends innocently to put forth a document that would seem to promise him a half share in the ownership of your business. How does the coding strengthen his case? It merely adds an aura of irreality to the whole thing. I don't understand it.

"Taking the translated document as it is, there's no evidence that I have been able to find that the financial assistance the document refers to ever occurred. If Gregory McElroy ever lent or gave Mr. Spall Sr. a cent, there's no record of it, not that absence of evidence necessarily implies the contrary. It's really troubling, this unnecessary element of the bizarre the coding provides."

"But can you prove the document is bogus?" Spall asked. "Lawsuits can be ruinous, and in a business like mine, all it takes is a touch of bad publicity, and the orders dry up fast."

"That's true of many businesses. I may or may not be able to demonstrate the falsity of the document," Schwartz said, "but I can certainly do what's almost as good, Mr. Spall."

"What would that be?"

CHAPTER THIRTEEN

"I can prove the coding is bogus," Schwartz said.

Chapter Fourteen

Believe it or not, I had plenty to do that evening and into the next morning, and I was, in fact, just caught up with the office routine when the package arrived by messenger. It was not unusual to receive a package of course, but they don't usually arrive by motorcycle, and the messenger is usually uniformed. This one wore good-quality black leather head to toe, counting a black helmet, and handed me the mini clipboard with the receipt to sign manually, and she took care of the electronic notification right there on the spot. She asked if there was any reply. I hefted the wrapped box, about the size and heft of a dozen or so checkbooks, or enough C4 to blow us all to kingdom come, and I said I'd have to ask after the addressee had opened the package. I invited her to follow me to the office. I had a feeling I'd seen her before, but I couldn't place her.

Schwartz laid down his current book when I came in carrying the package and trailing the messenger. "Addressed to you," I told him, handing it over.

He looked at it, picked it up with both hands, turned it over, flexed it. "It couldn't possibly contain an explosive," he said.

"You're pretty positive," I said.

"It would have gone off by now. There are still poisons to consider and various other possibilities."

"I notice there's no return address. Just handed it in at a Chicago station, paid cash, and away it went." He looked up at me suspiciously. "What do you think of this address?" He pointed at the laser-printed label. "I don't have Chicago addresses memorized, but unless I'm really out of touch, I would estimate that this would be half a mile or so into Lake Michigan, north of the aquarium."

"So, no reply?" the messenger asked. She had a rather deep voice, not quite husky, but getting there, not at all unpleasant.

Schwartz looked at the messenger. "How can I reply if I don't know who sent this?"

The messenger frowned. "I can take a text or voice or…"

"But I would still be addressing God only knows whom."

"You could open the package. That might tell you who sent it."

Schwartz nodded. The box was covered with brown paper, taped with masking tape, not the regulation fiber stuff. He opened his pocketknife, slit the paper all around the addressed side, lifted off a double layer of brown paper. A slightly squashed white shirt box was inside. He took the lid off carefully, and laid it aside on the paper. Inside the box was a manuscript, perhaps a couple hundred pages of ordinary 8½" × 11" printer paper. The top sheet read "Artificial Intelligence: The Case Against" about a third of the way down. There was a blue thumb drive loose at the end of the box.

Schwartz lifted the top sheet, and the next had the same title in the same place and, spaced several lines down, "by Stacy Hereford."

"Stacy Hereford," Schwartz said. "No middle name or initial, no letters after the name, just the name in the usual form."

"Is that who sent it to you?" the messenger asked. "Do you want to send a reply?"

"Well, Rainer," Schwartz asked, "do you think we should send a reply to this? Perhaps a confirmation of receipt? An acknowledgment that the manuscript arrived safely?"

"If you like, boss," I said, reaching for my notepad. "Fire away."

Schwartz laughed quietly but definitely. "Oh, I don't think that will actually be necessary, Rainer. Why send a written message when a spoken one will do?" He turned to the leather-clad messenger. "Don't you agree, Ms. Hereford?"

"I don't think that would be necessary, Mr. Schwartz," Stacy Hereford said. She laughed too. She had a good, full but not overbearing laugh.

I admit I was flatfooted, totally caught from behind. There was nothing to do but admit it, and I laughed too. As Grandma used to say, you can laugh or you can cry, and one feels better than the other.

"Please be seated, Ms. Hereford," Schwartz said, gesturing her toward the red leather chair and heading for his chair behind his desk. "Iced tea?" he asked her and got a yes. I went to the kitchen, got the day's fresh pitcher from the refrigerator, assembled glasses and so on, and carted it all to the office. Schwartz had kept things social while I was out, but when we all had full glasses, he sat back and asked her if she would care to explain what was going on.

"Well, Mr. Schwartz, and Mr. Zufahl," she said, turning from him to me, inclusively, "you have to understand that, on the one hand, I love my family, and in their own way, they love me, or believe they do, but on the other hand, there's simply no denying that they're all crazy. Dad's crazy. Mother's crazy. Grandpa's the craziest of them all."

"You realize we have already had reports of this problem," Schwartz said. "So far, your diagnosis seems to agree with our information."

"My Dad thinks that, with a little encouragement, this country can and will support another major league sport, and that sport will be cricket. He believes that Indiana, this basketball-crazed state, will somehow take to a sport that only a minority of English people really care about and that from Indiana, it will spread to the rest of the country." She drank iced tea.

"It's insane when you consider that spectator sports are close to if not in fact past saturation point; at any given time of day or night, there's sports on television or your computer, if not live, then recorded live on tape, of all the ridiculous terms I've ever heard. This is not unexplored territory, you understand.

"But Dad is a Hereford, and the Herefords are loaded, and if you're rich enough, you're not crazy. You may be eccentric or idiosyncratic, but you're not nuts. He has about as much chance of inspiring love of cricket in the hearts and minds of Americans as he has of curing cancer, but he's an idealistic visionary. He has vision, supposedly. So much more dependable-sounding than 'he has visions'.

134

"Cricket is not the passion of all Britons, in case you hadn't noticed their national football fetish. People do things for, by, and because of football that no one would ever do over cricket. It wouldn't, quite simply, be cricket. Never mind that the rules of cricket are utterly incomprehensible to most, if not all, Americans. Dad thinks he can deliver hot and cold running cricket matches, and once the whole thing has built up a head of steam, this country will be mad for it. He's mistaken, and you can't tell him so, because if he can't have you silenced, he'll just refuse to listen to anything remotely resembling good sense.

"Dad is fucking nuts, and he's going to pour the entire Hereford estate down that miles-deep rabbit hole unless somebody stops him, and it's one of the few good things about this mess that Grandpa won't let him have the money."

"Your grandfather Hereford controls the money?" Schwartz asked.

"Yes, and he's got the tightest fist you ever saw. But Dad has his own income, not that it's anything like what it would be if he'd inherited it from Grandpa. Dad can keep the dream alive, as he puts it, and he can get and has gotten substantial loans against the future as he thinks it will be. But even he isn't certain that Grandpa is leaving him the whole pile or anything like it."

"And your mother?"

"And my mother is crazier than my father. At least he just tries to become invisible and dreams of cricket putting American football in the shade. And, of course, he goes on with his father and my mother. But she is crazy and always has been. At least she's been crazy my entire life." Stacy sat back, looked hard at Schwartz, then at me. "You called me 'Ms. Hereford,' Mr. Schwartz."

"Of course," Schwartz said. "You were wearing lipstick, eyeliner, and, I believe, a touch of mascara."

"Right," she said, "and even though my parents hired you to find their missing son, you knew the truth when you saw it."

"Hold on a minute," I said. I turned toward Schwartz. "I realize, sir, that your acquaintance is at least as wide as mine, but it's different in a number of ways, and I'm here to tell you that a little lipstick and mascara doesn't really prove anything."

He gave a short laugh. "Of course not, Rainer, but a person wearing lipstick is probably a person who wishes to be considered female, if only for the nonce, and—"

Stacy Hereford nodded. "I can see how it could be confusing, especially with both my mother and my father telling you their son Stacy was missing, but I'd hate for you to be misled. Or to be in doubt at all." She stood up, unbuttoned her leather jacket, peeled it, as Schwartz tried to tell her she didn't have to convince us of anything whatsoever. She got down to a T-shirt and pants. "Oh, for God's sake," she said, "it's no big deal." She unbuckled her belt.

"Now, really, Ms. Hereford, you don't have to prove anything to me or Mr. Zufahl, for that matter—"

I sat there, kept my mouth shut. Stacy lifted the T-shirt and dropped the trousers, definitively proving what she wanted to prove.

"Well," Schwartz said, as she got dressed again, "that certainly settles that, although I'd have been willing to take your word for it. We were already aware that you were born female." That bit about taking her word for it wasn't even remotely true. He'd have been willing to take her doctors' words for it, but he can be surprisingly old-fashioned at times. It's not unpleasant, you understand; it's just the way he is sometimes.

"So you see, Mr. Schwartz, how it was, growing up with my parents both convinced that I was really a boy."

"That part is a little murky, Ms. Hereford," Schwartz said.

"By the way, you can call me Stacy," she said. "I mean, 'Ms. Hereford' seems a bit formal, now that you've seen me naked."

"Well," Schwartz said, "it's the formality that saves the situation, don't you think?" He was having a little trouble getting back to normal, so I thought I'd try to earn my keep.

"You said your parents were both convinced that you were really a boy," I said. "But it's pretty obvious you aren't, or weren't. How did they manage to ignore the reality?"

"My mother is the ringmaster of that particular circus," Stacy said. "You couldn't believe some of the things she got them up to. You've probably never heard of the MNC."

Schwartz shifted in his chair a bit. "The Mid-month Nature-study Club," he said. "Yes, we have heard of it. It came up in connection with a previous case." He turned to me, probably to get a chance to look away from her while he said, "As I recall, it was a dozen or so Northside couples who got together once a month to study their own sexual nature, or natures."

I helped him out. "Yes, and we came across it when a member, or rather a former member, was being threatened with blackmail."

"Well, there you are," Stacy said. "My mother got them involved in the MNC, not that I think Dad would have initiated such a thing, but he goes along with whatever she wants, so long as she leaves him alone about cricket and guns."

"Your father is interested in shooting?" Schwartz asked her.

"Well, yes, but it's more collecting them and refinishing them and just having them," she said. "He shoots, in the basement at home and at the Noblesville Sports Club, but with Dad, it's possession that's primary." She took a sip of iced tea to fill in the pause. "Cricket and guns, for God's sake. And aside from his two hobbies, he goes along with Mom on whatever she says. Up until kindergarten, so far as I know or remember, things were fairly sane, but once I showed the slightest aptitude for sports, anything physical really, and math and science, my mother got it into her head that I was a boy trapped in a girl's body."

"That's not really what one could call rare," he said. "I don't have the statistics to hand, but—"

"Transition isn't what one could call rare," she said, "but that's not what this was. It wasn't me; I was perfectly happy being a girl, playing sports, getting along with my friends, and all that. But my mother decided I was 'really' a boy, that I wasn't 'really' a girl, that I would eventually want to transition from female to male, and of course, since it was my mother deciding things, my father went along with her, and since that was how there would be a male heir, my grandfather did too.

"Since I was interested in boys, Mother decided I must be a gay boy in a girl's body, and they went along with that too." She looked hard at me, then at Schwartz. She nodded as if answering some silent question of her own. "You realize, of course, that I've seen that look before. I know it's hard to believe, but that's what money can do, buy you credibility. I mean, of course, it's difficult to get your head around, but all those years growing up, she kept the story straight—" She smiled at the phrase. "My mother managed my life the way she managed her own, nice and tight, totally scripted all the way. Private schooling at home, strictly supervised activities from kindergarten on up, and if anyone had any doubts, they kept them to themselves. Everyone knew which side their bread was buttered on. Money can buy just about anything. It's amazing, really, the things people will do for money. Money kept their membership in the MNC a secret, and it kept what was supposedly 'my secret' an open secret among family and close friends. I was raised as a boy, and of course, I had to go along with it. It's not as if I was ever consulted about the matter. I was told what I was supposed to be."

Stacy's expression changed suddenly from bemused to furious, but otherwise she didn't move a muscle. "Do you realize, Mr. Schwartz, how utterly helpless a child is when its parents, its entire adult family, are united in a conspiracy to deny the truth? I doubt it; I really doubt that you have ever considered that stark, cruel fact: a child is helpless in its parents' hands, and—"

"On the contrary, Ms. Hereford," Schwartz said, "as a father, I've often had to—"

"You are a father," she said, "not a monster. Not the assistant of a monster, like my mother. She is utterly insane, and she's dragged my father and grandfather in with her, and neither of them ever opposed her craziness, her one true lie."

She looked from one of us to the other. "All it would have taken," she said, "would have been a single word, one objection, and her house of cards would have been flattened. But for almost twenty years, God damn her to hell, that crazy bitch imprisoned me in her own little cell of lunacy. You tell a child of five she's really a boy in a girl's body, and what do you think she believes?"

138

"She believes she's a boy in a girl's body," Schwartz said quietly. "She believes what her parents tell her, of course."

"Yes," Stacy said. "I believed what they told me; I was a boy mentally and psychologically and emotionally and every other way, because they told me so, and I believed it—" Suddenly, the dam broke, and the tears were streaming down her cheeks. I reached over to hand her a box of tissues.

"You know," Schwartz said, "I have heard of parents like that, but this is my first direct encounter with anyone who has deliberately..." His voice trailed off. The look on his face was such that I was glad I hadn't inspired it. He cleared his throat, took a tissue for himself from the box on his desk. "This is unique in my personal experience, Ms. Hereford, and I believe I can say the same for Mr. Zufahl." I nodded assent.

"So, Mr. Schwartz, are you going to turn me over to my parents?" Stacy wiped tears from her face with another tissue, blew her nose decorously.

"Good God, no," Schwartz said, clearly glad to be able to say something positive, "and there is no way I could, in fact, do so. I was hired to find the Herefords' missing son, and you definitely do not fit that description. I will, of course, return the retainer, and—not really, of course—I will eat my expenses on the case, but rest assured, we are not turning you over to your parents." He turned to me. "Is the guest room ready for occupancy, Rainer?"

"As it happens, yes, I believe it is. I'll check things, just to make sure everything is okay," I said.

"Excellent. Now, Ms. Hereford, we can offer you a safe, clean, reasonable place to stay, if you wish to do so, or—"

"Now, that's really not necessary, Mr. Schwartz," Stacy said, but I could tell she was touched by the offer.

"Have you made other plans that must be canceled?" he asked.

"No, I thought I'd find a room somewhere anonymously," she said. "I have a pretty decent stash of cash."

"That might be less convenient than you'd like," Schwartz said. "Our guest room is on the second floor of this house, as are Mr. Zufahl's and my own, and from a security standpoint it would be hard to improve upon." He permitted himself a chuckle. "And since guests who stay with us aren't charged for the privilege, it won't eat into your cash reserves."

Stacy made some polite noises, but I could tell he'd made a sale. I excused myself, went upstairs to check the guest room, which is roomy, on the northwest corner of the second floor, away from the streets, that is, from 79th and Forest Lane. Like the other rooms, it has its own bathroom. Schwartz was being Schwartz when he designed that house; he couldn't imagine a bedroom having to share a bath. The linens and so on were in fine shape, and of course Stacy's luggage was basically what she had on and whatever was in the motorcycle saddle bags.

When I got back downstairs and proclaimed the guest room ready for occupancy, Schwartz asked Stacy if she'd like to freshen up. She just laughed at that idea. By now, we were getting close to dinner time. He discussed her dining preferences, volun-told me I would be picking up dinner once it had been decided on. Stacy expressed a hankering for Mediterranean food, and Schwartz suggested Canal Bistro. Stacy suggested that, while her return was still entre nous, she'd like to get some clothes and other articles, so I offered to take her by My Best Friend's Closet on the way to get the dinner order, and pick her up again on the way back, and we settled on that.

I should have expected it. By the time her clothing purchases were wrapped and ready to go, dinner was room temperature. Thank heaven for microwaves.

Chapter Fifteen

Friday morning Schwartz, Stacy Hereford, and I were in the office talking, with a decent homemade breakfast under our belts. Schwartz can cook when he wants to. We'd all slept well, and the weather conveniently cooperated with what Schwartz calls the pathetic fallacy. Our mood was good, and the sky was blue and the air was warm.

Schwartz was bringing Stacy up to date on the situation with her family, first with her parents and grandfather hiring us to find her, not that that was the way they had put it, and second with her cousin, Gordon Black. Stacy had known Allison Morgan, of course, but she hadn't heard of Allison's murder. She was shocked, but no more than one would expect. The two hadn't been especially close.

It was going on eleven o'clock when the doorbell began ringing with Steve Ripley's trademark persistence. When I opened the door as wide as the chain allowed, Inspector Mercer was giving Sergeant Ripley grief about that, but he stopped when I asked if there was something I could do for them. Mercer said I could open the door and get out of the doorway so they could come in. Just to stay in practice, I asked if they had a warrant, and Ripley replied that they didn't need a warrant for a social call.

"Oh, is that what this is, a social call?" I asked. I wanted to give Schwartz time to get Stacy out of sight if he deemed it expedient to do so, but I didn't want to make the police suspicious. "Well, in that case—" I shut the door, took off the chain, and opened the door wide, stepping back out of their way.

Without thanking me, the two representatives of law and order went

141

down the hall to the door to the office. By the time I had the door shut and had joined them in the office, Mercer was in the red chair and Ripley was in a yellow one, back against the wall so he could see the whole room. Stacy was nowhere to be seen. I assumed Schwartz had put her in the front room, which shares a bathroom with the office. The coffee pot, cups, and saucers were nowhere to be seen. If Mercer noticed his chair was warm, he didn't let on. He was saying to Schwartz, "I said before, and I say again, I'd ordinarily hesitate like hell to nominate a client of yours for a needle in the arm in Terre Haute, but this time I think you've stepped in it good."

Schwartz said nothing to that, which I thought was what it deserved. He glanced at me, and I nodded. I thought we both might be interested in what the police had to say about our client, Mr. Black. Inspector Mercer went on, "We have traced Black's rifle, the AR-15. It was made in Connecticut by Eastern Arms Ltd., which, by the way, I don't get, American companies using 'Ltd.' instead of 'Inc.,' but that's neither here nor there."

Schwartz interrupted quietly, "I suspect it's intended to give the name a touch of class, Inspector. Many Americans think of Britain as classy. Have you ever noticed that people use the word 'classy' when class is really the one irrelevant aspect of the matter? What some people view as 'high class' may be merely different from what they're used to. The typical sentiment of disliking the unfamiliar is replaced by an unthinking, or at any rate underthinking, assumption that the unfamiliar is superior."

Inspector Mercer dismissed that line of speculation with disdain flirting with rudeness. "The rifle was manufactured by Eastern Arms Ltd. of Hartford, and it was sold to a distributor in Sterling, Virginia, called Dominion Armaments. Dominion, in turn, included it in a shipment of guns that went to a gun show here last September. As you know, getting paperwork from a gun show can be hit or miss, but in this case, there's no problem. We have a bill of sale of that rifle, and a pricy telescopic sight for it, paid in cash, all information included, and the buyer's name is Gordon Black." He sat back in his chair. "There's also a silencer for it, but it's just a homemade piece of crap. No prints on it, no way to trace it. It worked, sort of, when we test-fired the rifle."

"Now, Mr. Mercer," Schwartz said in his most soothing tones, "as you say, we know that gun shows are notoriously lax about paperwork. Every show posts notices to the effect that all federal, state, and local laws must be respected, observed, obeyed, and we all know how hollow that assurance is. I have myself purchased a firearm or two at gun shows, and the principal concern is not keeping the ATFE happy." I thought that was interesting. Most people continue to refer to the Bureau of Alcohol, Tobacco, Firearms, and Explosives as the ATF. I decided Schwartz was being finicky about keeping the abbreviation up to date just to annoy our visitors.

Mercer leaned forward, jabbing down an index finger to emphasize his points. "Yeah, but in this case, the paperwork is, what's the word I want? Not 'extensive'; it's, ah, meticulous. The paperwork on this rifle is meticulous." He seemed pleased with himself for having found the right word to describe the written record.

"And that," Schwartz said, "is precisely what I find suspicious, Mr. Mercer. We know better than to expect anything like this meticulous record keeping at a gun show, and yet here you are: a nice, clear, all-spelled-out, all-blanks-filled-in concrete piece of evidence linking Gordon Black to the rifle. Really, do you take him for an idiot? If he had wanted to get hold of an AR-15 without a distinct paper trail, couldn't he have done so easily enough? I have no idea what sort of records you have about that particular gun show, but I'd be willing to guess that if I had attended it and had wanted to acquire a rifle without setting off red flags everywhere, I could have done so myself.

"Don't, Inspector, assume that because Gordon Black is a drunk, he must be an idiot as well. The same goes for you, Sergeant. As you know, both Mr. Zufahl and I are alcoholics, and you would not, I think, call us idiots." He gave them the opportunity to answer, or to call us idiots, but they just sat there. Despite their cocky manner, it seemed something about the case was bothering them. "Mr. Black is, in fact, a drunk, but that just means he's an alcoholic who hasn't stopped drinking; it doesn't make him stupid, just crazy. You gentlemen have both had enough experience to know that crazy isn't stupid, or vice versa.

"Mr. Black, you take it, planned Ms. Morgan's murder meticulously—"

That wasn't nice. Schwartz clearly wasn't trying to get the cops to stay for lunch. "—and he got a rifle and scope suitable for shooting her from his balcony, or from the roof, and he iced the cake for you by making sure there was a paper trail leading right to him. Please." Mercer and Ripley were trying to maintain a united front of confidence, and I admit they were good at it.

Mercer said, "Look, Schwartz, you know we're not taking anything for granted here, not with Black's connection to the Hereford family. We are definitely checking everything out. Nobody in their right mind wants to falsely accuse someone like that of murder."

"Or even truthfully," Sergeant Ripley contributed. "You can imagine the lawyers they'll have—"

Mercer overrode his subordinate. "Believe me, we're being thorough as hell on this one, and that's not always easy with kid gloves on, and believe you me, the kid gloves are definitely on, with this killing. But to me, Black feels good for this one; he's the ex-husband of the victim; he's in place at the time of the killing, no matter what he says about how much he was drinking when it happened." Mercer reached for a Salem Gold 100 that hadn't been in his shirt pocket for years now. He swore softly, then sat back. "But look, Schwartz, suppose for the sake of argument that you're right, that Black didn't kill Allison Morgan. Who did then? Aside from means and opportunity, who has a motive? She didn't have an enemy in the world, aside from her ex."

"Including her ex," Schwartz said. He went on, "We understand the anomalous position you're in, Mr. Mercer, but our belief is that he is innocent and that someone else murdered Allison Morgan and, to avoid taking responsibility for their actions, framed Gordon Black for the crime. I can tell you right now that I haven't the slightest idea who that person might be. Frankly, I consider this news further evidence that Mr. Black is innocent, not that he is guilty. A man of his financial resources, not unlimited but certainly well above average for a man his age, could obtain any weapon he might desire, legal or otherwise. He would know someone who knows someone who can acquire whatever item he wants." Schwartz failed to explain in excessive detail how he knows what he knows about these matters, thank heaven. "If he wants an item, he knows someone who can get it for him, and he's fully insulated by at least one layer and probably several.

"But instead, he goes to an Indianapolis gun show and finds a dealer of scrupulous honesty and the highest enthusiasm for federal firearms control, and he buys an AR-15 and scope, leaving a clear paper trail. When the bread crumbs are spread that thick, I have to ask who did the spreading. Maybe it wasn't Hansel at all, doling out a crumb now and then. Maybe someone wanted to make sure the trail of crumbs wasn't missed."

"Goddam your crumbs," Mercer said, just shy of a snarl. "We find evidence; we collect it." He patted his shirt pocket again, swore again. "Nobody, but nobody is trying to railroad Gordon Black. You don't railroad a Hereford in this town, and he's certainly enough of a Hereford to count. But then who the hell?"

"That is what I hope to discover," Schwartz said. "At the moment, I haven't a clue, Inspector, but I'm sure it wasn't Gordon Black." He offered tea, at last, but had no takers. He called off the mission, so I stayed at my desk. "Might I ask," he went on, "about the result of the test firing you have conducted with this rifle? I would assume that bullets fired from it match those taken from Ms. Morgan's body."

"Of course," Mercer said. "One of the slugs we took out of her was deformed enough to make it close to useless, but the other was in pretty good shape, and we're ready to take that to court and swear to it: that's the gun that was used to kill Allison Morgan."

"It would be tasteless," Schwartz said, "to offer a bet on that, so I won't. However, I will say this: I doubt very much that that rifle was used to murder Ms. Morgan."

"Now, wait a minute, Schwartz: I just said the bullets fired from it match one of the ones from the body, and—" Mercer hated to get into these situations with Schwartz, sitting across the desk. He turned his glare on me.

"Don't ask me, Inspector," I said. "I just work here; that doesn't mean I know what's going on. It sounds to me like Allison Morgan was shot with the rifle you found in Black's closet. But to add to Mr. Schwartz's comments, are we also supposed to believe that, having killed his ex-wife with a couple of bullets fired from his balcony, Black stows the rifle away in a closet in his apartment?"

Sergeant Ripley chipped in, "Should we tell them about the cartridge cases, Inspector?"

Mercer nodded, "Right, Steve. Sorry, Schwartz; I almost forgot to tell you about what I'm sure you will regard as further evidence of your client's innocence. We did a really close sweep along the ground below the east-side apartment balconies, and you'll never guess what we found."

"You found," Schwartz said, "two .223 cartridge casings with markings that indicate that they were ejected from the rifle you found in Mr. Black's closet." Mercer gaped, and Ripley suddenly sat up very straight. Both of them looked at Schwartz, which was handy for me, since I didn't have to manage my expression. He went on: "What else could it possibly have been, Inspector? It's the final bit of physical evidence; the casings complete the jigsaw puzzle. But a pleasing picture may not necessarily depict reality accurately at all. Beauty is not truth, nor is truth beauty, and it seems to me that the portrait of Gordon Black as the sniper in the night is just a little too perfect. It's too pat." He shook his head sadly, almost convincingly. "Who found the casings?" he asked, "and where and when?"

Ripley had his notebook out. "The casings were found a couple yards apart, six and eight feet, more or less, from the wall of the building, in a border of medium-sized river stone, about egg size, in a position consistent with ejection from the balcony of the apartment occupied by Mr. Gordon Black. Patrolman Rutger found them, about fifteen minutes into the search, yesterday at 14:45. Running a couple of empty .223 casings through Black's rifle—"

"Through the rifle found in Mr. Black's closet," Schwartz corrected Ripley, who remained unfazed.

"—held in a position consistent with aiming at a person standing on the path down by the canal, near where the body was found, and ejecting the empty casings, they flew out the right side of the rifle, bounced against the vertical rods in the railing around the balcony, and tumbled down to land six or seven feet south of the south end of the balcony."

"So you have the final piece of the puzzle," Schwartz said.

"And yet you're hanging on to Black as a client," Mercer stated, as if stating the law of gravity.

"I am," Schwartz said, "although I confess that I have no replacement for you to arrest. But surely you've confronted him with these discoveries, damning as they seem to be."

"Black denies ever going to a gun show, here or anywhere else. He says someone else must have bought the rifle and forged his signature, then planted it in his apartment," Mercer said. He shook his head. "He sounds almost paranoid about it, to tell you the truth. I mean, there's this vast conspiracy against him—"

"No," Schwartz said. "I'm sure it's not vast, indeed not a conspiracy at all, Inspector. Someone, some individual, killed Allison Morgan, and that same someone is trying to frame Gordon Black for it. It requires no conspiracy; only one person is breaking or bending the law; everyone else is innocently going about their business, more or less. He's not paranoid; he's defensive, which is a perfectly sane response to being attacked. If that person had a key, they could even have planted the rifle the evening of the murder, while Mr. Black was passed out in his living room."

"As I said," Mercer said, getting up to leave, "nobody wants to railroad a Hereford or a Hereford relation. As it stands, I don't have a choice about it. All the evidence says Black did it, and we still have newspapers and television in this town, and they'd eat us alive if we turn him loose without a damn good reason."

Schwartz said, "You don't think he's guilty, do you?"

Mercer said, "No, I don't. And not because he's your client. He just doesn't seem right for it to me. God knows I've known enough murderers in my time, and some of them were nice, quiet, peaceful folks who'd just let go for once at the wrong time. I know most of them tend to be a hell of a lot like you and me, and don't get me started on the other ones, the sociopaths. But no, I don't see Black as the murderer of his ex."

"Well," Schwartz said, "that is gratifying. We agree on fundamentals, Inspector. So far as I am concerned, I would like to be able to free Mr. Black by finding the person responsible, and I would like the Herefords, including Charles Hereford, to know that it was I who identified the murder. Aside from their fee for, or her fee actually, I need no applause."

"You're saying that if you find the killer before we do, you'll hand him over in front of the Herefords," Mercer said, "and so far as the media are concerned—"

"You will be seen to have removed a dangerous criminal from circulation and to have saved an innocent tax-paying citizen from wrongful imprisonment or even much worse."

"When you put it like that, it sounds too good to be true," Mercer said, "and that's usually an indication that it's too good to be true."

Schwartz smiled. "After all, Inspector, on a foggy night like that of the shooting, it would have been easy for Mr. Black to dispose of the rifle, even in a different section of the canal. I'm sure your check of the CCTV shows he never left the building, since the rifle was found in his closet."

"Wait a minute," Mercer objected. "You're saying he never left the building because the rifle was in his closet? That makes no sense."

"You're right, of course," Schwartz said. "I expressed myself poorly. It's really not important. Logic is great, and neither of us could get along without it, but we mustn't forget Marvin Minsky's definition of logic: 'what doesn't work in the real world.'"

Mercer offered to shake hands when they left, so at least Schwartz and I were provisionally human. For now.

I let Mercer and Ripley out, then turned to the front room. Stacy Hereford sat by the speaker she'd been listening to. Evidently Schwartz felt she should be up to date on current events. "Not one word about me," was all she said.

"None of their business," I told her. I opened the door to the office, and we joined Schwartz. He asked Stacy if she intended to get in touch with her parents, and as if on cue, the phone rang. I answered it. It was Anita Hereford, wanting an update on both cases. Schwartz got on the line, signaling me to let Stacy listen with me and asking Anita if she would arrange for me to see Gordon Black the following Monday. When she wanted to know about progress finding Stacy, he looked her daughter in the eye and told Anita that we were no closer to finding her son than we had been yesterday. She had a number of suggestions for a course of action we might take, none of it worth repeating, much less following. Finally, she said she'd call back after she'd talked with Gordon's lawyer. It didn't seem the right time to ask her for a recommendation.

Schwartz and I hung up, and he invited Stacy Hereford to stay with us awhile, not just overnight, for the foreseeable future. She was a bit taken aback, but when he pointed out the advantages of a place to sleep without alerting anyone's curiosity, she agreed. He asked her to give me a list of any toiletries she might need, and then she went out to her motorcycle, which she had brought into the garage, and came back in with a travel kit from the saddlebags.

We got carry-out from Pho Real, and she tucked away her fair share. Schwartz was positively maternal about the linens and so on in the guest bedroom. He invited her along on our trip to Muncie the next morning, and she said she'd see how she felt. We hit the hay.

Chapter Sixteen

That Saturday dawned clear and dry and almost windless, and the prediction was for fair skies all weekend. I checked for overnight messages, and there was nothing urgent to be done on anything professional, so after an early breakfast, Schwartz, Stacy, and I got into the Prius, Schwartz driving up to Muncie, me in shotgun, and her in the back seat with Schwartz's range box and motor box. *Frede,* separated into three sections, was in the trunk. We arrived at the Academy of Model Aeronautics flying field in plenty of time to help with the setup of the launchpads, electrical firing system, and the PA system.

It was a beautiful day, so we could expect a good crowd of flyers and spectators. There were several vendors, not nearly so many as there had been back before the crash of 2008, but enough to make browsing worthwhile. I left that to Schwartz, who was having a good time explaining things to Stacy, who seemed to be having a good time letting him do so. I helped run the HD extension cords out to the high-power pads, checking continuity, setting up the launch rails for the larger rockets, finishing off with emery cloth to remove any rust or other debris from the grooves the rockets' buttons would ride in on their way up the rails.

Schwartz was asked to serve as Range Control Officer for the initial hour or two of launches, most of which would be the smaller model rockets. He took a seat at the table, checked that the mike was on, then announced that the range was now cold and open, inviting folks to get their rockets on the pads. The Range Safety Officer, Sheryl Lynn Carlson, was doing a nice efficient job of checking rockets, getting the appropriate information, and passing the data on to Schwartz. I noticed that she was remarkably tactful when, now and then, she had to explain to a youngster why the rocket couldn't be flown as presented. Loose fins, unstable designs, and unsecured motors were the most common reasons, and she pointed out to the kids that, were she to allow the rocket to be flown, the results would be unfortunate. Nobody wants to watch their rocket come apart while everyone's watching.

When the near pads were full up, Schwartz waited until the last of the folks had returned to the spectator line, announced on the PA that the range was hot, and said that the first launch of the day would be the maiden flight of Roger Penwick's Renegade, flying on a C6-0 booster and a C6-7 second-stage engine. He remarked that this would be a high flight, asked people to watch for the booster, which would tumble after igniting the sustainer. Since it was a maiden flight, he counted down from ten, then pressed the red button. The black rocket took off with a whoosh, then staged perfectly, and the booster fell end over end back to earth, not six feet from the pad it had just left. There was a puff of talcum powder as the upper stage popped out the chute, and the Renegade came down safe and sound on the far side of the vendor shelter. I always seem to forget how fast rockets take off. Schwartz announced the next flight, a well-finished 1:100-scale Saturn V built by Sandy Ferrell. It flew well, but something went wrong with the parachutes, which stayed inside the two parts of the model. The rocket had been built so lightly that it suffered only cosmetic damage when it hit the ground. Sheryl remarked that she'd suggested that Sandy open the chutes up and dust them with talcum before rolling them again, but he hadn't done so. "Maybe next time," Schwartz said. I saw Stacy give him a quick glance with that remark.

The flying went well that morning, and after a while, Bernard Clay relieved Schwartz, and he and I took *Frede* out of the trunk, assembled it with screws except for the section where the body would separate for chute ejection. Stacy watched, asking the occasional question. Schwartz went with Terry Clinton to the table set up inside the vendor shelter, and Terry administered the written Level 2 test. Stacy and I watched the launches, most of which went well.

After the hours Schwartz had spent preparing for the written test, I wasn't surprised that he ripped through it pretty quickly, then went through it again, checking for careless mistakes. Terry graded the test and informed Schwartz that he'd made a perfect score, "just as I'd have expected of you."

Schwartz now had only to successfully fly and recover his rocket on a J or greater motor. Somewhat conservatively, he'd chosen an Aerotech J315 RMS Redline, which he assembled in his Monster Motors 54mm casing, while Terry observed, per the rules. He fed the assembly into the motor mount and secured it with the Kaplow clips. The fact is, I could give you a lot more technical information, but this is about as much as I understand and, I'd bet, as much as, if not more than you care about. Schwartz and I carried *Frede* out to the high-power pads, tilted the rail parallel with the ground, and eased the buttons into the rail, with some help from Stacy. Schwartz checked the cameras and the altimeter settings again, and then we lifted the rocket on the rail into a vertical position. There was no wind, so we didn't need to adjust the rail angle to compensate.

Schwartz took an igniter lead from his shirt pocket, slid it into the nozzle, and up into the slot in the solid propellant, taping it in place. There was a tile beside the pad, to hold the rear of the rocket above the flash plate. I ran the end of the extension cord around the base of the pad, below the plate, and Schwartz brought the igniter leads down and clipped the bared ends to the extension cord. The three of us walked back to the firing line, along with others who'd set up their own high-power rockets.

I got sodas from the shelter and we watched the latest batch of low-power launches, finishing with a crowd favorite, the Flis Kits A.C.M.E. Spitfire, a faithful instantiation of the rocket in the famous Far Side cartoon. About a foot and a half tall, it looks completely ridiculous, but it flies beautifully. Schwartz mentioned to Stacy that, the year before, members of a northern Indiana club had built an upscale of the Spitfire over six feet tall, and it had flown over a mile high. She asked him how high his rocket would go, and he told her he was hoping it might reach eight thousand feet AGL. She said, "Above ground level, as opposed to above sea level?" and he nodded. I wished we got along as well with clients as we were getting along with her.

Finally, and not to try your patience, the RCO announced that the next launch was Leo Schwartz's Level-2 attempt, flying his *Frede*, a Mad Cow Arrow on an Aerotech J315 Redline, with an expected altitude at apogee of eight thousand feet, and it may have just been my imagination, but the crowd seemed to get quiet as the count went down from ten, the button was pushed, and a puff of smoke was emitted from the base of the rocket. A split second later, that big pink needle was stabbing its way to the sky, and Schwartz was watching it go, and Stacy had hold of his arm, jumping up and down, crying, "Go, baby, go!" And I was doing the same thing.

The rocket hardly turned at all as it ascended into the cloudless sky, climbing on a red flame that seemed to last forever, trailing white smoke in as straight a column as you could ask for. At perhaps half a mile up, the propellant was exhausted, and the delay grain put out even thicker white smoke as the rocket continued to rise, coasting, coasting. The smoke ran out, and I lost sight of the rocket, then the RCO, watching with binoculars, announced, "We have an event!"

That meant that the rocket, having reached its highest point, had ceased ascending; the altimeter, having noted that fact, had sent a signal to the ejection charge, and the capsule of black powder had ignited, separating the upper and lower parts of the rocket and ejecting the drogue chute. Like most experienced flyers, Schwartz had included a generous amount of powdered chalk with the drogue chute, which had created the orange cloud the RCO had spotted.

We watched *Frede* descend under the small chute, the fin can hanging slightly higher than the nose-cone end, and it was clearly coming down right within the center of the flying area. No long walk today, thank heaven. At a hundred yards AGL, the main chute was ejected, and the descent slowed sharply for the last leg down to earth. Terry and Ed Stroh were congratulating Schwartz on a successful Level 2, and the RCO announced that the range was cold, and rockets could be collected. Stacy gave Schwartz an enthusiastic hug and told him that was the most fun she'd had in a long time. It was the first time I had seen her smile.

We broke *Frede* down into the separate sections and stowed it in the trunk, after taking out the altimeter, the camera, and the motor casing, which was still hot when Schwartz removed it from the mounting tube. He read off the stats from the altimeter, showing that the flight had reached 8122 feet AGL, and then we watched the flight on Schwartz's laptop. He'd set the cameras to start filming and transmitting when the rocket started to move, and for once, things went perfectly. The cameras were at the front of the middle section, pointing up at mirrors that reflected external mirrors that aimed straight downward at the fin can, launch pad, and ground. The action started with a puff of smoke, then the rocket rose up along the rail, and then the ground receded rapidly as *Frede* took to the sky. When the drogue chute ejected, the mirrors were pulled away by an auxiliary charge, and the camera, swaying below the shock cord to the chute, showed the ground coming up, considerably slower than it had fallen away. Then the main chute really slowed things down, to about twenty or twenty-five feet per second. We only watched it three times at the field. When the casing had cooled down, Schwartz disassembled it and cleaned it up before the residue could set.

Schwartz took another turn as RCO, and there were dozens of launches, from the smallest tumble-recovery rockets on A engines to a few really big ones, one on an M motor that took its rocket well over two and a half miles high. There were a number of unsuccessful flights, character-builders as Schwartz calls them, but nothing serious enough for tears.

When the time came to close down, we helped get the expensive and portable equipment stowed and locked in the club's trailer, but the launch pads and extension cords stayed in place for tomorrow's flying. Schwartz thanked Terry for his help with the test, and Terry, ever gracious, shrugged it off. We were still pretty psyched by the successful launch of *Frede,* and Stacy looked to be ready for more, but Schwartz explained that we really had things to do the next day. He talked projects with Terry for a while; then we got in the Prius.

I drove home, and Schwartz rode shotgun, with Stacy nodding off in the backseat.

When we got home, we brought everything in and got things put away in good shape. Some things can't be put off without penalty. Schwartz and I discussed the program for Sunday, which consisted of figuring out how to get into Allison Morgan's apartment. We finally decided that the police would surely have found anything she'd left. We wondered whether she'd have left anything with Gordon Black, in which case the cops certainly had it by now. Even if Gordon gave us permission to search his apartment, it had been given a good going over.

Stacy said, "Look, I know I'm a bit peripheral to this investigation, but after the divorce, Allison was pretty close to Guy Ungarn, if anyone."

"Guy Ungarn?" Schwartz asked her.

"Sure," she said, "the manager of Carl's Place—you know, the bar she was leaving that night. She was a regular there. Guy's gay, but she was about as close to him as anybody. If she had something to keep private, she might have asked him."

Frankly, it looked to me like a long shot, but we needed something. Schwartz asked Stacy whether she thought it was likely the police had learned this, and she said she had no idea. "You know the police better than I do," she pointed out. "Maybe they know about her and Guy, but since there isn't really much to know about them, maybe they don't." It seemed to make sense at the time.

So that was one item to check the next day. Stacy volunteered to introduce me to Ungarn, which couldn't hurt. After pizza from Bazbeaux, we called it a night.

* * *

Sunday was as nice as Saturday had been, except that we slept in rather than getting up to drive to Muncie. After a late homemade breakfast, with Schwartz showing off a bit with blueberry pancakes from scratch, more bacon than is really good for a person, and Vermont maple syrup or Maltese wild-thyme honey or both, Stacy and I headed for Carl's Place in Broad Ripple.

Carl's Place was in a smaller building just south of Helix Tower, where Gordon Black's apartment was. It was doing a good Sunday brunch business, and we found the manager, Guy Ungarn, supervising the pouring of a champagne tower, stemmed glasses forming a pyramid over a wide glass tray, the bubbly cascading down nicely. It was a California generic, of course. Stacy caught the manager's eye, and he nodded to her, then went on with filling the glassware, finished pouring, and turned the whole thing over to the waiting staff, then joined us at the bar, where we were nursing a couple ginger ales. It struck me that he looked familiar, but I couldn't place him.

Guy Ungarn seemed genuinely glad to see Stacy, and she introduced us. He said any friend of hers was a friend of his, which I took no more seriously than usual, but that's just habit. He was up to date on Allison Morgan's murder. "To think she walked out of here, and never made it home, it really gets me," he said.

"How do you feel about Gordon Black for it?" I asked.

"Well," he said, "cops on TV say we're likely to be killed by those closest to us, but I've really got to say I don't see it. I mean, when they were married—you know she was married to Stacy's cousin? When they were married, I used to see them here often enough. They lived where Gordon lives now, you know, so this was as handy a place as any. They always got along all right, when they were here at least. You never know how things are in private, of course, but frankly, I was surprised when they split." He asked the bartender for a Coke. "I don't drink," he said, "any more." I realized where I'd seen him before.

"Me either," I said.

"Friend of Bill?"

"Yes. You?"

"Well, yes and no. I go to meetings and all that, but frankly, I'm not that crazy about William G. Wilson, the philandering bastard. I think Lois put up with way too much from him, but what the hell? It was a different time, and you sure as hell didn't come by to get my opinion of Bill W."

"Right," I said. "What it is, Stacy's cousin is the cops' pick for her murder, and her mother has hired my boss and me to find a better candidate. She doesn't think Gordon did it, so we don't either."

"You know why Gordon and Allison split," Guy stated.

"Sure. His drinking," I said.

"He's an interesting case, Gordon. I never saw him drunk here, never had any problems with him, or them, in that line. But Allison told me once, and I'm only telling you this because you're trying to help him out, she told me that, once they got home, he'd go at it really hard, too hard."

"Controlled drinking in public, making up for lost time in private?"

"Exactly. Not what you could call an unusual situation in this world. Come to that, I was a bit like that myself, once upon a time. I'd watch my intake socially, you know; keep careful track of how much I was taking in, but when I got home, all bets were off. Played hell with a relationship or three."

"That does have a familiar ring to it," I said.

"And there I go again, dragging the conversation off track. Really now, what can I do to help?"

"Well," Allison said, "it seemed to me that, after she split with Gordon, Allison was as close to you as she was to anyone, and I was wondering if she might have left something with you."

"No, I'm afraid not," Guy said. "She did a fair amount of talking about how her marriage had gone down the drain, but as far as entrusting me with anything, no, I don't think so, and I'd remember that." He seemed to be ticking over memories. "I really don't think so."

"Could she have mentioned, like, you know, someplace she might have put something she didn't want found?"

"Not that I know of," he said, "but I think Margie might know. She was at least as well acquainted with Allison as anyone here." He watched a server across the main room, and when she dropped off an order at the kitchen slot, he signaled her over.

Margie Kincaid was about his age and mine, meaning she had ten years on Stacy. She said hi to Stacy, who introduced us, and Guy asked her if she knew of any place Allison Morgan might have stowed something for safekeeping, away from home. Margie gave it a good half-second's thought, said, "Sure. She'd have given it to me. Why?"

Stacy explained that we were looking for any evidence that someone besides Gordon Black had killed Allison. "Well, that's obvious," Margie said. "Gordon wouldn't kill her; he wouldn't kill anybody, but sure as hell not

Allison. He was crazy about her, still is, as far as I can tell." She stopped. "Could tell. I haven't seen him for quite a while."

"So," I asked her, "did she give you anything for safekeeping?"

Margie gave me a look calculated to let me know she'd heard better questions. "No," she said. She glanced around the room to see if any customers needed attention. "She didn't. But she told me something interesting that last night she was here, the night she was killed. She said she was glad to be out of that family, and she was going to finish up some business with them, and then she'd be done with them."

She saw a man and woman in the far corner of the room, both looking her way, trying to get her attention. "Got to get this." She went to finish up some business herself.

"She's as good as we've got," Guy said. "She won't tell you something just because she thinks you want to hear it. If she says Allison told her that, I'd say you can count on it."

"Thanks," I said. "It's not much, but it's more than I was expecting, to be honest." I was glad Schwartz wasn't there to hear me say that. I glanced at our glasses. "What do we owe you?"

Guy wasn't having any. "That's all right. But good luck finding out who killed Allison. You know as well as I do that you can't trust an addict or an alcoholic who's still using or drinking, but anybody who knows Gordon knows how far-fetched it is to see him as a killer. Sober or drunk, he loved her. He just loved booze more, but that just means he's crazy; it doesn't make him a murderer."

Stacy and I stuck around a few minutes more, and Margie came back, and I gave her and Guy each my card with contact information, in case they had a brainwave, and we left Carl's Place. I was glad to get away; it was a pleasant sort of bar, and everyone seemed to be having a good time, as I said to Stacy. "Too good a time," she said.

"Beg pardon?"

"Major Strasser's line in *Casablanca,*" she said, "when Louis protests closing Rick's bar."

"Ah," I said. On our way to the car we went by the apartment building, checked out the area under Black's balcony. There were no markers to indicate where the casings had been found, of course. I just wanted another look. I drove Stacy over to the drugstore on the west side of College Avenue, across from the Helix Tower. She had a few items to pick up. When she came out of the drugstore, I asked if she needed anything else, and she said no. I remarked that her fingernails were really great evidence that she was right and her folks were wrong about who she was. "You just don't see a lot of men with nails that long, or with clear polish," I said.

"Maybe you don't," she responded, "but I know quite a few guys who let their nails grow and even use polish." She looked out the window. "Generalizations are dangerous."

"Well, yes," I said. "Speaking of dangerous, it's a fact that nails can be. I mean, having nails long enough to be sharp can be—"

"Oh, mine are, definitely. And if you keep them filed to a fine edge—"

"Like you do?"

"As I do." Schwartz would have liked that, I thought.

"Just another example of things I don't know about and things I'm wrong about," I said. On the whole it didn't seem to me we'd had a completely wasted trip.

I phoned Schwartz about lunch, to see if I could pick up something, and he suggested asking Stacy. She asked if Sangiovese sounded good, and of course it did. I called ahead, then we drove down to pick the food up, and when we got back, Schwartz was more than happy with her choice.

I shared the sparse fruit of our inquiry with Schwartz, and he mulled it over. "Perhaps we can have a look at the accounting she was doing for the Hereford family," he said.

"She wasn't doing anything like that for me," Stacy volunteered.

"But your mother told us—"

"She meant that Allison was the Hereford family's accountant," she said. "She did the family business, the books for Mom and Dad and Grandpa, so all they had to do at tax time was sign and date the forms, write checks as necessary, collect dividends, blah blah blah. Yeah, I know; writing checks these days is supposed to be medieval, but that's what some people are used to, and that's what they're going to do."

It didn't seem an opportune moment to tell her how Schwartz felt about it. He likes to write checks, so he sees the outgoing funds. He's all in favor of automated income, but he does like to watch the outgo carefully.

Chapter Seventeen

That afternoon, Stacy talked over the situation with Schwartz and me, mainly with Schwartz, of course, so far as decision-making and advising were concerned, although she certainly made an effort to include me in the discussion. "The thing is," she said, "I have to be honest with them, and I tried that, but when you've been told one thing all your life, even if it's not true, you get used to behaving as if it is. Do you understand what I mean? Maybe if you had a daughter—"

"I have a daughter," Schwartz said, "and two grandchildren. I don't see that that grants me any special insight into your problem."

"I said my folks are crazy, and I meant it, but that doesn't mean I don't care about them, that it doesn't matter to me what they think."

"Worrying about what other people think is a waste of time, Ms. Hereford. In the program, we say that what other people think about you is none of your business." He'd told her earlier about the meetings he and I went to.

"That's easy for you to say, Mr. Schwartz," Stacy said. She looked at me.

I tried to look understanding, but told her, "I don't have a daughter, or a son either, for that matter, so I'm afraid I'm not much help." She looked utterly forlorn. I said, "Even so, I'll be glad to help in any way I can, if I can." It wasn't clear that that was helpful at all.

Schwartz said, "Besides your family, there's the matter of your job, Ms. Hereford. From what we were able to learn, it seems doubtful that your position will still be open." He turned a hand over. "But perhaps that's just as well, if I understand what you decided about Artificial Intelligence."

"Yeah, you're right about that," she said. "Even if the job were still there,

I'm not the one to be doing it."

"Am I correct in thinking that your doubts about the wisdom of creating Artificial Intelligence are sufficiently strong to prevent your continuing in such a role?"

"Oh, yeah. There's no way I can go on with that. That was anything but academic; they were into applications all the way, and the fundamental attitude was the economic exploitation of AI in business, especially in manufacturing, but there were subtler uses than that, much subtler. It hit me like an epiphany, Mr. Schwartz, that we are creating the monster that will dispense with us. Never mind climate change, pandemics, rogue asteroids, whatever external threat there may be—"

"Now, surely," Schwartz interrupted, "you're not exculpating humanity for climate change. I suppose, theoretically, there may still be some room for debate, but the scientific consensus seems to be that we did this ourselves. As for pandemics, that might be a mixed bag. You're aware of the problem of influenza as complicated by Chinese animal husbandry, I suppose."

"Chinese animal husbandry?"

"Chinese farmers raise pigs and ducks in close proximity, with the beasts and the birds sharing the same water puddles or wallows or ponds, whatever. So swine flu and avian flu are cooking away together, and a mutation in one or the other can readily become a new variety for people to try to develop immunity to. There are two to the eighth power, two hundred fifty-six different possibilities, two hundred fifty-six possible varieties of flu, and even if people do develop resistance to whatever new kind is released, the human life span is too short for any individual to develop resistance to all possible varieties. And an old variety can come around again, a century after it has first appeared, and no one who once had it is still alive."

"All right," Stacy said, "I'll drop the part about external or internal, whether we did what caused the problem or not. But AI is not a mountain-sized asteroid coming at us from space; it's something we're deliberately creating, ignoring the danger, or rather intentionally underplaying it, ostensibly in the name of science, really in the name of making money. Someone once said that ours is the only species that knows what is going to kill us: our own insatiable curiosity. William James once said that, with our symphonies and cathedrals, it's easy to forget that we are a predatory species and, alone among all others, the one species that can always be counted on to prey on our own kind." Stacy couldn't have known that quoting William James would be the key to Schwartz's heart.

He smiled at her beatifically. "Are you familiar with *Paradigms Lost,* Ms. Hereford? By John Casti?" She wasn't. "It's an examination of one-time big ideas that have had their day in the sun and have been quietly set aside because something better came along. At any rate, in the section discussing UFOs, the author points out that, while there are undoubtedly many hundreds of billions of planets capable of sustaining life in this universe, many billions that, in fact, do sustain life, and billions that have produced intelligent life, the immense distances between stars and even more immense distances between galaxies make it very unlikely that we have been visited by intelligent life from other worlds.

"An additional factor arguing against UFOs is the brevity of life and, according to some, of intelligent life."

"I'm not sure I follow you, Mr. Schwartz."

"The theory is that, whenever and wherever intelligent life arises, it is inherently unstable. Consider our own history: Until a millennium or so ago, artillery consisted of catapults, ballistas, trebuchets, and other devices for hurling sharp or heavy or burning or noxious objects at an enemy. The bow and arrow and the crossbow were one-man weapons for throwing arrows at the foe. There was Greek fire, or at least the idea of it, whether anyone actually made use of it or not."

Schwartz leaned back a bit. "Then someone in China invented black powder. Eventually, it was used in warfare, primarily as rockets to terrorize the enemy. Eventually it was used to make bombs, mines, explosives. You know Shakespeare's line about 'the engineer hoist with his own petard'?"

"Yes, but I'm not sure exactly what a petard is," she said.

"Well," Schwartz said, "it was essentially a hemispherical bomb suspended from a bipod. The idea was to get up to the castle door or drawbridge, lean the thing against the door, with the flat part of the bomb against the door and the fuse sticking out the round side, light the fuse, and get the hell away. If the engineer setting the thing up miscalculated on the timing of his own retreat, he could be blown up by the device himself."

"Pleasant."

"Of course," Schwartz said. "The name, by the way, is from the French, for 'breaking wind'. The medieval sense of humor always tends toward the earthy."

"And this has what to do with UFOs?" she asked.

"Ah, yes. A thousand years ago or so, black powder came to Europe from China, and before long everyone had rockets and bombs, and the next step was cannon and mortars of various sizes, down to one-man versions: firearms of all sizes. Black powder held sway until the middle of the nineteenth century, when nitrocellulose, nitroglycerin, and smokeless powder were invented. And for a century dynamite and its variants, TNT and so on, were the most powerful substances known for blowing things and people up, and then, in the nineteen forties, along came the atomic bomb and then the hydrogen bomb.

"So, yes, a case can be made that we, like any other intelligent life, are not long for this world. Without introducing a theological debate, you're familiar with the law of entropy, I assume."

"Of course: the general, inexorable tendency toward disorder," she said. "Creating order in one place merely shifts a greater amount of disorder somewhere else."

"Yes. Well, it seems to me that *Homo sapiens* has an overabundance of confidence in its own cleverness, that we always imagine that, faced with a problem, we can think our way out of whatever mess we're in. Whereas, again in my opinion, we are perfectly capable of painting ourselves into a corner, cutting off the limb we're sitting on, hoisting ourselves with our own petard. And, given our seemingly universal tendency toward hubris, the outlook may well seem grim. There is something in this universe of ours that doesn't like cockiness and likes to see it humbled."

"The way we're killing the earth," Stacy said.

"Well, perhaps, although I think Stephen Jay Gould made an excellent case, years ago, that we aren't killing Mother Earth. We may well be making this earth uninhabitable by us; we may be on the point of exterminating our own species, but the earth will get along fine without us. It got on fine without us for millions of years, and it will do so again, whatever changes we may have made to the climate, the oceans, the earth itself," he said.

"It's estimated that a millennium after we've ceased to be," he went on, "the only artifacts remaining to bear witness to our greatness will be Mount Rushmore, the pyramids, and the Great Wall. Even huge cities require constant upkeep to prevent everything reverting to ruin."

"Cheery thought."

"Yes," Schwartz said. "And what conclusions would emissaries from another planet draw from these relics of humanity?"

It seemed to me that he'd wandered pretty far afield from the point we had been discussing, and apparently, I wasn't alone. "What's all this got to do with my deciding what to do, Mr. Schwartz?" Stacy asked.

"Not much, really," he said, "but I've often found that overconcentrating on a problem is less productive than setting it aside and thinking about something else. Compared to the fate of the earth, the decision you have to make seems fairly manageable, don't you think?"

"Well, yes, it does," she said. "I need to tell my family once and for all what I am and, more to the point, what I'm not." She looked at him as if daring him to challenge her conclusion.

"Admirably stated," Schwartz said. Stacy looked at me, and I nodded to show her I agreed and was fully confident in her ability to do what needed to be done, without indulging in hubris, of course.

"I want you both to understand," she said, "that I'm not anti-trans." She looked at us, one after the other, then settled on Schwartz.

"Of course not," he said. "You can support justice for others, even if you yourself will not benefit directly. Many whites support equal rights for persons of color; many straights favor equal rights for gays, lesbians, and other non-cis people. I recall being moved, many years ago, by an article in *The New Yorker,* which included an interview with a trans banker, Michael, whose mother still displayed in her home a photo of her 'dead daughter'

Michelle. Michael said, and I paraphrase from memory, but I think I'm pretty close here, 'With all the difficulties and problems and hassles, those of us who have successfully made the change are among the few people on earth who have attained our heart's desire.' And that was what finally got through to me what it would be like to have been born with the wrong sort of body."

"I know the article you mean," Stacy said. So did I; it had been assigned reading my first year with Schwartz. "And I really have a lot less of a job to do than that. I just have to get through to my family that I'm happy being a straight woman. Dating men doesn't make me a gay man in a woman's body, after all."

Schwartz nodded in agreement but said, "You're quite correct, and while I wouldn't try to explain your family to you, I caution you to be prepared for resistance. Mr. Zufahl and I have encountered a few people with fixed ideas before now, and the fact that these ideas are completely, blatantly false does not usually make them easy to dislodge. On the contrary, the wrongest ideas can be the most difficult to dislodge."

"Like trying to talk sense to a bigot," she said.

"Exactly like that," he said, "because that is precisely what you're preparing to do. Heaven knows where your mother first acquired the idea that you were a transition candidate, but it's there; the seed got planted, and the idea has grown and flourished—in their minds. It will not be easy to extirpate, and it will probably not be possible to eliminate it entirely all at once. But patience and persistence should work in the long run."

"I wouldn't call it a seed that grew," she said, "more of an infection that festered."

"In any case, weed or infection, it will take work to get rid of it."

"I am so glad that I have you and Mr. Zufahl on my side," she said. I'd told her Rainer would be fine, but she stuck to formality, probably because Schwartz did. I'd seen it before. I'd see it again.

Chapter Eighteen

Monday morning Schwartz told me to call in the troops who were surveilling the Spalls for a conference after lunch. He said to tell them to wrap it up and bring anything with them that might be relevant, "unless by some miracle she picked this morning to go wild." He and I looked over the photos the boys had taken, not a single one of which showed anything out of bounds. "I wonder," Schwartz said, "how many of us could be watched that long without turning up evidence of wrongdoing of some kind on our part, or at any rate, something we'd rather the neighbors didn't know about."

Schwartz and I were still talking about Virginia Spall's striking lack of illicit behavior when Stacy came downstairs. Schwartz offered to fix her breakfast, but she snorted scornfully and said she was capable of fixing it herself, but it was getting pretty late, and why spoil her appetite for lunch? We discussed lunch, and Schwartz repeated what he'd said the evening before, that it would probably be best for her to stay out of sight for a while. He suggested carry-out for lunch, and we reviewed the options, and Stacy said German food sounded good to her. Since the Heidelberg Café is on the east side of town, on Pendelton Pike, well away from Carmel-by-the-Cornfields, Stacy rode with me after we'd phoned in our order. In addition to what we'd ordered for lunch, she bought a mixed bag of pastries, for which she paid cash, while I used my card for the wurst, potato salad, sauerkraut, red cabbage, and bread.

I was surprised when Stacy said she'd never been to the Heidelberg. She'd certainly never seen such an extensive collection of garden gnomes. I'd be ready to bet there were more on the premises than anywhere else in the state, maybe anywhere in the United States. She wondered why we translate *Gartenzwerg* as "garden gnome" rather than "garden dwarf," since the German *Zwerg* means "midget" or "dwarf," then she answered herself: "Because there really are dwarfs, or dwarves, and "midget" is considered offensive, and little people, real dwarfs, wouldn't appreciate being associated with the lawn ornaments." I said I could certainly see their point of view. "The German for 'gnome' is *Gnom* or *Erdgeist*, 'earth spirit,'" she went on. While she was talking, I looked over the offerings under the glass, and I tried to exercise self-restraint but finally caved and bought a half dozen of the various handmade pastries.

On the way back we discussed, among other things, the question of why red cabbage is called that, it actually being purple. Stacy suggested it was for the same reason that Yellow Cabs are called that, even though they're actually orange. "To complete the cycle," she said, "we'd have to think of something that's called blue, even though it's actually green."

"Well, there's Kentucky bluegrass," I pointed out, "which really is green, although I'd say it's a bluish green rather than the apple green of other grasses."

"I'd say that counts," she said. "And how about dog fanciers calling dogs blue that are actually gray? When I was a kid we had a Queensland blue heeler, and I used to ask why it wasn't called a gray heeler, maybe 'grey' spelled with an *e* since it's Australian, and later I found out that Queensland heeler and blue heeler are both nicknames for Australian cattle dogs. But I've heard other gray dogs called blue, and I don't get it."

"Maybe it's because gray is as close to blue as dogs get," I said. "Not at all red, not at all yellow, and—"

"But does that really make sense?"

"Well, maybe not, but dogs can be white or black or every shade of gray; they can be light or dark red, or brown—which is basically dark orange, right? But not purple, blue, or green, so—"

"So people would rather pretend the dogs are blue than accept the fact that there are no blue dogs," she said. It struck me that she was taking the whole matter very personally, as if she'd been asked to admit that gray was actually blue. By this time, I'd gotten off I-465 and onto Keystone, just a couple miles from home. The conversation lagged a bit. Then, "People would rather pretend than accept reality, most of the time," she said as I turned onto College Avenue.

When we got back, Schwartz had set the places at the kitchen table, and even after the generous helpings of authentic German food, there was room for Black Forest cake. We had barely finished when the crew arrived to assess the damage of the Ginny Spall investigation.

Schwartz told Stacy that he and I had to discuss another matter with some operatives, and she said she'd like to go to her room for a while anyway. There was a television and a well-stocked bookcase, with not-quite-current magazines filling the bottom shelf. If I didn't pay close attention, it would get to the point where Schwartz would want to keep her.

There wasn't really much to add to what we already knew. The subject had quite a few friends and quite a few good causes, and like anyone in her socio-economic bracket, she made the rounds of places to be seen, and there was absolutely nothing suspicious about anywhere she went or anyone she met with. The crew managed not to give the impression that they considered the job a failure, but it took some effort. As Paul said, "The way we ought to take it is that some people really aren't fooling around, which is good," but as Sonny pointed out, it was hard to believe that someone married to Ken Spall wasn't tempted.

Schwartz thanked the fellows for the Spall job so far, then told them he wanted the surveillance completely switched from Virginia to Kenneth. "I'd like the four of you to keep track of him as thoroughly as possible without letting him know he's being watched. Something has compelled him to hire us to watch his wife, who apparently needs no watching. It may be a guilty conscience; it may be nothing at all. The past few days, frankly, have been instructive, not always in a pleasant way, about the vagaries of human nature. No reasonable person expects people to always be reasonable, but I fear I have hitherto underestimated the element of randomness in human decision-making. So, let us find out if there is a rational explanation for

Kenneth Spall's suspicions about his wife."

Jonny, who thinks he should be doing my job but, in my opinion, wouldn't last a week at it, said, "But if there is a rational explanation for his suspicions, Mr. Schwartz, shouldn't we be looking at her to find it?" I love listening to him trying to pretend he's me.

"I expressed myself poorly," Schwartz said. "By 'rational explanation,' I meant some explanation that we might be able to understand, not necessarily misbehavior on Ms. Spall's part. It might well be some occurrence in Mr. Spall's business life or in his personal life aside from the marital aspect."

Paul, as usual, came up with the antidote to Jonny's ego. "If there's anything going on that could trigger suspicion on Spall's part, we'll find it, Mr. Schwartz."

We then spent about half an hour planning out the new program for keeping tabs on Spall. We ruled out any number of bright ideas from Sonny, Jonny, and Frank, mostly because they would have involved personal contact with the subject, and we didn't want him recognizing someone he'd met. It gave us an opportunity to try out some alleged advances in surveillance, and Schwartz gave his approval to trying out some long-range eavesdropping techniques, with the understanding that we would keep it at least defensibly legal.

At one point, I suggested running some questions past Colin, which Schwartz vetoed on the ground that Colin had done nothing to deserve to be placed in an ambiguous position, and the less he knew about what we were up to here, the less ambiguous his position would be. "I think it's fair to say that the five of us understand how far we can stretch the law and where the breaking points are. Colin, however, lacks experience with our work. He's invaluable for his technical expertise, which certainly far surpasses our own. It would not be right to expect him to take risks we accept."

He went on to describe the new subject, a.k.a. our client, his workplace, the business, and so on, and they had a number of good suggestions for keeping tabs on Kenneth Spall. As Schwartz explained, Spall's operation had grown to the point where he was overseeing a small army of workers, with a subsidiary supervisor present on each job managing a crew of five or six, depending on the size of the house in question. He had described the considerable training that went into getting a job boss ready, with the computer program at the heart of the matter, and the special modifications done to the shingles based on what the program told the crew, based on the measurements of the roofs.

Spall had said that the key to success was making sure the job supervisor knew the system inside and out, so that he—and he said he had tried to hire women supervisors, without success, and Schwartz and I had discussed afterward to what extent that might even have been true—so that he knew how to supervise others and how to take over any aspect of the work as necessary. Frank mentioned now that one way to keep tabs on Spall might be to hire on as an employee, but Schwartz pointed out that the time involved would probably be far more than we really wanted to devote to the project.

With the system having grown to branches in two dozen states, Spall's role was no longer hands-on, except in emergencies, and the training of job managers focused on heading off emergencies. Even so, it appeared that in good weather, he was pretty busy six days a week. As Schwartz was going over all that with the help, it occurred to me to wonder how difficult it had been for Spall to take time off to meet with us, and I made a note to look into that when the occasion arose. His office was in one of those new towers on North Meridian Street; at least that's the nominal address, although the entrance is actually from Pennsylvania Street, a block east of Meridian.

Schwartz told Paul to check into the possibility of short-term renting an office in that building, preferably on the same floor, and he got on it. Schwartz gave Sonny and Frank a bunch of instructions they didn't need, and he told Jon to wait to hear from Paul, which didn't go down particularly well with Jon, but that's the way it goes. Jon can't seem to get a clear and proper perspective on his importance vis-à-vis Schwartz Investigations. He really believes he should be holding down my desk chair, and since I decline to quit or drop dead, he's frustrated. At some things, he's good enough to make it worthwhile putting up with his ego as a freelancer, but he'd never last a week in the office with Schwartz. The only question would be which of them would break first.

171

After an hour of planning out the new Spall surveillance, Schwartz told them it would be unlikely to last two weeks. "If you find evidence of illicit activity on his part, sufficiently solid for our purposes, we can roll it up. From our interaction with Mr. Spall so far, I don't believe he could maintain a façade of virtue much longer than a week. If there's no sign of funny business in two weeks, then there's probably no funny business. He has no reason to think we've shifted our focus from Ms. Spall to him, so—"

I was surprised when Sonny said, "First time I remember a client paying to have himself shadowed. I mean, protected, sure, but—"

Schwartz straightened up a bit in his chair. I could tell he was nettled, whether any of the others noticed it or not. "Actually, gentlemen, we will not be billing Mr. Spall for this part of the job. Don't skimp on the job for that reason, but I think it proper that you be aware that we're maintaining at least that bare minimum of professional ethics."

Sonny tried backtracking. "I didn't mean to imply anything, Mr. Schwartz; I—"

"Of course not, Sonny," Schwartz said. "But it is a morally ambiguous situation. Strictly speaking, I suppose Mr. Spall should be informed that the surveillance on his wife is ended, and he will be, albeit not particularly promptly." He went on in that vein with the crew for a while. It was an interesting discussion of professional ethics, something you don't get much of in this business.

At last Schwartz had said what needed to be said. Paul said he'd let Schwartz and me and the others know what he found out about letting space close to Spall's office. If he was successful, they could set up a reception room as a front for the real operation in a morning or less.

The boys departed, and I went up to let Stacy know she had the run of the house again, and she came down. I had rocketry records to update, and Schwartz wanted to get back to his Fourth of July preparations. Stacy went with him to the gazebo or summerhouse out back, and she was watching him operate the arbor press on whistler rockets when I went out with a couple questions. The two of them made quite the picture, almost a father-daughter look, if your taste in such matters includes gloves, face masks, and breathing filters. He was even letting her stack the pressed rockets in the rack, awaiting the addition of headers and guide sticks. I watched while he let her open the tube clamp on a rocket, slip it off, and secure it around the next tube so it wouldn't split from the pressure. Very fetching.

Chapter Nineteen

Schwartz and I were getting settled before the Tuesday meeting started. I had a cup of that rather thin coffee, but he stuck with the iced tea he'd brought with him. Norman, an old-timer with quite a few years sober, who habitually introduced himself as a recovered alcoholic, rather than as a recovering one, which of course irked Schwartz, leaned over and asked us, "Did you know that God's first name was Andy?"

Schwartz took the trouble to stay civil. "Well, Norman, I hadn't realized God had a first or last name, for that matter. How do you figure that?"

Norman said, "It's from the hymn: 'Andy walks with me, Andy talks with me, Andy tells me I am His own...'"

I liked it, frankly, and Schwartz gave it a smile. When Norman turned to share the humor with the guy on his other side, Schwartz muttered, "Now that goddam song is going to be stuck in my head all day long. Just what I needed."

"Well, you could do worse," I said. "And by the way, you owe your kitty a dollar."

"Really?" he said. "I don't see how. Come to that, after that pointless, even feckless discussion of what to call the goddam pig, we find ourselves calling it the kitty. It's a pig and a kitty; nice trick. Don't tell Norman, for God's sake, or he'll try to make a joke out of it."

"It *is* a joke," I said.

"Well, yeah. How I could do worse, I mean; yes, I owe a dollar to the kitty. 'In the Garden' is an earworm, one of those tunes it's impossible to get out of your head once it's in. Perfectly adapted to make thought impossible, not to mention being theologically dubious, and—"

I objected, "How can you call it theologically—"

Schwartz gave me one of his paint-peeling looks. He quoted, " 'And the joy we share as we tarry there none other has ever known'? The speaker is so goddam special that he—you know it really has to be 'he'—is uniquely dear to Jesus, so that the joy they share is one of a kind, surpassing all other joys anyone else might have had—" Louise was calling the meeting to something like order, and Schwartz gave it a rest, thank heaven.

The meeting itself went all right. There were four AA chips given, one start-over, one for thirty days of continuous sobriety, one for nine months, and one for four years. Start-overs are always a source of mixed feelings, for me at least. It's too bad that someone went out, sometimes giving up a considerable stretch of sobriety, but it's good that they made it back. Lots of people who take a drink keep on drinking, crawl all the way into the bottle, and never make it back to AA. Today's start-over was Glenn, who had had a year and a half without a drink and had suddenly decided he deserved a reward and could handle just one drink. He'd been out about a week. Everyone welcomed him back and congratulated the one-month, the nine-month, and the four-year milestones.

The topic suggested for discussion was the Serenity Prayer. When it was my turn, I just said that I probably recite it to myself three or four times a day, on average, whether I knew who I was talking to or not. Schwartz said that he too found it indispensable, but that he liked to make one small adjustment, adding "and should," so that it ran, "the serenity to accept those things I cannot change, the courage to change those things I can and should change, and the wisdom to know the difference," so that he could keep himself reminded that there were many things in this world that he could change but that would be best left alone. He added that the difference he asked for the wisdom to know was the difference between things he should change and things he shouldn't, as well as between things he should have the serenity to accept and things he should have the courage to change, given that he should. Not for the first time, I got the impression that a number of people were wondering what on earth he was getting at. Not the end of the

175

world, after all. Nor is that exactly unusual in AA meetings, to put it mildly. The discussion continued, and for once we made it all the way around the room, and everyone got a chance to share.

Schwartz and I chatted with various other folks after the meeting, and on the way to the car he said, "Sure enough, that damned earworm is in there. I probably won't be capable of coherent thought all day long." I made sympathetic sounds, hoping he'd drop the topic. The last thing I wanted was to acquire the earworm myself. No such luck.

"The sheer unconscious ego," Schwartz said, "that lets a person imagine that they have this special relationship with God, which nobody but the speaker has ever had, directly contradicts the orthodox view that Jesus came down to earth to save all mankind. But people don't think of it that way. The whole notion of Jesus Christ as one's 'personal savior' seems to me dangerously close to the terminal uniqueness we see in some alcoholics, that egomaniacal sense of being so special, so one-of-a-kind that it's necessary to adapt AA, or Christianity, for that matter, to fit one's own particular requirements."

You can't just let him go on. "Well, of course 'terminal uniqueness' is an AA problem," I said, as I unlocked the car. I got behind the wheel.

He said, "I'm sorry to go on about this, but it's a really awful song when you look at it closely. It's saccharin, it's cloying, it's ultra-sentimental." He paused a moment. "It's repellent."

"It's very popular," I pointed out.

"That doesn't mean it's good," Schwartz said. "Quite the contrary. In fact, I think you could say that 'In the Garden' is to religious music what Warner Sallman's 'Head of Christ' is to religious art."

I thought about that as we pulled on onto 86th Street, then changed the subject. "What sounds good for lunch?"

"How about Thaiger Bistro?" Schwartz said. "Although you're headed the wrong way for it."

"I should have asked before I turned," I said. "Thai sounds great to me." I got into the left lane as we approached Meridian.

"I think I've been headed in the wrong direction all day long," Schwartz remarked. "The fact is that the change of plans with Mr. Spall has upset me more than I had expected, more than it really should, I think. We aren't screwing him over; we're just altering our view without telling him for a while. It's not wrong; it just feels wrong. A mental U-turn is probably just what I need right now."

Chapter Twenty

After lunch, I called Neil Parkinson, who said he'd arranged for me to see Gordon Black that very afternoon. I thanked him warmly, for Schwartz, and Neil said that under the circumstances, it really wasn't that big a deal. I got the impression, although Neil was far too good a lawyer to say so in so many words, that the circumstances had more to do with Gordon being a member of the Hereford family than with any general attitude of accommodating the public on the part of the Marion County criminal justice system.

Anyway, after finding parking in a recently created vacant lot within a couple blocks of the county jail, I left my Sig and holster locked in the Prius, because I don't like turning it over to the high-quality individuals employed at the lockup, and I went unarmed through the check-in procedure, which is always a pleasure. There's a real self-esteem problem at the jail, not confined to those confined there. Gordon Liddy once wrote that, after one has failed at all else in life, there remains open a career as a prison guard, and it doesn't seem to me that there's a whole lot of difference between the personnel in charge of prisons and those running jails. Jails and prisons, of course, aren't the same thing, but you wouldn't give a nickel for the difference once you pass through the first locked door.

We'd gotten the bird's-eye lowdown from Margie, but Schwartz had urged me to see if I could jar something loose from Gordon's memory. When he came into the visiting room, sat down at the table, he looked like he'd aged ten years. I realized, of course, that he'd never been anywhere like this, and it was bound to have an effect on him. For one thing, he had no legitimate access to cigarettes or alcohol. Naturally, I was aware that smokes and booze were available, but he'd either had the good sense or had been too frightened to make the sort of deal necessary to get either. Knowing how jailhouse plonk is made, I was glad he'd steered clear of that stuff, and that had nothing to do with AA on my part.

I've gone to help take a meeting to a few jails in the nine-county area, and it's always a reminder that there are many good reasons to stay within the law. I had no idea when smoking became verboten in jail, but I doubt a concern for the prisoners' health was the principal motivation. Anyway, Black didn't look great, but he didn't look all that bad either, so I took it that his family's standing in the community had carried over to a fair extent inside so far as basic living conditions were concerned.

We just looked at each other for a moment, then he said, "How are things outside?" and I realized it didn't matter how tenderly he'd been treated; the fact that he was inside was all that mattered to him.

"Making some progress," I said. "I won't ask how things are inside."

"Just as well," he said. "Is there any chance of—"

"There's no bail in murder cases," I told him, just as if that were news to him. I've seen this exact same phenomenon before. People locked up on a murder charge know perfectly well they aren't going to be turned loose, but they simply can't help asking. Just in case a miracle has occurred, they don't want to miss it. If you don't believe me, just get yourself arrested for murder and see how long it takes before you're asking the same question. It won't be long.

"Look," I said to Black, "I know you were asked about this before, but I want to see if you can maybe dredge something up that you've forgotten. Did Allison give you anything to hold for her, anything at all? A paper, a note, anything?"

"No," he said, "we really weren't exactly on the best of terms, and I don't think she'd have trusted me with anything important. I mean, I was drinking so heavily that she didn't really like to get together at all." It struck me how little time it had taken for Black to change to past tense about his drinking. But I've heard people say a day in jail is like a week in rehab, assuming you don't fall for the sort of temptation that puts you in debt to someone with more tattoos than teeth.

Nothing against tattoos, you understand.

"All right, then," I said, "who might she have left something with, if she wanted it to stay safe and not be found by anyone searching her or her place? The police have given her apartment a really good going over, and they know how to do that thoroughly, so if they haven't found it, I doubt it's there to be found, even if we could get inside. Who did she trust?"

"That's what I've been trying to think of," Black said. "Allison had friends, quite a few of them, but I really can't think of one she was all that close to. When we were married, we'd get together with various couples, you know, socially, to go out to eat, see a show, whatever. But I can't think of anyone she would trust with something really important. Have you tried her doctor or lawyer?"

I told him we'd talked to her doctor, following in the footsteps of the police, and neither we nor the police had found any evidence she'd had any more use for a lawyer beyond the divorce. Parkinson knew Steve Apfel, only a few years out of law school, said he had a good reputation so far as it went, but he wasn't the person you'd trust your guilty or even pseudo-guilty secrets with. Her doctor had cooperated as far as possible, but there was no help there either.

"Think back," I urged him. "It doesn't have to be all that recent. Did you exchange Christmas presents, for example?"

As God is my witness, Gordon Black blushed, as thoroughly as I've ever seen a man blush. "Oh, Lord," he said. "Christmas. I was so embarrassed. She came by the apartment a couple days before Christmas, and I hadn't gotten her a damn thing. I mean, the divorce was final only a couple months before, and I assumed that that was it, so I didn't... Anyway, she came over, and she was all dressed up to go out; I heard later it was a blind date she'd been talked into, and it never went anywhere. And there she was at the door, with this wrapped present, a book of early twentieth-century war poems, you know, the First World War, Sassoon and Owen, and so on." I nodded. "It was called *Poets of the Great War and After*, edited by somebody called

Simons or Simonson or something. I had mentioned to her once that I was really into the war poets, which was sort of true, once. In college, I mean, and I guess I was really just trying to impress her; that was before we were married, just going together, and I told her I liked Brooke, McCrae, Seeger, and the other war poets, and I couldn't believe she'd remembered that, and I was so embarrassed, but I invited her in, but she couldn't stay, and—"

"Did you unwrap the book while she was there?"

"No, afterward," he said. "I mean, Allison could tell I'd had a few drinks already; it was maybe seven, seven-thirty p.m., and she took off, and I went inside and unwrapped it. I read a couple of the poems, then set it aside."

"Do you know where it is now?"

Black looked really uncomfortable now. "Well, yes, but I can't get it back." He looked down at the table. "Look, you're going to think I'm terrible, with it being a present from my ex-wife and all, but I regifted it."

I just stared at him. "You—"

"Yes, I know that's terrible, but in January, I was seeing this girl, Jennifer Campbell, and she was into poetry, and it was her birthday, and I'd completely forgotten to get her something, so I got the book where I'd shelved it, and I wrapped it. I had wrapping paper and tape and ribbon and all that, and I dashed out and got a card at CVS across the street, and I gave Jenny the book."

I suppose the look on my face could have been better disguised. Black blushed again. I hadn't noticed until then that the pink from the first time had faded.

"Look, I know," he said, "and I had this ghastly moment when she was unwrapping it, when I thought perhaps Allison had written an inscription in the front of the book, as people do sometimes, but thank God she hadn't. But the editor had signed it on the title page. Frankly it was something of a dud as gifts go; whatever poetry she was into, it wasn't World War I stuff, pro or con." He looked down again, then up, and met my eyes. "We only saw each other a couple times after that, and that was that, I'm afraid."

"Do you happen to remember Jenny Campbell's address?" I asked him, trying to keep my voice neutral.

"Oh, sure, but I have no idea whether she kept the book." He recited the street number on Baur Drive, a few blocks southeast of Broad Ripple. He didn't recall her phone number.

"No problem," I told him. "Most detective work is eliminating possibilities."

"And 'whatever remains, however improbable, must be the truth,'" he misquoted, inappositely, but I didn't correct him. It was more of a lead than I'd been expecting, not that I was expecting much from this one. It's not difficult to ditch a book, or any present from an ex-flame, for that matter.

The guard said it was time to call it quits, so we did, without further formalities. But I told Black he'd hear from us as soon as we had something to report, and he nodded, headed back to the cells. He'd already learned to wait for the door to be opened. Quick study.

There's no feeling quite like walking out of a jail, being able to look up and see blue sky or stars or, in this particular case, gray rain clouds getting ready to burst. The funny thing is, it's the same feeling whether you're leaving after bringing an AA meeting to the incarcerated or you've been there on more personal business. Aside from the first visit with Gordon, the last time before this for me had been the Boone County clink in Lebanon, about a month earlier, and the stars had been shining as if just for us. The Marion County lockup is less than two years old, located on the Community Justice Campus, and it's a great example of how quickly a building can become depressing. Don't misunderstand me; I fully agree with Richard Pryor: "Thank God we've got penitentiaries!" and the same goes for jails too. You can trust a man who'd been married seven times, to six different women, at least on a subject like that.

On the stroll to the parking lot, I gave it some thought but came up with no better ideas than the truth, the partial, slightly abridged truth, and nothing but the truth. Heaven only knew how she felt about Gordon Black, whether she was aware he'd been arrested, whether she cared about him one way or the other.

When I got to my car, I did a quick search, got what purported to be Jennifer Campbell's phone number on Baur, and dialed it. She picked up right away, said it was the number I'd dialed, and asked who I wished to speak to. Probably had a roommate, or perhaps this was the roommate. I gave her a name and said I'd like to speak with Jennifer Campbell. She said, "Speaking," and I said I understood that Gordon Black had given her a book of poems some months ago and that I was interested in the book and would be willing to pay her for her copy if she still had it and was interested in selling it.

There was a pause, then she said, "You mean it's valuable or something?"

I wanted to ask what the hell "or something" might mean, but I said, "Well, I'm a collector, and this would almost complete my poetry of the First World War. It's not that the book is all that rare, but my understanding is that it's signed by the editor, and that would mean a lot to me." Well, so much for nothing but the truth.

"Could you go to, ah, fifty bucks?" she asked. I said sure. "How about a hundred?" she went on. This was beginning to look as if it could get pretty expensive if she thought she could keep on upping the price.

I waited to a count of ten Mississippi, then said, "Well, if the book is in good condition, with a dust jacket, and signed by Arthur Simmons, I think I could go to a hundred dollars." I still didn't know whether she still had the damn book.

"I'll take a look," she said. I heard her walking across an uncarpeted floor, sounds of books on a shelf being moved, then the phone was set down on some horizontal surface. Pages were being turned. "Yeah, it's signed by Arthur H. Simmons, dated August 1964. Is that what you're looking for?"

"Yes," I said, "that's exactly right. August of '64 would be the fiftieth anniversary of the start of the war."

"World War I?"

"Right," I said, "exactly." I was glad she hadn't guessed differently. "Look, if you're willing to part with the volume, I'd be happy to come by with the money this evening. I'm staying downtown at the Hyatt, but if you could give me directions..." Just a guy in town, looking for a book; no big deal.

Jennifer gave me directions, up Meridian to Kessler, Kessler east to Keystone, and so on, as if I didn't have GPS, and I told her I'd be there as soon as possible. She said it would probably take half an hour, forty minutes, at that time of day. I was ready to ring off when she said, "I don't know if I should accept a check."

"I wouldn't dream of offering you one," I said. "I prefer cash, if you don't mind."

"Um, no, cash will be fine," she said and rang off.

I called Schwartz to let him know what was happening, and he found it amusing. "So now you're a book collector, Rainer?"

"Well, no, sir, but Zachary Richards is," I told him. "I told her the book would be worth a hundred dollars to me, if it's in good shape and autographed by the editor, which she said it is, so I'll swing by her place on my way home."

"Wait, do you mean you're driving and talking on the phone?" I could hear Schwartz's blood pressure rising as we spoke. "You know perfectly well how I feel about multitasking, Rainer. Hang up at once. We'll talk when you get home. *If* you get home." He hung up. He says multitasking is one of the superstitions of our time. People think they can do more than one thing at once, and it really means they're screwing up more than one thing at a time.

Ignoring Ms. Campbell's directions, I came up Meridian but dodged over on Fall Creek to Keystone, which can save a couple minutes if you're lucky, and it burns a little less gas. When I got to her place, a pleasant neighborhood of one-story houses, sidewalks, mature trees, neither mansions nor apartment houses, I was pleased to see there was a parking space at the curb. As I went up the front walk, I noticed movement by the curtain in the picture window, someone holding what looked like a baseball bat. Cautious. I rang the bell, and a grim-faced young woman in office-not-quite-casual, not the one with the bat, opened the door immediately. I said I was Zach Richards and asked if she was Jennifer Campbell. Since she had a thick, jacketed, hardcover book in her hand, that wasn't the brightest question I'd asked all day.

She said she was Jennifer Campbell. Moving slowly so as not to cause alarm, I took out my wallet, extracted a nice new C note, and handed it to her. She took it, handed me the book, and thanked me. I told her she was welcome and it had been a pleasure doing business with her, which was a refreshing return to the truth at least, smiled and turned to go.

I heard the door bolt snap shut before I was off the small porch. They were definitely prepared to repel boarders. I wasn't surprised Gordon Black hadn't lasted with Jennifer Campbell. I certainly didn't want to get better acquainted with her or her roomie.

I called Schwartz to let him know I had the book and was parked and would soon be on my way home. It was a quick dodge over to Keystone, then through Broad Ripple, and up College to 78th Street. I put the car in the garage, went in the house, and brought the prize over to his desk. It hadn't been easy to resist the temptation to check it out, but I knew better than that, naturally. I told him, "A hundred bucks of expenses on the Hereford account," and handed him the book.

Schwartz took the book, looked at the front, spine, and back of the jacket, then slipped it off. He turned the jacket over; it was blank, as expected, on the inside. The front of the jacket had a sepia photograph of what I guessed was no man's land in France or Belgium, a field of pockmarked mud under an overcast sky, with three or four distant trees reduced to jagged stumps in the distance. The title and editor's name were printed above and below the photo. The same information, with the publisher's name, Steinfeld, occupied the spine. The back had a couple paragraphs of descriptive prose and a blurb in slightly larger type.

Schwartz laid the jacket aside and picked up the book itself. The cover was a dark green, with dulled silver type for the title, editor, and publisher on the spine. The front and back were plain, no printing. He opened the book, turned a few pages, noted the list of poets and their poems on the contents page. "Not a bad lot of choices," he said. "Not bad at all." He knows a lot more poetry than I do, and a lot more about poetry than I do, for that matter.

"Any obvious omissions?" I asked, just to stay with the examination.

"No, not at all," he said, "given that it's English-language only. And British English, come to that."

"No French or Flemish or Russian?"

"Or German either. It could have been called *British Poets of the Great War and After*," he said. "But that would have meant confessing to provincialism, and that would never do."

"Or maybe *British Poets against the Great War*," I ventured.

"Not really," Schwartz said. "McCrae's 'In Flanders Field,' for example…" He turned over the page. The contents ran to a second and a third page. Schwartz tipped the book back into his left hand, and the pages fell there. Except for the last few dozen or so. He held the loose pages down with his left hand. About a quarter-inch of pages stayed with the back board of the book, glued together around a shallow rectangular hole cut halfway down and close to the spine, a couple inches long, three-quarters wide, just large enough to hold a thumb drive with no space for movement.

"Well, well, well," said Schwartz. He took the steel letter opener from the jar on his desk, slid it down next to the thumb drive, and pried up carefully. The black plastic wafer slowly rose from its resting place, then came free. Schwartz didn't touch it. "Want to bet there's a spreadsheet or two on this?" he asked.

"No bet," I said. "So Allison gave Gordon a book she knew damned well he'd never open, with a little something safe inside for posterity."

"I doubt she intended it for posterity," he said, "although that's what we in fact are. If she'd thought her life was in danger, surely she'd have gone ahead and blown the whistle. Why don't we see if there are fingerprints on this first?"

I got the kit from my desk drawer, and Schwartz set the book aside on his, spread a clean 8½″ × 11″ sheet on his blotter, and used the letter opener to nudge the drive onto the sheet. I dusted it, he turned it over, and I did the other side. We checked it out all over, but there were only smudges, no worthwhile prints or partials.

"Would you agree that that's about what we'd expect?" Schwartz asked.

"Sure. It wasn't wiped, but normal handling of an object this small wouldn't ordinarily leave nice clean prints," I said. "Not that there would have been anything suspicious about a clean print. It could go either way."

"Yes," he said, wiping the powder off the thumb drive. "Why don't we see what's on this thing?"

"Yours or mine?" I asked.

"I bow to your superior expertise," he said insincerely. I nodded mock acknowledgment of the compliment, took the drive, and plugged it into my laptop. "Best copy the files, if any, and leave the originals unopened," he said. Right; thanks, boss. Up came a directory. There were half a dozen pictures on the drive, labeled "Gordon," "Anita," "Steven," "Charles," "Stacy," and "Family."

I copied them onto my computer and pulled the thumb drive out after checking that the copies were good. I got an envelope out of the drawer, wrote Allison's name and the date on it, put the thumb drive in it, and handed it to Schwartz. He took the envelope to the safe and tucked it in, made a notation in the petty cash book, took out a hundred-dollar bill, locked the safe, then came back, bringing a chair so he could watch comfortably. He handed me the replacement for the purchase of the book.

I opened one of the PDFs. It was a picture of Anita Hereford, in vacation togs, on a tropical veranda with ocean and beach in the background, a glass of something pinkish orange, with slices of lemon and orange and lime and a straw, in her hand. She was sipping the drink. I clicked on "Charles," and sure enough, there he was, right next to Anita, sitting rigidly upright in a deck chair, holding an identical drink but not sipping, dressed in tan shorts and a matching short-sleeve shirt with pockets. It was the same with the others: photos of Stacy, not on vacation, in profile, bent over a laptop; Gordon at ease on a sofa, in his apartment, I thought, a can of Bud Lite in one hand and a cigarette in the other; Steven, back on that tropical veranda, in blue shorts and a technicolor tropical shirt, with that same fruity drink, the light glinting off his glasses; and a group shot of the Herefords posed very stiffly in front of the fireplace at home, without Gordon. I couldn't see any obvious reason to tuck these innocuous shots on a thumb drive, much less hide the drive in a book of poetry. Schwartz sighed, went back to his desk, reached for his iced tea, then froze.

"How big are those files?" he asked.

I listed them, with that information. "Bigger than they look," I told him. "So

Allison hid files in family photos. Hmm." I googled the pertinent information and got busy.

An hour later I had played with those photos to my heart's content and then some, and I had exactly what I had started with, and I owed the pig thirty-some dollars.

I didn't have to say it; Schwartz did, going to the safe and retrieving the drive he'd just put away. "Give it to Colin," he said.

"Okay." I looked at my watch. "I should be able to catch him."

"I'll call him," Schwartz said. He reached for the phone and dialed. "Wait," he said. He was listening to a message. "He's out of town until Wednesday, a week from today," he said. "It will have to keep. Of course, if you'd like to keep trying, feel free to do so."

That didn't get the response it deserved; I was already in porcine hock far enough for the evening. "After all," Schwartz said, "you made plenty of progress for one day."

"I'll try again in the morning," I said. Then, finally, I recalled that we had a guest. I asked Schwartz, "Is Stacy—"

"Ms. Hereford decided to go see her family," Schwartz said. "I suggested it, in fact, while you were visiting Mr. Black. She was a bit trepidatious, but I assured her that her room would be waiting for her in case she wanted it." He looked at the clock. "Time for dinner, anyway," he said. "I expect we'll hear from her one way or the other before bedtime."

As it turned out, he was wrong about that, but we didn't know it at the time.

Chapter Twenty-One

As a matter of fact, we didn't hear from Stacy until the next morning. I took the call while I was having another try at the Hereford photos without success, and Schwartz was puttering in the basement. She said that, all things considered, the reunion hadn't gone too badly, at least not so badly as she had feared. But she asked if we'd rented her room out to anyone else, and I assured her it was waiting for her any time she wanted it, and it missed her. She said it was quite possible that she might want to take us up on that offer. It seemed to me from the intonation of her voice that she thought we might not be serious about that. I told her, "When Mr. Schwartz makes an offer, he means it. You are welcome any time, and you don't have to call first; just show up." She thanked me, and we rang off.

Just as the call ended, Schwartz came in, carrying a roll of two-inch duct tape, a two-liter plastic soda bottle, and an old imitation leather holster and revolver. I recognized it as his Russian Nagant M1895 revolver, as idiosyncratic a gun as any in his collection. For one thing, it's a seven-shooter, which has always struck me as odd. If you're not satisfied with six, why not go ahead with eight? And if you're not satisfied with six, why the hell not?

For another thing, the ammunition for it is downright weird, with the brass casing extended to completely enshroud the slug. It's a truly unique design, and that's a nice example of 'unique' not necessarily being good. As Schwartz has been known to observe, there are any number of reasons something can become and remain unique. Being one of a kind doesn't mean being superior to all others. It seemed the idea with the Nagant was to prevent the usual loss of power in revolvers when gases escape between the cylinder and the barrel. Whether it really made much difference is, as I understand it, undecided. Of course, I wasn't around to be asked my opinion in 1895, not that I would have been, had I been, anyway. Schwartz unlocked the cabinet where the ammunition is kept, took a box of shells for the Nagant from his left side pocket of his jacket, shook a few into his hand and put them in the same pocket, and returned the box to the cabinet, which he locked.

Schwartz suggested breakfast at Lincoln Square and a visit to Apex Firearms in Carmel, and he's the boss, so we saddled up. He brought the Nagant in its holster, stowing it in the glove box, which it barely fit into, and I drove.

Breakfast was excellent and substantial, as always, and with eggs, bacon, fried potatoes, and fried mush under my belt, I felt fully equipped to face the day as we headed north up Meridian to the City Center Drive exit. We took the rotary from City Center Drive to Carmel Drive, then turned in at the side road to the strip mall where Apex is located. Schwartz said something to the effect of his favorite places these days all being in strip malls. I suppose I could have pointed out that we'd just had breakfast in a freestanding restaurant and that we didn't live in a strip mall, but it didn't seem necessary, so I kept it to myself.

There were a few customers being waited on, but the clerks greeted Schwartz and me by name when we came in. It's that kind of place. While we waited for someone to be free, I checked out the shotguns and rifles on the walls and Schwartz looked over the handguns in the cases. Norman, a strongly built fellow in his thirties, with short-cropped hair so blond it was white, with a sidearm on his belt like all the other employees, was the first to finish taking care of his customer, and he asked us what he could do for us. He glanced at what Schwartz was unholstering and observed, "A Nagant," without noticeable enthusiasm. A uniformed Carmel cop, one of the other customers, looked over with interest.

Schwartz said, "If you were wanting to silence this piece, what would you go for, Norman?" He handed the revolver to Norman.

Norman pulled the hammer back to half-cocked position, flipped the loading gate up, then turned the cylinder slowly, checking to make sure the gun was unloaded. It was, of course, and he knew Schwartz and me better than to think we'd hand him a loaded gun, but safety means assuming nothing other than that everyone can make a mistake, so it's best to check just in case. My friend and helper had handed over his completed transaction form and credit card and was unobtrusively paying close attention.

"It's what, a 7.62 millimeter, .30 cal, right?" Norman said.

"Right," Schwartz said. "Suppose someone had reloaded the extended casings with .223 slugs with paper sabots, and they wanted to suppress the sound of firing. What would you recommend for a silencer?" He took a Nagant cartridge out of his pocket and set it on the counter. Norman laid the pistol down on the counter, picked the cartridge up, looked at it carefully.

"Flat-nose slug," he observed, "recessed into an extended neck. Damn, I don't think I've ever seen one like that." He looked back at the revolver. "Cost a factor?" he asked.

"Let's assume not," Schwartz said, "for the time being. And let's assume that the user has had opportunity to make sure the charge is low enough that the slug exits the barrel at less than the speed of sound."

"Well," Norman said, "you've got the slugs and paper patches coming out the barrel into the suppressor, and those gases already burning the paper pretty good." The conversation was gathering interest all around, and you could tell Norman noticed it and was working at not acting like he noticed. "So your bullet leaves the muzzle at below mach one, or anyway, it'll be exiting the suppressor below mach one." He considered the matter. "Do you figure he's pulled the slugs from live standard cartridges, or is he reloading empty casings, with new primer, powder, and so on, resizing the neck of the casings?"

"Well," Schwartz said, "I don't know. I'd think it would take a fair amount of expertise, not to mention nerve, to pull the slugs out of live cartridges. You'd have to drill the slug deep enough to get purchase with a screw turned into it, and I don't think I'd care to try it myself."

"Me either," Norman said. "It could be done, of course, with the proper tools, if you knew what you were doing, but I wouldn't want to do it." There was a murmur of agreement. Chet, another Apex employee, shook his head at the thought.

"So," Norman went on, "he's fired a few shots to get empty casings, and the necks will be slightly expanded, where the casing fits into the recess in the barrel, the reducing cone, so he's got the tools to tighten them down back to the original size."

"Which is going to weaken them a little," Chet put in.

"Exactly right," Norman agreed. "Of course, he's got unfired cartridges to match the used casings with. Someone's going to a hell of a lot of trouble with this, you know?"

"Absolutely," Schwartz said.

"And he's got .223 slugs, new ones, to wrap with paper. Now, any reloader could insert those into the casings; no big deal, although, I don't know, those sabots would complicate things a bit."

"Not really," Chet offered. "He just wraps them good and tight and a little over, with extra extending beyond the base of the slugs, feeds them in by hand, then presses them, so any extra gets shaved off by the mouth of the casing."

"Yeah, that would work."

"One complication," Schwartz mentioned. "These aren't new .223 slugs. They have all been fired from an AR-15 into gelatin or whatever, to get the rifling on them."

"And the paper wraps keep the Nagant rifling off them," Norman said. "The idea is to make it look like the shots came from an AR-15 when actually they were fired from the Nagant." He didn't make it a question. The atmosphere had become noticeably more somber. The Carmel policeman started to say something, then he decided to keep it to himself. Norman noticed. "Mr. Schwartz and Mr. Zufahl are detectives, Richard. And unless I'm mistaken, they're looking into—"

"We are sticking our nose into other people's business," Schwartz said, "but we're doing so at the request of a respectable taxpayer, so—"

"No, that's all right," the cop said with a smile. "This is fascinating, and it's none of my business either. Please carry on."

Norman turned to the laptop on the counter, typed, looked at the screen. "Well, that 7.62 mm or .30 caliber designation is not exact, as usual," he said. "The actual bullet diameter of the Nagant ammunition is 7.91 mm or .311 caliber."

He picked up a pencil and slid a scratch pad over. "That's .311 inches minus .223 inches, or .088 inches, divided by 2 equals .044 inches."

He turned on a calculator lying next to the scratchpad, checked his math, nodded. "The wrap needed would be about three sixty-fourths, a smidge over a thirty-second of an inch. About a twenty-fifth of an inch, a little less. No problem. You cut strips of tissue paper and wrap them nice and tight around the base of the slugs, and you're in business."

Chet said, "If you want to make sure there's no paper residue, you could soak a sheet of tissue paper in potassium nitrate, let it dry, then cut to size and wrap your slugs." Norman nodded. They could have been discussing the Dead Sea Scrolls. I glanced at Schwartz.

He said, "I knew we were coming to the right place." He went on, "Now, about the original question, what silencer would you recommend? I test-fired a couple shots in the basement this morning, using a two-liter pop bottle held on with duct tape, and the sound didn't disturb anyone upstairs, but that arrangement wouldn't be concealable. Or particularly reliable, for this purpose. I can't imagine anyone going to this much trouble, only to trust a makeshift silencer to keep things quiet. I'm thinking of something easily concealable under a coat."

"Well," Norman said, "as you say, if cost is no object, and if you're looking to make a close-up shot with a revolver look like a long-range shot with a rifle, it had better not be conspicuous, then I'd say you want a Gemtech Aurora II." Chet nodded in agreement. "See, the Aurora II is nice and compact, about three and a half inches long, an inch and an eighth in diameter. Weighs about eight ounces, which on a Nagant you're barely going to notice."

"So it would be concealable," Schwartz said, "under a coat, say."

"Oh, yeah. Say you take this holster here." Norman picked it up. "You fold the flap back around and secure it to make a loop for an eight-sling—" He was describing a belt for a shoulder holster formed in a figure eight to put one's arms through, with the belt crossing in back. "—and you have your holster under your left arm. You cut out the bottom to let the silencer stick through, but not completely, and you're in business. You could wear it under a jacket."

"I wouldn't try a quick draw with that," Chet commented.

"No," Norman said, "but after you shoot, you could just slide the piece right in there, and it's out of sight under your jacket."

"Now," Schwartz said, "to attach the silencer—"

"You'd just take off that front sight, machine about a half-inch of the barrel down to thread it for an adapter, and you're in business."

"So this Aurora II is an expensive suppressor. Why is that?"

"Well," Norman said, "it uses neoprene wipes and petroleum-jelly-filled spacer baffles. It's good for maybe twenty or thirty shots, and then it has to be sent back for factory servicing. There's really no practical way for the user to replace all that themselves."

"What's it cost?"

"The Aurora itself is about four hundred dollars, plus the two hundred for the tax stamp, of course. And then there's the wait, naturally." Norman meant the wait, up to about a year, for the ATFE to do the background check and issue the stamp. There's no pressure on the Bureau to expedite matters, so they don't. "And the servicing runs, what? About thirty dollars, I think. I could look it up."

"That's not necessary," Schwartz said, "and I appreciate your taking the time to explain all this." He holstered the revolver, put the cartridge back in his pocket. "So it would be possible to shoot someone at close range, with the Nagant firing suppressed rounds, to give the impression of long-range shooting."

"Oh, sure," Norman said, "although…" He paused. "Can you let me see that again?" Schwartz took the Nagant from the holster. "If you're talking about making it look like a sniper from an elevated platform—"

"Yes."

"—Then you'd have to raise your shooting hand, or hands, to get the angle right, and the trigger pull on this thing is pretty bad—"

"Ah," Schwartz said, "I think I see what you're getting at."

Norman checked the piece again to make sure it hadn't somehow gotten loaded again, raised it, pointing at a display case no one was standing near, and pulled the trigger. It clearly took an effort to keep the revolver pointed at the glass case across the room while he squeezed the trigger. The hammer, an evil-looking job with a long spur to strike the cartridge primer, went way back, then dropped forward with a loud click. "That's got to be a twenty-pound double-action pull," Norman said. He cocked the hammer, raised the gun, pointing across the room again, and squeezed the trigger till the hammer dropped with another loud click. "I'd say twelve pounds, even single action," he said. "I'd say your shooter had to cock the piece for each shot. Was it a single shot?"

"Two," Schwartz said, "in the back, from above, about six inches apart."

"So maybe he has it cocked already for the first shot," Norman said. The rest of us nodded to show we understood what he was saying. "Maybe he's even carrying the piece cocked, not that it's likely to get jostled, with a twelve-pound pull in double action, and he comes up on the victim, draws the cocked revolver, raises it high, pointing down at her, shoots her in the back. The victim starts to fall, and he cocks the gun again for the second shot, which for a lot of people means two hands, unless he's pretty strong—" Norman cocked the piece one-handed, with some effort. "And he shoots her again." He pulled the trigger. The hammer fell.

It was obvious from his reference to the victim as "her" that Norman, and the others for that matter, knew what shooting we were interested in. "That's not something just anyone could pull off," he said.

"Of course," Schwartz pointed out, "the first shot would have caused the victim to fall, or start to do so, and his aim would be easier for the second shot."

"Yeah," Norman said. "You're talking a pretty well-developed person here, physically, I mean. And that's a really nasty scenario we're talking about. I hope you catch the son of a bitch."

"So do I," Schwartz said. The Carmel cop nodded in agreement. Schwartz holstered the Nagant again, and we thanked Norman, nodded to the others, and took our leave. He was quiet on the drive back home, down Guilford to 116th, to College and south.

Chapter Twenty-Two

The fact is that Schwartz can do routine investigations when he feels like it; he just doesn't feel like it often. But somehow, the McElroy code had gotten under his skin, and that got him going on the background. He personally called Ken Spall twice as we prepared for the showdown with McElroy, and he learned that McElroy's grandfather, the purported author of the document, had been in the habit over the years of sinking his money in hare-brained get-rich-quick schemes and that he had in fact invested in Spall's father's enterprise.

Out of the blue that Friday morning, Schwartz was on the phone personally, leaving me to catch up on files, inviting Kenneth Spall, Geoffrey McElroy, and Neil Parkinson to a meeting at the office, and at three that afternoon, the five of us were gathered, along with a lawyer McElroy had brought along, Joseph Kennerly. Kennerly was a tall, lanky fellow of sixty or thereabouts, with a weathered, ruddy, clean-shaven face and a shock of snow-white hair, dressed in a black suit, dark red bowtie, and gleaming black oxfords. He carried a battered leather briefcase. He looked like central casting's idea of a senator.

We got iced tea distributed around the round conference table in the office, which seats six comfortably, disappointed Kennerly and McElroy by not offering anything stronger, but Schwartz assured them we were not discriminating; we just don't have alcohol in the house. McElroy even muttered that John Barrymore line about being in the house of the Borgias, but they got over it before too long.

Schwartz had his copy of the document and his worksheets in a folder he brought from his desk. He began by asking McElroy about the original coded document and Kennerly took a folder out of his briefcase. He opened it and took out half a dozen sheets of paper encased in plastic laminate. He handed them to Schwartz with the admonition that the paper not be removed from the protective plastic.

"That is no problem," Schwartz said. "Even without taking the sheets out, it's clear that we have a document printed on old paper by an old printer." Everyone took a closer look at the pages. "You can see that the edges of the sheets are not perfectly sharp, either at the sides or at top and bottom. The pages were originally from fanfold paper, not cut sheets, with micro-perforation that was used to produce what was considered near-letter-quality printing in the 1980s. The printing is also obviously from a dot-matrix printer, in NLQ, or near letter-quality, printing, with a fair imitation of Courier type."

Everyone, myself included, looked at the paper and the printing, and we saw what he was talking about. I've seen plenty of that kind of printing, and worse, going through old documents. Schwartz went on. "I know that some of us remember when this was about as good as you could get from a personal computer and a printer, before laser printers came along, and I know that few of us would care to go back to those noisy printers." So much for nostalgia.

"So we concede that the document may well have been composed on a 1980s computer and definitely was printed on an old dot-matrix printer. There's no disputing that. Now, here I have a decoded version of the file that Mr. Spall supplied us with earlier." He passed out copies to everyone else, giving what would have been my copy to Kennerly.

"The document may or may not have been written by a lawyer," he went on. "Did you, Mr. Kennerly, perhaps—"

"No, no," Kennerly said. "I know no more about this than you do, sir. I am here strictly in support of Mr. McElroy's interests."

"Just so. Now, the decoded document amounts to an agreement purport-edly between Godfrey McElroy, Mr. Geoffrey McElroy's grandfather, and Mr. Spall's father, Kenneth Spall Senior, in which Godfrey McElroy agrees to invest ten thousand dollars in Mr. Spall's business, which will implement the concept that, according to this document, Mr. McElroy rather than Mr. Spall originally conceived. That is, it credits Godfrey McElroy, not Kenneth Spall Senior, with the invention of the shingle modification that is at the heart of Mr. Spall's business."

Ken Spall looked like he was having a stroke. "It what?" he demanded.

"Here at the foot of page three and the top of four," Schwartz said. They all turned to page three and read. Schwartz went on. "Now, setting aside for the moment the bizarre nature of memorializing an agreement in code, let us focus on the content of the agreement itself. If we credit its veracity, Mr. Godfrey McElroy is clearly an equal partner in Mr. Spall Senior's business."

"But that's—" Ken Spall was ready to explode. Geoffrey McElroy looked smug, and Kennerly was reading the translated document, nodding occasionally, muttering to himself quietly.

Schwartz interrupted Spall's interruption. "The question then becomes, can we credit the document's veracity?"

Geoffrey McElroy spoke for the first time since we'd sat down at the table. "Well, I'm no lawyer," he said, "and that's why I asked Mr. Kennerly to come to the meeting. I don't know if the document is legally enforceable or not. If it is, that's one thing. If it's not, it seems to me at least that there's a moral interpretation that—"

Spall snapped, "I don't believe it for a second, and I think it's bogus. My dad never said a word about owing McElroy money; quite the contrary. He'd provided enough capital to get things off the ground, and my father repaid him, in full and with interest, and I'm damn sure the original idea was Dad's, not McElroy's."

"Okay," McElroy put in, "but suppose that was just your impression. Did your father ever say, in so many words, that the whole thing was his idea? I mean, you may have believed it just because he never said anything different. If I'd made a fortune off someone else's idea, I might be quiet about where the original concept came from." He wasn't having much luck with calming our client down; quite the contrary.

"The fact is," Schwartz said, "that all that is moot, beyond doubt."

"Now, just a moment, sir." The senator looked up from the decoded document. "I don't think you should be hasty in dismissing my client's claim, which this document seems at least to support. It seems to me that this deserves more consideration than you seem willing to give it." He looked back at page four. "Here, for example—"

Neil Parkinson put in an oar. "Counselor, if you don't mind, I think Mr. Schwartz may be ready to shed some light on the document's authenticity." He's not quite as distinguished-looking as Joseph Kennerly was, but he can hold his own in any legal discussion. He turned to the boss. "Mr. Schwartz, could we get to the point as soon as possible?"

Schwartz nodded. "The coded document is interesting in a number of ways," he said. "As I believe we all know, Mr. Godfrey McElroy taught chemistry and physics at North Central High School. The numbers in the coded document were striking in one respect: there were no numbers greater than 118, which, as it happens, is the number of known elements. Now, this is suggestive, and hardly for the first time. I recalled an episode of public television's *Mystery* series, a British crime drama, in which a former chemistry teacher left a message by choosing atomic numbers of elements whose chemical symbols, Cl, Ar, and K, spelled out the name of his killer. Why one would choose such a method is beside the point; in the episode in question, the victim was leaving a message that his killer would not recognize as such, placing the numbers in a church hymn chart.

"Now, Godfrey McElroy taught chemistry, so it seems plausible that he might have used the same method of leaving a message, for whatever reason. Without worrying about why he would have done so, let us take a look at how." He took out a set of sheets with a chart on them, passed them around. I have a copy of that chart right now; it looked like this:

Ac 89	Ag 47	Al 13	Am 95	Ar 18	As 33	At 85
Au 79	B 5	Ba 56	Be 4	Bh 107	Bi 83	Bk 97
Br 35	C 6	Ca 20	Cd 48	Ce 58	Cf 98	Cl 17
Cm 96	Cn 112	Co 27	Cr 24	Cs 55	Cu 29	Db 105
Ds 110	Dy 66	Er 68	Es 99	Eu 63	F 9	Fe 26
Fl 114	Fm 100	Fr 87	Ga 31	Gd 64	Ge 32	H 1
He 2	Hf 72	Hg 80	Ho 67	Hs 108	I 53	In 49
Ir 77	K 19	Kr 36	La 57	Li 3	Lr 103	Lu 71
Lv 116	Mc 115	Md 101	Mg 12	Mn 25	Mo 42	Mt 109
N 7	Na 11	Nb 41	Nd 60	Ne 10	Nh 113	Ni 28
No 102	Np 93	O 8	Og 118	Os 76	P 15	Pa 91
Pb 82	Pd 46	Pm 61	Po 84	Pr 59	Pt 78	Pu 94
Ra 88	Rb 37	Re 75	Rf 104	Rg 111	Rh 45	Rn 86
Ru 44	S 16	Sb 51	Sc 21	Se 34	Sg 106	Si 14
Sm 62	Sn 50	Sr 38	Ta 73	Tb 65	Tc 43	Te 52
Th 90	Ti 22	Tl 81	Tm 69	Ts 117	U 92	V 23
W 74	Xe 54	Y 39	Yb 70	Zn 30	Zr 40	

Schwartz went on. "A chart like this would be used in writing the message. The letters of the message would be replaced by the numbers, keying atomic symbols to atomic numbers. Now, referring to the chart, you can see that B, C, F, H, I, K, N, O, P, S, U, V, W, and Y occur alone, but some letters do not appear at all. There is no J or Q, first of all, and several letters, namely A, D, E, G, L, M, R, T, X, and Z, appear only in combination with other letters. This presents a problem in encoding some words, if the needed combination of letters is not available. Take 'the' for instance. The first two letters could be coded as 90, but how to code the 'e'? There is no number corresponding only to that letter. The last two letters, He, code as 2, but there is no individual number for 't'. '90 2' would code 'thhe', which is not satisfactory." He paused to let everyone look over the chart, and he waited until everyone had looked up.

"This problem has been surmounted with the parentheses. Parentheses around the first or last digit of a number indicate that the first or last letter of the corresponding symbol is omitted. Thus 'the' could be coded '9(0) 2' or '7(3) 2' or any of the other T numbers plus 2 for He, helium.

"Further, underscoring indicates that the letters of the symbol are to be reversed. If the letters 'ac' were needed, the code would be '89,' and to code 'ca' underscored '<u>89</u>' could be used."

I couldn't help it. "Or '20' for calcium would work," I said.

Schwartz nodded. "There are many cases where more than one possibility exists," he said. "But to return to the document before us. Just in the first few lines, we find certain numbers—" He took out another sheet, just the one, and laid it on the table. It read:

<u>118</u>, 103, 10(5) twice, 11(0), <u>117</u> three times, <u>108</u> twice, 11(5), and 117

<u>Og</u>, Lr, D(b), D(s), <u>Ts</u>, <u>Hs</u>, M(c), and Ts

Go, Lr, D, D, St, Sh, M, and Ts

I suppose my face was as blank as everyone else's, aside from Schwartz's, naturally. He said, "This is how the numbers in the first line are decoded. For example, '118' codes 'Og' and underscored it codes 'Go'; '103' codes 'Lr'; '10(5)' and '11(0),' both with parentheses, code the letter D, which doesn't appear as a letter by itself; and so on."

"All right," McElroy said, "but so what? It seems reasonable that my grandfather would have chosen a code like this; after all, he was a chemistry teacher, and I suppose the periodic table of the elements would have—"

"Was your grandfather also a psychic or a time traveler?" Schwartz asked softly. "I doubt it, in any case."

"Why would he have to be a, what, a psychic or—" McElroy sputtered.

"Because," Schwartz said, and I don't think I was the only one who mentally heard the trap snap shut, "your grandfather would have had to be remarkably prescient, in 1984, to be able to use the atomic symbols for the last dozen and a half elements. This document—" He tapped the coded version. "—is excessively up to date for an artifact from the 'eighties." He produced a periodic table of the elements. "It's not shown here, but the official names of elements 102 to 118 were decided upon well after the purported date of this document. Specifically, elements 102 to 109, Nobelium, Lawrencium, Rutherfordium, Dubnium, Seaborgium, Bohrium, Hassium, and Meitnerium, were not officially named until the 1990s, so their atomic symbols, namely No, Lr, Rf, Db, Sg, Bh, Hs, and Mt, didn't exist in 1984, and elements 110–18, namely Darmstadtium, Roentgenium, Copernicium, Nihonium, Flerovium, Moscovium, Livermorium, Tennessine, and Oganesson, symbols Ds, Rg, Cn, Nh, Fl, Mc, Lv, Ts, and Og, were officially named only in the twenty-first century, and therefore were unknown in 1984." I don't think I've ever been prouder of my boss than when I listened to him reel off those element names without a hitch. I told him so later, and he asked if I'd have known if he'd mispronounced one, and I had to agree that he had a point.

"So, amazingly enough," he went on, "forty years ago, your grandfather was aware of names and symbols from this century." He looked around the table, settled again on Geoffrey McElroy. "Of course," he went on, "there's a much simpler explanation. That is, you used an old printer, which for whatever reason was in working order, and old paper, which it's not actually impossible to find, to produce this utterly weird forgery."

Schwartz shook his head. "I won't bother to comment on how in heaven's name you ever thought you could convince anyone that this coded thing could be taken for an actual document; it doesn't really matter. The point is that the anachronisms prove that this is a recent forgery, not an authentic document from the mid-1980s. At the time this was supposedly produced, elements 101 through 118 were provisionally called unnilunium, unnilbium, unniltrium…, ununhexium, ununseptium, and ununoctium, and were symbolled Unu, Unb, Unt…, Uuh, Uus, and Uuo, for "One zero one, One zero two, One zero three…, One one six, One one seven, and One one eight." He waved a hand for the ellipses.

"Now, look," McElroy said, "I never claimed that this was…" He trailed off.

Joseph Kennerly looked like a very grim senator. "If I understand this correctly," he said, "the encoded document is clearly of very recent production, as evidenced by the use of modern atomic symbols," showing that he understood perfectly.

Schwartz nodded, said, "Yes, for example, oganesson was formally named in 2016, so the document cannot be older than that."

Kennerly looked at McElroy. "If you have attempted to entangle me in your scheme, sir, I can assure you that you have been unsuccessful." He got hold of his briefcase, rose. To the rest of us, he nodded, laid a card on Schwartz's desk, and said, "If I am needed further, you know how to reach me, gentlemen." I went with him to the hall and the front door. As I let him out, he said goodbye, muttering, "Of all the wastes of time—"

I went back to the conference table. McElroy was trying to dig his way out, but not doing well at it. He said to Kenneth Spall, "Now, I came to you in good faith, after coming across this coded message in my grandfather's papers, and—"

"You lie," Spall sneered. "You lie, and you're a liar, and there's nothing you can say that wipes that out. I'll bet you even got the idea from that *Mystery* program, you son of a bitch!"

"No," McElroy whined. "I've never even watched *Endeavour,* for God's sake; I didn't get any ideas—"

"Mr. McElroy," Schwartz interrupted, "no one has mentioned *Endeavour* until now. I referred to *Mystery* on PBS, but not to the specific program. You can't quit while you're ahead, because you're too far behind. You're only digging a deeper hole for yourself. I advise you to leave, sir, and hope that the morning's mail doesn't bring you a notice of a suit for damages. Mr. Parkinson, what do you think of our chances in a civil lawsuit, never mind criminal law for now?"

Parkinson was keeping a straight face, which can't have been easy. "I would say, Mr. Schwartz, that a civil suit for attempted extortion would be Mr. Spall's best choice, although I don't think you should so lightly set aside criminal charges. This is no either/or matter. Fraud comes in many varieties, and what we have here—"

McElroy was stammering. "Look, this is all a misunderstanding, see; I came to you in good faith with this document I discovered, and—"

"You came here in bad faith, with a lawyer who had the good sense to leave once he had a good whiff of your homemade fraudulent coded document," Schwartz said. "And by the way, what in God's name possessed you to code the damn thing in the first place? To tell the truth, I've got half a mind to sue you, just to get back for the insult you offered to my client, Mr. Spall, not to mention to myself, Mr. Zufahl, Mr. Parkinson, the citizens of the State of Indiana, the American people, and the rest of the human race. I have never seen such a patently, flagrantly, obviously fake piece of crap.

"I'll tell you what we'll do. You will sign and we will witness a document confessing to your fraud, admitting that the entire thing was your invention from start to finish, and relinquishing any and all claim to any part of Mr. Spall's business and to any compensation, real or imaginary, from Mr. Spall forever, so help you God."

Schwartz took a word-processed document from his folder, which I happened to know, since I'd composed it from his dictation, was worded rather less colorfully, and set it in front of McElroy. He laid a pen on top of it. "In return, I will attempt to persuade Mr. Spall not to sue you for everything you have, everything you ever have had or ever will have, unless you ever pester him again. From where I stand, that looks like a pretty good deal. From your standpoint, I think it looks better than that. You have engaged in a truly witless attempt at squeezing money from a man who owes you nothing, and you are evading punishment. Sign it. Now."

McElroy didn't even bother to read the document he was signing. It could have been a fan letter to the Dalai Lama for all he knew. I had to agree with Schwartz. He was getting off scot-free, and his coded agreement was the worst excuse for ingenuity I had ever seen. He got up as I signed as a witness on the line above my printed signature, dated it, and passed it to Parkinson. McElroy stopped at the door of the office, turned to Schwartz, and started to say something, decided against it. I went with him to see him out the door. He didn't say a word. When I returned, Schwartz had signed, and he handed the letter of agreement to Parkinson, who put it into his own briefcase.

Parkinson shook hands with both of us, then he seemed to want to ask a question, but he shook his head no and headed for the door. I went with him, not to make sure he made it out the door, but to open it for him. "You know," he said to me, "there are times when we need to be grateful for our opponents' shortcomings. Heaven only knows what possessed McElroy to use that preposterous code. If he had left the thing in plain English, using the 1984 printer and paper and so forth, he might have been able to fake it successfully, or at least with a better chance of success, not that I think he could actually have pulled it off. But he shot himself in the foot by putting it in that crazy code. That's really unique in my experience. What do you suppose made him imagine that doing that would improve his chances?"

"I don't think I'm spilling any family secrets by telling you that Mr. Schwartz is wondering the same thing," I said. "It makes no sense for McElroy to do what he did. Why did he do it that way? I don't know. He's crazy or stupid or both, and he's a goddam liar any way you cut it. I guess it comes down to this, why does anybody do anything?"

Parkinson didn't seem impressed, but he wasn't one to tell you so just for the hell of it. "By the way, Rainer," he said, "I wonder if you have heard this one. You probably have." He seemed a little shy about telling me the joke, whatever it was.

"Go ahead; try me."

"Very well. Do you know the difference between sanity and insanity?"

I thought a minute. "I think so, but I'd have a hard time putting it into words a lawyer would accept. What's the difference between sanity and insanity?"

"There are more of us," he said. He smiled, a little sadly, I thought, and he went to his car. I watched him drive off, the same direction as always. For some reason he always turns east not west onto 79th Street, then takes Kimlough Drive south to 78th, and from there to College. I have no idea why.

I stepped back inside, but Ken Spall was on his way out, so I opened the door for him. He seemed less delighted with the outcome than I might have expected, but I figured things were still sinking in for him. He managed to say goodbye, at least.

I went back into the office. Schwartz had put all the loose sheets in a folder for the case file. He fished out the first copy of the encoded "agreement" that wasn't really an agreement. "I hate to keep chewing this same old bone," he said, "but I simply cannot understand the point of encoding that document."

"Maybe to give Spall an excuse to ask you about it?" I ventured. "You did get a bit of publicity about solving that other code, for Viola Ketchum."

"'Publicity,'" Schwartz sneered. "Why in God's name would Mr. McElroy want Mr. Spall to show me the code?" I nodded at the pig, and he fed it. "For that matter, why would Mr. Spall want me to see it in its coded form? It makes no—" He stopped himself from having to continue stuffing Porky. "—sense for either of them to have the ridiculous agreement coded." He stared straight ahead. "So far as I can see," he finished.

Now, the fact is that the discussion continued like that for quite a while, but it didn't really get us any closer to an answer to any of our mysteries, beyond what I've already recorded here, so I'll spare you the rest. You're welcome.

Chapter Twenty-Three

The break, when it came, arrived out of the blue on Saturday. I had just finished with the usual morning chores, including a quick dusting, stacking the mail that wasn't junk or routine on Schwartz's desk pad, when the landline phone rang. I answered it, explaining that it was Leo Schwartz's office, Rainer Zufahl speaking.

It was Iris Warner. "Rainer, dear, did I get you up?"

"For God's sake, Iris, it's nine-thirty."

"Well, of course, it is, darling. Are you really up and about at this ungodly hour?"

"Of course," I said, not being in the mood for gushing affection. "Tell me, Iris, and I really think this is more appropriate from me to you than from you to me, but are you up and about at this time of day?" The fact is that Iris's hours are rather more flexible than mine. She used to be married to Buck Warner, whom you might have heard of, inventor, owner, and operator of WarnerCorp, a company that facilitates communication among various software used by doctors, hospitals, clinics, nurses, and insurance companies, without which everything would—I am told by those who know such things—either move more slowly or, according to our tech friend Colin, come crashing to a dead halt. Iris can sleep till noon if she so chooses, and she so chooses pretty often. She seldom hits the hay much earlier than I get up, which puts a bit of a crimp in our relationship, but so far, it had seemed worth it to both of us. At any rate, a phone call from Iris to the office number this early must mean something was stirring.

It was. "Well, Rainer, my sweet, I just wanted to invite you to a birthday party." I ran through a mental list of relatives' and friends' birthdays, but came up empty. "It's going to be the biggest birthday bash this sorry town will see all summer," she went on. "Ginny's inviting anyone who's anyone, and that, of course, includes me, and I thought, now, who would I like to pluck from obscurity to be my escort, date, and boon companion to this shindig? And who do you think I came up with, dear heart?"

"That should have been 'whom' both times," I said. Frankly, I'm not bothered by the fact that Iris and I generally move in rather different circles, or social strata, nearly so much as I'm bothered that occasionally she deigns to invite me up to her level. Indianapolis is not one of those cities with a really old-money elite class. Pharmaceuticals, medical equipment and supplies, motor vehicle and aircraft parts and products, and of course the Motor Speedway, and there you just about have it. Class is determined by money, almost exclusively. Naptown is, as Schwartz likes to say, the biggest goddam town you'll ever see.

"You are a pedant," Iris said, "and a spoilsport pedant at that. Here I get up at the crack of dawn—" As if she'd ever seen a dawn upon arising "—and you're a grouch. I have a good mind to take my invitation back."

"You can't take it back," I said. "You haven't issued it yet. Who's Ginny, and whose birthday is she celebrating?"

"She's my good friend Ginny Spall," Iris said, "and she's celebrating her husband Ken's fiftieth, that's who. Or whom."

"No, 'who' is fine." I was trying to stay calm and quiet, as if I were somehow going to break the bubble. "So…your good friend Ginny is planning a birthday bash for hubby. Hmm. No doubt she's really putting on a party."

"Well, if you call renting the Indiana Roof for dining and dancing for a couple hundred couples putting on a party. And the thing is, it's a surprise. Between us, Ken's a bit of a stick, not that you'd know him." There was a pause, as if Iris was thinking something over. I decided I'd better try to hold up my end of the conversation, if possible without sharing information Iris didn't need to be burdened with.

"Okay, my sweet," I said, "I guess I was just startled by a call from you so early in the day. Er, when is this party, anyway?"

"So you can check your crowded social calendar?"

"Of course," I said. "I mean, you know how it is. Weeks go by without a glimmer of social interaction, and suddenly everyone wants me at the same time." That was far enough from the truth to allay suspicions. "When is it?"

"His birthday is July 9," she said, "which conveniently enough is a Saturday. Ginny reserved the date months ago, and she's kept the whole thing a secret. Ken isn't all that big about socializing, which makes it a little tricky. There are people he likes, and there are people he does business with, and there are people who just must be invited, if you know what I mean."

"Of course, of course. I'm sure she's taken every precaution to prevent Ken from finding out about this party."

"Oh, absolutely," Iris said. "We had lunch yesterday, and she was telling me all about it, how she's been meeting friends and acquaintances who must make the cut, and—"

"She didn't invite you until yesterday?"

"Oh, good Lord, Rainer; she asked me weeks and weeks ago. I haven't invited you until today because, well, I wasn't sure you'd want to come."

"You weren't sure I'd want to come? How could you doubt it, dear heart? Let you drag some second-choice to the event of the season? Am I so heartless?"

Schwartz came into the office, nodded a greeting, and sat down to check the mail. He turned to the latest issue of *American Fireworks News* first, as I'd expected. Iris and I chatted a couple minutes more, then we wound it up and rang off.

I swiveled in my desk chair to face Schwartz. He finished a paragraph, or maybe it was a diagram he'd been scrutinizing, and then, finally, he looked up. He could tell I had news, but what kind was just the first thing he'd have to face that morning.

"Relax," I said. "I bear glad tidings. At least I think they're glad tidings." At that point, the phone rang. Heaven only knew what Iris had forgotten to say. I picked it up, got as far as saying whose office it was, and Paul Surcutt interrupted me.

"Rainer," he said, "I just found out what Virginia Spall has been up to. It's a surprise fiftieth birthday party for her husband."

"Hold on a second," I said. I covered the mouthpiece. To Schwartz: "You'll want to pick it up. It's Paul, and damned if he hasn't got the exact same news I just got from Iris and was about to pass on to you." Back to Paul: "Your timing is impeccable. I was just about to tell Mr. Schwartz exactly what you're about to tell him. Go ahead."

There was a perfectly understandable pause at Paul's end, then he said, "God, Rainer, I'm sorry to step on your toes. Would you rather go ahead—"

"I wouldn't think of it," I said. "I got it by pure chance, and I bet you dug it up by hard work. Just tell him." Schwartz looked ready to fire someone, and Paul wasn't present. "Don't worry about it," I told Paul. "Go ahead and tell Mr. Schwartz."

"All right," he said. "Ginny Spall has been arranging a surprise birthday bash for her husband, a real mother of a blowout at the Indiana Roof, dinner for a few hundred couples, a small orchestra selected from the ISO, the works. I don't have all the details yet, but two sources have confirmed their invitations, for July 9, and apparently, she's decided that this will be the occasion that will put the rest of the social summer in the shade."

"Indeed," Schwartz said.

"Yes, sir, and she's been hand-delivering the invitations for the past six weeks, with everyone sworn to strict secrecy. From what I've been able to find out, Ken Spall has no idea about this, and her supposedly suspicious movements—" Paul broke off a moment. "How'd you find out about it, Rainer?"

"Oh, you know how it is up here in the social stratosphere," I said, "you can see the whole world spread out beneath you, open to your every—"

"Ms. Warner called him up this morning to ask him to escort her," Schwartz said, bringing me back to earth. "Apparently, she assumed he'd be free even at this late date."

Paul didn't answer right away, then he said, "Well, I'm sorry about that, Rainer. I hope you have a great time."

I had a suitable reply, but I didn't want to feed the pig, so we kept it civil, and we were so careful about that that Paul almost rang off without dropping the real bomb. He said, "I suppose you've got the yearbook too."

"What yearbook?" Schwartz and I said together.

"The Broad Ripple High School yearbook with the picture of the swim team," Paul said.

"The swim team?" Schwartz asked.

"The swim team that Ken Spall, a junior, and Geoffrey McElroy, a sophomore, were on together."

Schwartz and I looked at each other. "So," he said, "Mr. Spall and Mr. McElroy were teammates and have been acquainted for over thirty years, not for about a year, as we were told. Paul, you have delivered the goods. Do you have a copy of the yearbook?"

"Yes, sir."

"Please bring it with you when you come."

"Yes, sir, I will."

"I look forward to seeing it." Schwartz leaned back, closed his eyes, opened them, and sat up again. "Very fine indeed." He and Paul and I hung up together.

"So," he said, "you'll be accompanying Ms. Warner to the Spall birthday party." He was obviously pleased at the thought of my spending an evening on best behavior. He can really be insufferably smug at times, but today he desisted, beyond the bare minimum. "And so we get to the bottom of Ms. Spall's supposedly suspicious movements. A surprise party. Well, well."

"It's technically a satisfactory answer to the question Spall posed," I said. "However, I can't help wondering if he'll see it that way."

Schwartz gave me a look. "He asked us to find out what his wife was up to, and we found out. Indeed, setting aside your conversation with Ms. Warner, we got to the bottom of the problem in a perfectly legitimate way. True, serendipity stepped in, but barely before Paul's call. In fact, you hadn't told me what Ms. Warner had told you before Paul told us both what he'd found out."

It was obvious that he was ready to send Spall a bill for services rendered, the sooner the better. "But," I pointed out, "Spall isn't the sort of guy to just take our word for it. I mean, you can't expect him to be satisfied with 'Oh, we discovered that there's a perfectly innocent explanation for your wife's behavior, and you'll just have to trust us, hope you don't mind.'"

Schwartz smiled. He had really taken a dislike to the client, and not just because of that cockamamie coded agreement. "No," he said, "nor can we simply ask him to wait until July eleventh."

"Ninth," I said.

"The following Monday," he said, "keeping things businesslike, even hypothetically." He glanced at the clock. Lunch was still a little while away. "No, I really don't see any alternative, assuming we're not willing to just swallow the costs, to spoiling the surprise."

"We could load the search expenses onto the coded-agreement invoice."

"Search?" Schwartz said. "You mean surveillance, don't you? In any case, you can't be serious. There simply isn't enough time or trouble to carry the men's hours."

"Well, no," I admitted, "not really. Look, I don't like Spall any better than you do, and I would hate like hell to eat the money we've spent on the surveillance. So I agree with you: we have to tell Spall what his wife has been up to." I thought about it for a few moments. "The fact is," I said, "he should be happy with that result. His wife doesn't have anything on the side; quite the contrary. She's going to one hell of a lot of trouble to throw him a really memorable party for his half-century mark, and he ought to be appreciative."

"We had the impression, did we not, that Mr. Spall was actively looking for evidence of infidelity, grounds for a relatively painless divorce?... From our meetings so far, would you say he still loved his wife, or is he looking for a pretext to get rid of her?" After twenty years of happy marriage, Schwartz really has a hard time understanding people whose experience has not paralleled his own.

I gave it some thought. "That's an interesting question," I said. "You know, a couple of hours ago, I might have said he was looking to call it quits, going down for the third time." Schwartz made a face at the mental image. "But you know, now that I give it some thought, I think he's been burned twice, and he's just afraid this is going to turn out the same way as the first two marriages, and so he might as well head it off. From what Paul turned up, Spall had to pay alimony both times, although there were, and still are, no children.

"But," I went on, "it's very possible that the whole thing is in his head. In all the reports, there's not a whisper of a hint that there's anything wrong with his marriage, apart from his suspicions, and we've just got proof that those are unfounded. So maybe what he needs is just a good stiff dose of marriage counseling."

I looked at Schwartz, and he looked at me. He could see it coming, and he didn't like it much. "And you, sir, are just the person to administer said dose. Forgive the personal observation, which I sure as hell wouldn't dream of making if it weren't professionally necessary, fitting, and appropriate, but frankly, I can't think of anyone more qualified than you are to give him a good straight talk on the subject of marriage." I sat there waiting for an explosion and possibly release from employment.

Schwartz sat there, impassive, then he cleared his throat, said, "You owe the pig, three times, Rainer." I breathed again as I got my wallet out, pulled three ones out, and fed the pig. Schwartz wasn't looking mellow, to put it mildly, but whatever he was feeling, he kept inside. "Yes," he said finally, "we really have no choice, aside from the unacceptable one of eating our expenses, but to inform Mr. Spall of his wife's efforts to give him a fiftieth birthday to remember." I'm no mind-reader, but I knew he was thinking that Freda hadn't made it to his fiftieth birthday, but she'd have made it special if she had. From what I've heard in passing over the years, she made life special for him.

"So shall I call Spall and let him know we've got a final report on his wife?" The doorbell rang. I went to let Paul in. He had an old high-school yearbook with him, and I congratulated him on coming up with the goods.

We went into the office, and Paul handed Schwartz the book, which had a few Post-It notes flagging the appropriate pages. The swim team was the best feature, but there were two other pictures of groups Spall and McElroy both belonged to. Schwartz let Paul know how welcome this item was. It was clear that Spall had known McElroy a lot longer than he'd let on. I wondered why, and I suspected Schwartz did also.

"It will certainly keep until this afternoon," he said. "How long has it been since we ate at the Canal Bistro? And would you join us, Paul?"

Paul begged off, for a dental appointment he couldn't put off any longer, and Schwartz and I wished him well with that. He said he'd just be able to make it on time, and he left, with more congratulations from Schwartz.

It didn't seem the right moment to point out that we'd had carry-out from there quite recently. "Long enough," I said. "I could really see the gyros salad today."

"Not to mention baklava and Turkish coffee."

"I've been wondering about their tiramisu," I said.

"You know, we could order both and split them."

"Absolutely." Another crisis averted through food. "I'll drive," I said.

"Excellent."

The drive down was uneventful, and we got there early enough to snag a parking space in the lot next door. It was a beautiful day, so we ate on the terrace alongside the canal, the same canal Allison Morgan had been found in, but on the north side, farther east. The sun was shining in a cloudless sky, and the awning was just wide enough to give us shade.

Schwartz ordered the lamb kebab with house salad, and I went for that gyros salad, which would have been enough, but the desserts would make room for themselves.

While we were waiting, Schwartz got onto one of his topics. He'd just reread several Poe stories, and he said it was characteristic of Poe that they stayed fresh, no matter how often he'd read them.

"The truly amazing thing about 'The Gold Bug,' one of Poe's most well-known, most successful stories," he said, "is that he pulls it off at all. I'm certainly not at all au courant with Poe scholarship, to put it mildly—"

"And to put it in French," I put in, just to let him know I was paying attention. He's so fond of quoting Orwell's six rules for avoiding bad English, it's always a pleasure to point out when he's violating one himself. A pleasure that I enjoy only when it seems safe, naturally.

"I'm not at all up to date with Poe scholarship," he went on, "and there are doubtless dozens of articles I haven't read on this very subject, but the improbabilities in the story are striking. You've heard me say a hundred times—" He paused for a comment, but I figured I'd interrupted him enough for the time being. "—that fiction has to be plausible, but reality suffers from no such constraint. Yet in this story, he sweeps the implausibilities under the rug so deftly that the reader never notices, or at any rate, is not brought up sharp by them, and he pulls it off. I mean, it's so interesting that the series of unlikely events and circumstances never distracts the reader."

"For example?" I asked dutifully as Stephanie brought our iced teas.

"Well, for starters it's not at all clear when the story is set. It was published in 1843, and the nameless narrator begins the story 'Many years ago, I contracted an intimacy with a Mr. William Legrand,' and later he describes the day of his visit to Legrand, the very day that Legrand found the gold bug, 'About the middle of October, 18—, there occurred, however, a day of remarkable chilliness.' Now, why would the narrator pick such a day to trek out to Legrand's hut on the island? He doesn't say, except to note that he hadn't seen Legrand in some time. All right, he visits Legrand on a remarkably chilly day, and Legrand has just discovered the gold bug, and his servant, Jupiter, has found a piece of parchment stuck in the sand in the ruins of a boat, which he uses to pick up the bug without getting bitten. A chilly day, but a busy one, to be sure.

"Now, the events occur 'many years ago,' in the early nineteenth century, therefore more than a hundred years after Captain Kidd was hanged in London on May 23, 1701, ostensibly for murder, but really for piracy."

"Really?" I said.

"Yes. He killed a mutinous crew member with a bucket, and that was the pretext for hanging him. Anyway, that piece of parchment had been buried in the sand for well over a hundred years, on a low, sandy island exposed to the weather of the South Carolina seacoast. And after a century, it's still there for Jupiter to find. Right. Jupiter sees it sticking out of the sand enough to be noticed, picks it up, and wraps it around the bug to avoid getting bitten, which package Legrand sticks in his pocket. Legrand and Jupiter encounter Lieutenant G—— from the fort, who is out strolling the

216

island in the unseasonably chilly weather for God knows what reason, and God also knows why Poe couldn't be bothered to think up a last name for him. Knowing of the initialed lieutenant's interest in entomology, Legrand lends him the bug, but the lieutenant takes the bug without the parchment wrapper, which Legrand sticks back in his pocket, for no other reason than that it will be needed later to advance the plot. The bug itself, however, is safely handed over to Lieutenant G——, so that it will be necessary, later, to draw it for the narrator.

"Later, sitting before the fire made necessary by the chilly weather, Legrand is describing the gold bug to the narrator, and he decides to sketch it but finds there's no paper, although pens and ink are in good supply. Had there been a sheet of paper to hand, the rest of the story wouldn't have happened, so we have to believe there wasn't so much as a used sheet with a blank back suitable for an illustrative sketch. Ah, but Legrand finds the dirty parchment in his pocket, turns it over to find a clean spot, and, for whatever reason, uses just a corner for his drawing. He hands the piece of parchment to the narrator, and right on cue, his dog jumps on the narrator, who pets and holds off the beast with one hand while holding the parchment near the fire with the other, just long enough to let the heat warm just that corner on which the sketch was made. The dog having served its purpose, the narrator looks at the parchment, not at Legrand's sketch but at the newly visible drawing of a skull, which he criticizes as a poor drawing of a bug without antennae, but never notices that the skull is drawn in a reddish color quite unlike the ink Legrand used for his sketch."

Stephanie brought the food, and we tucked in. Schwartz left off the "Gold Bug" discussion for the moment, to concentrate on his kebab, and I shoveled in gyros, lettuce, arugula, spinach, and that delicate dressing. It was a perfect day in May.

We had split the tiramisu and the baklava, and I was alternating bites along with the thick Turkish coffee, when Schwartz said, "You're right, at that. I should talk with Mr. Spall, and we definitely will have to spoil the surprise aspect of the party, if not the party itself. We don't have to tell him the details, just the fact that his wife is planning a surprise fiftieth birthday party."

I was surprised it had taken him no longer than that to accept the reality of the situation. It wouldn't be easy for him, but we both knew he was the one with the experience, not I. I said I'd call Spall about an appointment.

When we got back, despite the holiday traffic, I made the appointment with Kenneth Spall for the following Tuesday, May 31. It was, of course, Memorial Day weekend, also known in these parts as Race Day weekend. Getting anything other than a hangover accomplished then is a near-miracle in Indianapolis, so I was lucky to get hold of him on the Saturday before he left "for the lake" with Ms. Spall. He didn't specify what lake they were going to, and I didn't ask. I made sure he understood that this was regarding his original problem, the surveillance of his wife, not that encoded pseudo-agreement. We agreed on ten Tuesday morning.

Schwartz suggested that I call the Herefords to make an appointment to discuss the situation with Stacy. He suggested I try for just Stacy and her parents, leaving her grandfather out of it if possible. I got Steven on the line, and after he quizzed me on what he called my unaccountable prejudice against cricket, we agreed on Tuesday afternoon at three o'clock, since they were all going to the Race, then up to their place on the lake Monday. As Schwartz said, that would also give Colin plenty of time to get those files decrypted.

Chapter Twenty-Four

The Race got run Sunday, with no serious injuries to the drivers at least, which is always a relief. Years ago, when I was in high school, I went to the Race when the father of a friend had an extra ticket, and he was right when he told Brian and me that everyone should go once, just to see what it was like when a third of a million people congregated for a single event. "It'll change your view of human nature," he'd said, and he was right. Things are pretty well cleaned up these days; the old Snake Pit is well-patrolled, and it's not terribly unsafe for women, assuming that hordes of drunks don't offend them. Back when, it was very different.

Anyway, the 500 was run, and I was glad we weren't part of the crowd slowly oozing out of the Speedway. Monday was Memorial Day observed, and we caught up on neglected routine chores. Schwartz took the car, although I offered to drive him, and he got flowers and took them to Crown Hill Cemetery. While he was out, I updated the pyrotechnics files, inventorying the chemicals and verifying the amounts on hand. Schwartz is meticulous about recording purchases, but he tends to be just a bit careless about noting what he's used and how much is left. I checked the equipment, too, just to make sure he hadn't added some instrument or other without telling me, even though I knew better.

He'd bought a couple or six kits since the last update of the rockets inventory, and of course, I had the data from *Freda*'s successful flight to record. At least that was file transfers, not manual data processing, which naturally involves serious proofreading. I finished off the time typing up a complete summary of all the interim reports Paul and the others had submitted, with a chronological list of Virginia Spall's meetings with friends and acquaintances. And, of course, I lowered the flags to half-staff in the morning and raised them at noon. As I have said, Schwartz doesn't refer to his military service much, but some things just have to be done properly, at least at 7912 Forest Lane.

On Tuesday morning, Ken Spall called to verify that he was expected at eleven. I said he was, and I was a little surprised that he arrived on time. Schwartz and I were ready for him. After ushering him into the office, taking tea and coffee orders, and supplying them, I excused myself, leaving Schwartz and the client alone. As instructed by Schwartz earlier, I went around the corner to the short hallway with walk-in closets. Inside the one adjoining the office, I opened a panel noiselessly. The wall and the back of the bookcase there were cut out in a rectangle. The back of the bookcase was lined with black fabric stretched thin. There was a space conveniently left between the books on the shelf at eye level. The closet was dark; the office was well-lighted. Between the books, I had a ten-inch-high, six-inch-wide view of the office, and sound came through just fine.

Schwartz wasted no time in getting to the point once enough time had elapsed for me to take up my listening post. He told Spall flat out that we had discovered what his wife was up to, that he had no grounds for divorce or separation or even complaint. Referring to the report summary I'd written the day before, he read Spall the list of people Ms. Spall had met with, with Spall sputtering, trying to interrupt what was, after all, a not very exciting recitation.

When he was done with the list, Schwartz closed the file folder on the report, looked at Spall, who had gotten quiet finally, and asked whether he had any idea why his wife would have met with all these people. For once, Spall was at a loss. It was interesting to watch and listen to the change as Schwartz eased out of the severe mode and into a more sympathetic attitude. "Mr. Spall, can you really not guess what's been going on?"

"No," Spall said, as if he'd been asked his address and couldn't recall it offhand. He looked every day of his age at that moment.

"It's really quite simple," Schwartz said. "You have a birthday coming up in July, Mr. Spall."

"Right, my fiftieth," he said. He sat up straighter. "Are you saying—" He looked at Schwartz as if noticing him for the first time. "All this activity has been—"

"Preparation for a surprise party," Schwartz said, "in honor of your fiftieth birthday." He drank the last of his iced tea. "Your wife has gone to an inordinate amount of trouble to give you a truly memorable birthday party, and your suspicions of her behavior have been totally unwarranted, unjustified, and unfounded." He waited until he had Spall's eye.

"Your wife loves you, Mr. Spall, and however you feel about her, you can at least appreciate her affection for you—" Schwartz raised his left hand abruptly, the signal for me to return to the office. Spall was suddenly crying, and Schwartz wanted help with that.

I got there quickly, in time to grab the box of tissues from my desk and hand them to the client. He didn't sob or whimper, just sat there weeping and wiping his eyes, and in a minute or so he had it back under control. He begged our pardon, and Schwartz assured him he wasn't the first to be moved to tears in that office. He could have said in that chair.

It took Spall a while to get it out, but it was clear that he'd let his previous lousy marriages color his view of this one. He'd been in agony, he said, afraid that Ginny was planning to take him to the cleaner's the way the first two wives had done.

It was pushing lunch back by the time Spall was settled down. Schwartz told him, "There remains one matter still to discuss, Mr. Spall. Your wife has gone to a great deal of trouble to arrange for this surprise party. Can you manage to behave for the next, what, almost seven weeks, as if you suspect nothing?"

"Why, yes, I think I can," Spall said.

"Very well, then," Schwartz said, "I hope you can. As it happens, Mr. Zufahl has been invited to your party, as the escort of one of the guests, and he will be well-placed to observe the proceedings. We will postpone billing you for the surveillance of your wife until the week after your birthday, and I will be frank with you: the cost of the work will, of course, be covered, but if

Mr. Zufahl reports a deficiency of surprise in your demeanor, there will be a surcharge, by no means a moderate one, on the invoice." He paused a few seconds, no doubt imagining how much he'd like to soak Spall for if he couldn't keep up the pretense.

"It is my opinion," he went on, "that you are a very fortunate man, Mr. Spall, and frankly, in many ways more fortunate than you deserve." Spall nodded in agreement and had to dab away some fresh tears. "Your suspicions of your wife were unworthy of you, and her.

Schwartz went on in that vein awhile, but you get the idea, and there's no point in getting embarrassing about it. It ended with Spall saying he'd gladly pay any invoice we'd like to submit, right now, and Schwartz repeating that we'd wait until after the party. I noticed that Schwartz had kept things as vague as possible, not mentioning the venue, for example, so Spall wouldn't have to act surprised for all of it. Spall insisted on shaking hands with both of us, thanking us, with more tears starting, before he left.

The door had barely closed behind him when Schwartz asked if Hollyhock Hill was open, and I said I'd be glad to check. For the best fried chicken in the state, yes, I would. They were, and I asked him, "Light meat or dark or both, just chicken or dinners?" He said two dinners, both light and dark, and I said I'd pick it up.

I ran over in the gray Cobalt, paid, and carried the carton out to the car, wondering, as always, why we don't get Hollyhock Hill chicken more often than we do. When I got home, Schwartz had the table set in the kitchen, and I unpacked the chicken, mashed potatoes, gravy, green beans, whole-kernel corn, and salad with oil and vinegar dressing. As usual, I had forgotten to get dessert, and as usual, we didn't need it.

I went over the revisions to inventory with Schwartz after lunch, and all that was jake, to use an expression he disapproves of. When that had been taken care of, he asked if I had any thoughts about the coding of the phony agreement, and I confessed I was as clueless as ever. "Well," he said, "far-fetched as it might be, I think Spall may have colluded with McElroy, in an effort to remove half his business from the divorce lawyers. As an old friend, McElroy might have agreed to take a half share legally, which would in fact have remained in Spall's hands."

"That is far-fetched," I said.

"Yes, but it fits in a really strange and convoluted way. If McElroy ostensibly owned half the business and if Spall was expecting a third divorce, then he'd have protected half of the company from any settlement with his wife."

"And the coding?" I asked.

"Served as an excuse to involve us," Schwartz said.

"Well, to involve you," I said. I thought about it. "Are you going to confront Spall with this theory?"

"Oh, God, no." He looked at the clock. "There's no way to prove anything; the whole thing is just too screwy for words. And the sooner we're done with Mr. Spall, the better."

"There remains the birthday party."

"Which you, not I, will attend," he said with obvious satisfaction.

I looked at it. "I think you're right," I said. "There are some things it's better just to leave alone."

"And this definitely seems to be one of them," Schwartz said. "I don't want to think about that crazy agreement any more."

I couldn't argue with that.

Things were pretty quiet until three, when the Herefords arrived, all four of them. Schwartz had given me careful instructions, so I had six identical glasses ready, washed, wiped, and very discreetly labeled.

From our standpoint, the meeting was a success, but it's doubtful that any of the Herefords, including Stacy, would have agreed. Charles, in an even louder windowpane check suit than before, light blue with navy stripes, assumed he was in charge, and naturally, he snagged the red leather chair in front of Schwartz's desk. Anita took the yellow chair to his left, then Steven, who immediately slid down and forward, and Stacy took the chair closest to my desk.

Charles opened up with an outraged outburst: "I understand you've been filling my grandson's head with a bunch of—"

"Shut up!" Schwartz bellowed. He seldom raises his voice, but when he does, it's effective. Charles Hereford sat there as if he'd sat on a nightstick and didn't know what to make of it, his mouth still open. "This meeting was arranged at my behest," Schwartz went on, more quietly but quite firmly, "and you, sir, were not invited. Ms. Anita Hereford and Mr. Steven Hereford are my clients, and I have extended my hospitality to their daughter, Stacy Hereford, as well—"

Charles found his voice: "Their *son*, you son of a bitch!"

Schwartz brought his arm up and pointed at Charles Hereford, and he snapped at me: "Another word out of his mouth, Rainer, and you will eject him from this house. With as much force as necessary, or as you feel like using, whichever is greater."

Charles gaped at Schwartz, who went on: "You remain here by sufferance only, sir. After the reception Mr. Zufahl and I received at your home, we owe you no more than the basic requirements of human civility, and you strain our patience. You will listen, and you will do so in silence."

Charles stared. The other Herefords looked as if they hoped they weren't next in line for Schwartz's anger.

"We are not here to debate that matter," Schwartz said, "that is your problem, not mine, thank heaven." He turned to me. "Rainer, let's offer iced tea." No one objected when I stood and went to the kitchen. I took the chilled pitcher from the refrigerator, filled the ice bucket, stuck in the tongs, and got the glasses arranged with them on the tray so that I'd be sure to get the right glasses to the right people.

When I returned to the office, Steven Hereford was making a point, or thought he was. He said and then repeated, "There are no coincidences."

Schwartz had clearly had enough of the client, or at least the male one. "That's one of the most common myths abounding today," he said, nodding to me to start serving. I'd already put coasters out on small tables between the chairs so they had somewhere to set the glasses I filled and handed to them. "People hear someone or other, usually a character on a police show, say, 'There are no coincidences,' as if observing that there's no free lunch, and they believe it. On cop shows, it's used as shorthand to mean that suspicious occurrences should not be overlooked, and that's fine, but to go around believing that there are no coincidences is simply mindless. There are coincidences all the time. Most of them are not suspicious, don't mean anything significant, and aren't worth worrying about, but they do occur. So kindly stop saying there are no coincidences unless you wish to take your case elsewhere." Any opportunity to avoid work, even at this late stage. He really is shameless.

Hereford wasn't ready to concede. "So give me an example," he challenged Schwartz.

"No problem," Schwartz said, barely bothering to conceal his self-satisfaction. "Rainer, have you thrown out today's paper?" He knows perfectly well I keep a week's worth minimum in the basement. Today's was on a table near the door. I got up to fetch it. "Let me see the puzzle page." The only part he really gives his full attention to. I handed it to him. He'd done the crossword, the Jumble, the Boggle, and the Sudoku, as usual, ignoring the horoscope and the bridge column. He'd also done the Cryptoquip on the reverse side, and for all I knew, he'd read Dear Abby and Ask Carolyn. "How likely do you suppose it would be," Schwartz asked Hereford, "that a famous Vatican church would be mentioned in a puzzle on a given Sunday?"

Hereford knew he was being taken for a ride. "You mean the Sistine Chapel? Not likely, I suppose," he said, "but certainly possible."

"How likely that it would be mentioned in two different puzzles in the same paper on the same day?"

"Well..."

"The Jumble has six jumbled words with circled letters that complete the sentence 'After they cleaned up when Michelangelo was done painting the ceiling, it was a –' and of course the circled letters are rearranged to spell 'Pristine Chapel'. The crossword's clue 110 across is 'Like a famed Vatican chapel,' and the answer, equally obviously, is 'Sistine.'" Now, assuming that the crossword and Jumble authors didn't collude, which seems a safe bet, the two references to the Sistine Chapel are clearly a coincidence. A meaningless one, no doubt, but a real one. Therefore I'd appreciate it if you'd have the kindness to help me retain my respect for my clients by refraining from

225

parroting that nonsense about the nonexistence of coincidences."

It had been a long holiday weekend, and you want to make allowances, but it occurred to me that Schwartz was getting tired when he let 'retain/refrain' and 'nonexistence/coincidences' clutter his speech. Or maybe he just didn't feel like bothering.

Steven Hereford was objecting. "Still, I don't see that you've proved anything by that. A couple of references in the Sunday paper—"

"Any theory worth the name is disprovable, in theory, and one exception is sufficient to call for reassessment of the theory. The exception proves, in the sense of tests, the rule. Your theory was that there are no coincidences. Just because you hear it parroted by actors on television doesn't make it true. I just pointed out a coincidence; if a coincidence exists, this disproves the notion that there are no coincidences."

Schwartz leaned back. All four Herefords had sampled their iced tea. Stacy and her mother were ready for more, and I supplied it. Steven's glass was three-quarters full. Charles's was only an inch down, but at least he'd drunk some of it. It was obvious that Schwartz had had enough of the Hereford family, and now that the essential mission was accomplished, I could just see him trying to piss off the client. "Want another example? How about two? 'Yosemite,' as its pronunciation should make clear, has nothing to do with semites, Jew or Arab. And, regardless of pronunciation, Ashkenazi Jews are not, needless to say, Nazis. 'Yosemite' means 'killers,' which is one tribe's name for another, and 'Ashkenazi' refers to Germany, which was much of the Holy Roman Empire, sometimes called the Holy Roman Empire of the German Nation, or Sacrum Romanum Imperium Nationis Germanicæ, or das Heilige Römische Reich Deutscher Nation." Schwartz was being deliberately obnoxious now, and I saw that I'd better intercede if we wanted to keep the client long enough to send a bill. Anita and Steven looked as if they were wondering why they were there. Steven had slouched another inch.

"Granted that there are coincidences," I said, "we were discussing Stacy's return to her family."

Charles Hereford snapped, "To *his* family," and gave me one of his looks, defying me to throw him out. It was obvious he was never going to get over his conviction that I was an ill-mannered lout. I looked at Schwartz, and he shook his head briefly, so I tried to return Hereford's look with one of civilized manliness and greater confidence than I really felt. Once someone of a certain type has you pegged, there's very little you can do to change their mind. And there I was, taking his inventory for him. I held his gaze until he returned it to Schwartz.

"Now, what is this nonsense about Stacy?" he demanded. "I warn you, sir, if you have attempted some sort of 'deprogramming' my grandson, I'll have you in court—"

"There's no deprogramming to it, Grandpa," Stacy said. The three older Herefords turned to look at her. "You are all three engaged in a conspiracy, and you have been, my whole life, and you've been at it so long you believe it's true, but it's not. You don't have a grandson. I am not a man trapped in a woman's body. I am not a gay man in a woman's body. I'm a straight woman, or as straight as it's possible to be straight after twenty years of your craziness, your obsessive delusion. All of you, Mom, Dad, Grandpa—all of you are nuts! You did such a number on me that you had me convinced, so long as I lived at home, under your control, but it's not true, and I had to get away from you to realize that it was all nonsense." Her parents said nothing, just looked stunned. You'd have thought the topic had never been raised before.

Stacy stood up, turned to Schwartz, and asked, "Is my room upstairs still available, Mr. Schwartz?"

Schwartz nodded. "Of course, Ms. Hereford." She headed for the door, crossed the hall to the stairs. He nodded to me, glanced at Charles Hereford,

Charles erupted, "Goddamn you, it's 'Mr. Hereford,' you bastard! You've brainwashed my grandson, and I'll—" But I was there to help him out of his chair, whether he wanted to leave it or not. He was plenty wiry for a man his age, but I was able to get him to his feet without undue violence, and his son and daughter-in-law were getting up too. Believe it or not, I did a quick check to make sure all four glasses were still there. Anita and Steven managed to take charge of Charles and steer him out of the office, still sputtering, and I followed them to the door and closed it gratefully after them. I was glad I wouldn't have to share a ride back to Carmel with the three of them.

When I got back to the office, Schwartz had the carton ready for the glasses, with paper labels to affix to them. He held the pitcher while I siphoned the tea from the glasses, taking care not to contaminate anything. The carton had spacers to keep the glasses separated, and we got it packed and ready for—well, you really don't need to know who it was ready for. Getting DNA testing, especially unofficial, express service, is not actually illegal, but when you have a contact at a lab who is sufficiently grateful for services previously rendered that he'll rush your job and do it for free, you'd be doing them no favors by naming them. Let's leave some things unsaid. As I've mentioned, the detective business is about discretion, among other things. Besides, a former client who didn't get soaked in a blackmail case is unlikely to want publicity.

So, being discreet and all, we got the glasses the Herefords had used all packed, Schwartz took the pitcher to the kitchen to pour the tea into the sink, and I drove the package to a location not five miles from 7912 Forest Lane, and I explained that we'd be interested in what the saliva might tell us. Our former client said he could have results by close of business tomorrow unless it was a real rush job. I told him that would be fine, and I made a point of telling him the client, in this case, was loaded, so he shouldn't be shy about billing us. He said he wouldn't think of it; it was a privilege to assist Mr. Schwartz and myself on a case, and he hoped the results would be satisfactory. Funny how getting out from under a blackmailer affects a person's feelings. I told him it was a pleasure to see him and I hoped he and the family were all well, and he filled me in about his adorable grandchildren, and I assured him I'd give Mr. Schwartz his regards.

Chapter Twenty-Five

Schwartz picked up the call from Colin at about nine on Wednesday morning. There went May. Colin had had enough of time off, or enough of sun and surf, or maybe of just not working. He'd gotten our message and called to see what he could help us with. As I headed for the door, Schwartz was saying, "Oh, good, Mr. Beardsley. It's been a bit more than we can deal with here, but I'm sure you'll be able to handle it readily. No, it's no emergency; it's been waiting five days here and a while elsewhere before that, but Rainer is on his way to your office with it. I hope you'll find it an interesting problem."

I drove to Broad Ripple, handed Colin the thumb drive, and he said Schwartz had explained what we had. "There may be more than one file hidden," he said. "I'll check it right away, let you know what I find, okay?" I told him that was fine. One of the many things I like about Colin is his modesty. He tries to make you feel as if you're only handing him a problem because you have something more urgent to take care of; you could do it just as easy yourself, but you're kind enough to let him help out. Also, he never pads his bills.

Anyway, I left the thumb drive with Colin, and it took maybe ten minutes to drive back to Windcombe, and when I came into the office Schwartz was on the phone. It was Colin, letting Schwartz know how he was coming on the files. I thought he could at least have let me get home before calling to say he'd solved our problem. I got on the line with them. Colin said each photo had one embedded Excel file and a Word file of notes. He was printing out hard copies of all of them and copying the files themselves to disk. "I could email them to you," he said, "but I'd rather keep everything off the Cloud, if that's all the same to you."

"Of course, Mr. Beardsley," Schwartz said, "and we appreciate your discretion. Should I ask Rainer to pick them up while the car is still out?" I glared at him, but he didn't notice or pretended not to.

"You might give it another fifteen minutes," Colin said, "let me get it up to an even hour, and I'll print out a bill for you." He rang off, and Schwartz and I looked at each other.

Schwartz said, "Division of labor is a wonderful thing, Rainer, and other people have the right to make a living too. You can't be sore about Colin's expertise; after all, consider the things you can do that he can't."

"Sure," I said, "and by the way, you may recall that Colin has preferences regarding payment for small jobs."

"Of course. Get cash from the safe, and use your judgment. You know he tends to undervalue his services, not to mention his time. Don't be profligate, but—damn it, Rainer, you know what I mean." I nodded at the pig on my way to the safe, and Schwartz got out his wallet.

I drove down to Broad Ripple, parked in front of Colin's house and office, rang the bell. I identified myself, as if that were necessary, and the buzzer signaled that the door was open. He had the whole package ready: hard copies of the files, a disk, and the original thumb drive. The invoice was on top of the manila envelope. "She wasn't trying to make it hard to find," he said. "You can tell by the way she encrypted the files that she could have been a lot stealthier, if she'd wanted to. She just didn't want to leave everything out in the open."

"Okay," I said. "Are there any special features I need to know about, so we don't have to bother you again?"

He said, "Well," which was about the last of it I understood, until he finished with, "so no, not really; it's all pretty straightforward. And as you see, I have the invoice ready, and I gave you guys a break, seeing as how you're always good customers and basically make life more interesting, and—"

I glanced at the invoice, and of course, Schwartz was right; it was ridiculously low for what he'd done, so I got out the wallet and counted out double what he'd charged. He tried to object, but I told him, "In appreciation for your promptness and discretion, as always. I would hate to tell you how long I tried to find what was in there."

"Oh, of course," he said. "She was pretty good at it, you can tell, and while I certainly didn't peruse the files any more than necessary, I'd say she was a pretty damn good accountant. Good enough to catch—" He let it hang. "You'll see when you look at it. And as far as I'm concerned, I've never seen any of these files, or the thumb drive, for that matter."

"Excellent," I said, "and as mentioned, we appreciate your discretion."

Colin scooped the bills up and stuck them in his pocket. "No problem," he said. "After all, you were never here." He loves that line. He walked to the door with me, and we shook, and he closed the front door behind me. I have no idea what would happen to someone who tried to get past that locked door, but I doubt that it would be pleasant.

When I got back to the office, Schwartz was out back working on another rocket, an up-scale of the Estes Wacky Wriggler, which is a model rocket divided into half a dozen sections strung on a cord between the nose cone and the fin can. The sections are interlocking so that the pressure of the engine's thrust forces them together in a temporarily rigid cylinder, then when the ejection charge blows, the sections separate, a chute pops out, and the rocket returns to earth in pieces connected only by the cord.

His up-scale used plastic Folgers Coffee cans for the sections, with lids attached to the bottoms, the air-tight ridge cut out so that the cans were linked loosely. He had made the fins, which were parallelograms, out of lightweight plastic honeycomb sign material, and the nose cone was a shell made of single-sided corrugated cardboard built in concentric rings around a quarter-inch dowel. He was smoothing spackling compound over the SSCC, working from the tip downward toward the base, which was another Folgers can. I told him I had the files from Colin and I was going to take a look at them.

"Of course," he said, "and when appropriate, you might check with—" naming the grateful former client "—about the DNA samples." I said I would. I stood there a couple of minutes. There are few forms of entertainment that equal watching someone work who knows what they're doing. It's too bad there's no money in amateur rocketry. Well, there is money in it, but from our standpoint it's outgo, not income.

I tore myself away and got back to work before Schwartz had a chance to tell me to do so. I went into the office, got out the laptop that never interacts with the internet, and transferred the files Colin had found onto its hard drive. Since he'd taken the trouble to print hard copies, I thought I'd have a look at them, and I was glad I did. In fact, I didn't even get around to looking at the files on screen, just went over the paper. After half an hour or so, I realized Schwartz should have the same thing to look at, so I dusted off the old photocopier in the corner and ran the sheets through. I sorted his copies and clipped each of the spreadsheets to its text notations and set them on his desk blotter, half a dozen sets labeled "Charles," "Anita," "Stacy," "Family," "Gordon," and "Steven," staggered, with a Post-It note on the one at the right.

It took some willpower, but I went through the other five spreadsheets and Word notations, just to make sure there was nothing else hinky. There wasn't, so I was able to spend most of my time on the one that mattered. Colin had been right about Allison: she was a good accountant. She had to be good to catch what she'd caught. It was too bad she'd been too ready to think she could handle what she'd uncovered.

Schwartz came in only a few minutes after I had finished making notes about the files, printed them out, and laid a hard copy next to the other sheets on his desk. He sat down, glanced at the paper, and said, "I gather you've learned some things from all this."

"That I have," I said. "Allison Morgan was a good accountant, and she was honest, and she thought she could control things she couldn't, and that got her killed."

"Indeed." He picked up my summary notes, skimmed them, then read them over again, slowly. He laid that down, picked up the "Steven" hard copy, read Allison's notes carefully while I did my best not to be distracting. He went over the Excel spreadsheet, referring to her text file now and then. He picked up a pen, started to make a notation, but set it down without making a mark.

He looked up at me. "You realize, of course," he said, "that we are legally obligated to let the police have this."

"Well, yes," I said, "if it's relevant to their investigation. The question is, is it?"

"Oh, come now. Do you seriously have any doubt about it?"

"No."

"Good. Neither have I. It blows the lid right off the case, doesn't it?" He sighed. "Call Inspector Mercer, please."

I picked up my phone, ran down the list, and punched Mercer's number. It went to message. I called Steve Ripley's number and got him. "What do you want?" he answered rudely as Schwartz picked up the phone.

"Oh, nothing much," I said. "We just happen to have evidence regarding a murder, and—"

"The only murder I give a damn about," Ripley said, "is one we already have the perp for."

"Yes," Schwartz said, "and since the person you have incarcerated is, in fact, innocent, we thought you'd be interested in the evidence that exculpates him and focuses attention on the actual murderer."

Ripley uttered a couple syllables we needn't concern ourselves with, then was silent. Sure, they had Gordon Black locked up, but whatever he might think of Schwartz or, for that matter, me, he knew we weren't in the habit of making prank calls. Also he had heard Inspector Mercer say he wasn't convinced Gordon Black was it. The silence deepened. Finally, Schwartz said, "Mr. Ripley, are you there?"

"Yeah, I'm here," Sergeant Ripley said. "Evidence, you say? What kind of evidence?"

"Financial spreadsheets," Schwartz said, "with pertinent notes by the victim of the murder, which I'd be reluctant to discuss over the phone. Mr. Zufahl and I have an appointment this afternoon, but if you'd like to come by this evening—"

"By God," Ripley said, "if you're clowning about this, Schwartz, I'll—"

"Very well," Schwartz snapped. "We have attempted to fulfill our legal obligation to bring relevant evidence to the attention of the police, but if the police refuse to pay attention to that evidence, we will simply proceed—"

"No, goddammit, wait a minute," Ripley said. He was silent for a moment, thinking, no doubt. "I'll talk to the Inspector, and one of us will get back to you, probably within half an hour. I'm not sure where he is, but I'll find out. Hold on until you hear from us, all right?"

"Very well, sir," Schwartz said. "Have a good day."

There was a pause as Ripley considered various options, then he said, "Yeah, you too," and hung up. So did we.

I turned to Schwartz to ask him if we wanted to arrange a nice gathering, but the phone rang. I picked it up. It was our former client letting us know that he was done with the DNA analysis and had prepared a report. I told him I'd be right there to pick it up.

"While you're out," Schwartz said, "you might pick up dinner. What sounds good to you this evening?"

"Well, it's not exactly on the way, but I've been thinking about Chinese today."

"Excellent," he said, "I'd like Szechuan shrimp, with an order of pot stickers, and a spring roll." He handed me cash.

On the way to that address I'm not sharing with you, I called Chinese Inn and put in an order, adding egg fu yung, Szechuan beef, and more pot stickers to Schwartz's order. Jessica said it would be ready in twenty minutes, and I said I would be there then. I drove to the ex-client's house, and he gave me back the carton with the glasses in it, with a neatly typed report on top. I asked him what we owed, and he said nothing; he was eternally in our debt and all that. I told him Schwartz had told me that the next time we would insist on paying, and he said that, in that case, he would be happy to prepare an invoice for zero dollars and zero cents, and we could pay that in whatever way we liked. We shook on it. I don't care how corny it seems; it's nice to know somebody feels that way about you. I didn't look at the report.

Chinese Inn, however, is insistent about payment, which is fine, considering we'd get about three meals apiece from our order. As with the DNA report, I left the food alone, although it was pure torture, all the way from 96th and College down to Forest Boulevard, over to Windcombe Boulevard, then 79th, and Forest Lane. Schwartz came out to help carry the food and the other carton in.

As we laid out the food and set the table, Schwartz said that Steve Ripley had called back to say he and Inspector Mercer would be by at seven-thirty or eight. We had time to eat in a civilized manner. I had a number of questions I'd have liked to ask, but Schwartz doesn't like to discuss business during meals. He pays me, so we stuck to current news. He noted that the state legislature was having another go at the Kinsey Institute for Sex Research. "If they were capable of learning from history," he said, "they'd know that this has all happened before. Way back in the fifties, not that long after the Institute had been invited to the campus, some geniuses in the state legislature decided they could make political hay by attacking it. They invited the president of the university, Herman B. Wells, to come up for a talk, and they told him that they thought the state could do without the Kinsey Institute, that they'd consulted with the legal advisors, and the lawyers said that the legislature had the authority to decline to fund programs, such as the Kinsey Institute, that they deemed inappropriate, and what did he think about that?

"Dr. Wells told the legislators that he had also consulted the lawyers, and they agreed that the legislature could indeed shut down any programs it didn't care for by declining to fund them. Well, they hadn't expected that this would be so easy, and naturally it wasn't. Dr. Wells went on to say that he had consulted further with the lawyers, and they had assured him that, as president of Indiana University, if he believed that the university was being subjected to undue interference with academic freedom, he had the authority to shut down Indiana University.

"Now, Herman B. Wells was a lot of things, by any standard, but he was not widely noted as a wacky funster. One hesitates to make generalizations about elected officials, but apparently, even in a 1950s Indiana State Legislature, there was nobody quite stupid enough to think that Herman Wells would mention the idea of closing down IU just for grins. Nobody thought he was bluffing. So, after a certain amount of hemming and hawing, they thanked Dr. Wells for coming to visit with them and wished him a safe and pleasant journey back to Bloomington. He asked whether they wanted to discuss the Kinsey Institute further, but they assured him that, so far as they were concerned, the university was in his capable hands, and that was by God that."

"Well," I said, "that's a hell of a story. I wonder if the state legislature, or the current president of IU, remembers that."

"We'll see," he said. "My mother was a student at IU at the time, and it was one big deal back then." As he finished eating, he said, "I'd hate to bet that things are better, politically, now than they were in the 'fifties. And Dr. Wells has been gone a long, long time."

We talked further as we put away the leftovers and soaked the plates and utensils, and then the doorbell rang.

Through the one-way mirror on the front door, I saw law and order waiting on the stoop. I let Inspector Mercer and Sergeant Ripley in. They weren't chatty, but they weren't hostile either, since they were fully aware we wouldn't have made a claim like we had just for the hell of it. As usual Mercer took the red chair, and Ripley moved a yellow one so he sat with his back to the wall.

Schwartz had gotten the book of poetry from the cabinet where it had been locked up, and he explained, without extraneous detail, how it had come into our possession and how he had found the hidden compartment for the thumb drive. While he was talking, I printed a set of the Excel and Word files for them to take with them. He explained that we, that is, I, had tried to decrypt the pictures on the thumb drive, without success. "So you took it to your pal Beardsley, no doubt," Mercer growled.

"Indeed," Schwartz said, "and there's nothing culpable about that. Mr. Zufahl was able to open the PDFs, and he noticed that the file size of each was much greater than it would have been for simple pictures."

"And this was when?" Ripley wanted to know.

"Mr. Beardsley was out of town until yesterday," Schwartz said. "And until we knew for certain that there were files embedded in the pictures, we—"

"You kept it for yourself," Mercer said. "You had a book that the victim had given her ex-husband, and you kept it the hell to yourself for the better part of a week, until you could get your pet Geek Squad working on it."

"There was really no reason to consider the material suspicious," Schwartz began, but Mercer cut him off.

"You've got a goddam book of poetry with a hidden compartment cut out of it containing a thumb drive with files on it that are, that are…I mean, they're obviously larger files than they look like, so they're—"

"Anomalous," Schwartz said.

"Yeah, anomalous files on it, and you don't think the police could shed some light on it, so you save it for a week for Beardsley to decrypt. My God, Schwartz, that's pretty raw, even for you."

"We received the decrypted files only this morning, Mr. Mercer," Schwartz said, cool and calm, "and until we were able to examine them we had no reason to believe that they might shed light on Ms. Morgan's murder. Now that we have examined them, we are, of course, ready to turn them over to you."

"You're goddam right you're turning them over to us," Mercer said. I got up and retrieved the hard copies of the spreadsheets and textual notes and passed the whole stack to him. "What the hell is this?" he wanted to know.

"That," Schwartz said, leaning back, "is a set of hard copies of the files that were hidden in the six PDFs on the thumb drive. Five of them, so far as we have been able to tell, are perfectly innocuous. But the sixth is another matter. It's the spreadsheet labeled 'Steven Hereford' and the text labeled 'Steven Hereford Notes.'" He turned to me. "We haven't asked if you gentlemen would care for some iced tea. It may take a while to go over that material, and some refreshment might be welcome." Mercer just nodded, and I headed for the kitchen.

So help me, Steve Ripley came with me, offering to help. He probably wanted to make sure I didn't sneak out and let the air out of their tires. I carried the fresh pitcher of Constant Comment iced tea and the ice bucket, and he brought the glasses on a tray.

Schwartz was talking and Mercer was making pencil marks next to some lines on the spreadsheet. Schwartz had supplied him with a lightweight drawing board to lay his papers on. Ripley and I got the tea passed around and we sat down again, but Steve pulled his chair up to observe what Mercer was marking. "The point is," Schwartz was saying, "is that all but the 'Steven' spreadsheet balance; everything adds up, at least in a way. There are various seemingly innocuous but unexplained transfers out of the accounts. But 'Steven' does not. There are, how shall I put it, gaps. Amounts appear without explanation. Totals are greater than the sum of their parts." He shifted to the text notes. "If Ms. Morgan's analysis is correct, and I assume it is, Steven Hereford has 'borrowed' extensively from the accounts of other members of his family and even more extensively from the combined family account. Only Gordon Black's account shows no amounts unaccountably missing."

"So how much—" Mercer wanted to know.

"A hundred thousand here, two hundred thousand there, and almost a million from the family account. It comes to over one point three million, and that's just for the past year. Apparently Ms. Anita Hereford first hired Ms. Morgan to do the accounts only last year. There's no telling how much money was 'borrowed' previously."

"So you figure Steven Hereford killed Allison Morgan because she found out he was stealing from the rest of the family?" Mercer looked skeptical.

"Well, that may be how it worked," Schwartz said, "or it may be that Ms. Morgan let Steven Hereford know that she'd found out what he was up to."

"And maybe she tried to put the squeeze on him?"

"I would hope not," Schwartz said. "I would be sorry to find that a person of her ability would stoop to blackmail."

"She wouldn't be the first, you know."

"I would also be sorry to finger someone for killing a blackmailer, Mr. Mercer." Schwartz tapped the spreadsheet. "But from reading her notes about the spreadsheets, I get the definite impression that Ms. Morgan was taking the high road. She was going to report the facts as she had found them. She was going to expose Mr. Hereford, not squeeze him."

"So what was he using the money for?" Mercer asked. "To finance that cricket thing he's trying to get going?" He looked as if he couldn't think of anything less prepossessing than cricket.

"There's no way to tell from these figures where the money was going," Schwartz said. "He may have put it in overseas bank accounts; who knows?"

"There'll be some record somewhere," Mercer said. "Even if the money's all gone, it will leave a trail."

"And that, gentlemen," Schwartz said, "should be enough to exculpate Mr. Black."

Mercer nodded. "Okay, Schwartz," he said. "Accepting your explanation of the timing, which I might as well since I can't do anything about it, it makes a pretty good case. At least a start of a case."

"And Gordon Black," Schwartz said.

"Can be released once we have Steven Hereford in custody. Which we will take care of right away. Excuse me." He took out his phone, punched a number, and spoke. "This is Mercer, Jackson. Yeah. I need an arrest warrant, two IMPD officers, and a carful of Carmel cops who know how to behave with the country club set." He looked at his watch. "Yeah. For Steven Hereford. Right. You have the address handy? All right. Come to Leo Schwartz's office, 7912 Forest Lane. Right, a couple blocks east of College. Right. Meet me here, and Sergeant Ripley and I will lead the way. Okay. And remember, we're arresting a prominent citizen at his home in Carmel, so just tell the Carmel cops to meet us at—"

Schwartz suggested, "Gray Road and 126th Street."

"Have them meet us at Gray Road and 126th Street, okay? No names to them at this point, just in case. Right. Yeah, I doubt it too, but you never know, do you? It's always possible that, you know…. Yes, that should do it." He hung up.

"Are you that worried about the Carmel police?" Schwartz asked blandly.

Mercer didn't even take offense. "You never know," he said. He drank iced tea, reached once again for the phantom pack of cigarettes. "You know, at first, I really thought that Black kid was it. Ex-husband, drunk most of the time, probably pissed off. I don't know." He finished his tea. "Rifle right there in the closet, still loaded."

Schwartz, at least, tried to be sympathetic. "By the way, I noticed one item in the spreadsheet that might be traceable. Last September, there was a gun show here at the State Fairgrounds, and there's a withdrawal that would cover the cost of an AR-15 and a Russian Nagant Model 1895 revolver."

"What the hell is a Russian Nagant Model 1895 revolver?" Mercer wanted to know, "and what the hell has it got to do with this murder?" He picked up his empty glass, and I refilled it. "Hell, so Steven Hereford shoots Allison Morgan, probably from Black's own balcony while Black is passed out, wipes the rifle clean but leaves it, still loaded, in Black's closet."

"With his eyesight?" Schwartz asked. "He couldn't use a telescopic sight, especially at night. But close up…" He went on to outline his theory about using a silenced revolver, close up, and he showed Mercer his own Nagant, demonstrated its action, and let Mercer experience the very heavy trigger pull and the strength needed to cock the piece. He had got most of it explained when the IMPD car pulled up in the driveway.

Mercer got the papers gathered, and I gave him a manila envelope to put them in. He and Ripley left, spoke to the officers in the new car, and got in theirs. The other car backed out, Ripley pulled out in front of it, and they headed up Forest Lane and turned left on Forest Boulevard South Drive.

Chapter Twenty-Six

Well, the law was off to arrest Steven Hereford and Schwartz and I weren't invited to join them. I had just a moment to feel neglected, but then I thought of the DNA report we hadn't even looked at, and I perked up, although I had no idea what we were looking for. This was a nice example of Schwartz's fondness for not telling me why we were doing things, although I could speculate, naturally. After all, there are really only a small number of things DNA testing can tell you.

Schwartz took the typed report and read it while I ran the glasses back to the kitchen. It didn't take long. When I returned to the office he handed it to me. I sat down at my desk to go through the report. "Well, well," I said.

"Indeed," Schwartz said.

"So what put you onto it?" I asked him.

"Nothing substantive," he said. "Just a hint of intuition, I suppose. It occurred to me that not everything might be as it seemed, especially with people who belonged to the Mid-month Nature-study Club."

Not to keep you wondering, the report made it clear that Stacy's mother was indeed Anita, but her father was Charles, not Steven. Steven was Stacy's half-brother, not her father. Exactly what that meant to us, I had absolutely no idea. Schwartz said that the only real question was whether Stacy knew; we could assume that Charles certainly, Steven probably, and, of course, Anita definitely knew the score.

Schwartz set the report aside and looked at the clock. "We just have time to make it to Mercy Road," he said. It seemed like a good idea to me: the only AA meeting I know where cross-talk—talk directed to another alcoholic—is actively encouraged.

I drove, and on the way up to 116th Street Schwartz held forth further about his latest obsession. "The narrator and Legrand trade words about Legrand's lack of talent in drawing," he said, "and then the narrator hands the parchment back to Legrand, and the two of them never look at the parchment together. Legrand sees that the drawing—coincidentally exactly on the other side of the parchment from his sketch—is not the one he made, and after some decidedly odd behavior, he puts the parchment in a wallet and locks the wallet away in a drawer, something Captain Kidd would have been well-advised to have done himself.

"The part of the story where Legrand heats the parchment, bringing out the coded message, then decodes the message itself, is one of the few passages that actually seem to make sense. He sees the drawing of a baby goat, a kid, which tips him to whose message this is, and a message written in digits and punctuation marks, including parentheses, bracket, asterisk, dagger, double-dagger, and pilcrow—"

"'Pilcrow'?" I said.

"Or pilcraft, or paragraph mark," Schwartz explained. "How familiar these symbols would have been to a seventeenth-century pirate, I don't know. But at least the decoding makes sense. The message itself, of course, is another matter. Imagine invisible ink that survives a century of exposure to the weather. The treasure is buried on the mainland, not far from the island where the parchment was found. Are we supposed to believe that Kidd wrote the coded message on the parchment in invisible ink after burying the treasure but before returning to his ship? Or did he write it all out beforehand, then make sure to bury the treasure exactly where the code said it would be? And what's with the ruins of the boat, anyway? If the message was important enough to encode and then write out the encoded message in invisible ink on parchment, for whom was it intended? Was Kidd afraid he'd forget where the treasure had been buried? Was he leaving the message for someone else who would know how to warm up the parchment to make the coded message visible and who would then know how to decode the damn thing? And why would Kidd be so goddam careless with the precious parchment anyway? He just stuck it in a pocket so that the first time he had to blow his nose, he'd drag it out with his handkerchief. Please."

"Well," I said, "it does seem a bit unlikely, at that. But, look, it's hardly less likely than the coded agreement McElroy and Spall came up with, and that's real world. And by the way, you owe the pig a dollar when we get home." He ignored that sidebar.

It was a good meeting, with anonymity as the topic, even though neither Schwartz nor I spoke. Sometimes that's for the best. We spent a little time chatting with folks after the meeting. That one always goes by fast, with fifty to sixty or so men and women present. It's a popcorn-style meeting, meaning that rather than going around the room in seating order, anyone can contribute. It gets to be like an auction at times.

So, we drove back home with the windows down, very pleasant. Schwartz was seated at his desk and I was headed for mine when the house phone rang. It was Steve Ripley. "The inspector thought you deserved to know," he said, "that Steven Hereford was not at home when we arrived this evening, and neither was Stacy. Charles and Anita were home but say they have no idea where Steven and Stacy might be." There was a pause. "I don't suppose—"

"No," Schwartz said, "we certainly did not warn anyone that the police were coming. Why on earth would we? After sending you to arrest the killer of Allison Morgan? Please."

"Well, right," Ripley admitted. "That would be pretty pointless." He had a hard time accepting anything from Schwartz at face value. That at least was understandable.

* * *

The next morning Schwartz made buckwheat pancakes with wild-thyme honey, crisp bacon, and rye toast. We had finished washing up when the phone rang. Inspector Mercer wanted to know what we knew about his missing suspect and the suspect's daughter. Schwartz didn't enlighten Mercer about Stacy's true relationship to Steven, not to mention Charles, but told him we knew pretty much what he did, although we were probably

243

more conversant with how the killing was done.

Mercer wanted to know more about the mechanics of firing a .223 bullet from a .30-caliber revolver, and Schwartz explained the business of loading cartridges with saboted slugs that had been run through what was supposedly Black's AR-15. He said that the Nagant had been chosen because, being a revolver, there would be no ejected casings to worry about, and it was, so far as he knew, the only revolver that could be silenced. Mercer asked how we knew Hereford had a Nagant, and Schwartz told him we didn't; it just seemed the only piece of the puzzle that fit. What about the silencer? Mercer wanted to know, and Schwartz snapped that a person standing close enough to shoot someone in the back didn't want to attract a crowd, even in Broad Ripple on a Saturday night. He went on to say that getting the body into the canal was the surest way to obliterate any traces of powder burns or paper from the sabot, although with the type of silencer used those would have been minimal anyway.

I got the impression that Inspector Mercer was less than satisfied, but he didn't seem able to put anything further into words, and he just said, "Well, thanks so much for the instruction and, by the way, if you happen to hear from Steven Hereford, you will let us know, right?" Schwartz assured him pleasantly that we would call him immediately, should we run across his murderer. Mercer has a tough job, and even though he knows Schwartz is publicity-shy, he has a hard time putting up with either of us.

I called Anita Hereford just to ask whether there'd been any sign of Steven or Stacy, and she said no, neither of them had been heard from. She sounded like she was about at the end of her rope. I told her I'd let her know if we heard anything, but she made no promises. I couldn't hold it against her. Having the police show up to take your husband into custody is no picnic, even if the husband isn't on hand. Maybe especially; I don't know. Of course, the police had been through the house, and no matter how polite they'd been about it, that wasn't the sort of thing the Herefords were used to.

Schwartz gave me a nice list of errands to run, including the bank, the grocery, and Target, but asked if I could be back before noon. He wanted to hit the noon meeting at St. Luke's Methodist, the Brown Bag Discussion meeting. I said sure, and I made it pretty snappy getting the jobs done. I realized later he'd wanted some privacy for a phone call to Paul.

Meanwhile, Gina had come by with the kids, and I'd just missed seeing them. I felt bad about that; they're always mood improvers. Josh was slow to start talking, which Schwartz tells me is pretty usual for hearing children of Deaf parents, but he's catching up fast. I wonder whether his speech will rub off on his little sister or if she'll have a hard time getting a word in edgewise. I suppose we'll see.

Schwartz has said, way more than once, that his daughter saw him drunk, but his grandchildren never have, and he wants to keep it that way. One more reason to stay sober is a good thing.

Chapter Twenty-Seven

The AA meeting was coming up in a quarter hour or so. We'd left home in time for the pre-meeting meeting, casual conversation with others who'd arrived early. Schwartz was talking with Dinah, who was asking him questions about fireworks. It seemed her husband, Sean, was thinking about getting into pyrotechnics after seeing Schwartz's backyard display last year. Dinah wasn't sure it was a great idea, herself, but she wanted Schwartz's take on Sean's suitability to the hobby.

"Well, I don't really know Sean that well," he said, "but I seem to recall that he was smoking last July, and the truth is that you just can't smoke while you're making fireworks, so maybe it'd at least force him to refrain from smoking for whatever periods of time he spends with pyro activity. It's like in firearms and rocketry: the three most important rules are Safety, Safety, and Safety."

"I'm not sure he can go an hour without a cigarette," Dinah said.

"Well, a lot of things can be done in half-hour sessions," he said a bit doubtfully. "Most likely he'd spend the money on basic introductory the kit, which is a couple hundred or two and a quarter, something like that, and that would be comparable to how many cartons of, what's he smoke?"

"Marlboros," she said. "They're about sixty a carton."

"So the kit would run about the same as four cartons of cigarettes," Schwartz said. "How much does he smoke?"

"Oh, at least a pack a day, maybe a pack and a half."

"So the kit would cost less than a month's worth of Marlboros," he said, "so the worst that could happen, even if he didn't complete all the projects, it would sit there, and it wouldn't have cost him an arm and a leg."

"Now, that sounds like Sean," she said. "I can see him spend a bundle on it and then sort of just lose interest."

"If he gets just the kit and doesn't go nuts for expensive tools," Schwartz said, "it will limit the cost," not that that was advice he'd ever taken himself. He had bought an arbor press and built the pedestal for it, and the pressure gauge, not to mention a dozen or so tools for rockets, fountains, gerbs, and motors in diameters from quarter-inch to inch and a half, in eighth-inch increments up to one, quarter-inch thereafter. He had good-sized stores of fuels, oxidizers, and additives, aluminum in a dozen sizes of particles, from flakes to powder, magnalium, copper, steel, iron, zinc, and so the hell on. I should know; I regularly update the inventories. As I mentioned to Schwartz when he was looking into buying a couple suppressors, the ATFE has enough reason to check into his pyro supplies; signing up for the two-hundred-dollar tax stamp for each silencer would just wave another red flag. He ignored me. If I couldn't stand being ignored part of the time, I'd have a different job.

Actually, Schwartz typically had got in touch with the Bureau and discussed his fireworks plans and found out the storage requirements, and he'd coughed up for the solid steel, fire-resistant, lockable vaults, suitably protected from the weather to maintain structural and functional integrity, as required for completed, ready-to-use fireworks and for the various chemical constituents. He had as safe an operation as a factory making hundreds of times his output, and he liked to point out that most chemicals are pretty safe in isolation; you just want to be cautious about mixing them.

Personally, I don't see it. I like fireworks, all right. But the time, money, and effort Schwartz puts into it is his business. It's his hobby, among others, and he's never gotten into trouble with pyrotechnics, rocketry, firearms, or books. Running a private detective agency, like military service, on the other hand, has cost him in ways that don't show. I can't begrudge him relaxation, except when he's using the hobby to avoid work.

At any rate, it was time; we went in and got seated, and the meeting got started; Stanley read the AA Preamble, Beverly read How It Works, and Kathleen, who was chairing the meeting, asked for a topic. Virginia, a relative newcomer, maybe in her late twenties, suggested the First Step, which is "We admitted we were powerless over alcohol and that our lives had become unmanageable." I was a little surprised at that; Virginia tends, like a lot of newcomers, to stay pretty quiet and just soak up sobriety from the room. In fact, as Schwartz affirmed to me later, this was a very positive sign that she was beginning to feel part of the group, part of the fellowship of AA.

Kathleen asked who would like to start the discussion, and Daniel, an elderly man a few seats to our left, said that his name was Daniel and he was an alcoholic, and everyone said, "Hello, Daniel" or "Hi, Daniel" or whatever. He said that he appreciated the topic, that the First Step was always relevant to alcoholics, no matter how long it has been since their last drink. "It's interesting that we use time to say how far we are from the last drink, and we use space to say how far we are from the next one. I mean, I hope that last drink, my most recent drink, the one that I took twenty-four years ago, is the last drink I ever take, but the fact is that the next drink is waiting there for me, only a hand's reach from my mouth. Two dozen years since the most recent one, less than a yard to the next one." He looked around, probably to check people's faces, making sure he at least seemed to be making sense. I know that feeling.

"'Powerless over alcohol'? Well, I'd say to myself, as I poured the first drink of the day, 'I won't get drunk tonight.' If you are pouring a drink, that's a pretty pointless thing to say, since every day before has started out with a drink, then another, and so on, to pass-out time. And if you don't intend to get drunk, why are you pouring the first drink? You never have *a* drink. And was my life unmanageable? Well, I was doing things I didn't want to do, and I wasn't doing things I wanted to do. That's unmanageable." He looked around again. "Anyway, that's quite enough out of me." He beat the timer by four seconds. Everyone thanked Daniel.

Chris, late teens or early twenties, to Daniel's right, said she would just listen, and when you're still feeling the aftermath of detox, that's often not a bad idea at all, and we thanked her.

Sid, one closer to us, around forty or so, gave his name and his reason for being there and added his sobriety date. He had a few months over five years of continuous sobriety. He said, "I have to agree with Daniel: I had no choice in the matter. Having a drink seemed the only option. I'd had a drink every other goddam night for the last fifteen years, so it seemed the normal, natural thing to do. I was a goddam robot that turned booze into hangovers, dry heaves, blackouts, piss, and regrets. Isak Dinesen got it pretty much right: 'What is man, when you come to consider the matter, but an ingenious mechanism for transforming, with infinite variety, the red wine of Shiraz into urine?'" A deep sigh from Schwartz informed me that Sid was not quoting quite correctly. Okay, I thought, we'll doubtless look that one up when we get home. "Not just red wine either, lady: wine, beer, every kind of hard liquor, and it's all about a chemical, alcohol, that turned me into an orangutan with shoes on. God, the things I did drunk that no sane person would do."

He said that was enough out of him. To his right, the other side of Schwartz, Patricia, about sixty, said, "I agree with what's been said. I had no choice: I had to drink. There was no alternative; I had no idea how to get through a day, any day, without a drink. Now, it's different. I am no longer powerless over alcohol, because I don't drink it. I have a choice now: I can decide not to drink today. Maybe I'll decide to have a drink tomorrow, but today I decide not to drink. It's my free decision, my choice, not to drink, rather than to drink and ruin my life completely. I tell you, the things I did drinking, things I did drunk, I don't want to ever do again, and I'm lucky I got out of it when I did. I have had enough of being alcohol's bitch. I'm done." That last could have meant she was done with drinking or done with talking, probably both.

We told her thanks, then Schwartz said his name was Leo, and he was an alcoholic. "I think this is turning out to be a great meeting today," he said. "Great topic. I had a hard time realizing the core importance of AA meetings, helping me get over my terminal uniqueness, helping me understand the fundamental fact that I'm not alone, I'm just one of a lot of people doing this together, I'm part of a voluntary fellowship of people who have the same problem with alcohol, and by staying in touch with my sponsor and with other alcoholics, by spending time with people who are dealing with their problem, which is the same problem I'm dealing with, I find it easier, friendlier, pleasanter, more enjoyable, to live life sober rather than to crawl back inside the bottle. It's utterly amazing to me that I actually know people who come to meetings and do things together outside meetings, and these people actually come to the meetings and do outside things, and it's all about our staying sober.

"Thanks for showing up for this meeting, to help me stay sober. I pass."

We thanked Leo, and it was my turn to share. I don't know what it is, but I can come up with these brilliant insights and pithy slogans and all that, while the conversation is going around, and the minute it's my turn to share, my mind becomes a blank slate, and no chalk in sight. "I'm Rainer, and I'm an alcoholic," I said, "and I'd also like to thank you all for showing up to help me stay sober. The fact is, on my own, I drink, and I drink alcoholically, not normally, not socially. I'm an antisocial drinker. I need you guys to stay sober. By myself, alone, on my own, *I* will drink. *We* stay sober. Thanks for coming here today to help me stay sober."

I was thanked, and it was Abdel's turn to share. He's about thirty, from Lebanon, that is, from the country, not Lebanon, Indiana, the county seat of Boone County, although he told me once he'd driven up to Lebanon to see what it was like, and he said it was as unlike anything in the country he came from as one could imagine. As a fluent speaker of Oxbridge English as well as Arabic, both local and standard, and French, and as he put it, enough Hebrew and Greek to get in trouble, he'd come to Indiana as a technician installing and servicing computer systems for law firms, medical practices, and other quasi-professional businesses. Less than a month after he arrived here, he'd been hired away by a customer, which had meant, as he put it to me once at Bazbeaux, a nice improvement in his income and "sudden access to multiple ways to ruin my life. Do you know what it's like to be an Arab in Indiana? How about an alcoholic Arab in Indiana? Or an atheist Arab in Indiana? Or an alcoholic atheist Arab?" He diagrammed the terms on a paper napkin:

alcoholic Arab atheist
alcoholic atheist Arab
Arab alcoholic atheist
Arab atheist alcoholic
atheist alcoholic Arab
atheist Arab alcoholic

"We have six combinations of three words, arranged as adjective-adjective-noun, and to be honest, I try to see subtle distinctions, but they don't really exist, because...." He added a word to each line:

alcoholic Arab atheist person
alcoholic atheist Arab person
Arab alcoholic atheist person
Arab atheist alcoholic person
atheist alcoholic Arab person
atheist Arab alcoholic person

"So you see it's actually three adjectives and a noun, and it really doesn't matter what order the descriptors occur, the facts that I'm an Arab, an alcoholic, and an atheist are all equally true. So many reasons to be disliked. But the truth is, I don't drink, and I don't criticize, much less threaten, another person's religious beliefs."

That was at Bazbeaux, several months ago, and I'd kept the napkin. Now, Abdel was sharing. "I believe what I believe, you believe what you believe, and what's important is not our beliefs, but rather how we behave, how we treat other people, alcoholics and earth-people alike."

Abdel shook his head a bit, sadly. "It's okay for different people to believe different things; it seems to me that we need to leave each others' beliefs alone. I think that's the first step in civility. In cities, we have lots of people living close to each other, and civility is the art of living in a city gracefully and well. Difference of opinion is healthy; it makes horse races possible. We need to leave each others' beliefs alone and yet be ready to help out anyone who might be in need of it. I really don't think it matters what we believe about God. I think what matters is how we treat each other, period. Nobody in this room cares two hoots about my beliefs. My behavior is what matters. And that is definitely enough out of me."

Thanks, Abdel. Hello, Hester. "I can't believe, looking back at it, that I not only tried to help raise two kids, stay married to my husband, and hold down a steady full-time job and do it drunk most of the time, but I actually pulled it off pretty well. I mean, the girls were six and eight when I finally realized it wasn't working, and I had to do something about my drinking. I was a wine snob, boy. I drank almost only good California whites and reds and roses and blushes and, on occasion, wines not so good, but at least as powerful, and yes, I was powerless over alcohol as long as I kept pouring it down my throat. And my job, my marriage, my house, my kids, were all teetering on the verge of disaster. The girls are grown now, one a senior at North Central and one a sophomore at IU. But if I want to destroy my marriage and my career and what's left of my life, I can take a drink. No, thanks."

The sharing went on for another ten minutes, we joined hands, said the Our Father and ended with "It works if you work it." I chatted with Abdel a while after the meeting. He said it was difficult for him to have a social life; I gathered from things he'd said that alcoholics are even less popular within the Muslim community than elsewhere in central Indiana. Pleasant as life in this neck of the woods can be, Naptown is not a Mecca of tolerance and understanding. Nor, it seems, is Mecca.

"I mean, I want to fit in," he said to me and Robert, who had come over. "I dress American, I behave American, but the fact is that white Americans notice that my skin is by no means pale. American women don't want to go out with some guy who will drag them off to life in the eleventh century, and I can't blame them. And women in the local Arab community do not date. I know, I bore you with my complaints; I'm turning into an embittered, tiresome old man."

Robert said, "I wouldn't call you old, man."

"Thanks." Abdel had a pleasant voice and a nice sense of irony. "I suppose…" I would have liked to hear what he supposed, but just then, Leo got my attention, and we headed for the door.

"I apologize for dragging you away," Schwartz said, "but I'm afraid you were not aware that Robert was going to try to date up Abdel."

"Oh," I said. "I knew Robert was gay, but Abdel has always seemed straight."

"Abdel has that quality very few people have fully: he's like a mirror of the person or persons he's interacting with. You see yourself reflected in him, and only yourself. Most of us are people-pleasers; we want to please, by whatever means necessary, and we try so hard we mess it up, and it's very unsatisfactory for everyone. But Abdel is a very interesting fellow, in my opinion. If I were gay, he would definitely be my type."

I freely admit I have zero gaydar. I don't know why, but subtle signs that most people get elude me. I stood and talked with Schwartz, next to the car, and we watched Abdel's Toronto Orange Chevette follow Robert's red Ram onto 86th Street, then over to Meridian and north toward downtown Carmel. Schwartz said, "Maybe it will work out for them, who knows?"

"Who knows, indeed?" I said. "I really would like to see things go well for Abdel. The guy deserves a life, and I hope it turns out okay."

We went home to a late lunch, for us, which was not at all bad. Gina had left a casserole of pasta and meatballs, sausage, tomato sauce, cheese, olive oil, and herbs, and it was heavenly. I washed up while Schwartz put the last remnants of the leftovers away. "Enough for another lunch for two," he said. "We may need to be here at midday tomorrow."

"I don't suppose you'd like to let me in on what's going to happen tomorrow," I said.

"Well, if you insist," he said, sitting down at the table, tea in hand. "I suppose I really should, at that." I drank iced tea with him as he explained what was next. It was actually quite pleasant, feeling that I was needed for the occasion. "That feeling of uselessness and self-pity will disappear," indeed.

Chapter Twenty-Eight

Schwartz explained what we were up to, and, without liking it, I could understand that he hadn't wanted to burden me with excessive details. Paul had managed, legally if not quite ethically, to find out when the Hereford house had been built, by whom, and what the plans showed. It had cost a few well-distributed bucks, but it seemed worth it, even if we could never bill Anita for finding her son, excuse me, daughter.

"So," he said, "we have a pretty good idea where Steven is, and, in all likelihood, Stacy, as well. I'd feel bad about letting that wretch escape, but I'd feel even worse if harm came to her. I think we might want to call Mr. Mercer."

I tried to get in touch with Mercer but was told he was in a meeting and couldn't be interrupted. I tried Steve Ripley, but he wasn't available either. As I had feared, the unavailability of the cops gave my boss an excuse to fall back on his current favorite topic. He leaned back and got comfortable.

"Any way you look at it," Schwartz said, "it makes no sense at all." He tapped the stack of books on his desk pad. "And that business in the message itself about sitting in the bishop's hostel or castle or whatever it is, looking in such and such a direction with a telescope, with the implication that you can only see that skull on the seventh limb up on the left from that particular vantage point... Did Captain Kidd climb the tree and nail the skull to the limb himself, then discover it could only be seen from that one place? Or did he locate the seat and look around for a limb that he somehow knew couldn't be seen from any other point, and only then climb up and put the skull there? Neither sequence makes the slightest bit of sense; there's no way either version of events is feasible, probable, or even conceivable.

"And anyway, ignoring all that, suppose that he gets one of his assistants to climb the tree and reach the seventh limb on the left and nail the skull there, the limb has to be thick enough that, a hundred years later, after it's died, which Jupiter has told him it has done, it will still support the weight of Jupiter, who is clearly a good-sized man if he can climb that blessed big tree. We're expected to believe that the difference between a bullet dropped from the left eye of the skull and one dropped from the right eye is only three inches. So that dead limb is no more than three inches thick at the point where the skull has been attached. Yeah, right.

"And again, about that skull. It has to have been altered, since the eye socket holds and protects the eyeball. If Jupiter—or anyone else—dropped the gold bug or a lead bullet into one of the eyes of an unaltered skull, it would just stay there. The bones forming the back of the eye socket, through which the optic nerve passes, would have held such an object. So apparently, Captain Kidd removed that rear part of the eye socket so a bullet could be dropped through it. Gross, but necessary, and you'd think that someone as morbid as Poe would have latched onto that factoid. But no, there's no mention of any such alteration, probably because Jupiter was engaged in dropping the gold bug through the eye, and the skull was fixed facing away from him, outward from the tree. It's not mentioned whether the mandible was included with the skull, but at any rate, the bug falls through the skull, apparently undeflected by the dead limb it's nailed to and is lowered to the ground, and Legrand drives a peg at that point. Measuring out fifty feet from the nearest point on the base of the tree through the peg supposedly locates the buried treasure."

I was just about ready to reach for a gun myself when the phone rang. It was Sergeant Ripley. He filled us in on their morning. Apparently, it had been a really jolly meeting in the Deputy Mayor's office, with all the top brass explaining to him and, more to the point, to Inspector Mercer that the Hereford lawyers had been really emphatic about the consequences of accusing an upstanding tax-payer like Steven Hereford of jaywalking, much less murder. Never mind that Hereford was a resident of Hamilton County, not Marion; his many business interests were so crucial to the health and well-being of central Indiana that the mere whisper of iniquity was not to be tolerated. And never mind that he couldn't be found. And so on. As Ripley put it, the fix was in.

Schwartz said he doubted that the fix would stay in, but Ripley had spent the morning getting his ass chewing second- and first-hand, and he sounded, if not cowed, then certainly discouraged. Being an honest cop is by no means always easy, and Schwartz was clearly controlling himself on the phone. He knows Mercer and Ripley as well as anyone who doesn't actually work with or live with them, and it was obvious he was sorry to have been one of the causes of their situation.

Ripley finished up, said he was going to see if the inspector wanted a quiet drink, didn't make a point of the fact that he wasn't inviting us to join them, and hung up.

"Well," Schwartz said, hanging up his phone, "that wasn't entirely unexpected. But the fact is, we now know where Steven Hereford most likely is, perhaps where Stacy is as well. So what do we do about it?"

"I say we go get them," I said.

"With what to open the door? We have the plans for the house; we know where the secret panic room is and how to reach it, but how do we get into the house? Stealth? No chance. They, or at least he, will be expecting us."

"Look," I said, "Iris knows everybody, and I'd bet you she knows someone inside the gate."

Schwartz looked at me steadily for a minute. "Really? Someone she could ask for a favor like that?" He didn't like the idea of owing Iris a favor.

"I'd think so," I said. "Let me give her a call."

He nodded, and I used my cell rather than the office phone. She answered on the second ring.

"Do you know how long it's been since you called?" Iris demanded. "I don't know why I even answered your call, Rainer. I mean, granted, I have other things to do—"

"Iris, my sweet, I come on bended knee to beg a favor of you."

"I just bet your knee is bended," she said. "Naturally, you call when you want a favor." It went on like that for a while, and I thought Schwartz was going to throw something at me, so I tried to get around to the point.

When I finally got through to her that we really did need her help, that did the trick. "Let's see, who do I know well enough to ask a favor who has the bad taste to live in that godawful, pretentious, so-called community? Oh, sure, Jamie Atchinson. You know her; you met her at the Art League fund-raiser last year."

I said I couldn't place her. "Oh, you know, the woman who does those pastel pseudo-Mondrians, freehand, mind you; no tape." The light came on. This was not someone I'd trust to walk my dog, if I had a dog, much less trust to get us past armed guards.

"Oh, I don't know, Iris, I'm not sure she'd be—"

"Oh, get serious, Rainer; it's just a little favor. She'll be delighted to help on a case."

"'Help on a case'?" I said. "She'll blab all over Carmel that—"

"No, she won't," and I noticed an icy quality to Iris's voice that hadn't been there before. "You've got to get over the idea—"

"Okay, okay," I said. "Can you arrange for her to tell the guards at the gate that she's expecting us? I mean, they've seen us before, coming to the—well, coming to another residence. Can she be convincing enough to get us past the front gate?"

"Oh, sure," Iris said. "I'll tell her you're undercover, on a job, and it all hangs on her telling the guard who calls that she is expecting you."

"Well, that has the advantage of being perfectly true," I said. "We should tell the guard that we're expected at the Atchinson residence, by Ms. Jamie Atchinson, and—"

"You'd better say by Mr. Stuart Atchinson," she said. "Or by Mrs. Stuart Atchinson. Yes, I know. It's the twenty-first century, but some habits die hard with some people."

"All right, light of my life," I said. "What's her address, in case we're asked?"

Iris gave me the address and promised to call Jamie right away and set it up. She said if there was a hitch or she couldn't get in touch with Jamie, she'd call right back; if we didn't hear back from her, it was a go. We finished with the amenities and hung up.

Schwartz had only heard my end of the call, but it was enough. He was ready with some pointed comments, when the phone rang, not five minutes after I'd hung up with Iris. It was Iris. She said it had occurred to her that, although she'd said not hearing from her meant everything was all right, we might worry that something had happened. I asked her if Mrs. Stuart Atchinson was expecting us, and she said no, but Mrs. Atchinson had told the guard at the gate that she was, and her name would get us in.

I thanked Iris, said I'd let her know how things went when I had a chance, and she told me to give her a call if we needed bail.

Schwartz called Paul Surcutt to arrange a set of text messages. There were half a dozen messages; all Schwartz had to do was text Paul the appropriate digit, and Paul would take the necessary steps. If Schwartz needed to elaborate, he could do so in the text, following the message number. It struck me as unnecessarily elaborate to drag Paul in on this, but fortunately, as it turned out, Schwartz overruled me.

Schwartz said we'd probably want to be as quiet as possible, and that included firearms. He went to the cabinet in the basement and came back with the two suppressors he's legally entitled to own. By the way, you probably know this, but the correct term is 'suppressor,' not 'silencer,' since the device lowers but doesn't eliminate the sound. If you want to buy one, go to a gun store, pay your money, get photographed and fingerprinted, pay another two hundred dollars for the tax stamp, one per suppressor, and wait about a year.

"I should have had the foresight to get a .40 and a .45," Schwartz said, and I wasn't in any position to argue. I'd been against getting suppressors at all, but a couple of years ago, he'd gone ahead and bought a Gemtech suppressor for a .22 and a SilencerCo for a .380, which would also work for a 9 mm. People think suppressors are all James Bond, silent assassin devices, but the mundane truth is that the legislation was passed back in the '30s, during the Great Depression. People were using suppressors on rifles, poaching game from the wooded estates of the wealthy, just to put meat on the table. So naturally, those who didn't have to shoot their food got laws passed, and anyone who couldn't shell out two hundred bucks plus the cost of the device itself could do without. As Schwartz likes to quote someone or other, "the law forbids rich and poor alike to sleep under bridges."

Anyway, Schwartz got his S&W M&P Bodyguard .380 and attached the suppressor to it, and I did the same for the Walther P22, and he talked while we waited for twilight. At this time of year, that's pretty late.

"Now Poe's trigonometry gets crazy," Schwartz said, as if I'd never go crazy listening to him go on about literature. "It's not stated how far the gold bug falls from the tree, but choosing the wrong eye throws things off enough that the first dig misses the treasure entirely. When Legrand realizes that Jupiter has confused left and right, his correction is explicitly only about three inches, that is, about the distance between an adult's eyes, pupil to pupil. Again, the line is drawn from the tree through the peg, out fifty feet. According to the narrator, this moves the dig 'several yards.' The smallest construction that I can place on 'several' yards would be 'three,' and that's pushing it. Let's say it's three yards, or nine feet. So the distance from the tree to the peg is to three inches, or one-quarter of a foot, as fifty feet is to nine feet." Schwartz wrote on his memo pad:

$d/3" = 50'/9'$

$d/\frac{1}{4}' = 50'/9'$

$4d = 50'/9$

$d = 50'/36 = 1.3888...' = 1'-4\frac{2}{3}"$

"By giving the distance from the tree to the dig as only fifty feet and the change in the peg as only three inches, Poe has painted himself into a corner. How on earth could one determine the 'nearest point' of the tree to the peg so exactly? It just doesn't work."

Schwartz snorted. "Never mind that a hundred years have gone by, and the parchment with its invisible ink intact after a century's stormy weather is still legible once it's heated up just right, how the hell does a tulip tree's size remain unchanged, and a skull stay nailed to a dead limb and—oh, and by the way, how on earth did someone, Kidd or accomplice, manage to climb up there and nail a skull to a limb with a spike long enough—a foot or so, I'd estimate—without breaking the limb or falling out of the tree?"

"I think I'm beginning to see what you're getting at," I ventured.

"My God, I'd hope so," Schwartz said. "All that stuff I've said about fiction having to be plausible, whereas reality doesn't—forget it. I was wrong. Poe may have deliberately set out to pile up as many implausibilities as he could, for all I know. The real point is that it just doesn't matter: if the storyteller is good enough, and God knows Poe was good enough, no matter how many times the bastard uses the n-word, all the improbabilities just don't matter. Okay; I owe the pig another dollar as well. Do you or I or any rational being believe Captain Kidd drew a juvenile goat as a demibuttocked rebus of his own name, and a freaking skull to make sure we know it's a pirate's coded message?"

"I notice," I said, giving away the fact that his obsession with the story had led to my actually reading it, "that the n-word occurs only in Jupiter's speech. Legrand uses lowercase 'negro,' which nowadays is itself considered offensive, of course, even capitalized, except by the UNCF, I suppose, and I think the narrator does too, but neither of the white men would be so vulgar as to say the really bad n-word."

"I think that's one subtlety we should grant Poe," Schwartz said, getting his wallet out. He took two dollar bills out and stuffed them into the slot on the pig's mouth. "I'm going to have a very wealthy grandson one of these days." He glanced out the window. It was getting dark and would be by the time we got there.

We went to the garage. I drove the Prius, just in case we ended up needing to leave in a hurry. That mild-looking baby has a bomb under the hood. We headed up Meridian to Carmel, went over 126th Street, and turned in at the guard's gate. As previously, one guard came out, and the other stayed inside the booth, and he didn't even try to act like he didn't have a weapon on his lap. They took security seriously, which, after all, is a good, healthy, sensible attitude. As Schwartz remarked after they'd checked with Mrs. Stuart Atchinson, security would be a lot more effective if people didn't find it inconvenient. We drove toward the Atchinson house, on the same side of the compound at the Hereford place, which we found quite convenient. We didn't have to put on a show for the guards.

I drove past the Atchinson residence on the way to the Hereford place, but then Schwartz had an idea. He surprised me. He'd got the Atchinson phone number when I talked with Iris, and he called, putting it on speaker. Ms. or Mrs. Atchinson answered. He identified himself, and she sounded as if she'd been hoping he'd call. He said, "As I believe Ms. Warner explained, we're working a case, Ms. Atchinson—"

"Oh, please call me Jamie."

He didn't even make a face. "Sure, Jamie. We're working a case, and we may need to leave our car somewhere while we approach the house, and I wonder—"

"You could leave it here," Jamie said. "There's a circle in front of the house— " As Schwartz had noticed when we drove past. "—or you could park inside the garage. My husband is out tonight, and—"

"Actually, in front of your house would be ideal," Schwartz said. "As you know, our cover story is that we're calling on you, and—"

"Great!" We were really making Jamie's day. "If you're going to the Hereford house, you could come in the front door here and go out the back way, and it's not too far at all." We hadn't mentioned the Hereford house. Thanks, Iris.

"That would be perfect," Schwartz said. "We're only a couple of minutes away."

"I'll see you then," she said. "Looking forward to it." We rang off.

"She'll probably bake cookies," Schwartz remarked.

"Well, it'll be good to have somewhere that's not suspicious to park the car," I said.

"Certainly," he said. "Of course, if we were half smart, we'd have thought of that ourselves, rather than having to rely on the intelligence of Ms. Warner's friend Jamie."

"Yeah, but it's sounding like she's our friend Jamie too."

Chapter Twenty-Nine

We returned to the Atchinson house, pulled in the drive, which curved around in a circle in front big enough to set Schwartz's house in, along with the lawn and shrubbery and trees. Schwartz muttered, "Neo-Georgian" as we got out and went up the entry path. I was reaching for the bell when the door opened wide. "Mr. Schwartz, Mr. Zufahl, do come in!" Ms. Atchinson said, loud enough to tip off the neighbors. We were really playing this one to the hilt.

Schwartz and I went in, and our hostess closed the door. "Can I offer you something to drink?" she asked, then she corrected herself, "But you don't drink on duty, do you?" It was becoming clear that she wasn't on duty herself. "But that doesn't apply to private detectives, does it, now?" she went on.

Schwartz said, "In this case, Jamie, we're trying to stay sharp, so thank you, but we'd better pass for now." For just a second, I thought he was going to tell her we were alcoholics, but of course, he'd realized we didn't want to get involved in a history of AA at this point. "I wonder," he said to her, "if you know Anita Hereford well enough to call her and make sure she's all right."

Jamie nodded, but said, "You know, Mr. Schwartz, I know Anita, and I like her, but I don't think I have her number on my phone." Schwartz held up his phone, she held up hers, and shortly she did have Anita's number. It rang and rang, didn't go to message, and no one picked up. Schwartz looked at me, then at Jamie, then me again.

"That's not good," I said. "Would you have Stacy's number?"

"No, but you do," Schwartz said. I tried it; got the same: rings but no answer.

"I'm afraid," Schwartz said to Jamie, "we need to get over there, and we may need to get inside the house without—"

"If it will help, Mr. Schwartz," Jamie said, "I can tell the police I tried calling and called you." Neither Schwartz nor I said so, but that would be about as much help as waterwings, but why hurt the feelings of someone who wants to help?

Schwartz just nodded to her, and he told her, "We would like to leave inconspicuously, Jamie, and we may need to pick up our car in a hurry, so don't count on seeing us again soon. You've been a great help. Many thanks, and Anita Hereford will probably want to thank you too."

"It was my pleasure," she said, and I bet it was at that. She explained the layout of backyards, hedges, fences, and so on, and how to get over to the Hereford house. She asked if we had a flashlight; Schwartz had his and showed it to her. She asked if he'd put new batteries in it, and he didn't even get short with her, just assured her he had. She paused a moment, as if trying to think what, if anything, we'd forgotten, then she led us down the hallway to a kitchen the size of Schwartz's office, and let us out the back door. "Be careful," she whispered once we were headed across the back yard. I waved assent to her, and we disappeared into the dark.

Schwartz is good at night work, and I think I know where he got that way, which is why we never discuss it. He was in the lead all the way, and we found that, whatever else you might think about gated communities, this one had really well-maintained back yards. We had to detour around a koi pond at one point, and I was glad Schwartz was in the lead.

It couldn't have been more than a quarter-hour, and Schwartz had slackened the pace, when I realized we were approaching the Hereford residence from the rear. Schwartz stopped, got close to my ear, whispered, "Now we'll see about their security." He put on surgical gloves. So did I.

He went to a back door that opened onto the patio and swimming pool, got close to it, shone the light on it briefly, tried it, and it opened. "Easy," he said. "Too damn easy." He eased the door wider. "If there's an alarm," he whispered, "it's a silent one." He went in, and I followed. Technically it was still entering, and the law was not on our side.

We were in what would have been the mud room in a more modest dwelling; God only knows what the Herefords called it, if anything. The room and adjoining hallway and kitchen were dark. With Schwartz leading the way, we headed down the hall, staying close to the wall on our right, going around a seemingly interminable series of tables and stands holding vases of flowers, small statues, and vases without flowers. I decided that if I were ever a millionaire, I'd go for a clutter-free approach to interior decorating. Then I decided that there was no point in being so considerate of burglars.

Well down the corridor, light shone into the hallway from a room on the right. I guessed it was the room where Charles Hereford had made it clear that he wasn't interested in hiring us, not that we'd asked him to. Schwartz stood a moment, then pointed in that direction, held up a finger, pointed to himself, then pointed right. He held up two fingers, then me, and then I shook my head. I wasn't getting it at all.

Schwartz leaned close, whispered, "I'll go in by way of the adjoining room here on our right—" It was dark as hell, so I was glad I wouldn't be trying to make my way through it without knocking something over. "—You count fifteen seconds from when I give the signal as I go in there, and on fifteen you go in that door." He pointed at the beam of light into the hallway. "Try not to shoot the client," he said, then he stepped quietly forward, toward the dark doorway. He held up a finger, then started in. I began counting, slowly stepping down the corridor toward the light.

"Fourteen. Fifteen," I said to myself, and I swung into the lighted room. Charles Hereford lay sprawled in an armchair, head back, face upward, mouth open. An upside-down saucer and an upset teacup lay nearby. Anita Hereford lay prone, face to her left, between a spilled cup and saucer. Schwartz was entering the room from the connecting doorway on my right. I got to Charles, he to Anita, and we checked them. They were breathing but unconscious. Schwartz murmured, "Watch for interruptions," as he took out his phone.

I stood there, ready to face down anyone who'd disturb my boss while texting. He let Paul know the situation, muttering while he texted, so I knew he'd asked Paul to send cops and ambulances with EMTs, and all. "We've got a few minutes," he said as he put the phone away. "Let's not waste them. God knows what was in those coffee cups. I wonder where Donovon is, and the rest of the staff."

I thought that was a pretty good question myself. Schwartz went to the front door, unlocked it, turned on the front lights, and turned back to face me. "The panic room is on the second floor, toward the back," he said, "and I'm assuming that's where Steven is, with Stacy. It's accessible from Charles's bedroom in front, and from there there's a back way down a narrow stairway to the basement. According to the plans, the stairway from the ground floor runs under the stairs from the safety room. Of course, both doors lock from the inside. If I go upstairs and attack the door from Charles's room, maybe Steven will get spooked into taking off by the back way, with or without Stacy. What do you think?"

"I don't know," I said. "Steven might try to stay holed up with Stacy."

"Right," he said. "If he's still there when the police come, it'll be up to them to deal with him. I'd like to have Stacy safe when they get here, if that's all right with you. I think it's worth a try."

"Okay, I agree. You're right; it's worth a try. Stacy's safety is the main thing, right?"

"Absolutely. I'm afraid if he thinks he's cornered, and he will be, with no way out, he'll just try to take her with him."

"To hell with that," I said. "I'll get down to the basement."

"See you on the other side," Schwartz said, and he headed down the hall toward the stairway.

Chapter Thirty

I went back down the dark hall again, faster now that we weren't trying very hard to be quiet. Now, it was just our best guess that Steven and Stacy were still in the house, but they hadn't been found by the search of the house by the police, and a nationwide alert hadn't found them. I realized that, if Steven had left the safety room already, I'd best not make a lot of noise going downstairs, so I trod on the sides of the steps, putting my weight down carefully. I needn't have bothered; the house was built like a cathedral, and those stairs were solid as stone.

When I got down to the basement, I paused on the landing. It was perfectly quiet down there, and the lights were on. The basement was completely finished, no expense spared. In the near right corner was a tool bench with an extensive set of gunsmithing tools, all neatly arranged on shelves, racks, and boxes. Next to it were three gun safes, side by side, and I was ready to bet that there was a Nagant revolver fitted with a suppressor in one of them. Probably still with five live cartridges in it, for that matter, with saboted .223 slugs replacing the blunt originals.

The right side of the basement, as I faced it, was a firing range, twenty meters long, twice the length of Schwartz's, with an extensive angled backstop. I could see how, with a setup like that, Steven could easily have collected his .223 slugs and prepared those cartridges for up-close murder. About halfway down the left side of the room, there was a door, almost certainly to the outside.

I heard pounding overhead, faintly, but it must have been serious for the sound to reach me all the way from the second floor to the basement. I briefly wondered what Schwartz was using to create that much racket. At least there was no shooting, I thought, but then I realized I would only have heard shots if someone other than Schwartz was firing.

Suddenly there was another noise, closer, overhead. Someone was on the stairs, not worried about keeping quiet. It sounded like more than one person. I stepped back, between the workbench and the firing line of the shooting range, so that I could see the entire big room. The steps got louder as they came down to the basement. The door from the stairway swung open, and Stacy came through, with Steven right behind her.

Steven was holding a leather briefcase in his right hand, God knows why, and with his left, he held on to a rope with a loop around Stacy's wrists, in front of her, pulling, pushing her, shoving, and dragging her along with him as he came into the room. "Hold it!" I sang out, and I raised the Walther.

Steven swung Stacy around in front of him as he faced me, forcing her between us. He pulled her with him as he worked his way toward the door down the left side of the room. "Come on, Stacy!" he snarled, "You're coming with me." There was nothing fatherly about his stance now. Or brotherly, for that matter. It occurred to me that he probably had that briefcase stuffed with negotiable securities, or cash, or whatever he thought he'd need to live somewhere else. A ridiculous thing for me to be worrying about in the circumstances.

Stacy yelped in pain as Steven gave a vicious yank on the rope. Her eyes were wide, on me, pleading for release from his grip. I said, "Remember that thing I didn't know about your fingers, Stacy?" To my surprise, she managed to nod. Hereford gave her another nasty jerk. "Now might be a good time to try it," I said.

Stacy nodded understanding, and suddenly she got twisted around and managed to get her hands loose and up, then she scraped both clawed hands down Steven's face. He yelled in pain, "You bitch!" and reflexively thrust her away from him, letting go of her and the briefcase. I swear I thought I saw her smile at the epithet as she fell to the floor and began scrambling toward me, staying low. I kept the Walther P22 leveled at him. With the suppressor extension, it was pretty easy. "You don't have your shield anymore, Hereford,"

267

I said. "Give it up while you can."

He glanced at the .22 automatic in my hand, snarled, "Pea-shooter," and pulled back his gray jacket with his left hand, reaching with his right for an oversized shoulder holster holding a really large revolver. It looked to me like a Smith & Wesson Model 500, a .50-caliber magnum.

"Don't do it," I said, as he got his hand on the big S&W and drew it from the holster. He swung it around toward me and fired one-handed from the hip. The revolver boomed loud as a cannon in the closed room, and I swear I felt the wind as the slug passed by my head and slammed into the wall behind me, and it was all one terrifically loud sound. Just then Schwartz emerged from the stairway, his pistol in his hand at his side.

The heavy recoil of the .50 cal kicked Hereford's Smith back and up, and it pushed him back toward the wall, but he started to bring it down again. Before he could get off a second shot at me, or at Stacy, or at anybody else, for that matter, I double-tapped him with my .22, aiming for high center mass. As usual, I pulled both shots a little to my right. His left. Two black dots appeared on his snowy-white shirt front, just above the pocket, and immediately blossomed into a red, red rose. Steven Hereford stared at me as if he'd caught me using the wrong fork, then the massive revolver clattered on the floor, his knees buckled, and he went down.

Acknowledgements

I owe more than I can ever repay to Cindy Bullard, my agent, and to Shawn Reilly Simmons, my editor, for encouragement, invaluable suggestions, expert guidance, and keeping me on track. Without them, it wouldn't have happened.

For technical advice, assistance, and suggestions, I would like to thank Harry Gilliam, formerly of Skylighter, Inc., Ned Gorski, of Fireworking.com, Terry Bush and Mario Perdue, both of Rocketeers of Central Indiana, and V. A. Atkins, Ty Jester, Ethan Nichter, and Bill Whitley, of Pinnacle Firearms. Any errors, mistakes, and misconceptions are of course my own.

The following people deserve my heartfelt thanks for their encouragement and support, moral and otherwise: Miguel Alçaron and Alex Jones; Fred and Elizabeth Alexander; Frances Blake; Lawrence Block; Kristi Decke; Steve Fraser; Pat Gallagher; Don Gary and Eva Cheung; Carolyn Garlock; the Reverend Allan Harlan; Brad Hellyer; Richard Hendel; Carol Hommel; James N. Hullett; Frances Gayhart Hutchinson; Kate Janeway; Nyle Kardatzke; Bill Kirklin and Jennifer Zehr; Michelle Lacy; Mike Lester; Peter Lindenbaum; Pat, George, and Vivian Lynch; Sean, Brynne, Caleb, and Gwen McFall; the Reverend Chester Minton; Ross Murray; Tim Rimedio; Rob and Linda Rupp; Lou and Phyllis Savka; Jud and Martha Vaught; Deborah Wilkes; and Tim Witsman.

And most of all Kim, now and forever.

About the Author

Lewis Vaught grew up on a farm in central Indiana. He has been a farm hand, a surveyor's assistant, a student, an injection-mold operator, a bookmobile driver and librarian, a teacher of German and English, an amusement park ride operator, a "steamship" (diesel, actually) pilot, a dance-hall meeter and greeter, a teacher of EFL in Dortmund, North Rhine Westphalia, a reader, a writer, a proofreader, a copy editor, an editor, a programmer, a book designer, and a (barely) managing editor. He is a member of the PGI, the ILS, and the NAR, among other things. He lives in Indianapolis with a border collie, not terribly far from his daughter and her husband and their kids. *Things People Do* is the second Leo Schwartz mystery.

AUTHOR WEBSITE:
  https://tinyurl.com/ycxenccj

Also by Lewis Vaught

Crime in Italy, Level Best Books (the first Leo Schwartz mystery)